BIONIC

BIO NIC

KOREN SHADMI

Top Shelf® PRODUCTIONS

BIONIC
KOREN SHADMI

Bionic © 2020 Koren Shadmi.

Published by Top Shelf Productions, an imprint of IDW Publishing, a division of Idea and Design Works, LLC. Offices: Top Shelf Productions, c/o Idea & Design Works, LLC, 2765 Truxtun Road, San Diego, CA 92106. Top Shelf Productions®, the Top Shelf logo, Idea and Design Works®, and the IDW logo are registered trademarks of Idea and Design Works, LLC. All Rights Reserved. With the exception of small excerpts of artwork used for review purposes, none of the contents of this publication may be reprinted without the permission of IDW Publishing.
IDW Publishing does not read or accept unsolicited submissions of ideas, stories, or artwork.

Editor-in-Chief: Chris Staros.

Design Assistance: Tara McCrillis.

Printed in Korea.

ISBN: 978-1-60309-478-8

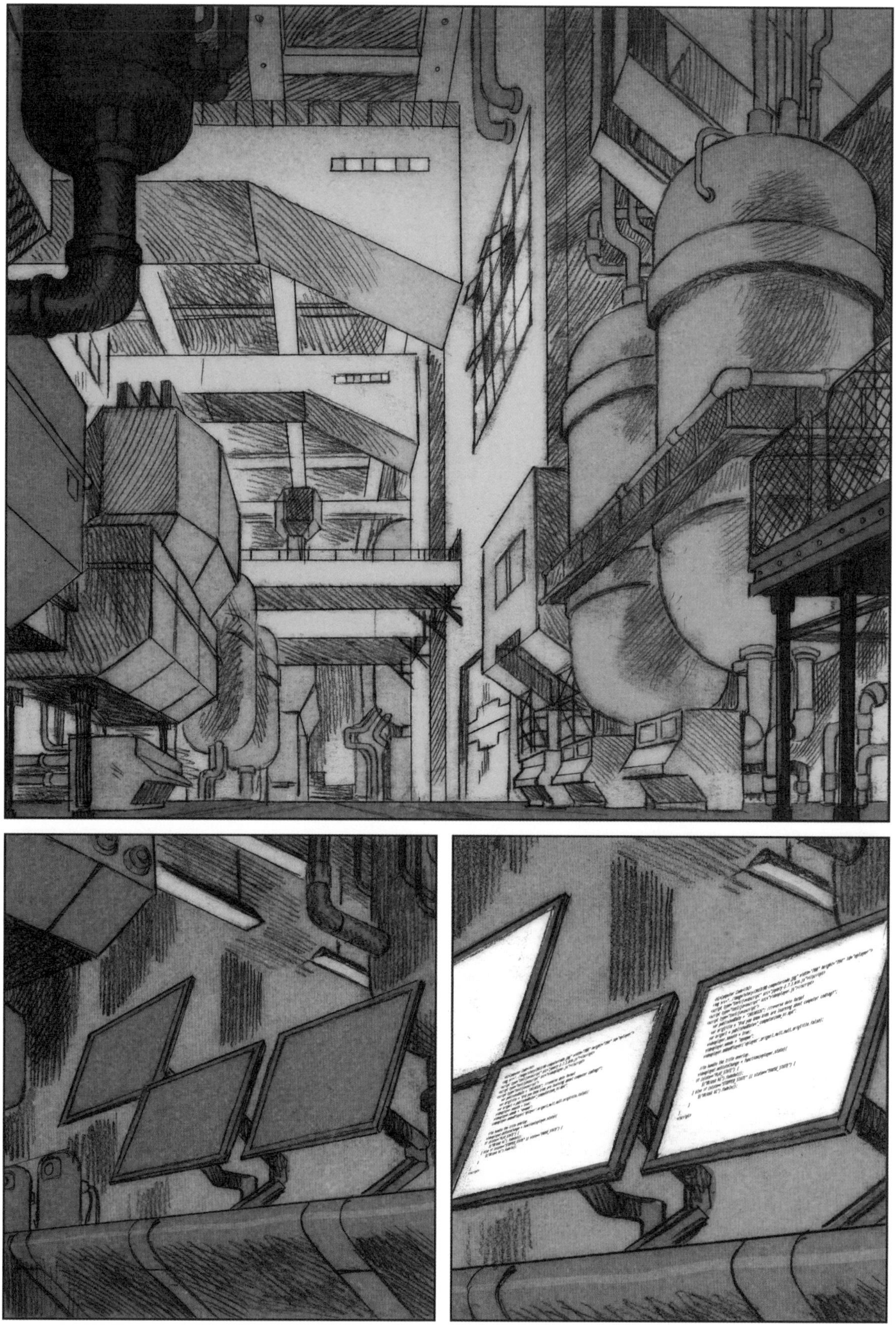

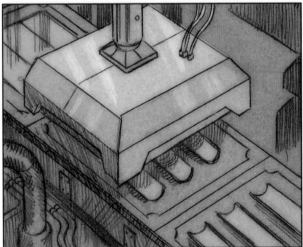
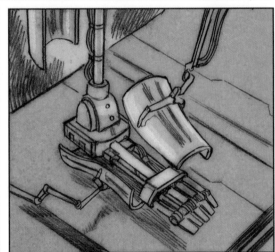
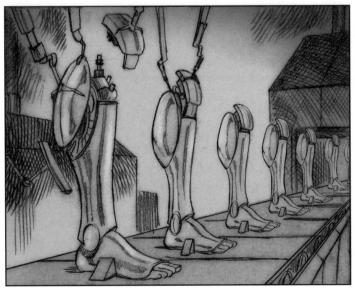
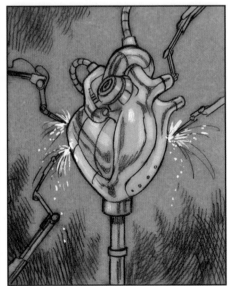

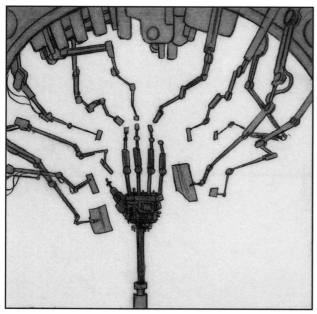
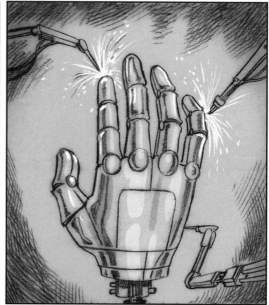

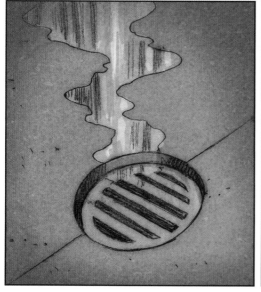
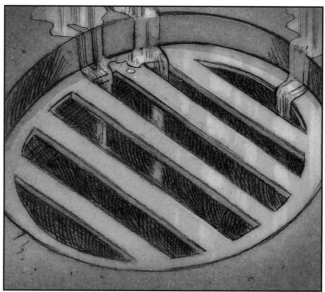

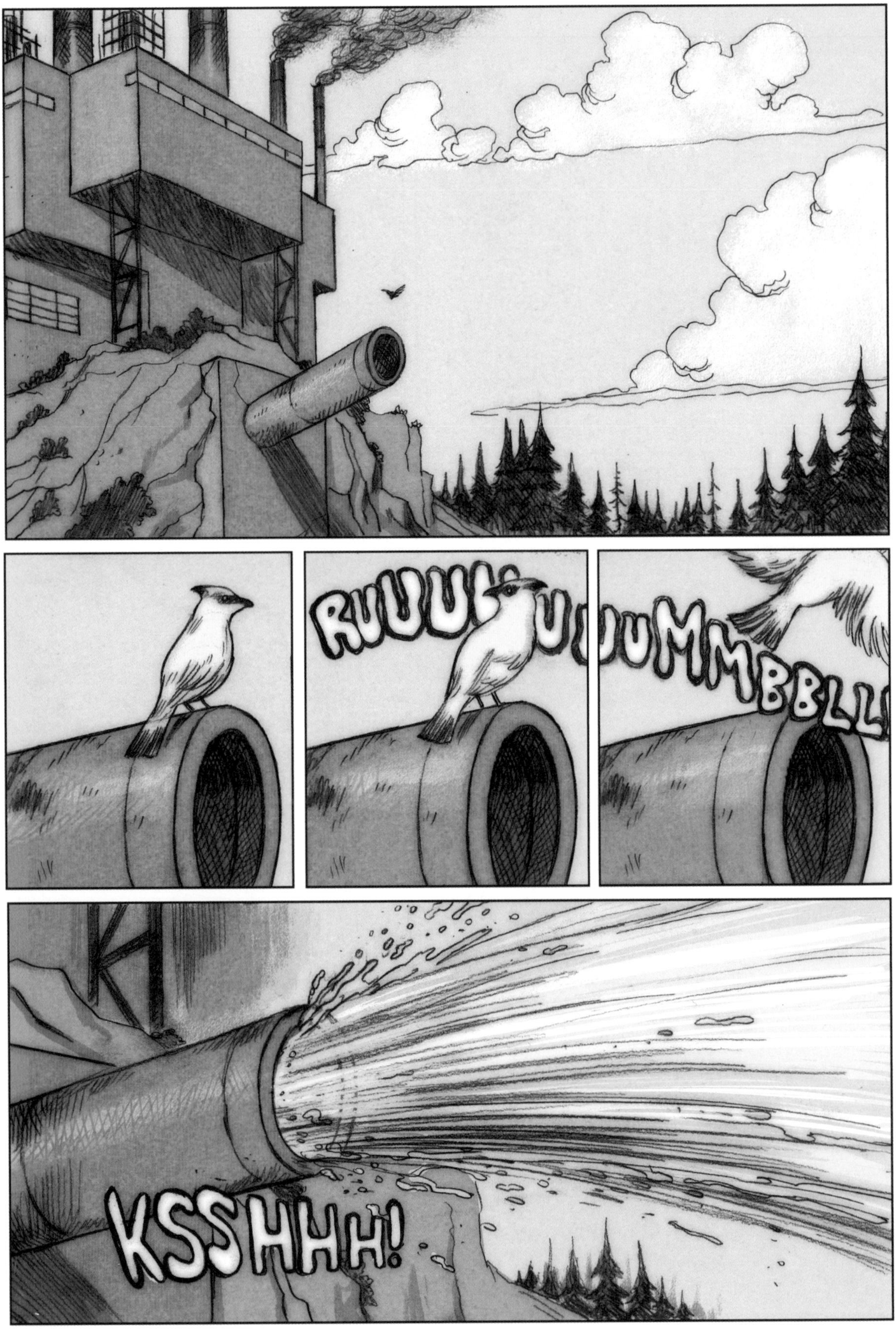
RUUUUUUUMMBBLL
KSSHHH!

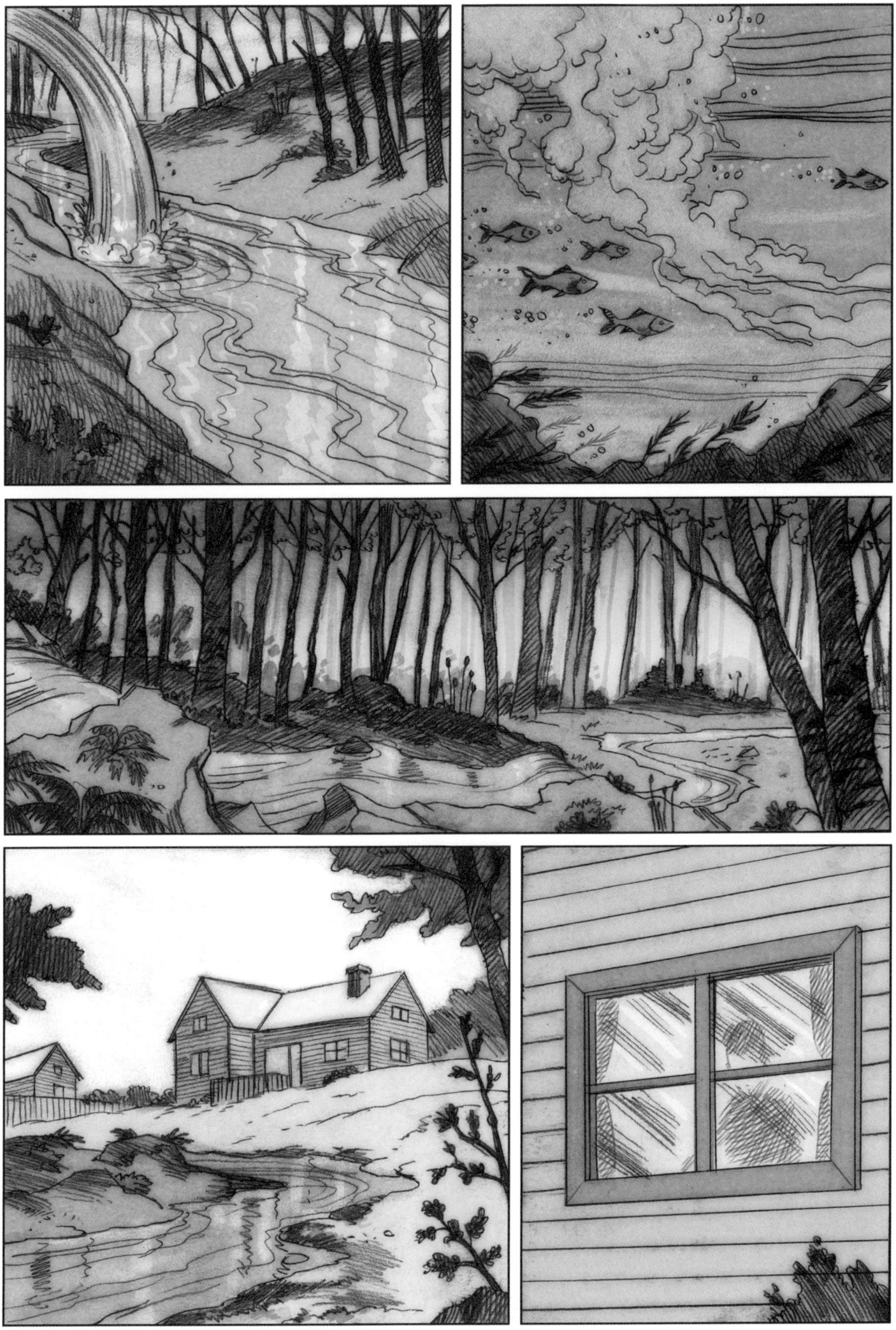

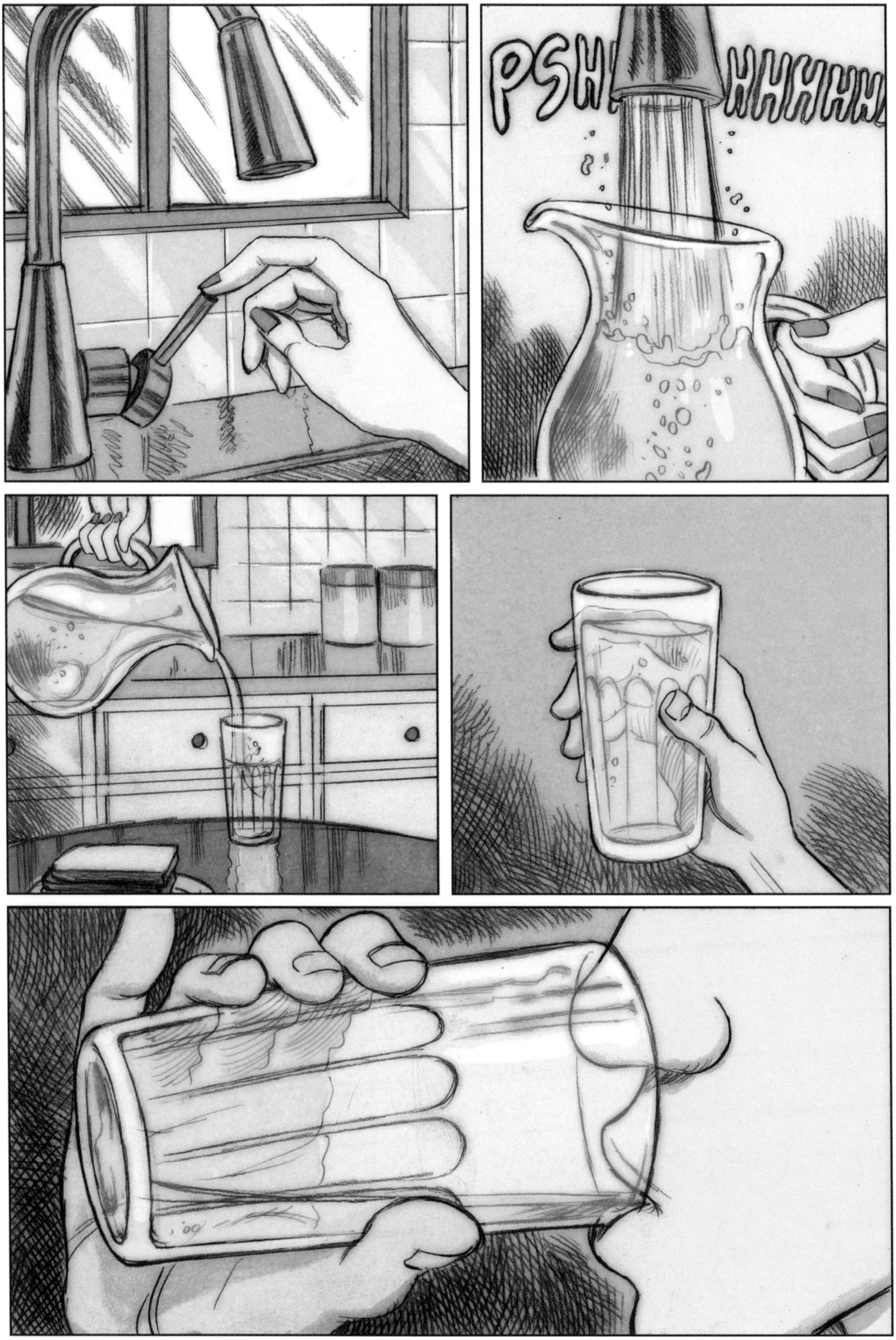
PSH HHHHHH

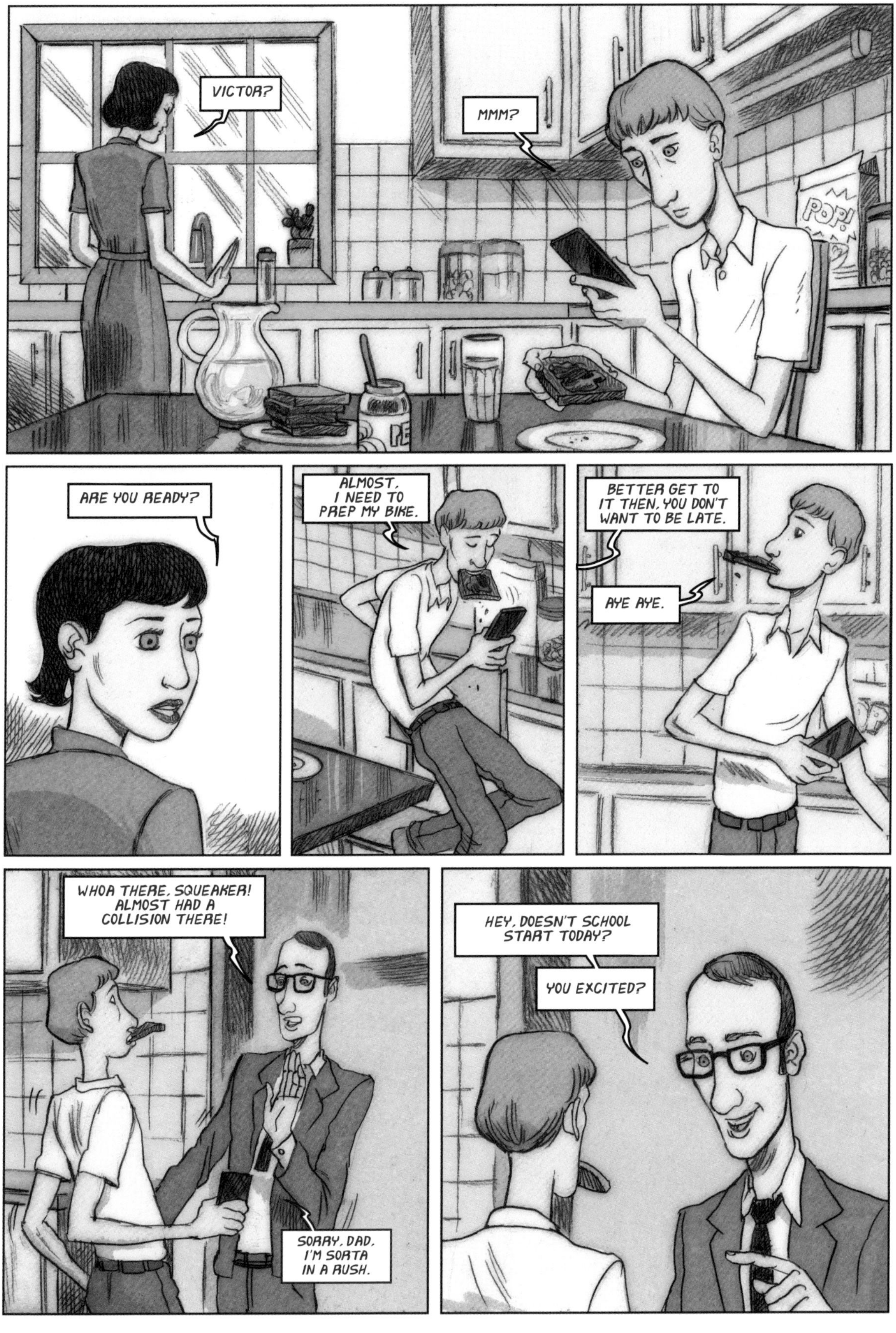
VICTOR?
MMM?
ARE YOU READY?
ALMOST, I NEED TO PREP MY BIKE.
BETTER GET TO IT THEN, YOU DON'T WANT TO BE LATE.
AYE AYE.
WHOA THERE, SQUEAKER! ALMOST HAD A COLLISION THERE!
SORRY, DAD, I'M SORTA IN A RUSH.
HEY, DOESN'T SCHOOL START TODAY?
YOU EXCITED?

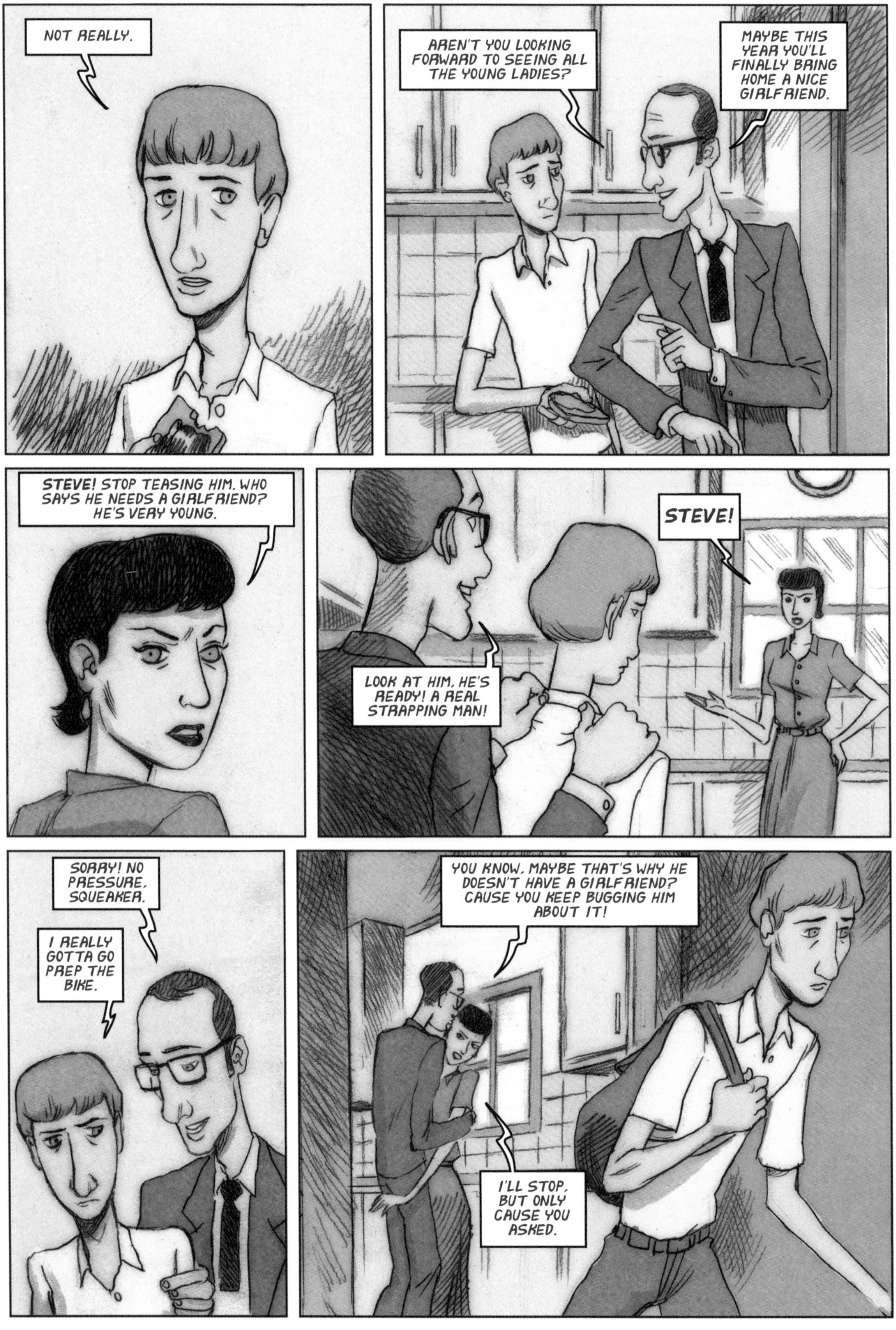
NOT REALLY.
AREN'T YOU LOOKING FORWARD TO SEEING ALL THE YOUNG LADIES?
MAYBE THIS YEAR YOU'LL FINALLY BRING HOME A NICE GIRLFRIEND.
STEVE! STOP TEASING HIM. WHO SAYS HE NEEDS A GIRLFRIEND? HE'S VERY YOUNG.
LOOK AT HIM. HE'S READY! A REAL STRAPPING MAN!
STEVE!
SORRY! NO PRESSURE, SQUEAKER.
I REALLY GOTTA GO PREP THE BIKE.
YOU KNOW, MAYBE THAT'S WHY HE DOESN'T HAVE A GIRLFRIEND? CAUSE YOU KEEP BUGGING HIM ABOUT IT!
I'LL STOP, BUT ONLY CAUSE YOU ASKED.

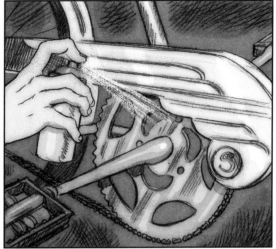
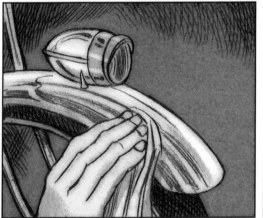
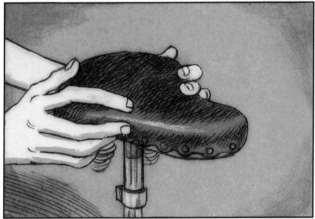

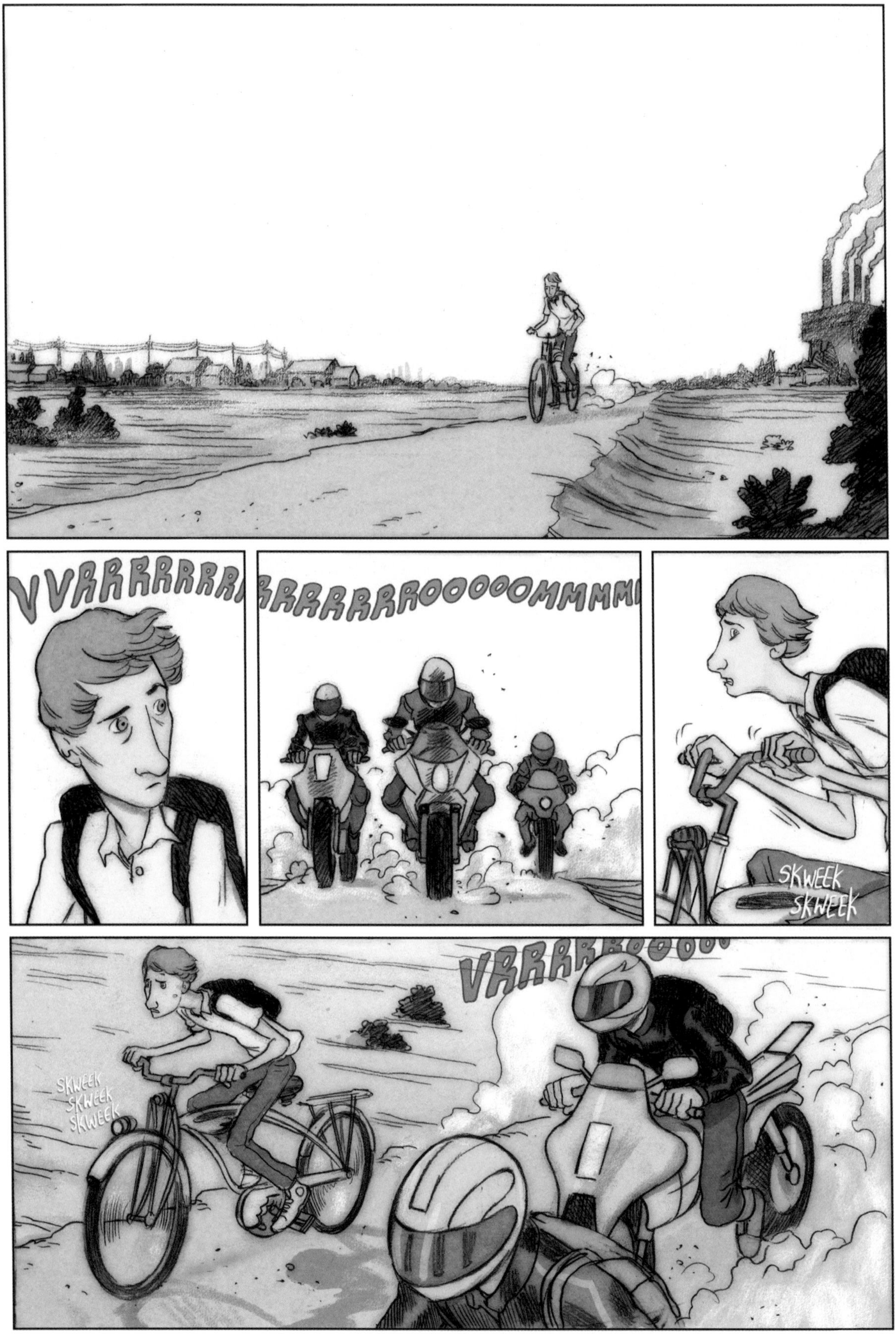

VVRRRRRRRR
RRRRRRRROOOOOMMMMM
SKWEEK SKWEEK
SKWEEK SKWEEK SKWEEK
VRRRRROOOOO

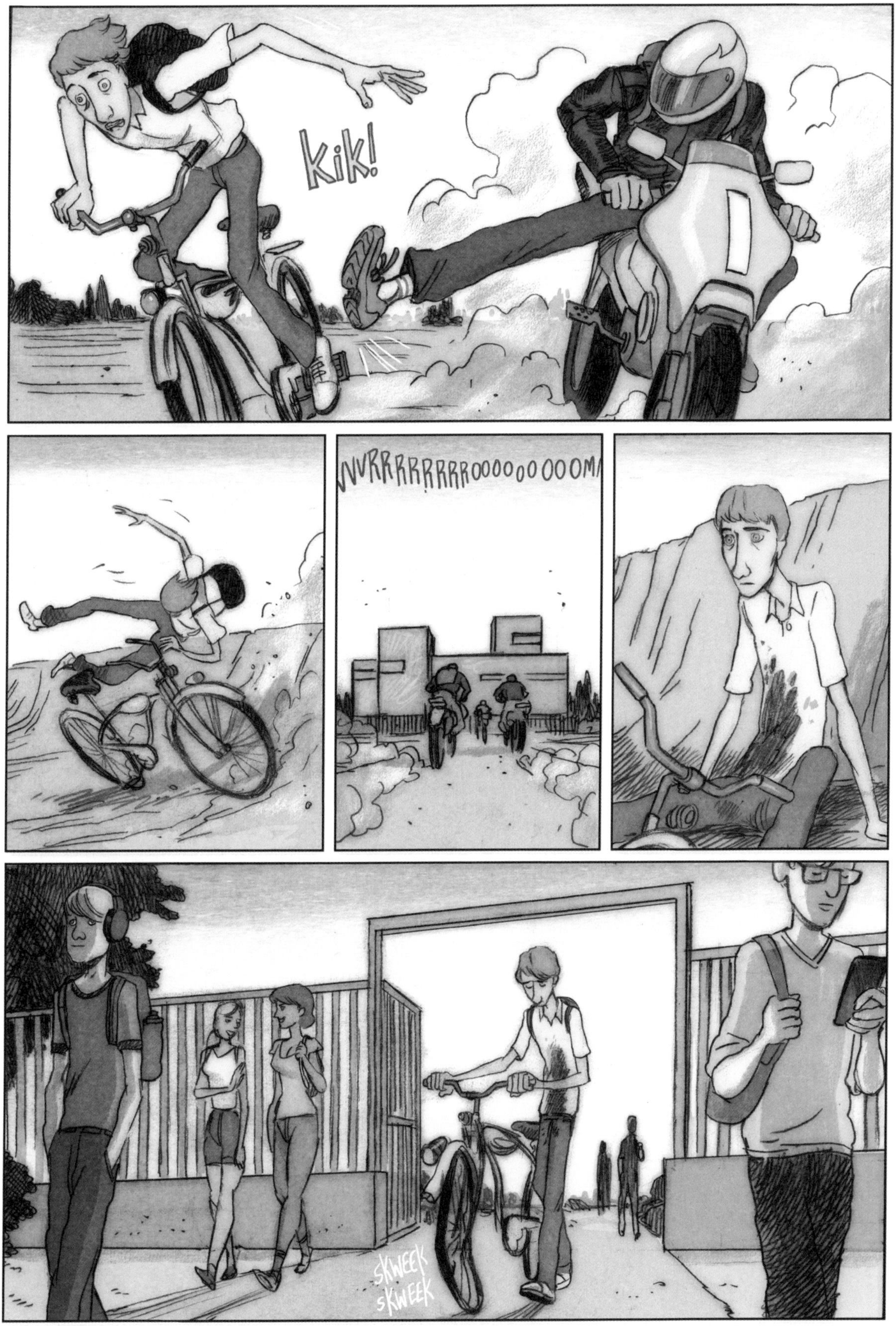
kik!
VVRRRRRRRROOOOOOOOOM
sKWEEK
sKWEEK

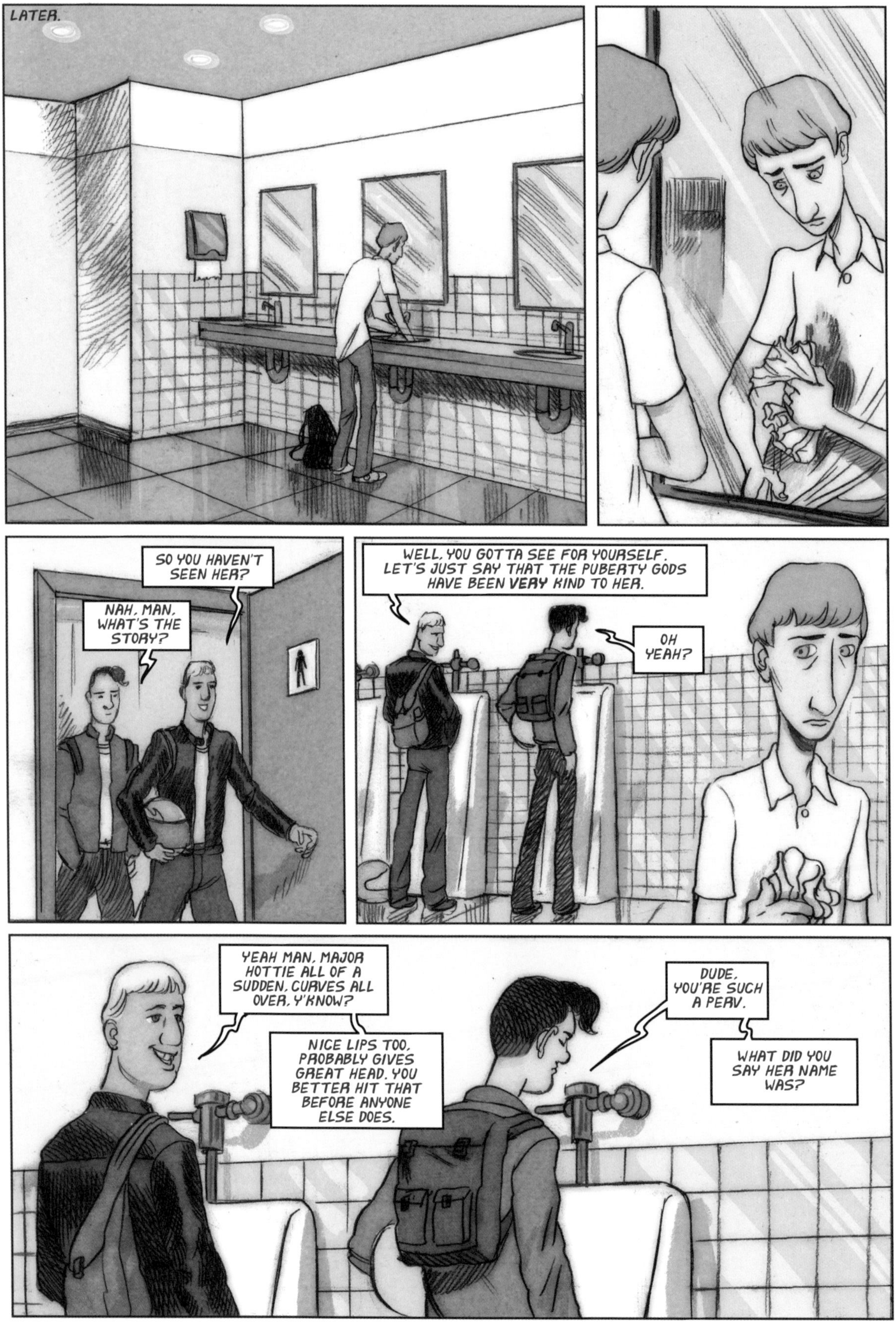
LATER.
SO YOU HAVEN'T SEEN HER?
NAH, MAN, WHAT'S THE STORY?
WELL, YOU GOTTA SEE FOR YOURSELF. LET'S JUST SAY THAT THE PUBERTY GODS HAVE BEEN VERY KIND TO HER.
OH YEAH?
YEAH MAN, MAJOR HOTTIE ALL OF A SUDDEN, CURVES ALL OVER, Y'KNOW?
NICE LIPS TOO, PROBABLY GIVES GREAT HEAD. YOU BETTER HIT THAT BEFORE ANYONE ELSE DOES.
DUDE, YOU'RE SUCH A PERV.
WHAT DID YOU SAY HER NAME WAS?

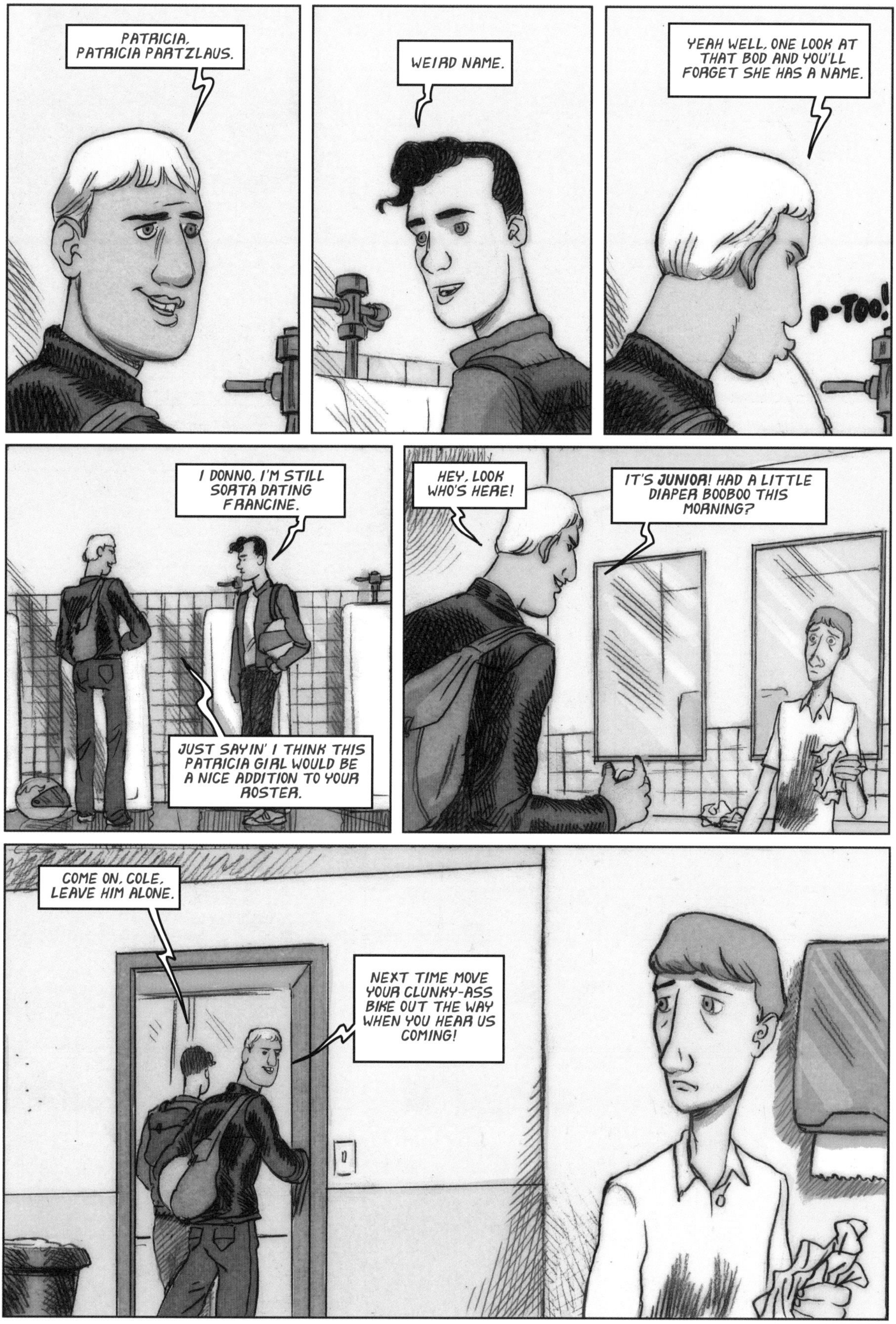
PATRICIA, PATRICIA PARTZLAUS.
WEIRD NAME.
YEAH WELL, ONE LOOK AT THAT BOD AND YOU'LL FORGET SHE HAS A NAME.
P-TOO!
I DONNO, I'M STILL SORTA DATING FRANCINE.
JUST SAYIN' I THINK THIS PATRICIA GIRL WOULD BE A NICE ADDITION TO YOUR ROSTER.
HEY, LOOK WHO'S HERE!
IT'S JUNIOR! HAD A LITTLE DIAPER BOOBOO THIS MORNING?
COME ON, COLE, LEAVE HIM ALONE.
NEXT TIME MOVE YOUR CLUNKY-ASS BIKE OUT THE WAY WHEN YOU HEAR US COMING!

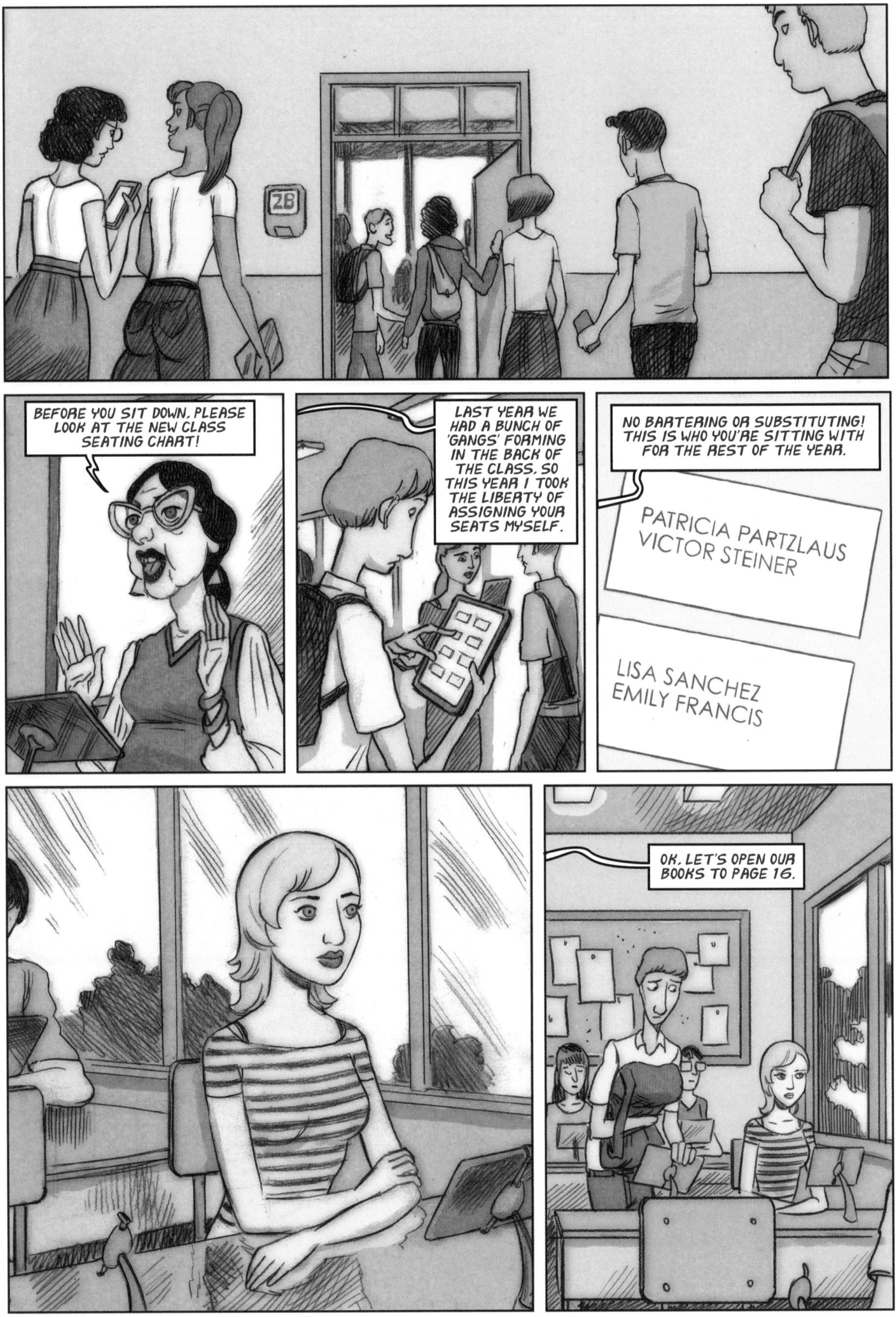

2B
BEFORE YOU SIT DOWN, PLEASE LOOK AT THE NEW CLASS SEATING CHART!
LAST YEAR WE HAD A BUNCH OF 'GANGS' FORMING IN THE BACK OF THE CLASS. SO THIS YEAR I TOOK THE LIBERTY OF ASSIGNING YOUR SEATS MYSELF.
NO BARTERING OR SUBSTITUTING! THIS IS WHO YOU'RE SITTING WITH FOR THE REST OF THE YEAR.
PATRICIA PARTZLAUS
VICTOR STEINER
LISA SANCHEZ
EMILY FRANCIS
OK, LET'S OPEN OUR BOOKS TO PAGE 16.

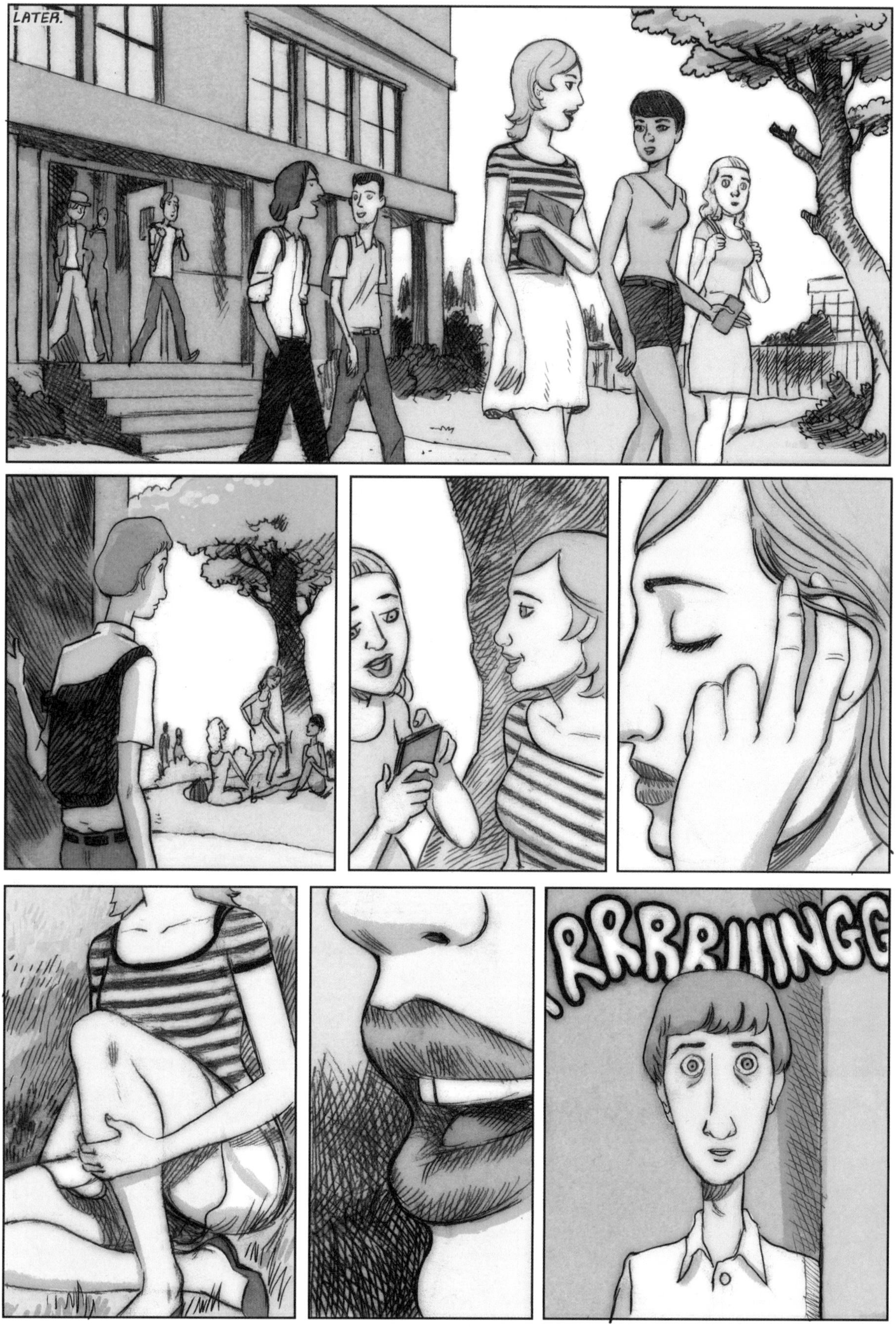
LATER.
RRRRIIINGG

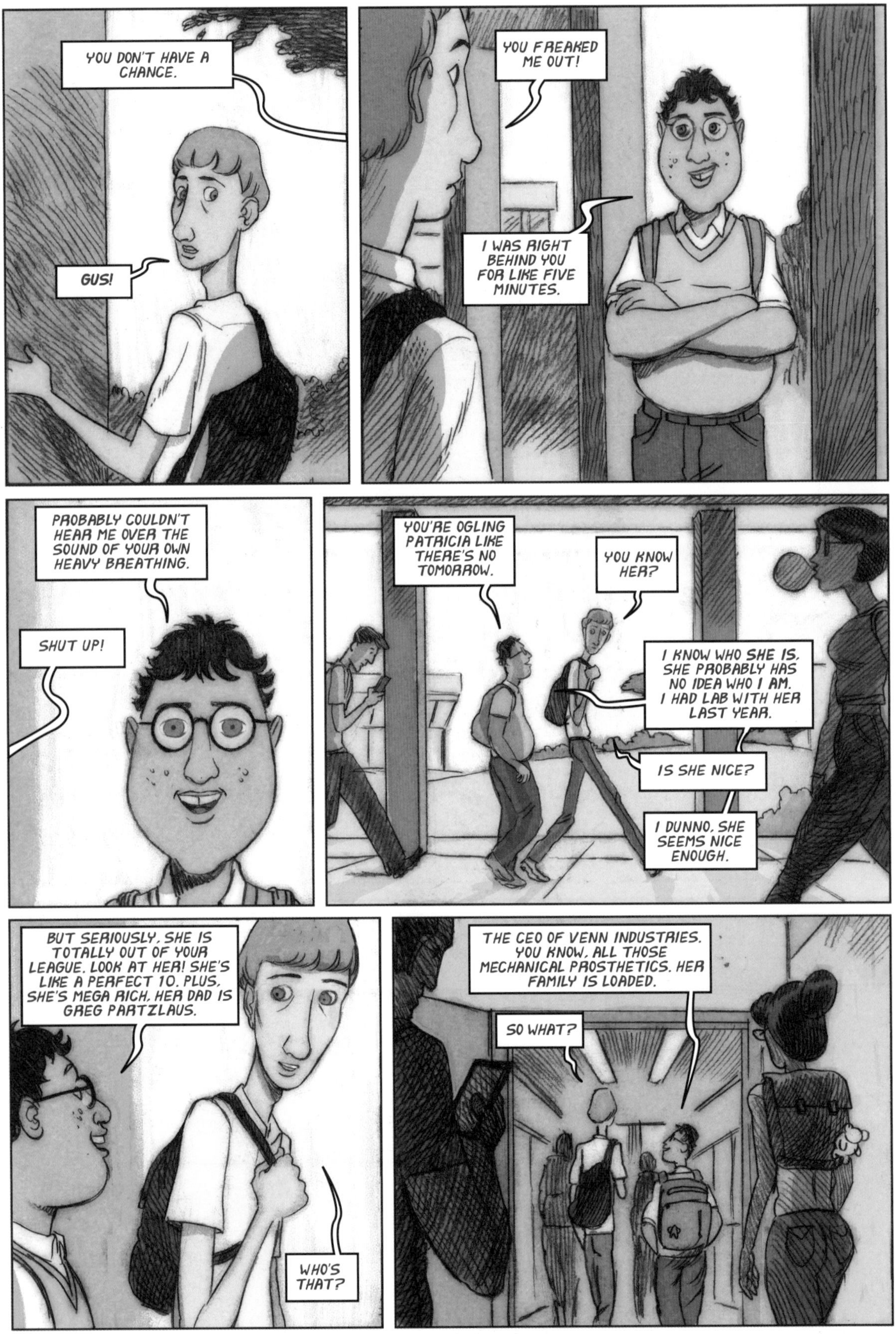

YOU DON'T HAVE A CHANCE.
GUS!
YOU FREAKED ME OUT!
I WAS RIGHT BEHIND YOU FOR LIKE FIVE MINUTES.
PROBABLY COULDN'T HEAR ME OVER THE SOUND OF YOUR OWN HEAVY BREATHING.
SHUT UP!
YOU'RE OGLING PATRICIA LIKE THERE'S NO TOMORROW.
YOU KNOW HER?
I KNOW WHO SHE IS. SHE PROBABLY HAS NO IDEA WHO I AM. I HAD LAB WITH HER LAST YEAR.
IS SHE NICE?
I DUNNO. SHE SEEMS NICE ENOUGH.
BUT SERIOUSLY, SHE IS TOTALLY OUT OF YOUR LEAGUE. LOOK AT HER! SHE'S LIKE A PERFECT 10. PLUS, SHE'S MEGA RICH. HER DAD IS GREG PARTZLAUS.
WHO'S THAT?
THE CEO OF VENN INDUSTRIES. YOU KNOW, ALL THOSE MECHANICAL PROSTHETICS. HER FAMILY IS LOADED.
SO WHAT?

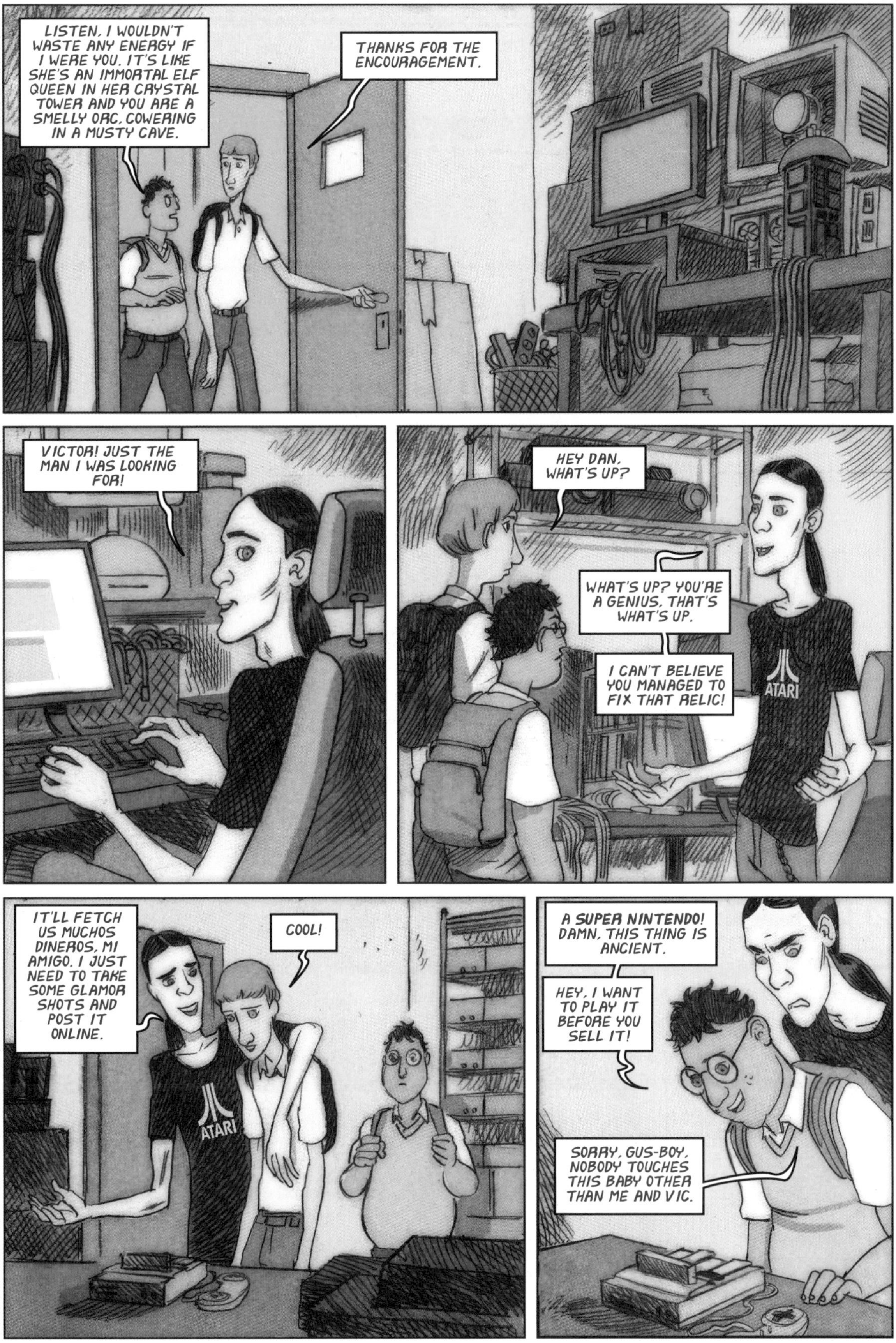
LISTEN, I WOULDN'T WASTE ANY ENERGY IF I WERE YOU. IT'S LIKE SHE'S AN IMMORTAL ELF QUEEN IN HER CRYSTAL TOWER AND YOU ARE A SMELLY ORC, COWERING IN A MUSTY CAVE.
THANKS FOR THE ENCOURAGEMENT.
VICTOR! JUST THE MAN I WAS LOOKING FOR!
HEY DAN, WHAT'S UP?
WHAT'S UP? YOU'RE A GENIUS, THAT'S WHAT'S UP.
I CAN'T BELIEVE YOU MANAGED TO FIX THAT RELIC!
ATARI
IT'LL FETCH US MUCHOS DINEROS, MI AMIGO. I JUST NEED TO TAKE SOME GLAMOR SHOTS AND POST IT ONLINE.
COOL!
ATARI
A SUPER NINTENDO! DAMN, THIS THING IS ANCIENT.
HEY, I WANT TO PLAY IT BEFORE YOU SELL IT!
SORRY, GUS-BOY, NOBODY TOUCHES THIS BABY OTHER THAN ME AND VIC.

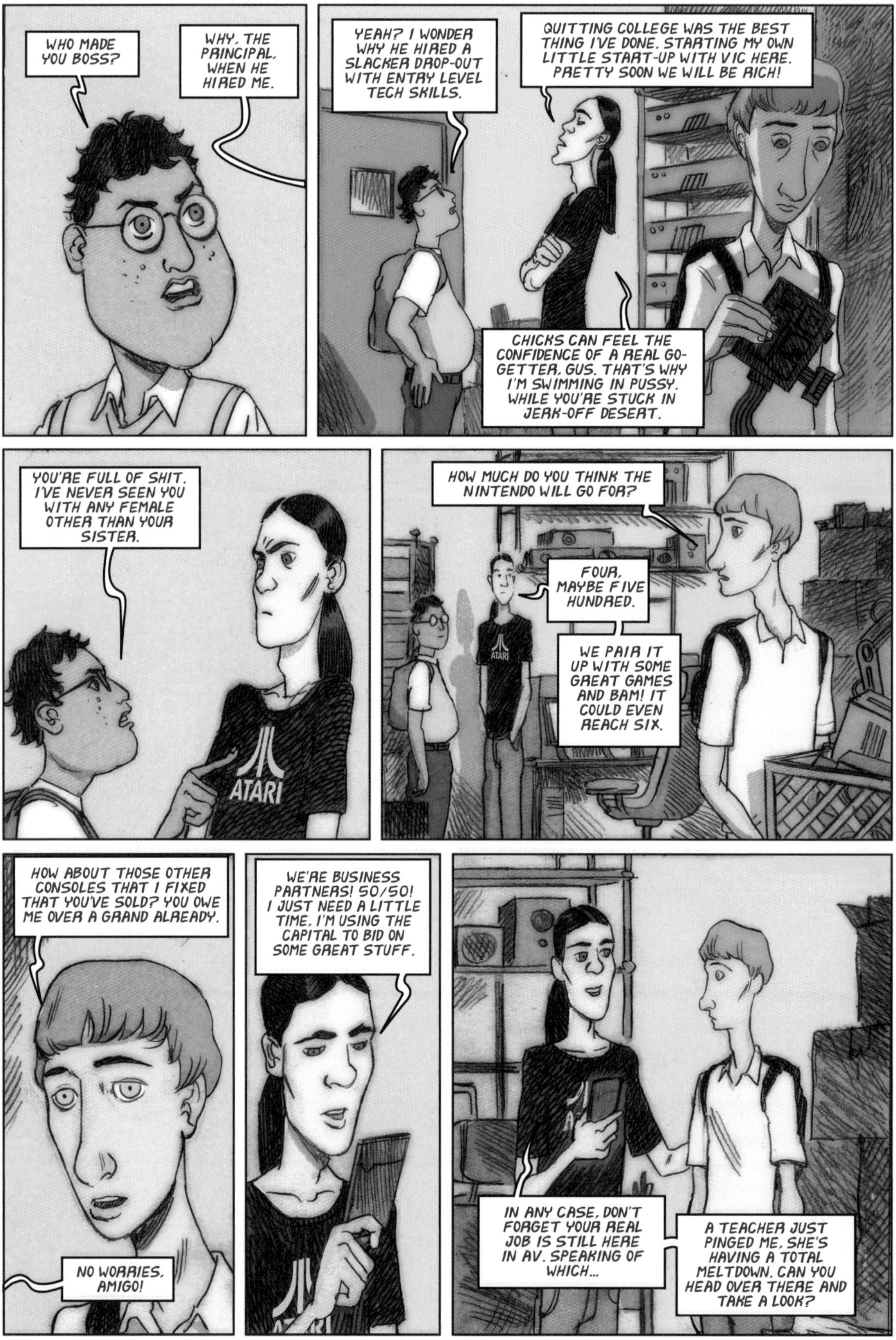
WHO MADE YOU BOSS?
WHY, THE PRINCIPAL, WHEN HE HIRED ME.
YEAH? I WONDER WHY HE HIRED A SLACKER DROP-OUT WITH ENTRY LEVEL TECH SKILLS.
QUITTING COLLEGE WAS THE BEST THING I'VE DONE. STARTING MY OWN LITTLE START-UP WITH VIC HERE. PRETTY SOON WE WILL BE RICH!
CHICKS CAN FEEL THE CONFIDENCE OF A REAL GO-GETTER, GUS. THAT'S WHY I'M SWIMMING IN PUSSY. WHILE YOU'RE STUCK IN JERK-OFF DESERT.
YOU'RE FULL OF SHIT. I'VE NEVER SEEN YOU WITH ANY FEMALE OTHER THAN YOUR SISTER.
ATARI
HOW MUCH DO YOU THINK THE NINTENDO WILL GO FOR?
FOUR, MAYBE FIVE HUNDRED.
WE PAIR IT UP WITH SOME GREAT GAMES AND BAM! IT COULD EVEN REACH SIX.
ATARI
HOW ABOUT THOSE OTHER CONSOLES THAT I FIXED THAT YOU'VE SOLD? YOU OWE ME OVER A GRAND ALREADY.
NO WORRIES, AMIGO!
WE'RE BUSINESS PARTNERS! 50/50! I JUST NEED A LITTLE TIME, I'M USING THE CAPITAL TO BID ON SOME GREAT STUFF.
IN ANY CASE, DON'T FORGET YOUR REAL JOB IS STILL HERE IN AV. SPEAKING OF WHICH...
A TEACHER JUST PINGED ME, SHE'S HAVING A TOTAL MELTDOWN. CAN YOU HEAD OVER THERE AND TAKE A LOOK?

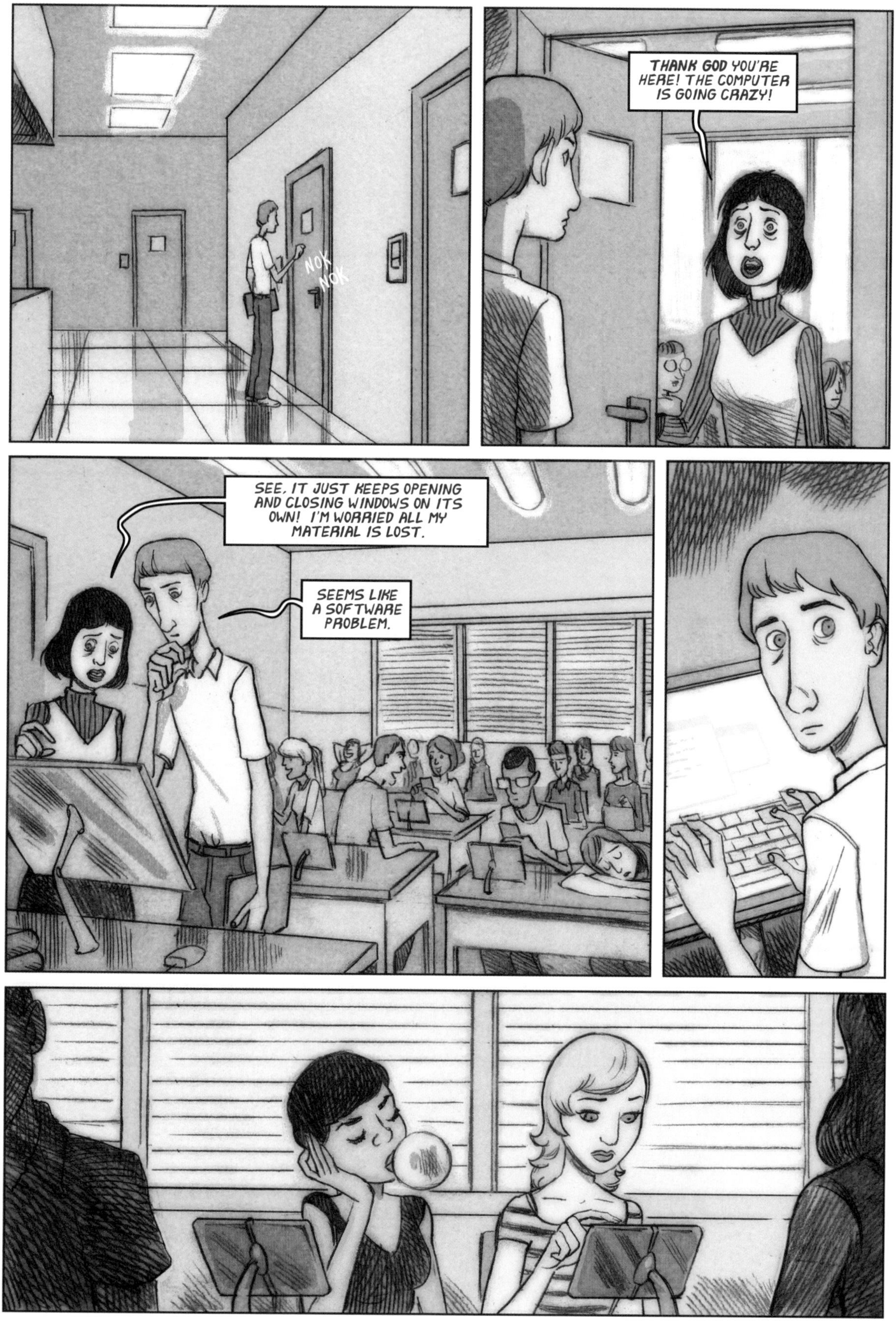
NOK NOK
THANK GOD YOU'RE HERE! THE COMPUTER IS GOING CRAZY!
SEE, IT JUST KEEPS OPENING AND CLOSING WINDOWS ON ITS OWN! I'M WORRIED ALL MY MATERIAL IS LOST.
SEEMS LIKE A SOFTWARE PROBLEM.

PING!

BRAD Wants To Be Your Friend!

HOLY SHIT!

APPROVE

clik!

WHY'D YOU DO THAT? YOU SHOULD HAVE WAITED A FEW DAYS!

WHAT'S THE BIG DEAL?

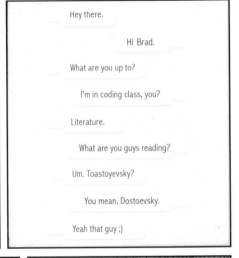

Hey there.

Hi Brad.

What are you up to?

I'm in coding class, you?

Literature.

What are you guys reading?

Um. Toastoyevsky?

You mean, Dostoevsky.

Yeah that guy ;)

TOASTOYEVSKY?

I'M SURE HE'S JUST JOKING AROUND!

WHY DON'T YOU LET ME TYPE?

I'LL MAKE SURE TO LURE HIM IN FOR YOU.

I CAN HANDLE THIS!

WELL? ANY LUCK? I HAVE TO GET ON WITH CLASS.

LET ME TRY SOMETHING ELSE.

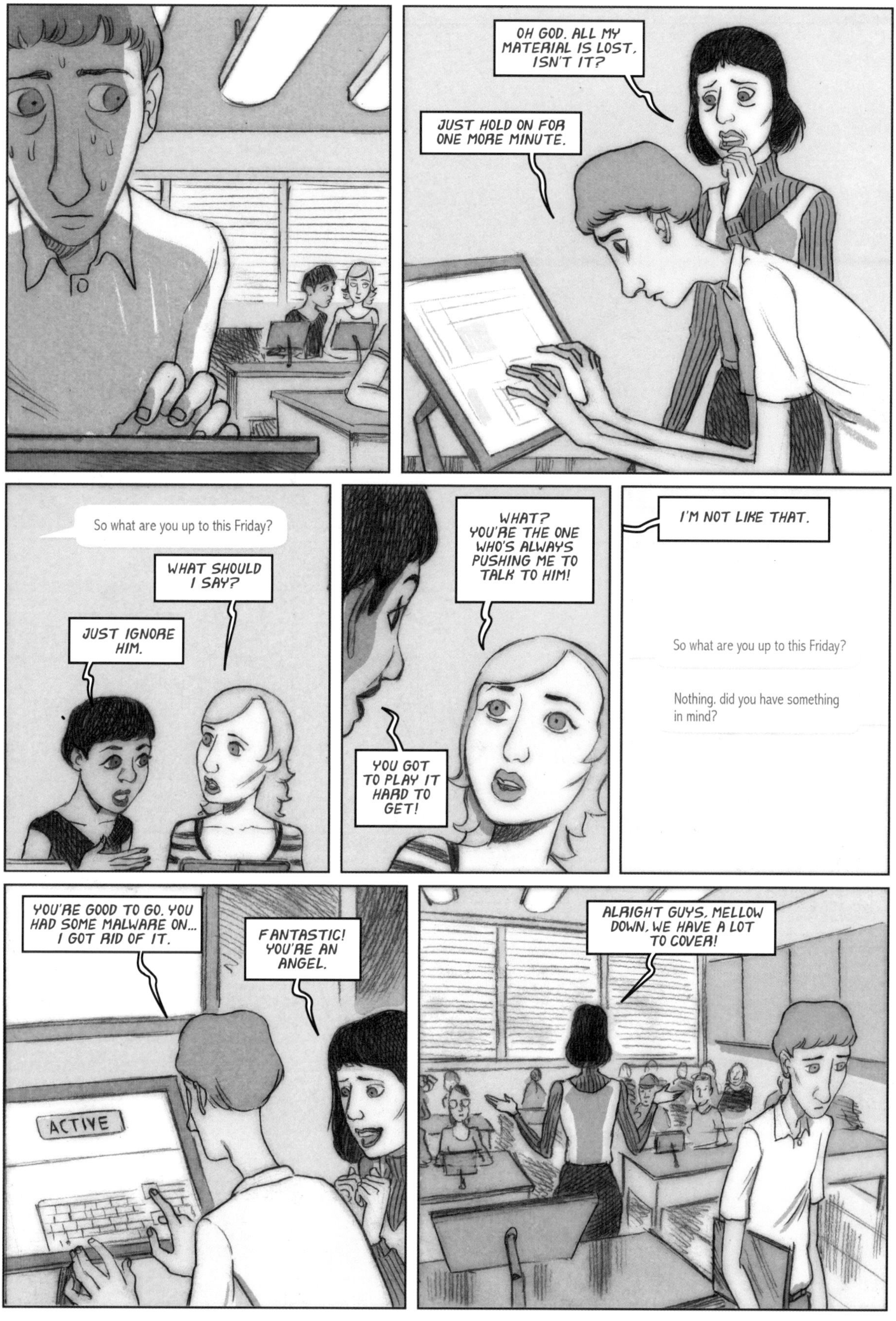
OH GOD. ALL MY MATERIAL IS LOST, ISN'T IT?
JUST HOLD ON FOR ONE MORE MINUTE.
So what are you up to this Friday?
WHAT SHOULD I SAY?
JUST IGNORE HIM.
WHAT? YOU'RE THE ONE WHO'S ALWAYS PUSHING ME TO TALK TO HIM!
YOU GOT TO PLAY IT HARD TO GET!
I'M NOT LIKE THAT.
So what are you up to this Friday?
Nothing, did you have something in mind?
YOU'RE GOOD TO GO. YOU HAD SOME MALWARE ON... I GOT RID OF IT.
FANTASTIC! YOU'RE AN ANGEL.
ACTIVE
ALRIGHT GUYS, MELLOW DOWN, WE HAVE A LOT TO COVER!

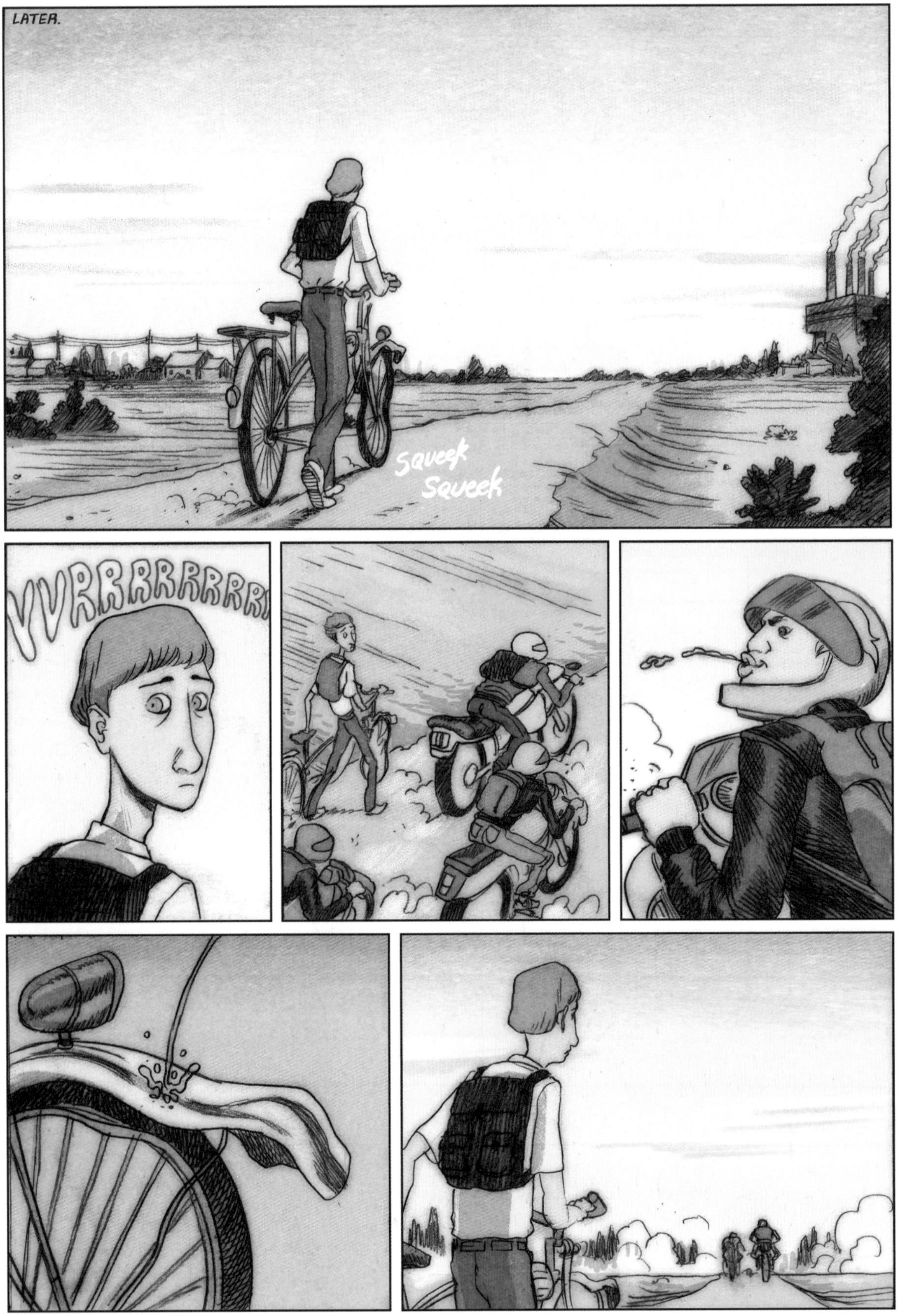
LATER.
Squeek
Squeek
VVRRRRRRRRR

Friend request sent. Waiting for approval.

```
  people.data.users
onse    client.api.statuses.us
   'Got', len(response.data),
n(response.data)    0:
date    response.data[0]['crea
date2   datetime.strptime(ltda
ay   datetime.now()
long   (today ltdate2) days
                            s twe
taltweets     len(response.dat
 j   response.data:
   j.entities.urls:
       k   j.entities.urls:
       newurl   k['expanded_u
       urlset.add((newurl, j.

.sci.screen_name, 'has not twe
```

Profile Unlocked

PATRICIA'S PHOTOS

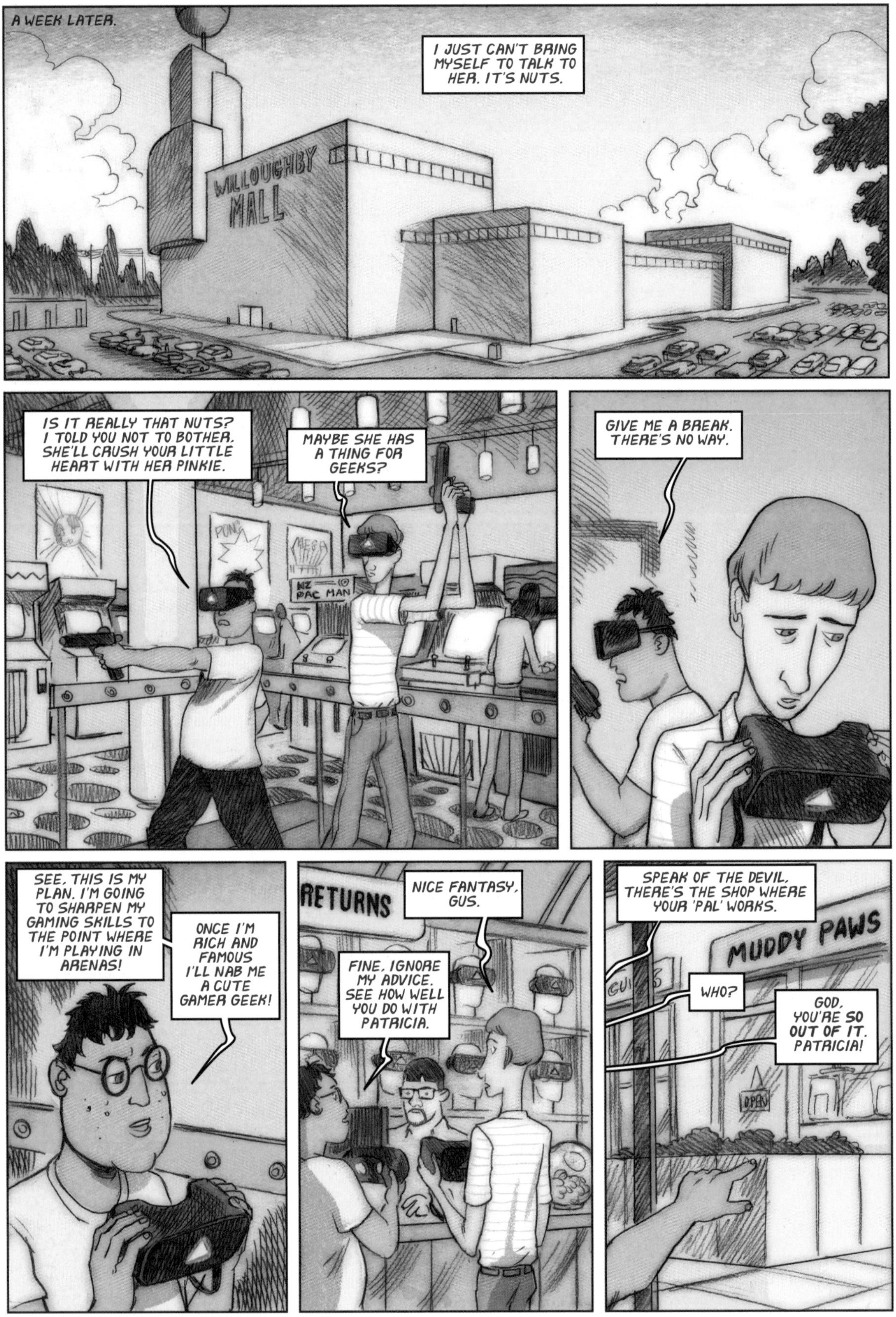
A WEEK LATER.
I JUST CAN'T BRING MYSELF TO TALK TO HER. IT'S NUTS.
WILLOUGHBY MALL
IS IT REALLY THAT NUTS? I TOLD YOU NOT TO BOTHER. SHE'LL CRUSH YOUR LITTLE HEART WITH HER PINKIE.
MAYBE SHE HAS A THING FOR GEEKS?
PONG
PAC MAN
GIVE ME A BREAK. THERE'S NO WAY.
SEE, THIS IS MY PLAN. I'M GOING TO SHARPEN MY GAMING SKILLS TO THE POINT WHERE I'M PLAYING IN ARENAS!
ONCE I'M RICH AND FAMOUS I'LL NAB ME A CUTE GAMER GEEK!
RETURNS
NICE FANTASY, GUS.
FINE, IGNORE MY ADVICE. SEE HOW WELL YOU DO WITH PATRICIA.
SPEAK OF THE DEVIL. THERE'S THE SHOP WHERE YOUR 'PAL' WORKS.
MUDDY PAWS
WHO?
GOD, YOU'RE SO OUT OF IT. PATRICIA!
OPEN

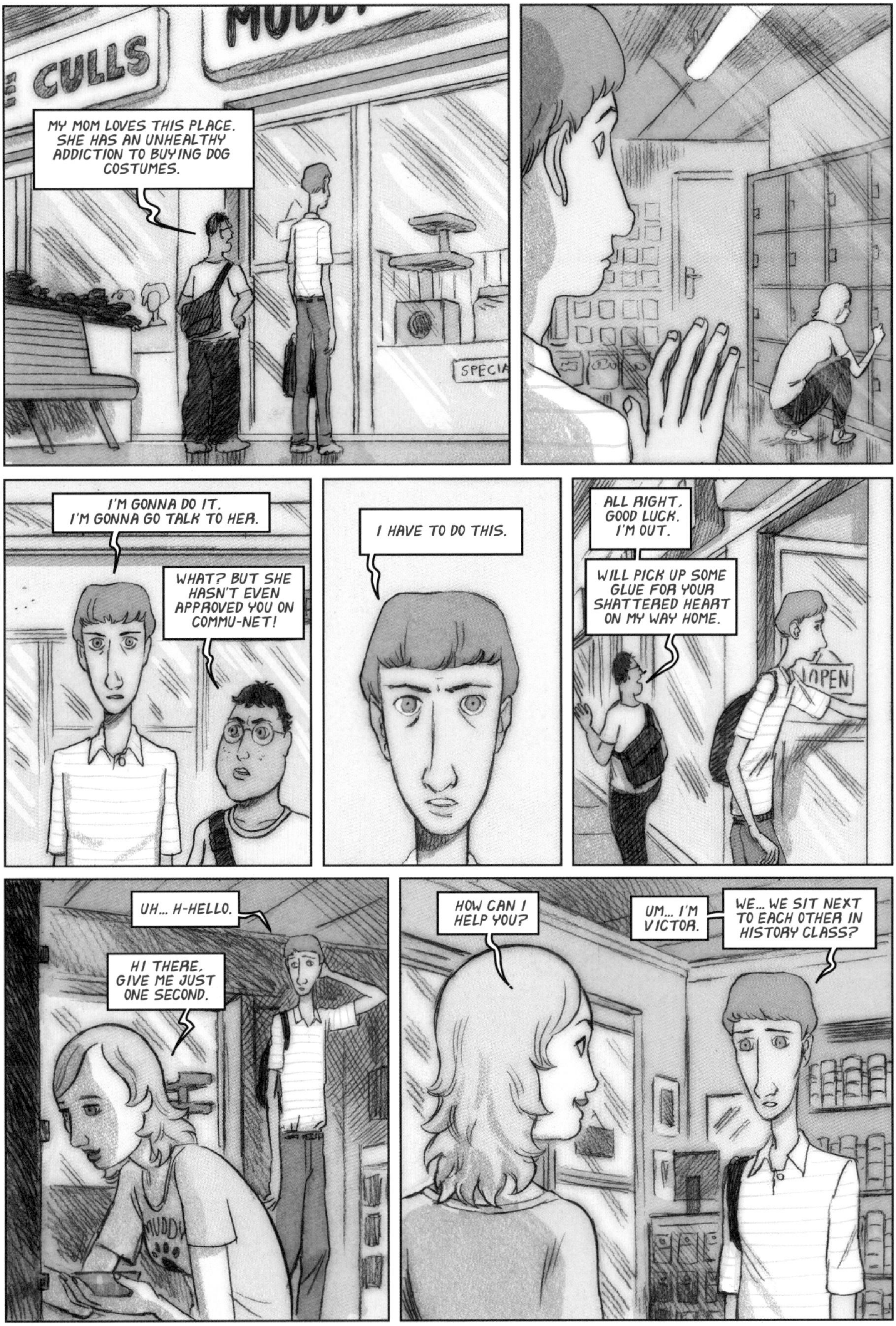
CULLS
MUDD
MY MOM LOVES THIS PLACE. SHE HAS AN UNHEALTHY ADDICTION TO BUYING DOG COSTUMES.
SPECIA
I'M GONNA DO IT. I'M GONNA GO TALK TO HER.
WHAT? BUT SHE HASN'T EVEN APPROVED YOU ON COMMU-NET!
I HAVE TO DO THIS.
ALL RIGHT, GOOD LUCK. I'M OUT.
WILL PICK UP SOME GLUE FOR YOUR SHATTERED HEART ON MY WAY HOME.
OPEN
UH... H-HELLO.
HI THERE, GIVE ME JUST ONE SECOND.
MUDDY
HOW CAN I HELP YOU?
UM... I'M VICTOR.
WE... WE SIT NEXT TO EACH OTHER IN HISTORY CLASS?

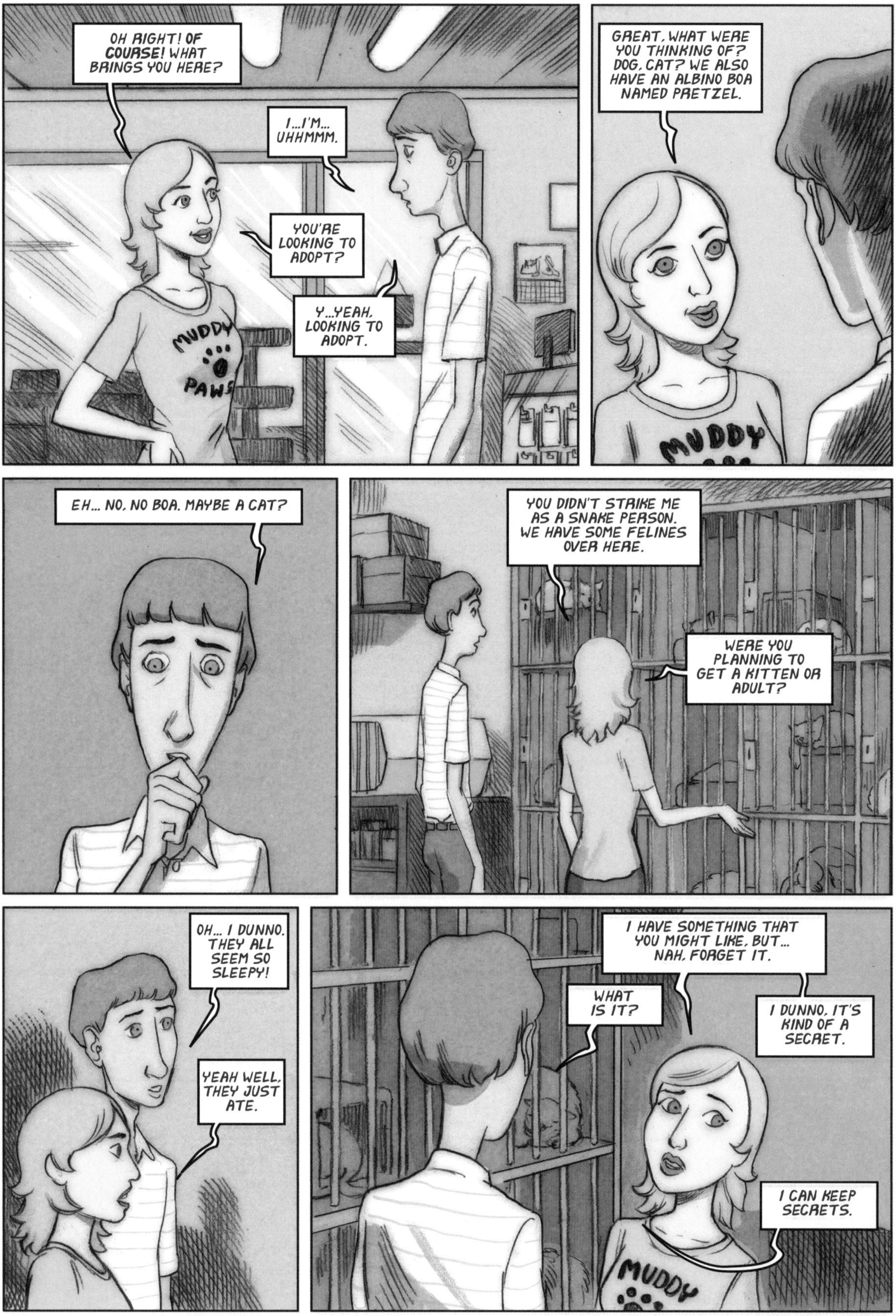
OH RIGHT! OF COURSE! WHAT BRINGS YOU HERE?
I...I'M... UHHMMM.
YOU'RE LOOKING TO ADOPT?
Y...YEAH, LOOKING TO ADOPT.
MUDDY PAWS
GREAT, WHAT WERE YOU THINKING OF? DOG, CAT? WE ALSO HAVE AN ALBINO BOA NAMED PRETZEL.
MUDDY
EH... NO, NO BOA. MAYBE A CAT?
YOU DIDN'T STRIKE ME AS A SNAKE PERSON. WE HAVE SOME FELINES OVER HERE.
WERE YOU PLANNING TO GET A KITTEN OR ADULT?
OH... I DUNNO. THEY ALL SEEM SO SLEEPY!
YEAH WELL, THEY JUST ATE.
I HAVE SOMETHING THAT YOU MIGHT LIKE, BUT... NAH, FORGET IT.
WHAT IS IT?
I DUNNO, IT'S KIND OF A SECRET.
I CAN KEEP SECRETS.
MUDDY

OK. YOU CAN'T SAY A WORD TO ANYONE ABOUT THIS.

I SWEAR I WONT.

WATT.

COME OUT!

WOW! WHERE DID YOU GET HIM?

I CAN'T REALLY TELL YOU.

OH... OK, WHAT HAPPENED TO HIM?

I'M NOT SURE. HE'S VERY SWEET THOUGH.

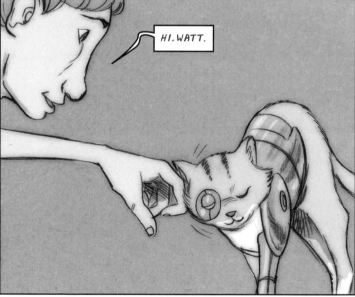

HI, WATT.

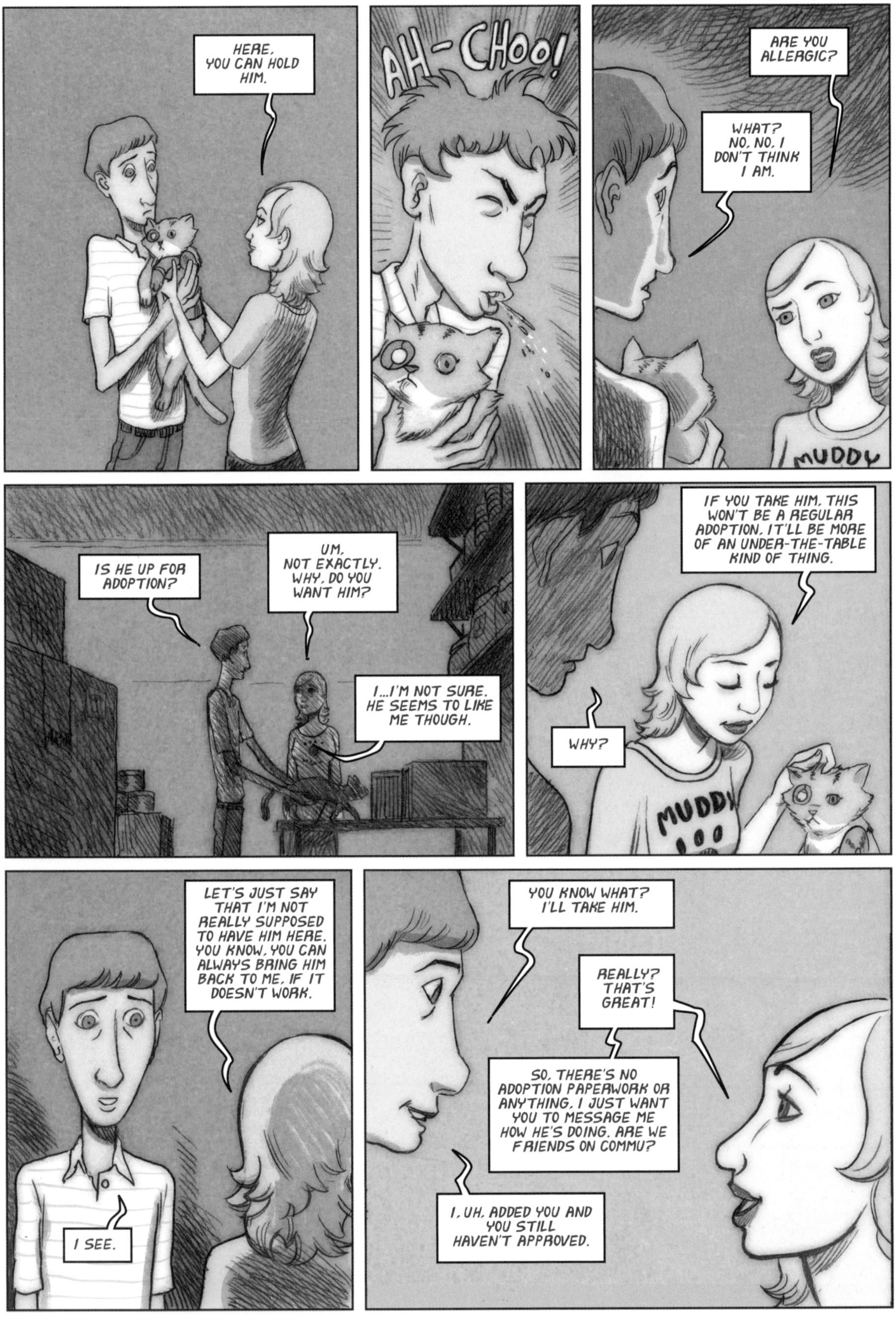
HERE, YOU CAN HOLD HIM.
AH-CHOO!
ARE YOU ALLERGIC?
WHAT? NO, NO, I DON'T THINK I AM.
MUDDY
IS HE UP FOR ADOPTION?
UM, NOT EXACTLY. WHY, DO YOU WANT HIM?
I...I'M NOT SURE. HE SEEMS TO LIKE ME THOUGH.
IF YOU TAKE HIM, THIS WON'T BE A REGULAR ADOPTION, IT'LL BE MORE OF AN UNDER-THE-TABLE KIND OF THING.
WHY?
MUDDY
LET'S JUST SAY THAT I'M NOT REALLY SUPPOSED TO HAVE HIM HERE. YOU KNOW, YOU CAN ALWAYS BRING HIM BACK TO ME, IF IT DOESN'T WORK.
I SEE.
YOU KNOW WHAT? I'LL TAKE HIM.
REALLY? THAT'S GREAT!
SO, THERE'S NO ADOPTION PAPERWORK OR ANYTHING, I JUST WANT YOU TO MESSAGE ME HOW HE'S DOING. ARE WE FRIENDS ON COMMU?
I, UH, ADDED YOU AND YOU STILL HAVEN'T APPROVED.

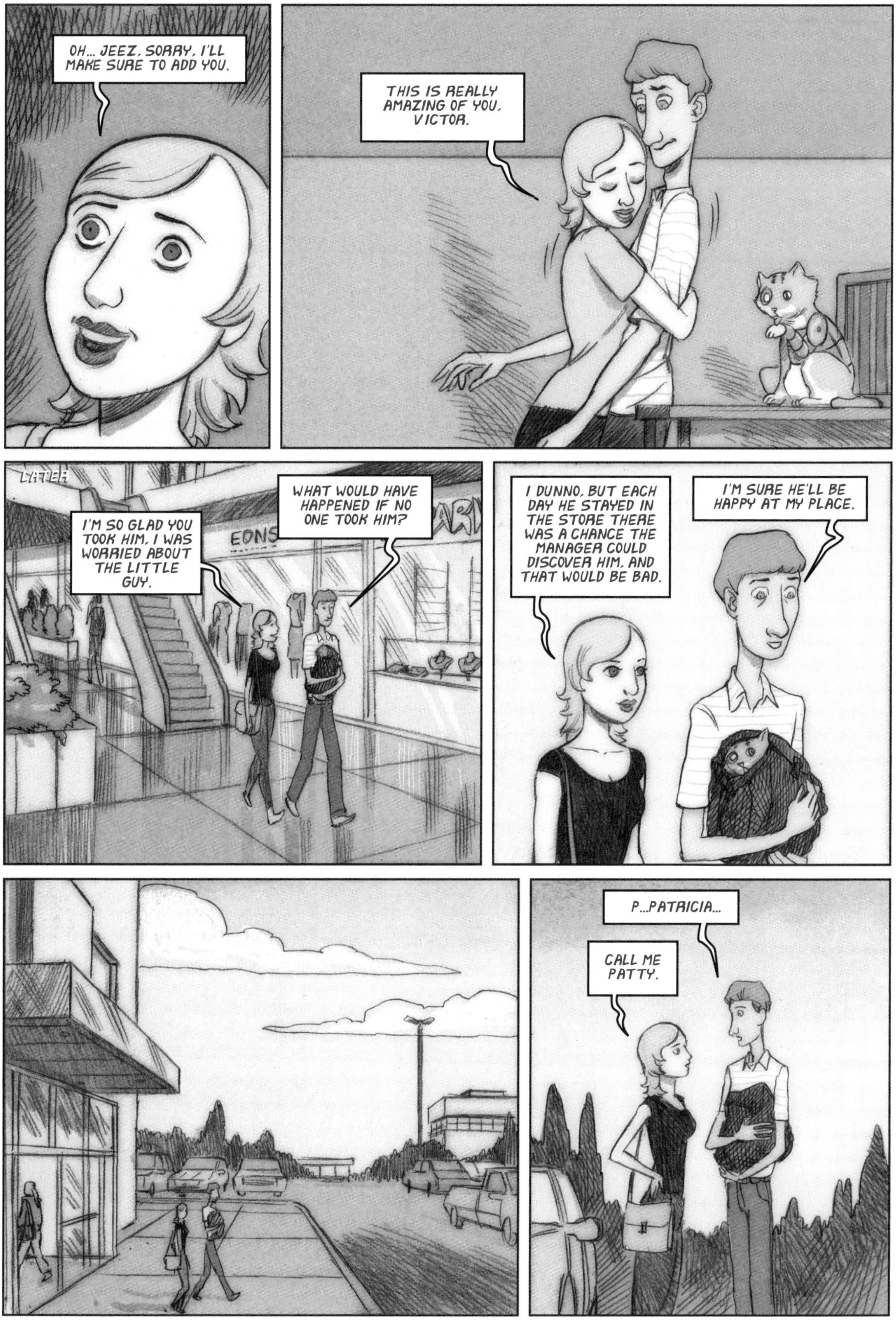
OH... JEEZ, SORRY, I'LL MAKE SURE TO ADD YOU.
THIS IS REALLY AMAZING OF YOU, VICTOR.
LATER
I'M SO GLAD YOU TOOK HIM, I WAS WORRIED ABOUT THE LITTLE GUY.
WHAT WOULD HAVE HAPPENED IF NO ONE TOOK HIM?
I DUNNO, BUT EACH DAY HE STAYED IN THE STORE THERE WAS A CHANCE THE MANAGER COULD DISCOVER HIM, AND THAT WOULD BE BAD.
I'M SURE HE'LL BE HAPPY AT MY PLACE.
P...PATRICIA...
CALL ME PATTY.

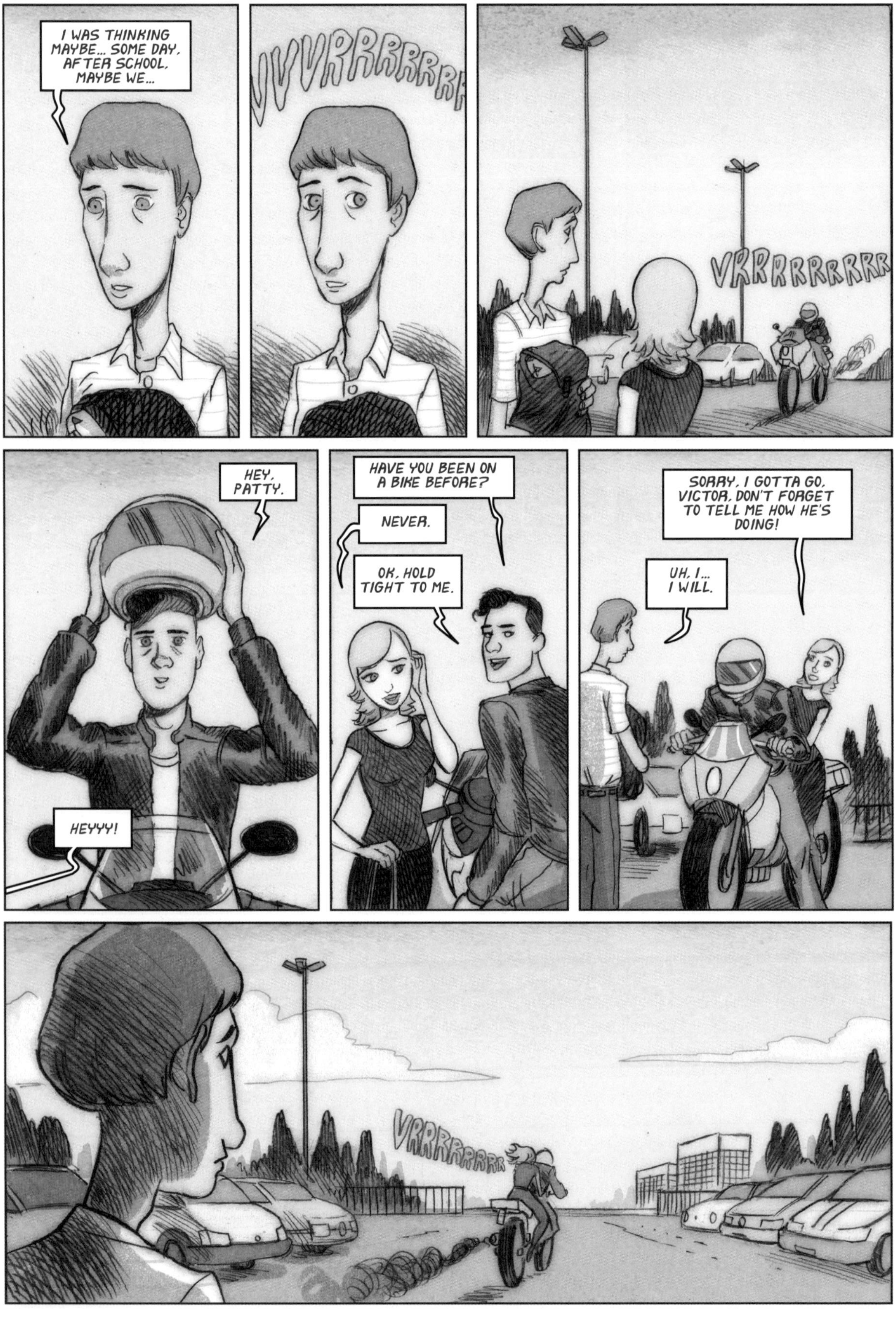
I WAS THINKING MAYBE... SOME DAY, AFTER SCHOOL, MAYBE WE...
VVVRRRRRRRR
VRRRRRRRRR
HEY, PATTY.
HEYYY!
HAVE YOU BEEN ON A BIKE BEFORE?
NEVER.
OK, HOLD TIGHT TO ME.
SORRY, I GOTTA GO, VICTOR, DON'T FORGET TO TELL ME HOW HE'S DOING!
UH, I... I WILL.
VRRRRRRRR

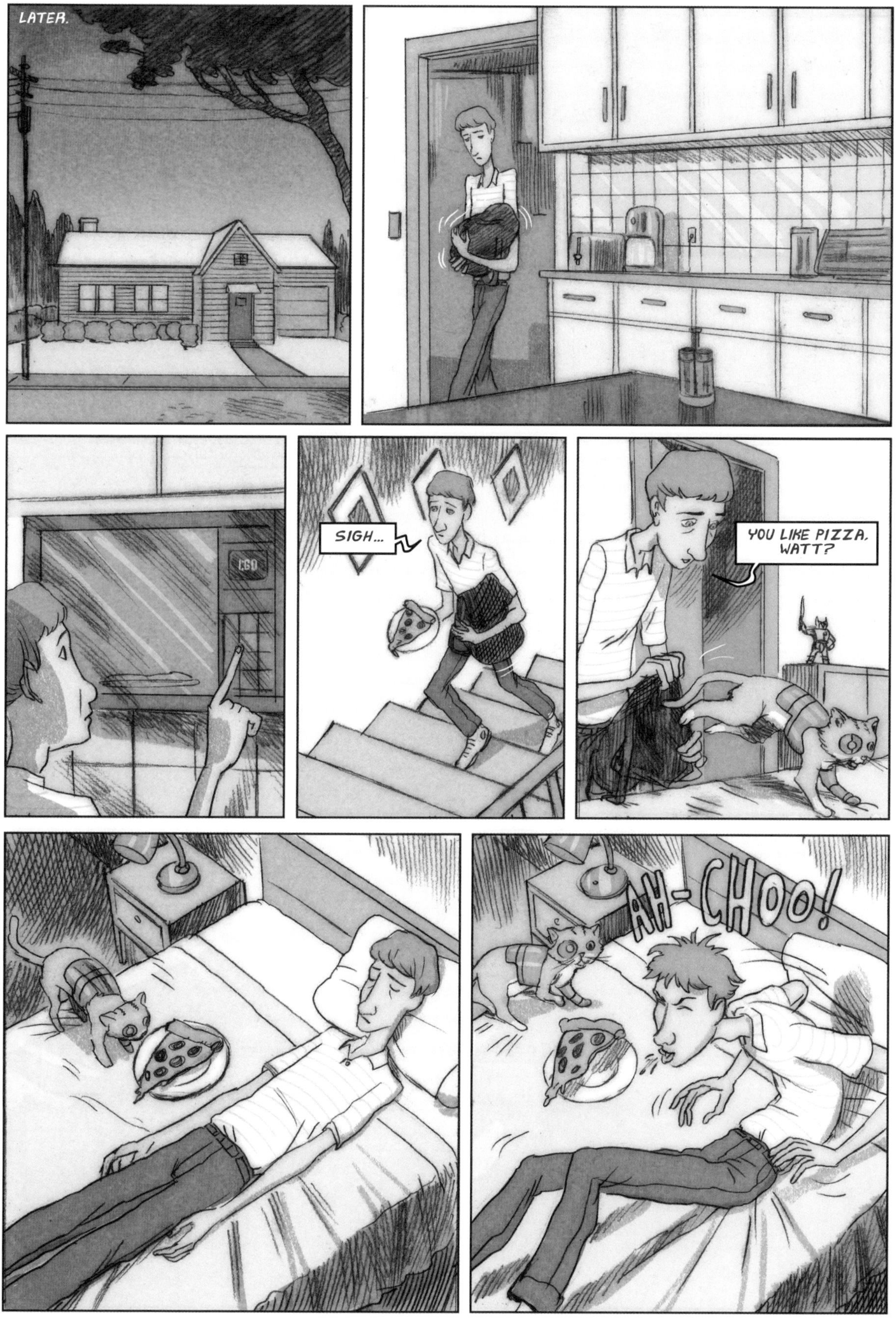
LATER.
SIGH...
YOU LIKE PIZZA, WATT?
AH-CHOO!

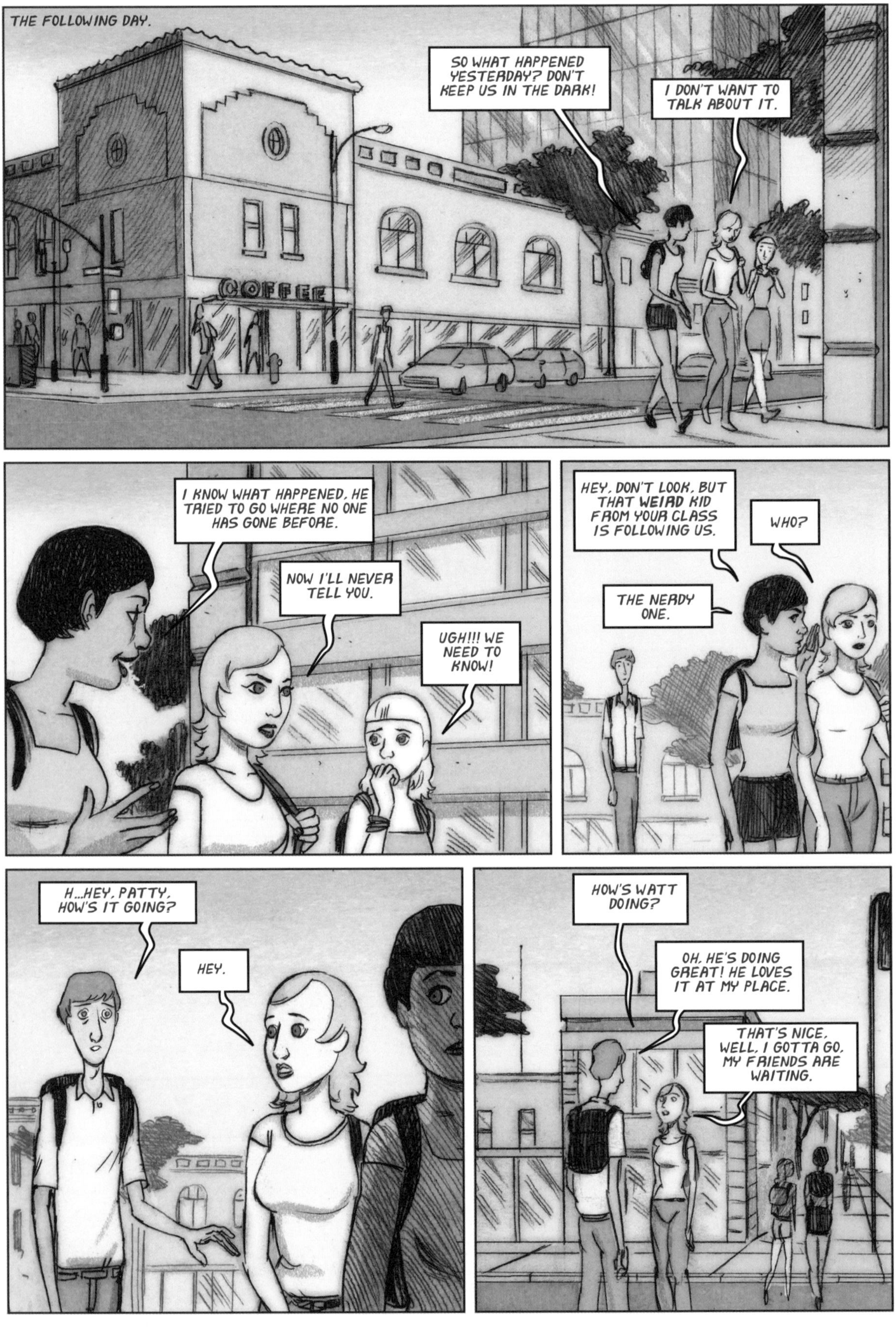
THE FOLLOWING DAY.
SO WHAT HAPPENED YESTERDAY? DON'T KEEP US IN THE DARK!
I DON'T WANT TO TALK ABOUT IT.
COFFEE
I KNOW WHAT HAPPENED. HE TRIED TO GO WHERE NO ONE HAS GONE BEFORE.
NOW I'LL NEVER TELL YOU.
UGH!!! WE NEED TO KNOW!
HEY, DON'T LOOK, BUT THAT WEIRD KID FROM YOUR CLASS IS FOLLOWING US.
WHO?
THE NERDY ONE.
H...HEY, PATTY, HOW'S IT GOING?
HEY.
HOW'S WATT DOING?
OH, HE'S DOING GREAT! HE LOVES IT AT MY PLACE.
THAT'S NICE. WELL, I GOTTA GO, MY FRIENDS ARE WAITING.

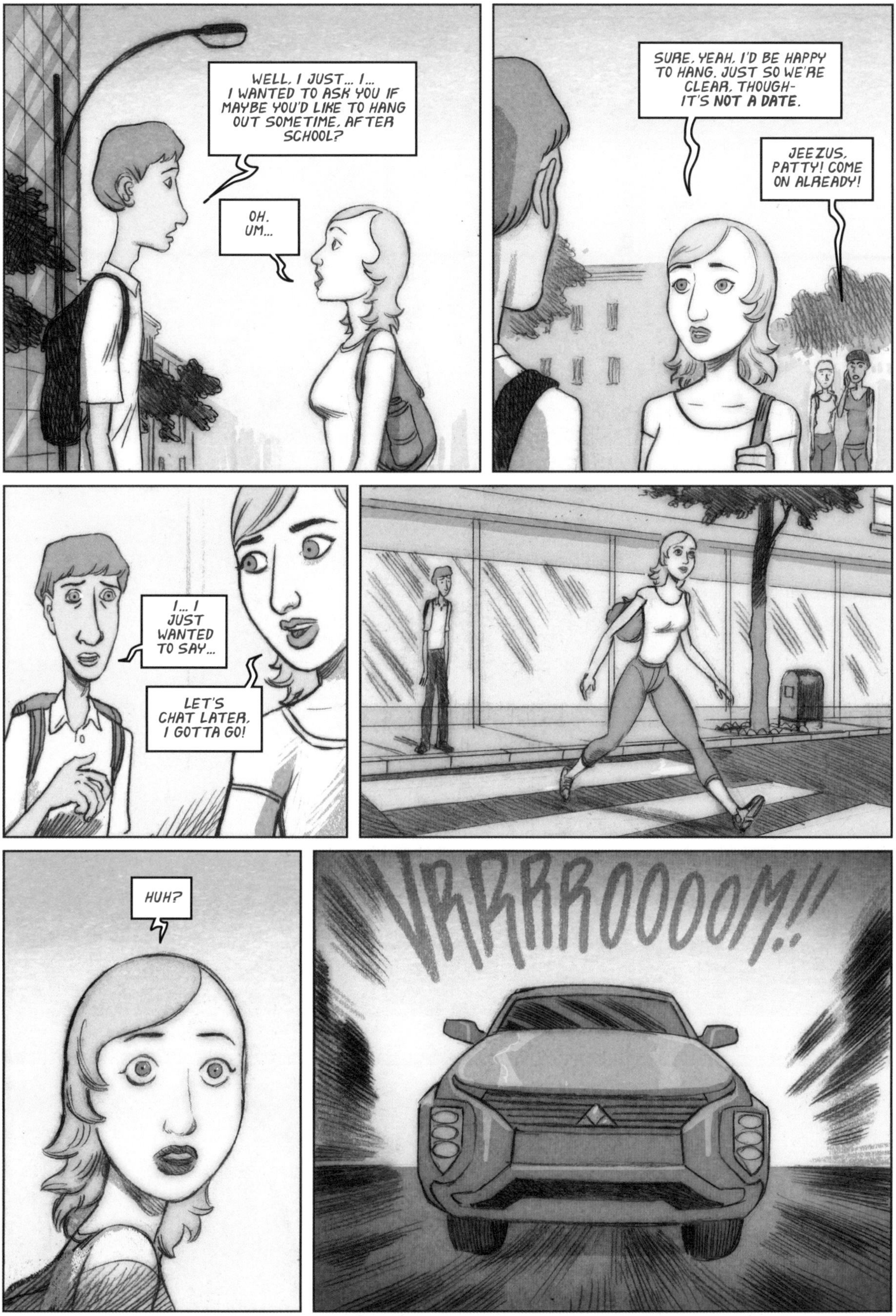
WELL, I JUST... I...
I WANTED TO ASK YOU IF MAYBE YOU'D LIKE TO HANG OUT SOMETIME, AFTER SCHOOL?
OH. UM...
SURE, YEAH, I'D BE HAPPY TO HANG. JUST SO WE'RE CLEAR, THOUGH-
IT'S NOT A DATE.
JEEZUS, PATTY! COME ON ALREADY!
I... I JUST WANTED TO SAY...
LET'S CHAT LATER, I GOTTA GO!
HUH?
VRRRROOOOM!!

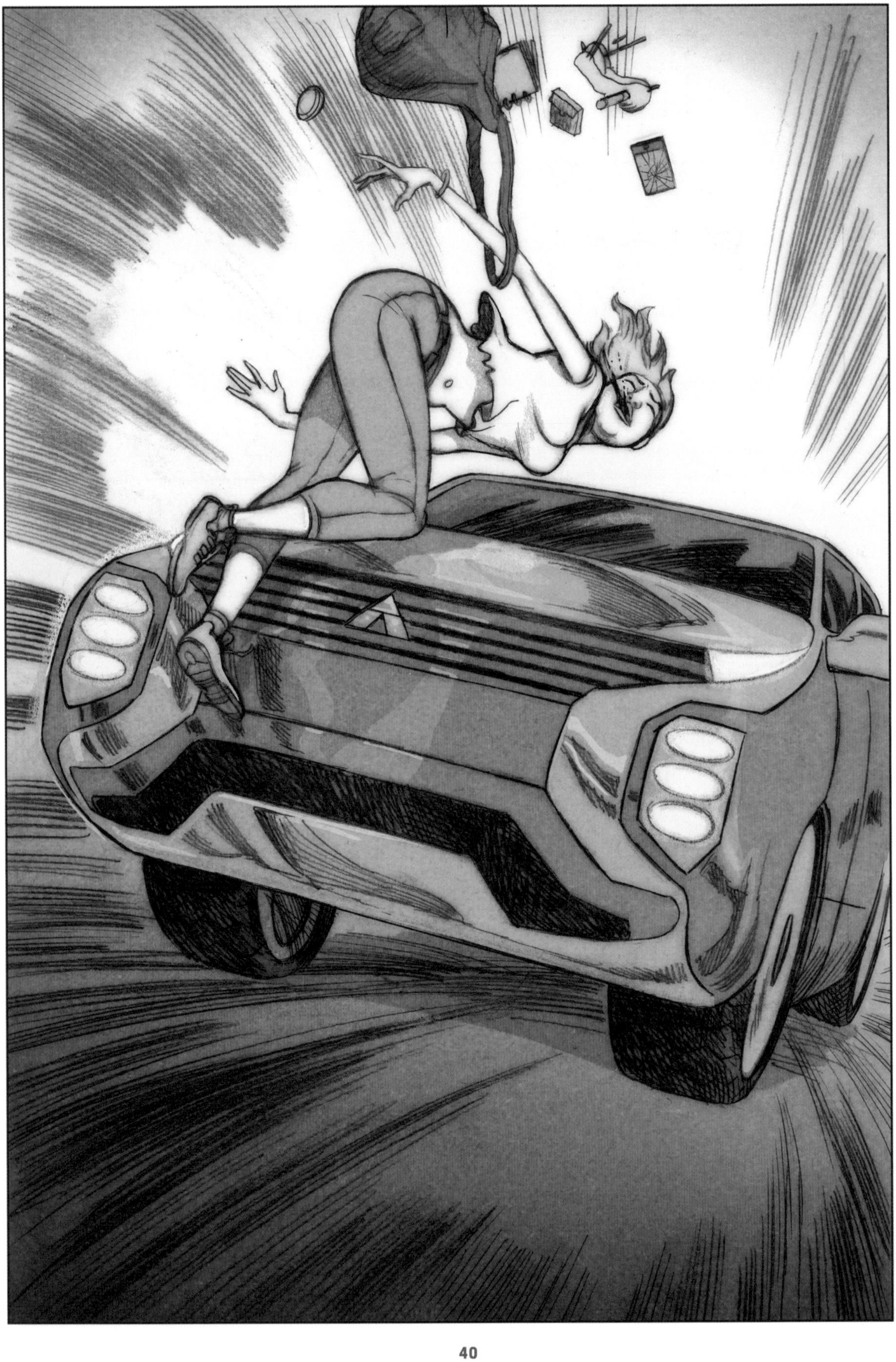

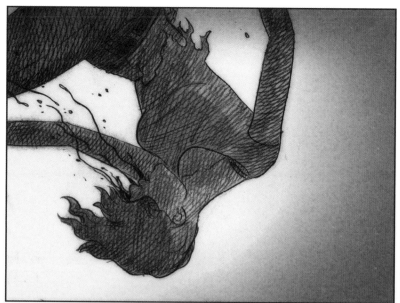

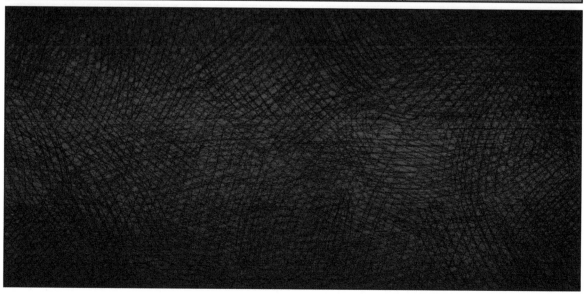

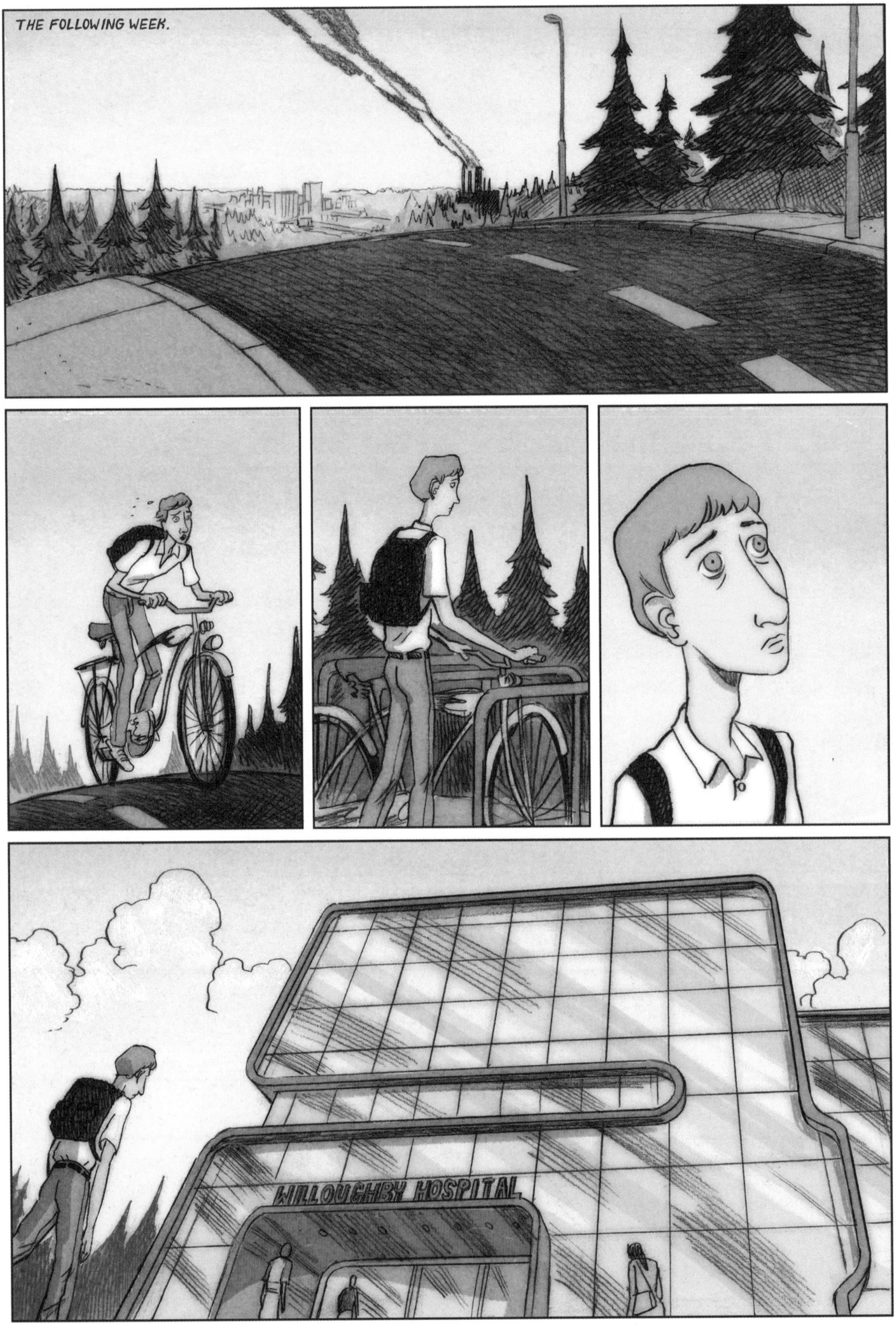
THE FOLLOWING WEEK.
WILLOUGHBY HOSPITAL

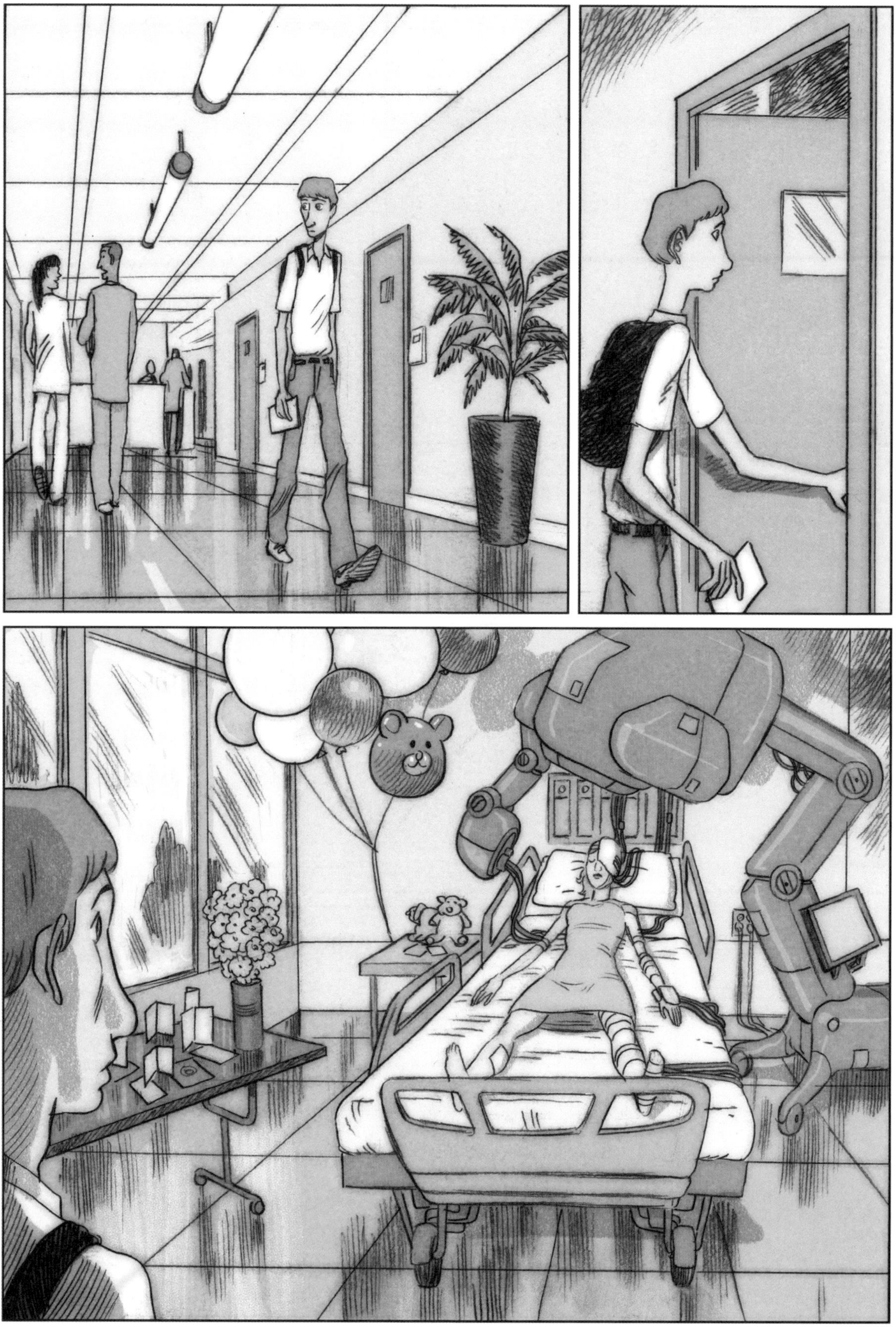

HEY. I... I HOPE YOU DON'T MIND THAT I CAME.

I WAS SURE YOU DIED.

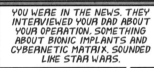

YOU WERE IN THE NEWS. THEY INTERVIEWED YOUR DAD ABOUT YOUR OPERATION. SOMETHING ABOUT BIONIC IMPLANTS AND CYBERNETIC MATRIX. SOUNDED LIKE STAR WARS.

YOU HAVEN'T MISSED MUCH AT SCHOOL IN THE LAST MONTH, JUST A LOT OF BORING ASSIGNMENTS.

OH, THE SCHOOL B-BALL TEAM WON SOME BIG TOURNAMENT.

NOT SURE WHO THEY WON AGAINST, IT'S NOT REALLY MY THING. APPARENTLY BRAD HELPED WIN THE GAME.

44

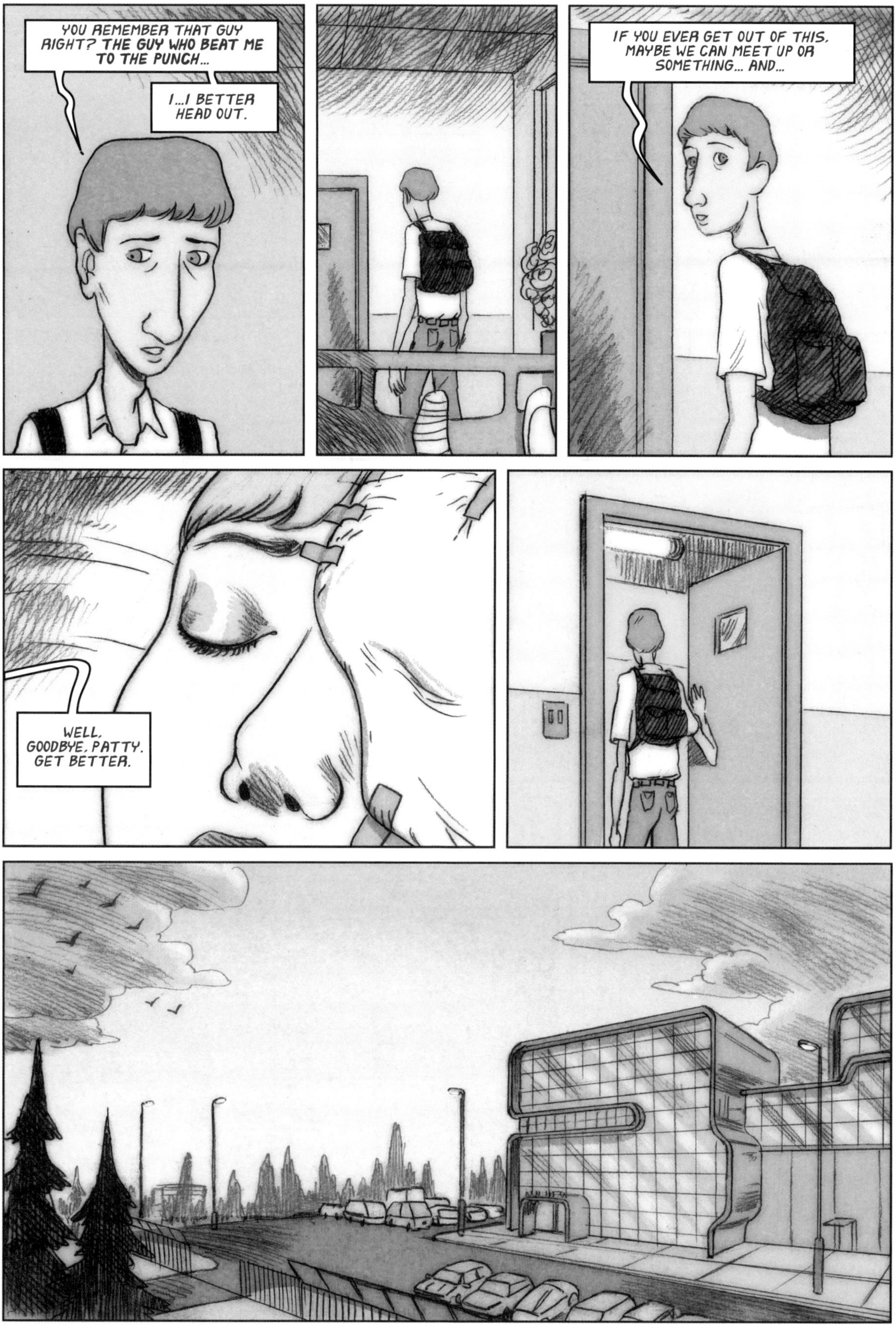
YOU REMEMBER THAT GUY RIGHT? THE GUY WHO BEAT ME TO THE PUNCH...
I...I BETTER HEAD OUT.
IF YOU EVER GET OUT OF THIS, MAYBE WE CAN MEET UP OR SOMETHING... AND...
WELL, GOODBYE, PATTY. GET BETTER.

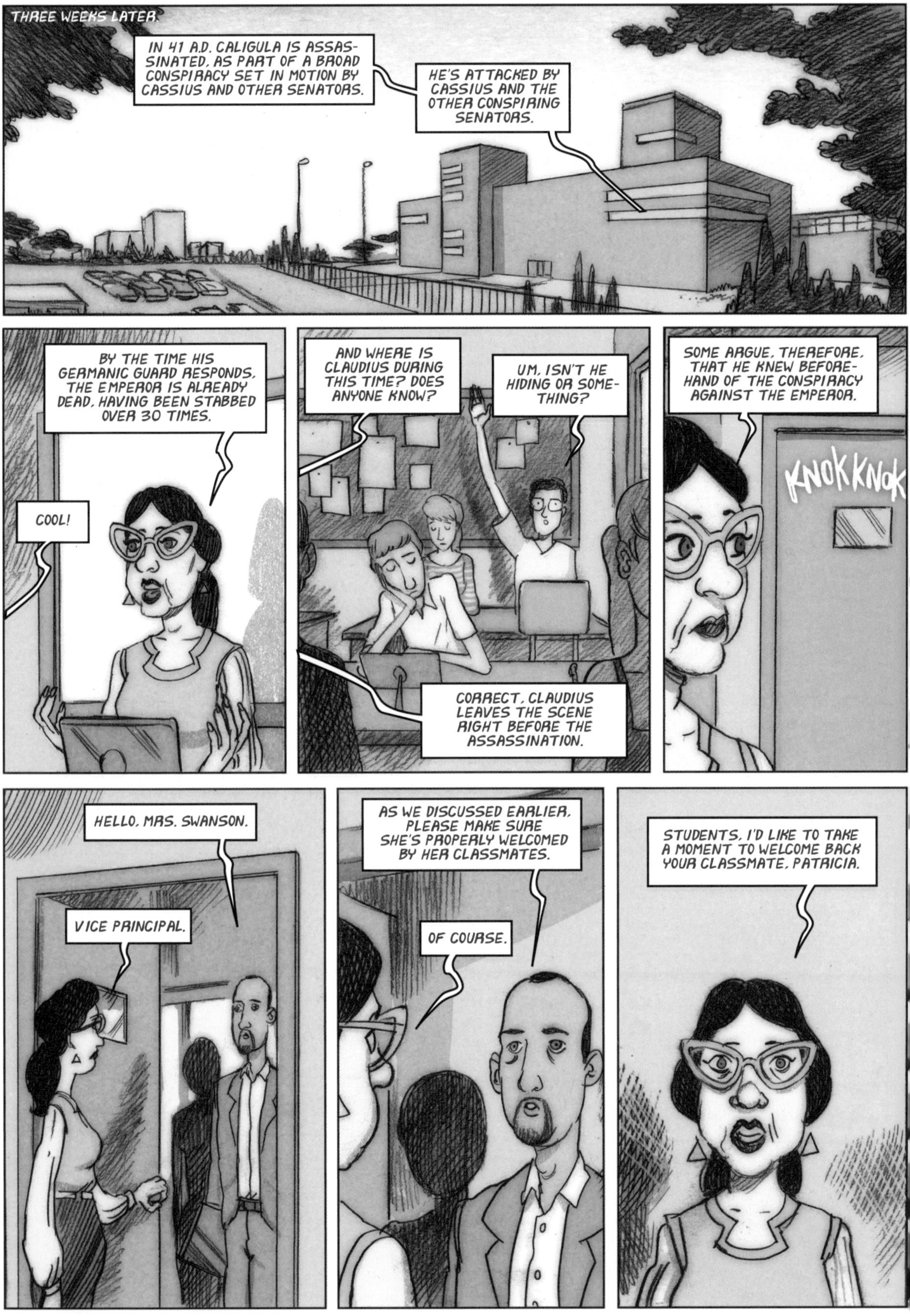
THREE WEEKS LATER.
IN 41 A.D. CALIGULA IS ASSASSINATED, AS PART OF A BROAD CONSPIRACY SET IN MOTION BY CASSIUS AND OTHER SENATORS.
HE'S ATTACKED BY CASSIUS AND THE OTHER CONSPIRING SENATORS.
BY THE TIME HIS GERMANIC GUARD RESPONDS, THE EMPEROR IS ALREADY DEAD, HAVING BEEN STABBED OVER 30 TIMES.
COOL!
AND WHERE IS CLAUDIUS DURING THIS TIME? DOES ANYONE KNOW?
UM, ISN'T HE HIDING OR SOMETHING?
CORRECT. CLAUDIUS LEAVES THE SCENE RIGHT BEFORE THE ASSASSINATION.
SOME ARGUE, THEREFORE, THAT HE KNEW BEFOREHAND OF THE CONSPIRACY AGAINST THE EMPEROR.
KNOK KNOK
HELLO, MRS. SWANSON.
VICE PRINCIPAL.
AS WE DISCUSSED EARLIER, PLEASE MAKE SURE SHE'S PROPERLY WELCOMED BY HER CLASSMATES.
OF COURSE.
STUDENTS, I'D LIKE TO TAKE A MOMENT TO WELCOME BACK YOUR CLASSMATE, PATRICIA.

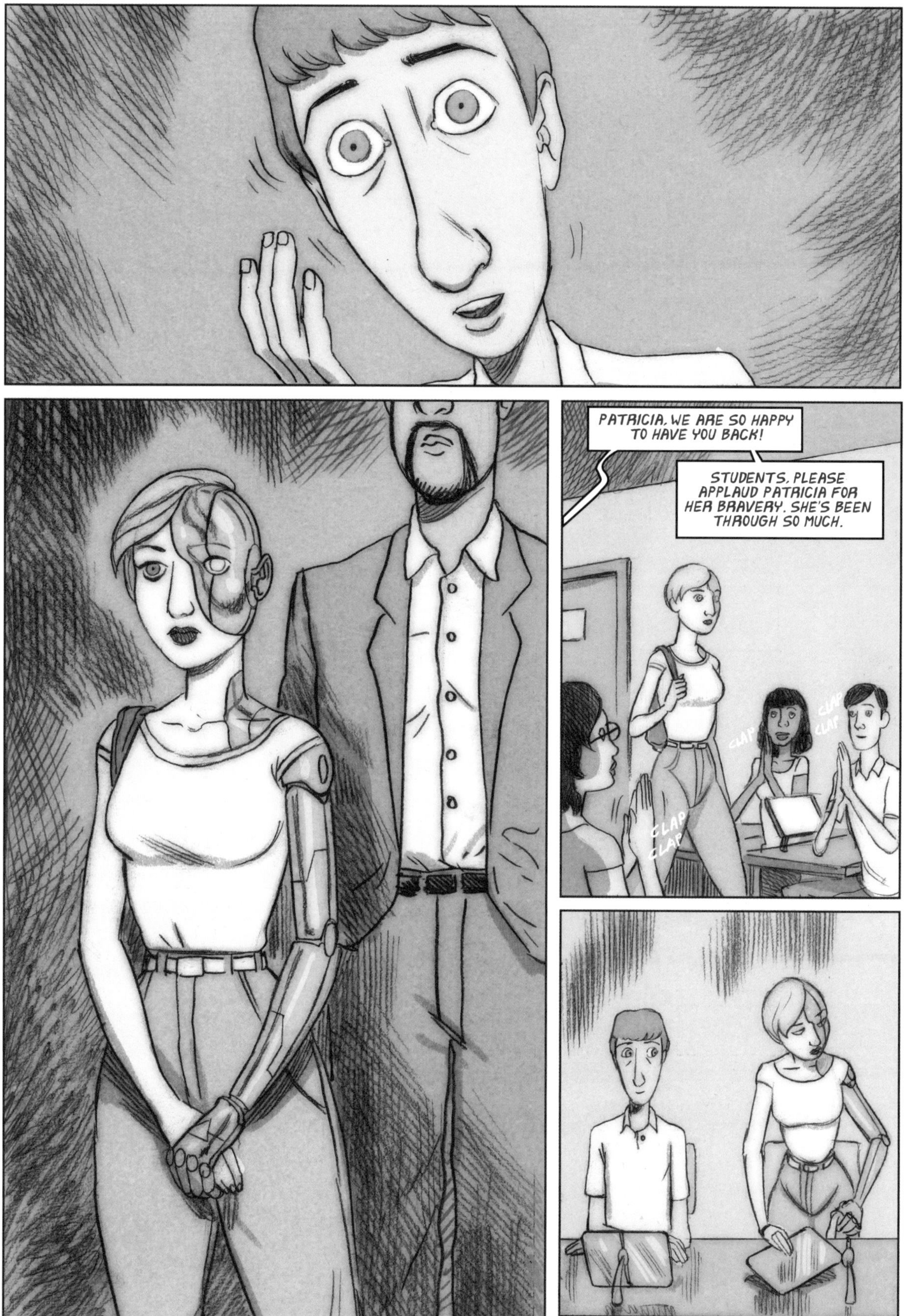
PATRICIA, WE ARE SO HAPPY TO HAVE YOU BACK!
STUDENTS, PLEASE APPLAUD PATRICIA FOR HER BRAVERY. SHE'S BEEN THROUGH SO MUCH.
CLAP CLAP
CLAP
CLAP CLAP

GUS! GUS!!!

HEY! WHAT THE FUDGE?

DID YOU SEE?

SEE WHAT?

PATRICIA! SHE'S BACK!

OH YEAH. ALL CYBERNETIC AND STUFF. I SAW.

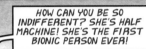

HOW CAN YOU BE SO INDIFFERENT? SHE'S HALF MACHINE! SHE'S THE FIRST BIONIC PERSON EVER!

TECHNICALLY, THERE'S ALREADY BEEN EXTENSIVE BIONIC IMPLANT OPERATIONS DONE IN CHINA. I BELIEVE WONG MEI WAS THE FIRST TO HAVE OVER 50% OPERATIONAL MECHANICAL PARTS.

THANKS, MR. KNOW-IT-ALL, I STILL THINK IT'S PRETTY COOL.

YOU'RE WELCOME.

WAIT, WAIT. YOU MEAN TO TELL ME... HOLY SHIT!

YOU'RE NOT OVER HER!

WHAT'S SO WEIRD ABOUT THAT?

NOTHING, NOTHING WEIRD ABOUT CRUSHING ON A ROBOT.

WELL, AT LEAST NOW SHE'S FINALLY IN YOUR LEAGUE.

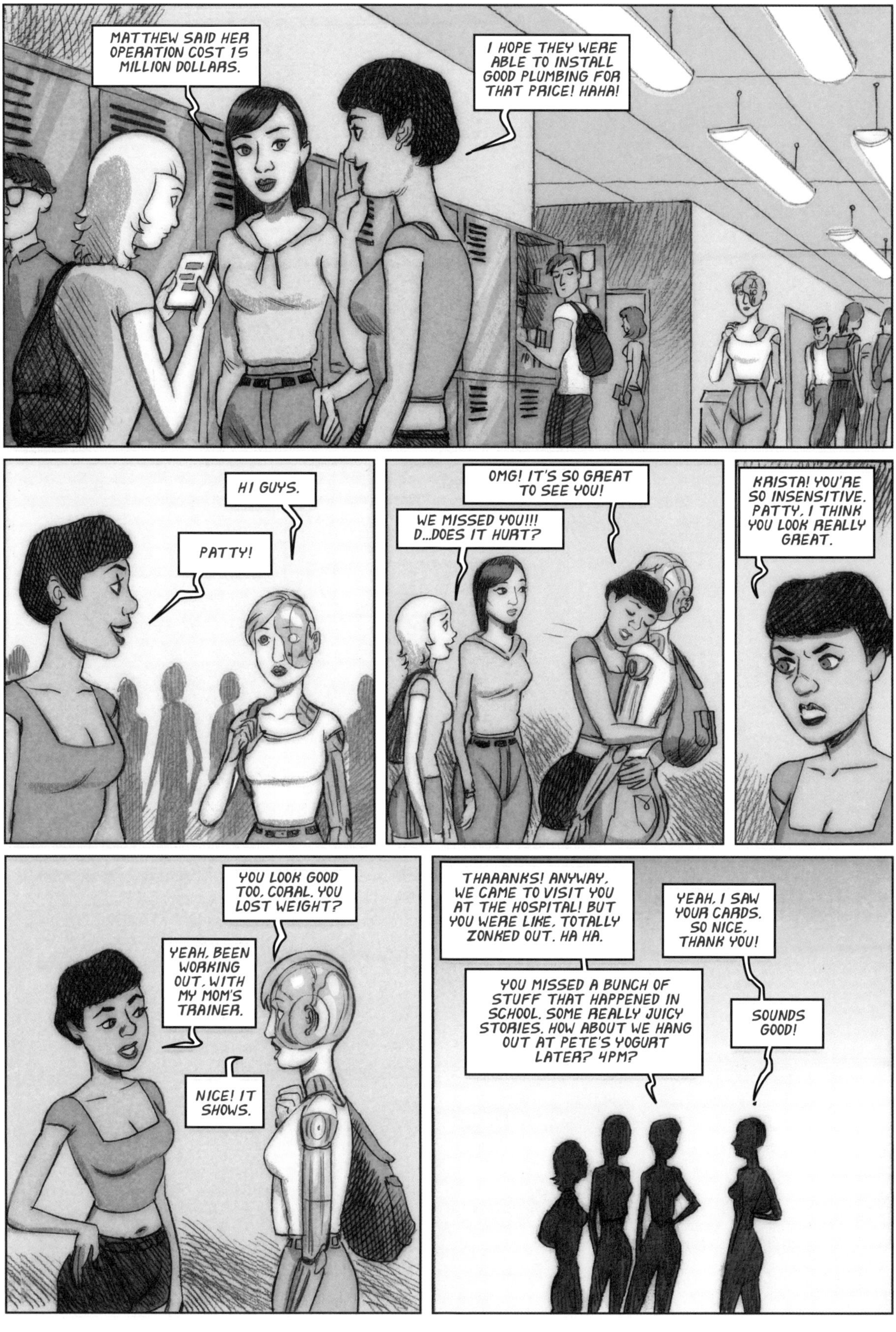
MATTHEW SAID HER OPERATION COST 15 MILLION DOLLARS.
I HOPE THEY WERE ABLE TO INSTALL GOOD PLUMBING FOR THAT PRICE! HAHA!
HI GUYS.
PATTY!
OMG! IT'S SO GREAT TO SEE YOU!
WE MISSED YOU!!! D...DOES IT HURT?
KRISTA! YOU'RE SO INSENSITIVE. PATTY, I THINK YOU LOOK REALLY GREAT.
YOU LOOK GOOD TOO, CORAL. YOU LOST WEIGHT?
YEAH, BEEN WORKING OUT, WITH MY MOM'S TRAINER.
NICE! IT SHOWS.
THAAANKS! ANYWAY, WE CAME TO VISIT YOU AT THE HOSPITAL! BUT YOU WERE LIKE, TOTALLY ZONKED OUT. HA HA.
YEAH, I SAW YOUR CARDS. SO NICE, THANK YOU!
YOU MISSED A BUNCH OF STUFF THAT HAPPENED IN SCHOOL. SOME REALLY JUICY STORIES. HOW ABOUT WE HANG OUT AT PETE'S YOGURT LATER? 4PM?
SOUNDS GOOD!

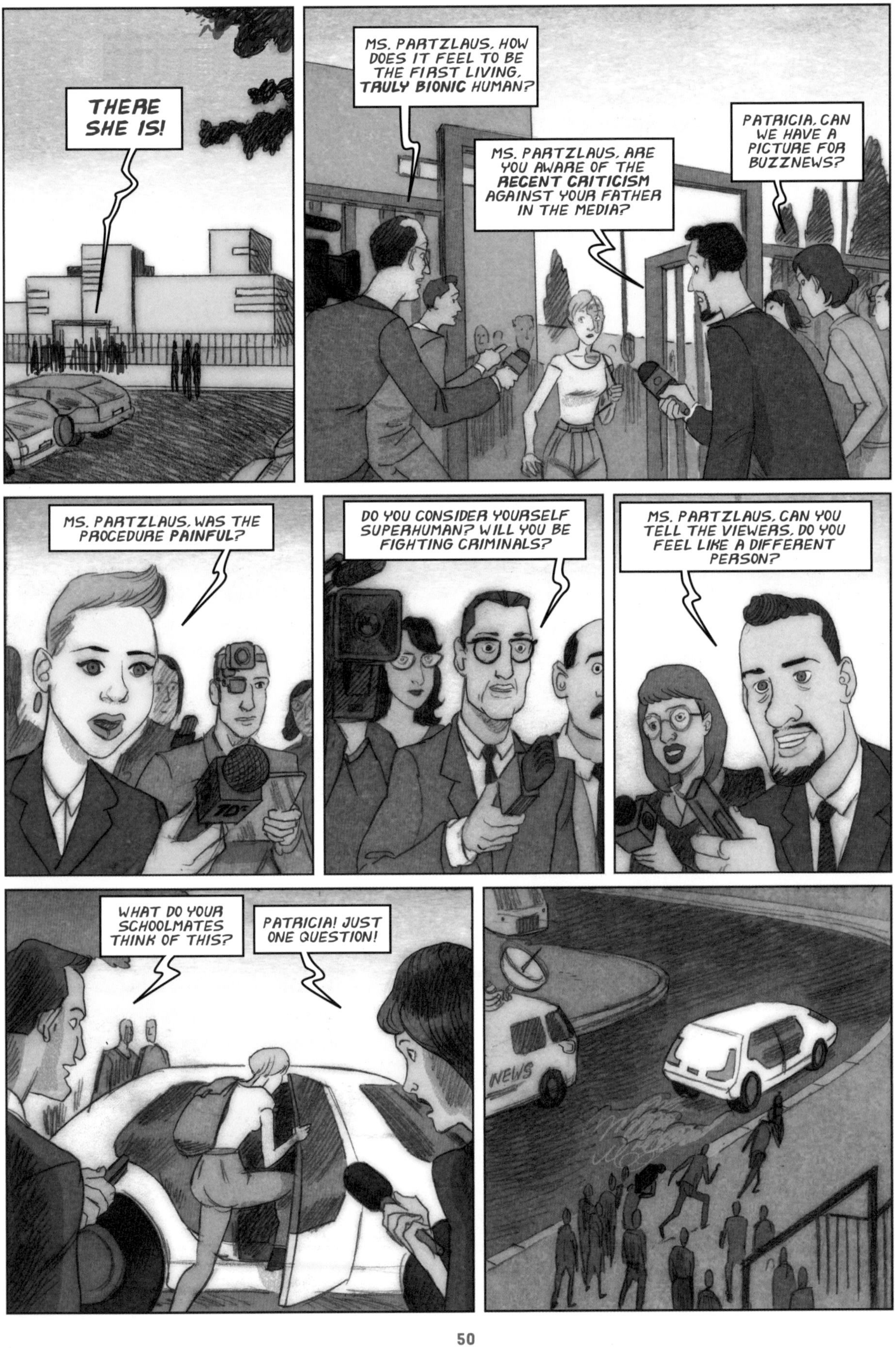
THERE SHE IS!
MS. PARTZLAUS, HOW DOES IT FEEL TO BE THE FIRST LIVING, TRULY BIONIC HUMAN?
MS. PARTZLAUS, ARE YOU AWARE OF THE RECENT CRITICISM AGAINST YOUR FATHER IN THE MEDIA?
PATRICIA, CAN WE HAVE A PICTURE FOR BUZZNEWS?
MS. PARTZLAUS, WAS THE PROCEDURE PAINFUL?
TD
DO YOU CONSIDER YOURSELF SUPERHUMAN? WILL YOU BE FIGHTING CRIMINALS?
MS. PARTZLAUS, CAN YOU TELL THE VIEWERS, DO YOU FEEL LIKE A DIFFERENT PERSON?
WHAT DO YOUR SCHOOLMATES THINK OF THIS?
PATRICIA! JUST ONE QUESTION!
NEWS

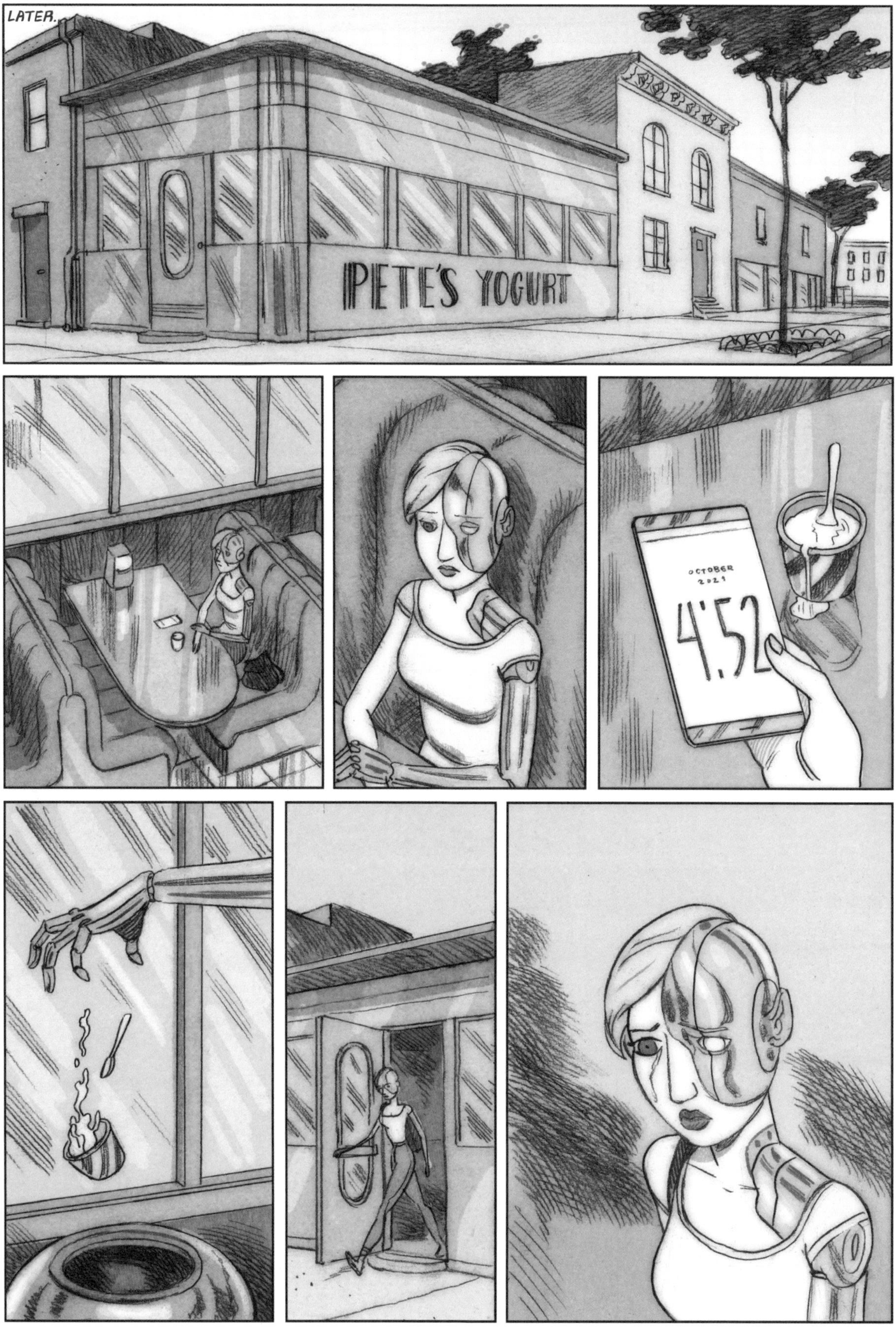
LATER.
PETE'S YOGURT
OCTOBER
2021
4'52

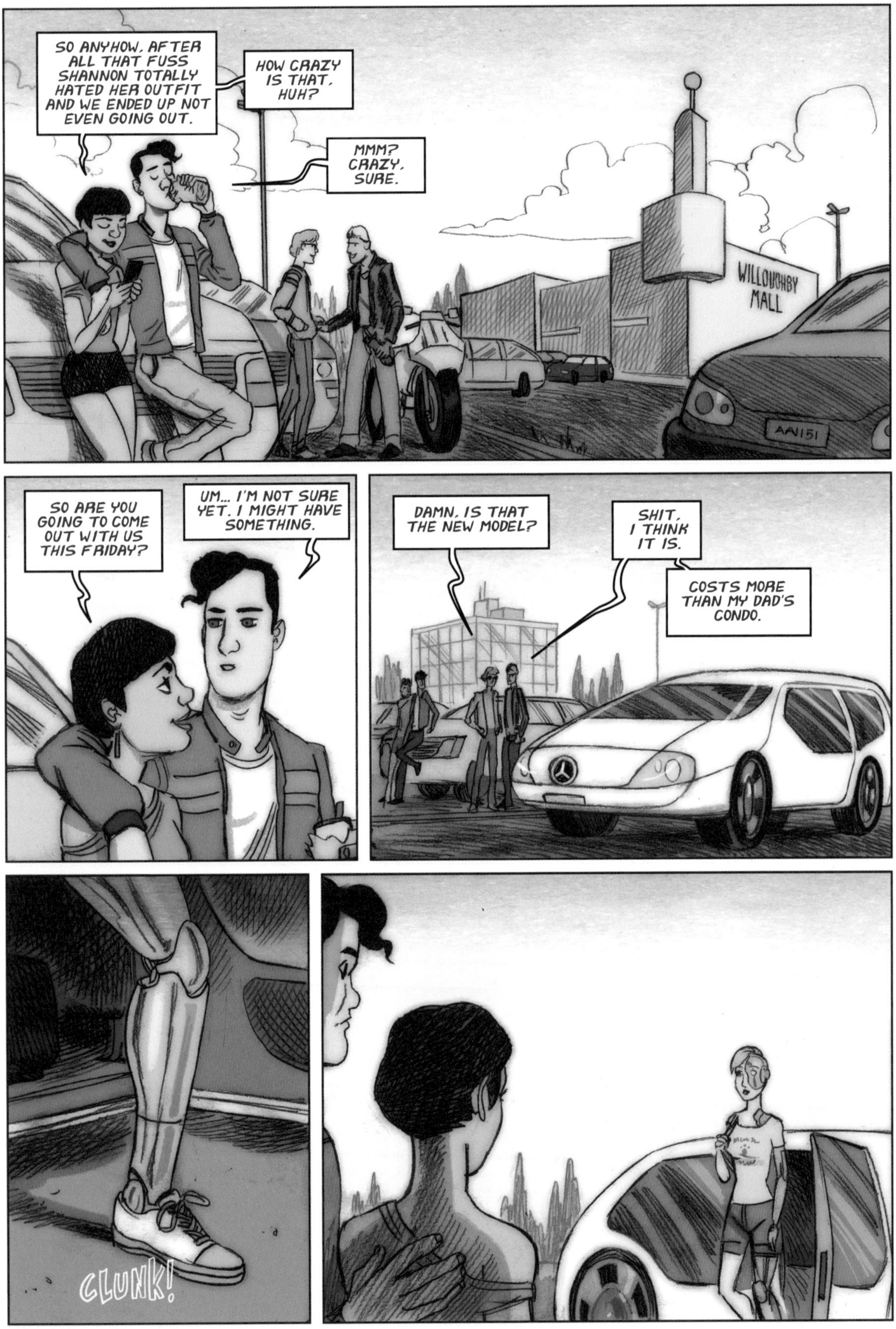
SO ANYHOW, AFTER ALL THAT FUSS SHANNON TOTALLY HATED HER OUTFIT AND WE ENDED UP NOT EVEN GOING OUT.
HOW CRAZY IS THAT, HUH?
MMM? CRAZY, SURE.
WILLOUGHBY MALL
SO ARE YOU GOING TO COME OUT WITH US THIS FRIDAY?
UM... I'M NOT SURE YET. I MIGHT HAVE SOMETHING.
DAMN, IS THAT THE NEW MODEL?
SHIT, I THINK IT IS.
COSTS MORE THAN MY DAD'S CONDO.
CLUNK!

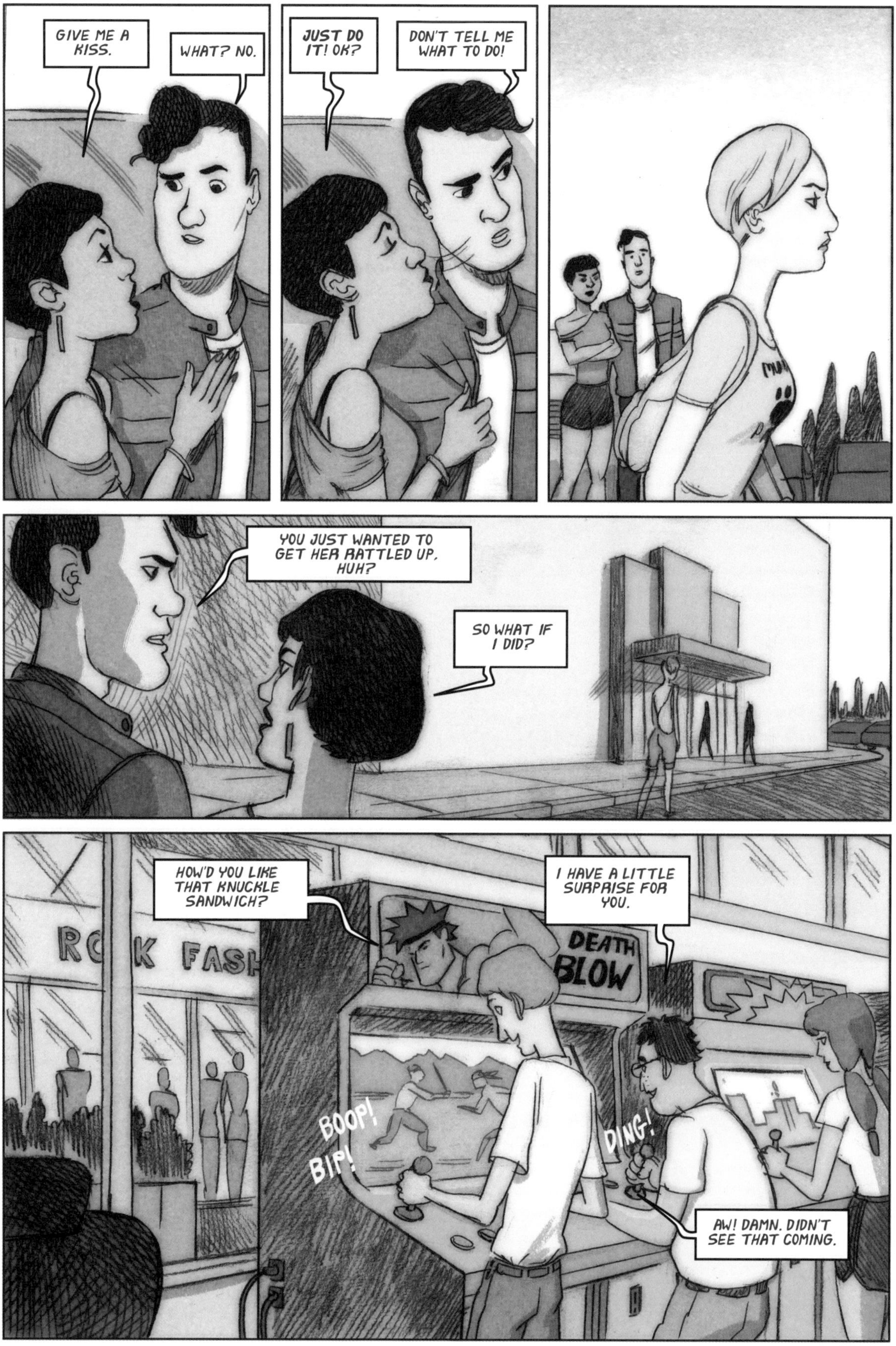
GIVE ME A KISS.
WHAT? NO.
JUST DO IT! OK?
DON'T TELL ME WHAT TO DO!
YOU JUST WANTED TO GET HER RATTLED UP, HUH?
SO WHAT IF I DID?
HOW'D YOU LIKE THAT KNUCKLE SANDWICH?
I HAVE A LITTLE SURPRISE FOR YOU.
DEATH BLOW
BOOP!
BIP!
DING!
AW! DAMN. DIDN'T SEE THAT COMING.

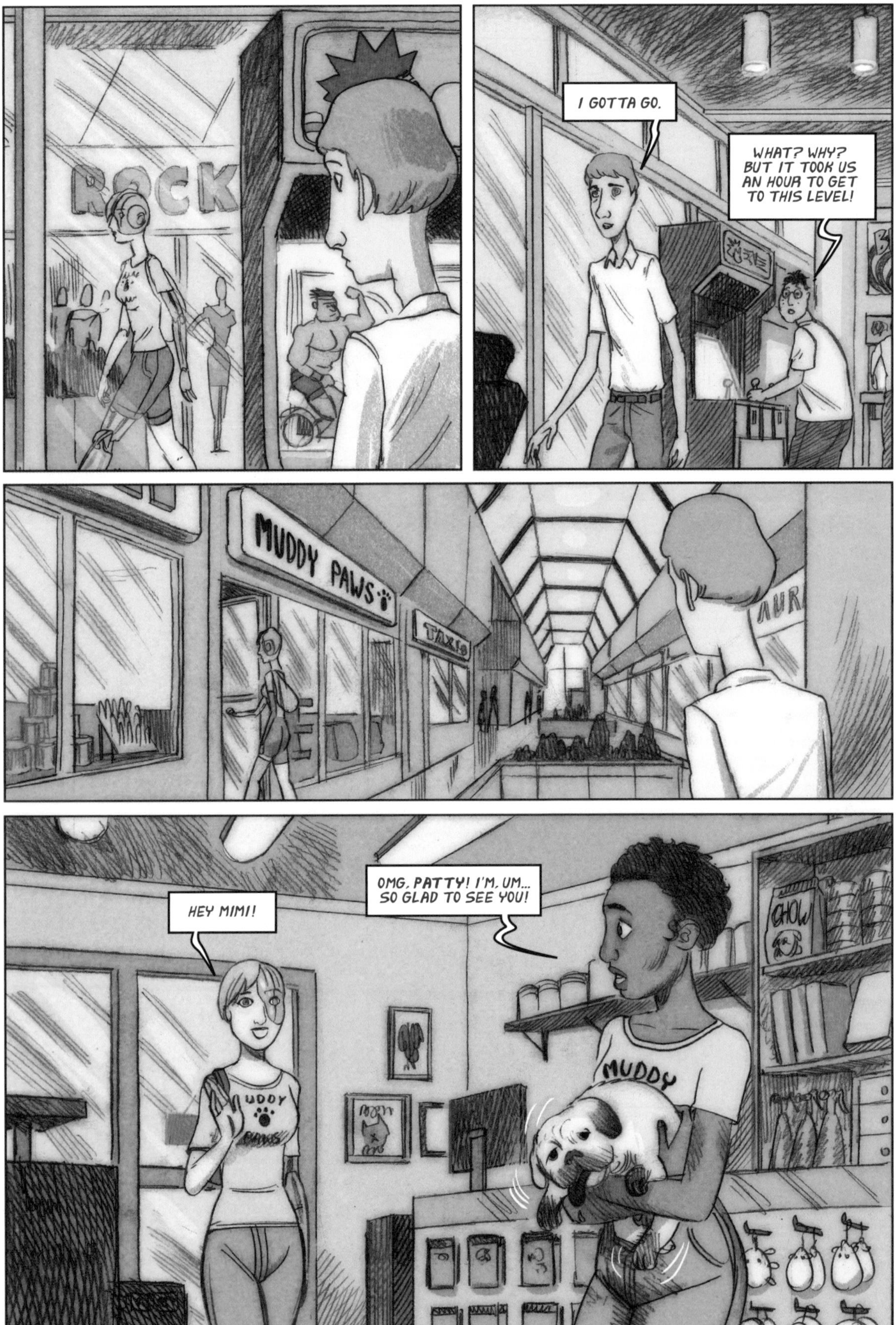
ROCK
I GOTTA GO.
WHAT? WHY? BUT IT TOOK US AN HOUR TO GET TO THIS LEVEL!
MUDDY PAWS
TAXIS
HEY MIMI!
OMG, PATTY! I'M, UM... SO GLAD TO SEE YOU!
MUDDY
CHOW

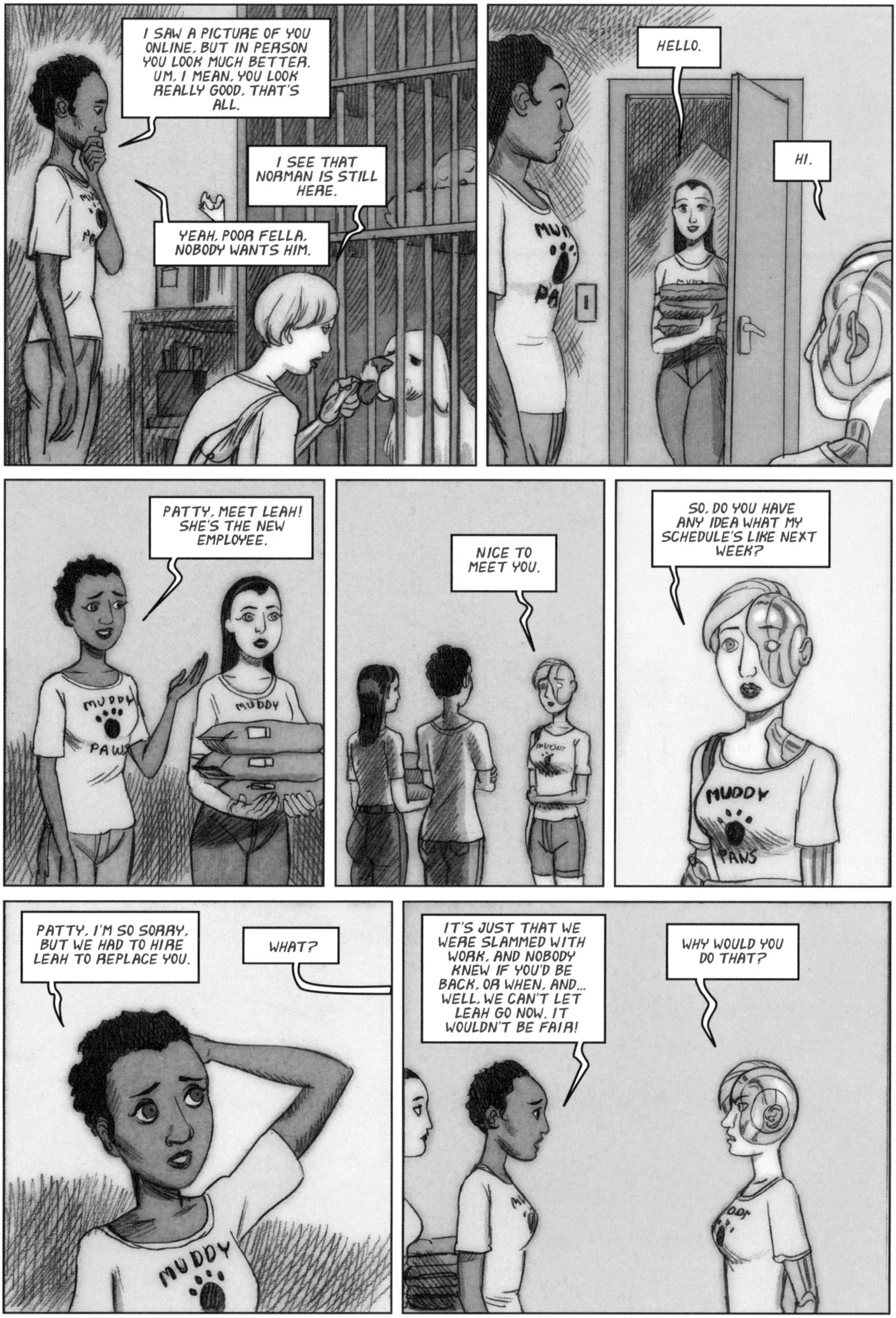
I SAW A PICTURE OF YOU ONLINE, BUT IN PERSON YOU LOOK MUCH BETTER. UM, I MEAN, YOU LOOK REALLY GOOD, THAT'S ALL.
I SEE THAT NORMAN IS STILL HERE.
YEAH, POOR FELLA. NOBODY WANTS HIM.
HELLO.
HI.
PATTY, MEET LEAH! SHE'S THE NEW EMPLOYEE.
NICE TO MEET YOU.
SO, DO YOU HAVE ANY IDEA WHAT MY SCHEDULE'S LIKE NEXT WEEK?
PATTY, I'M SO SORRY, BUT WE HAD TO HIRE LEAH TO REPLACE YOU.
WHAT?
IT'S JUST THAT WE WERE SLAMMED WITH WORK, AND NOBODY KNEW IF YOU'D BE BACK, OR WHEN, AND... WELL, WE CAN'T LET LEAH GO NOW. IT WOULDN'T BE FAIR!
WHY WOULD YOU DO THAT?

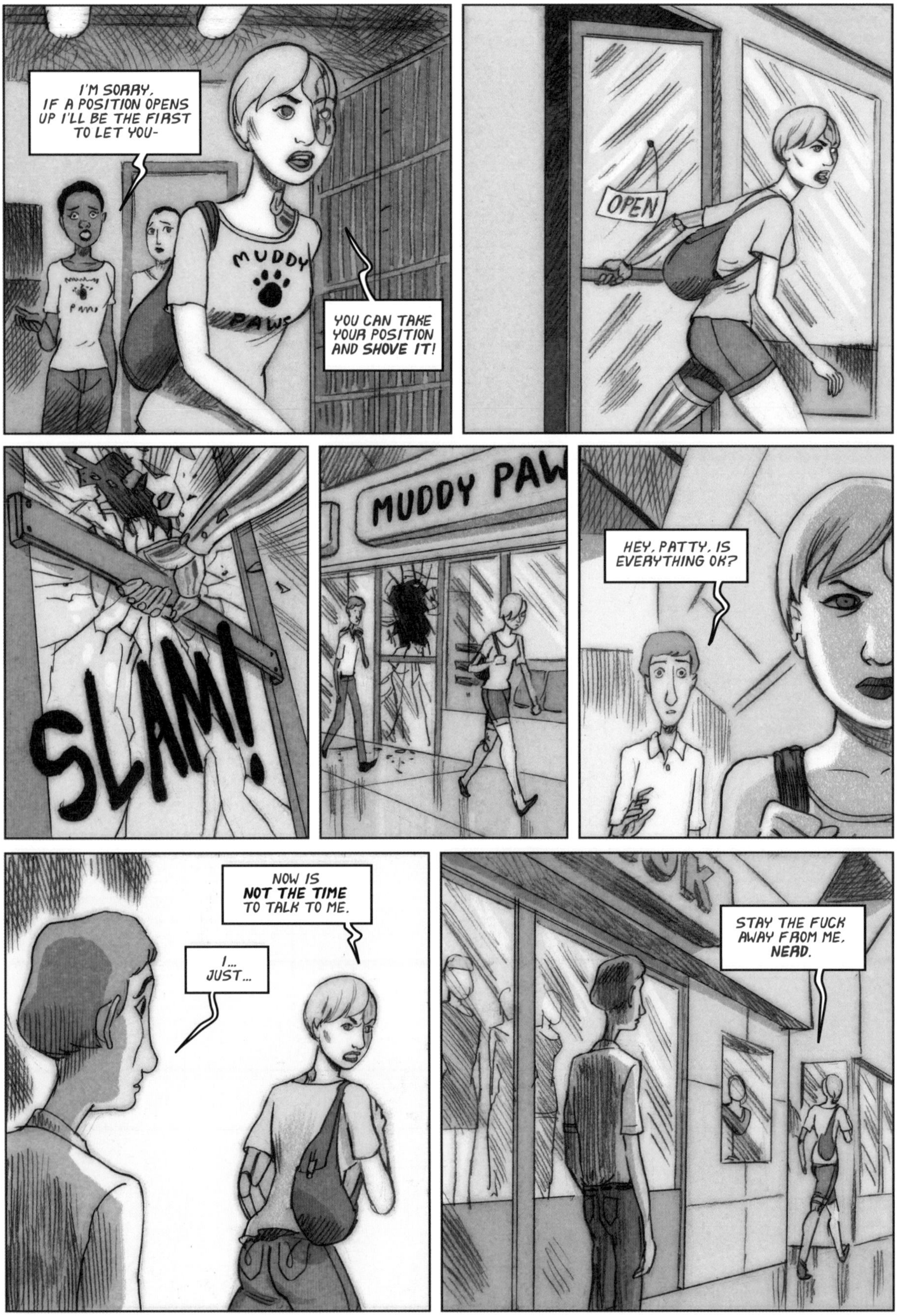
I'M SORRY, IF A POSITION OPENS UP I'LL BE THE FIRST TO LET YOU-
YOU CAN TAKE YOUR POSITION AND SHOVE IT!
MUDDY PAWS
OPEN
SLAM!
MUDDY PAW
HEY, PATTY, IS EVERYTHING OK?
NOW IS NOT THE TIME TO TALK TO ME.
I... JUST...
STAY THE FUCK AWAY FROM ME, NERD.

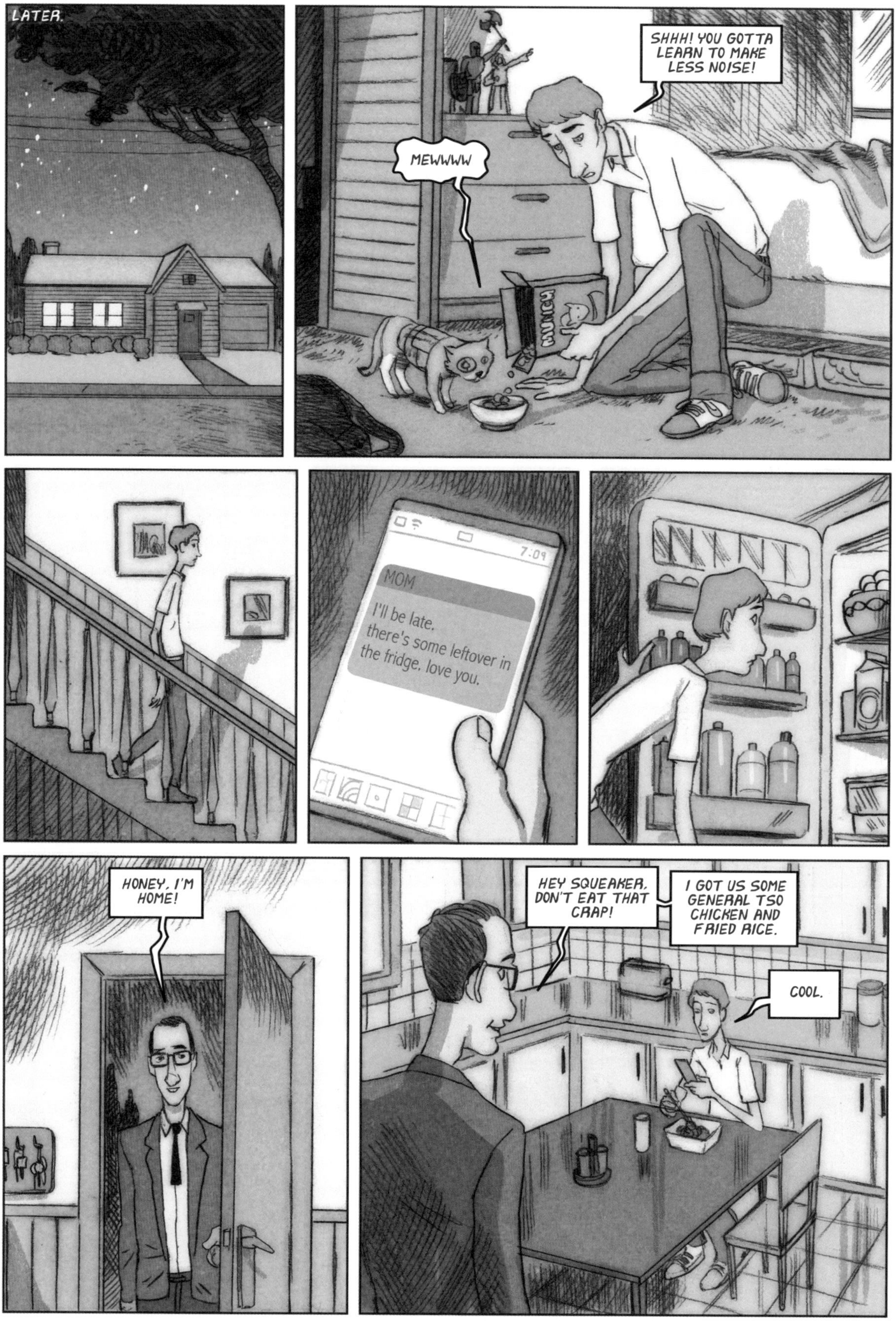
LATER.
SHHH! YOU GOTTA LEARN TO MAKE LESS NOISE!
MEWWWW
MUNCH
MOM
7:09
I'll be late.
there's some leftover in the fridge. love you.
HONEY, I'M HOME!
HEY SQUEAKER, DON'T EAT THAT CRAP!
I GOT US SOME GENERAL TSO CHICKEN AND FRIED RICE.
COOL.

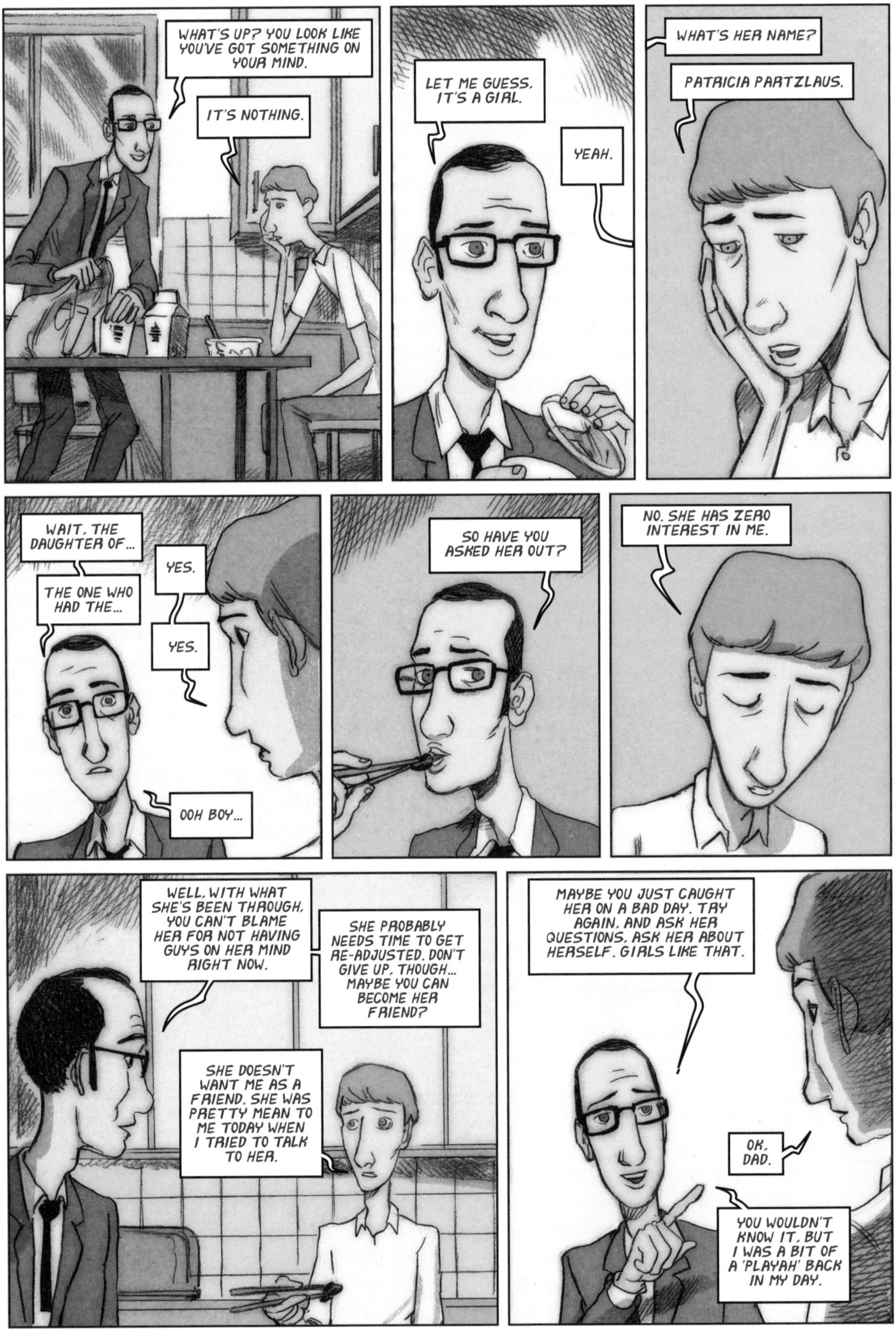
WHAT'S UP? YOU LOOK LIKE YOU'VE GOT SOMETHING ON YOUR MIND.
IT'S NOTHING.
LET ME GUESS. IT'S A GIRL.
YEAH.
WHAT'S HER NAME?
PATRICIA PARTZLAUS.
WAIT. THE DAUGHTER OF...
YES.
THE ONE WHO HAD THE...
YES.
OOH BOY...
SO HAVE YOU ASKED HER OUT?
NO. SHE HAS ZERO INTEREST IN ME.
WELL, WITH WHAT SHE'S BEEN THROUGH, YOU CAN'T BLAME HER FOR NOT HAVING GUYS ON HER MIND RIGHT NOW.
SHE PROBABLY NEEDS TIME TO GET RE-ADJUSTED. DON'T GIVE UP, THOUGH... MAYBE YOU CAN BECOME HER FRIEND?
SHE DOESN'T WANT ME AS A FRIEND. SHE WAS PRETTY MEAN TO ME TODAY WHEN I TRIED TO TALK TO HER.
MAYBE YOU JUST CAUGHT HER ON A BAD DAY. TRY AGAIN, AND ASK HER QUESTIONS. ASK HER ABOUT HERSELF. GIRLS LIKE THAT.
OK, DAD.
YOU WOULDN'T KNOW IT, BUT I WAS A BIT OF A 'PLAYAH' BACK IN MY DAY.

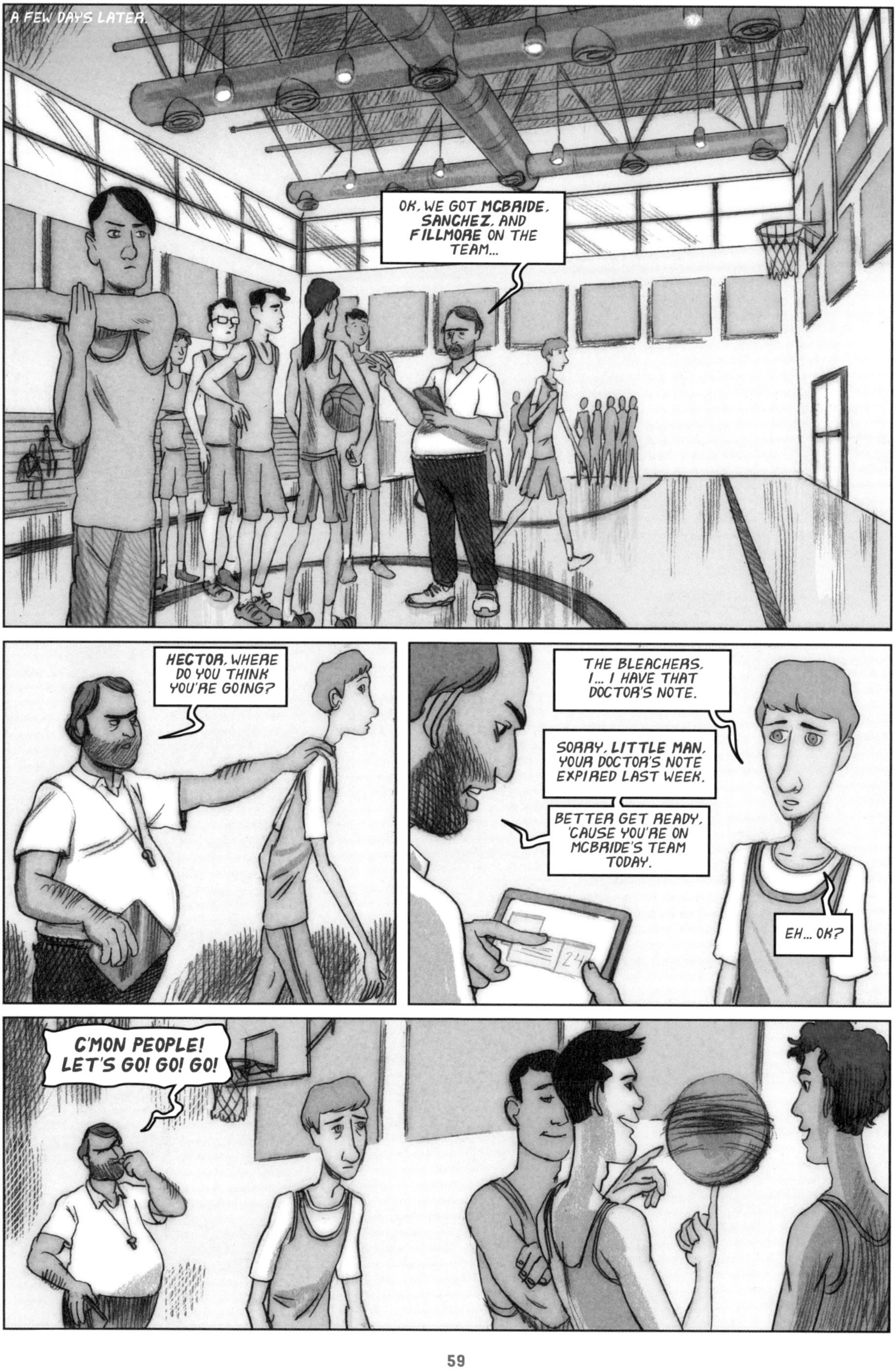
A FEW DAYS LATER.
OK, WE GOT MCBRIDE, SANCHEZ, AND FILLMORE ON THE TEAM...
HECTOR, WHERE DO YOU THINK YOU'RE GOING?
THE BLEACHERS. I... I HAVE THAT DOCTOR'S NOTE.
SORRY, LITTLE MAN, YOUR DOCTOR'S NOTE EXPIRED LAST WEEK.
BETTER GET READY, 'CAUSE YOU'RE ON MCBRIDE'S TEAM TODAY.
EH... OK?
C'MON PEOPLE! LET'S GO! GO! GO!

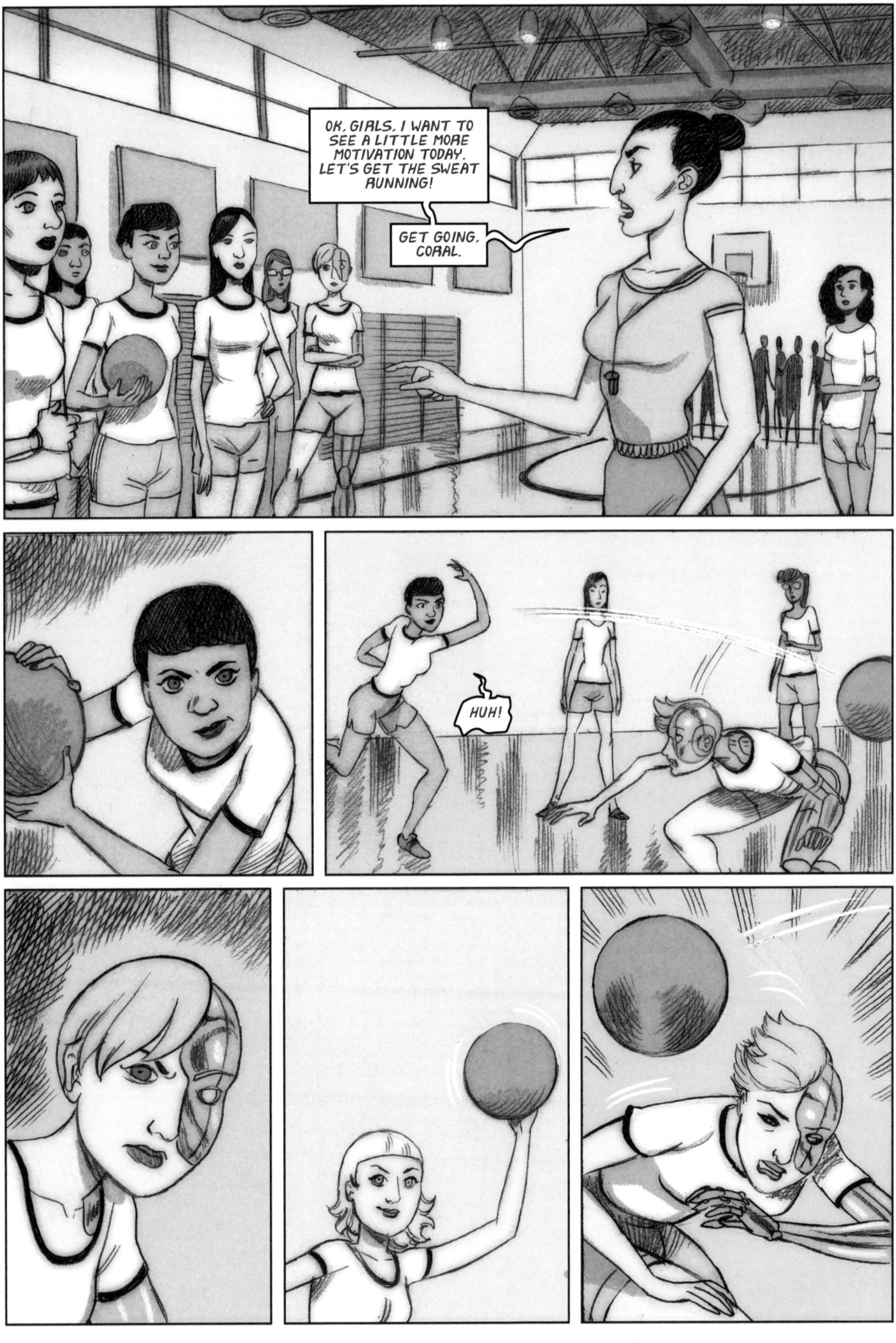
OK, GIRLS, I WANT TO SEE A LITTLE MORE MOTIVATION TODAY. LET'S GET THE SWEAT RUNNING!
GET GOING, CORAL.
HUH!

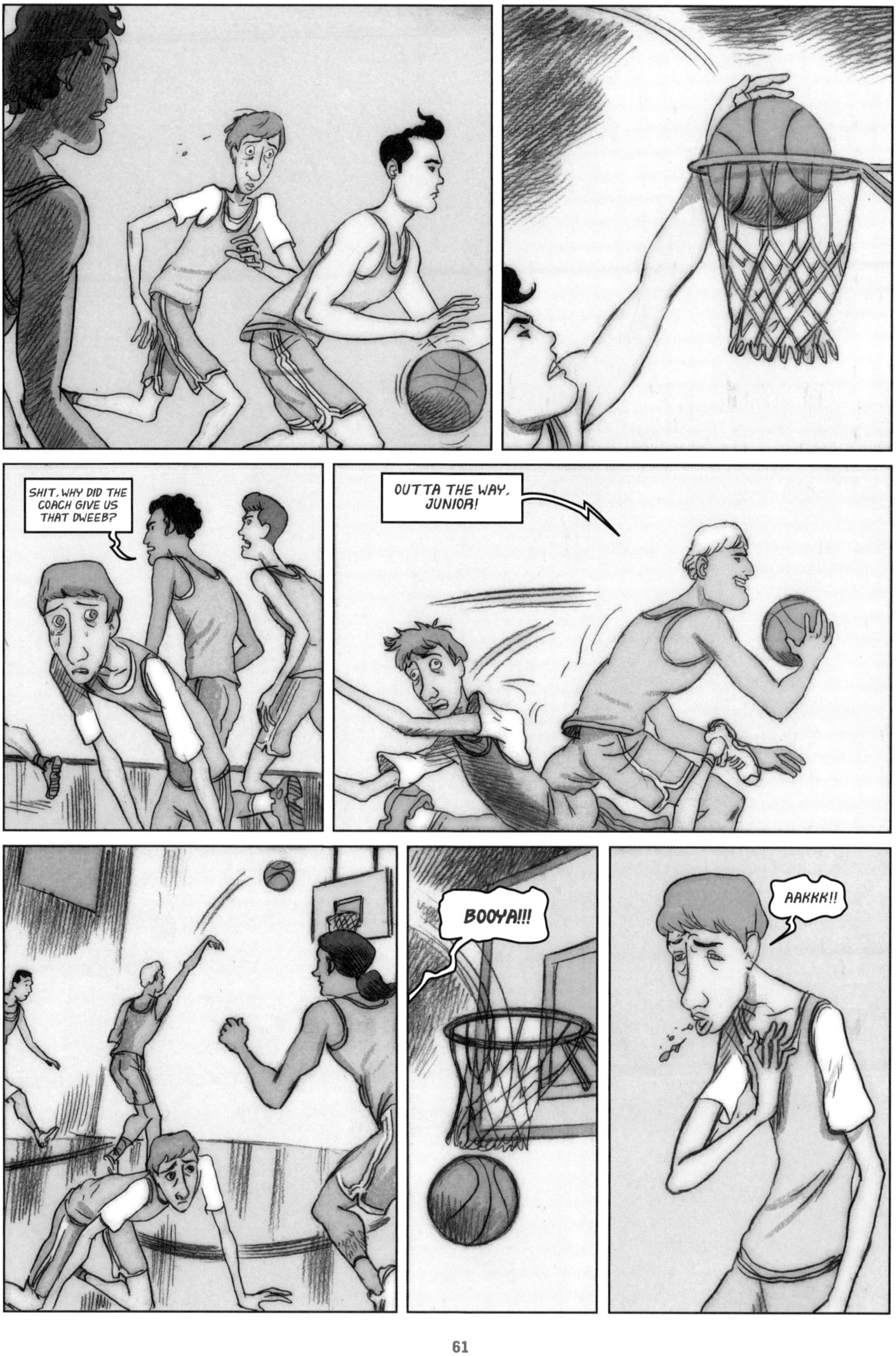
SHIT. WHY DID THE COACH GIVE US THAT DWEEB?
OUTTA THE WAY, JUNIOR!
BOOYA!!!
AAKKK!!

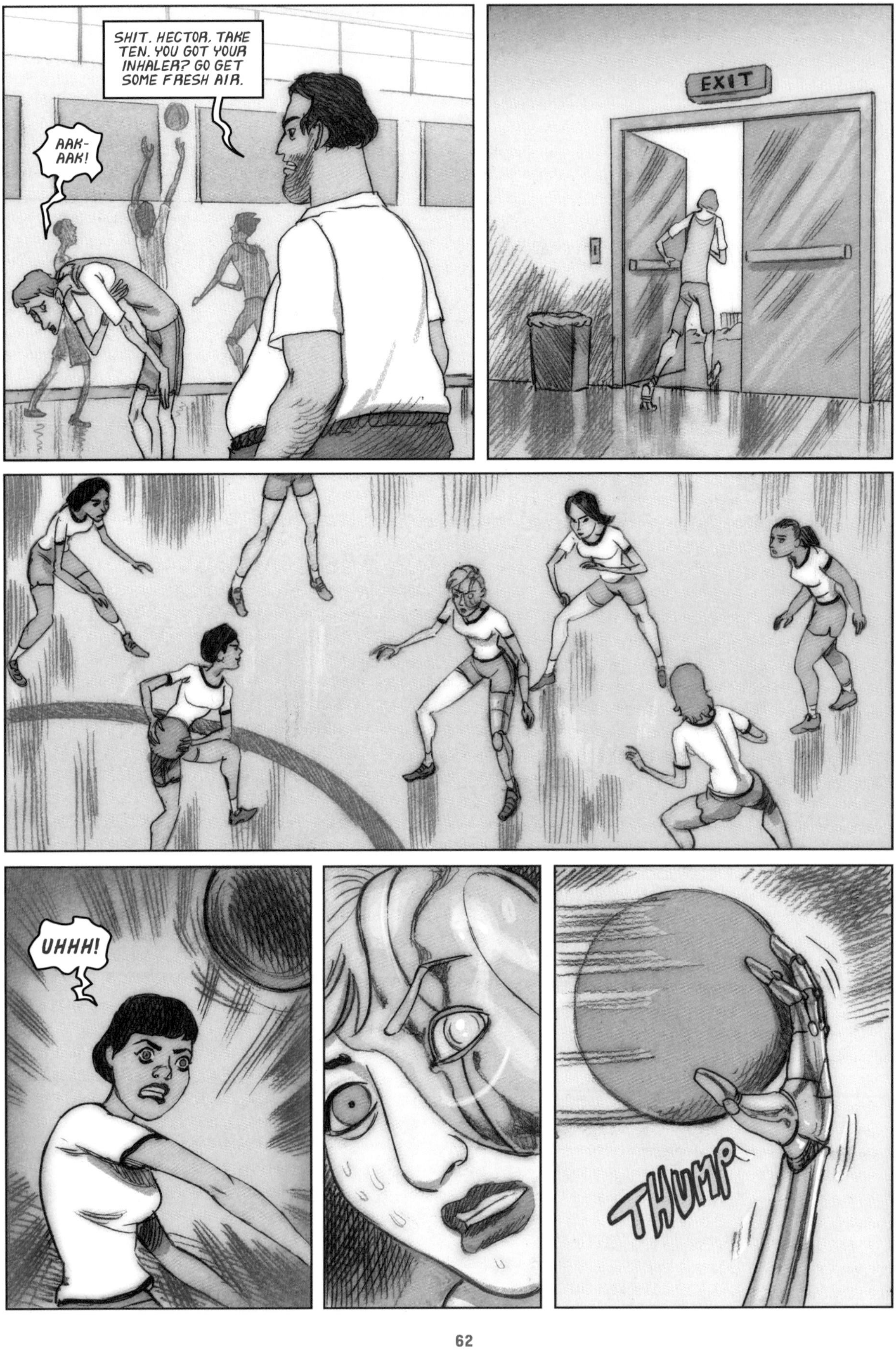
AAK-AAK!
SHIT. HECTOR, TAKE TEN. YOU GOT YOUR INHALER? GO GET SOME FRESH AIR.
EXIT
UHHH!
THUMP

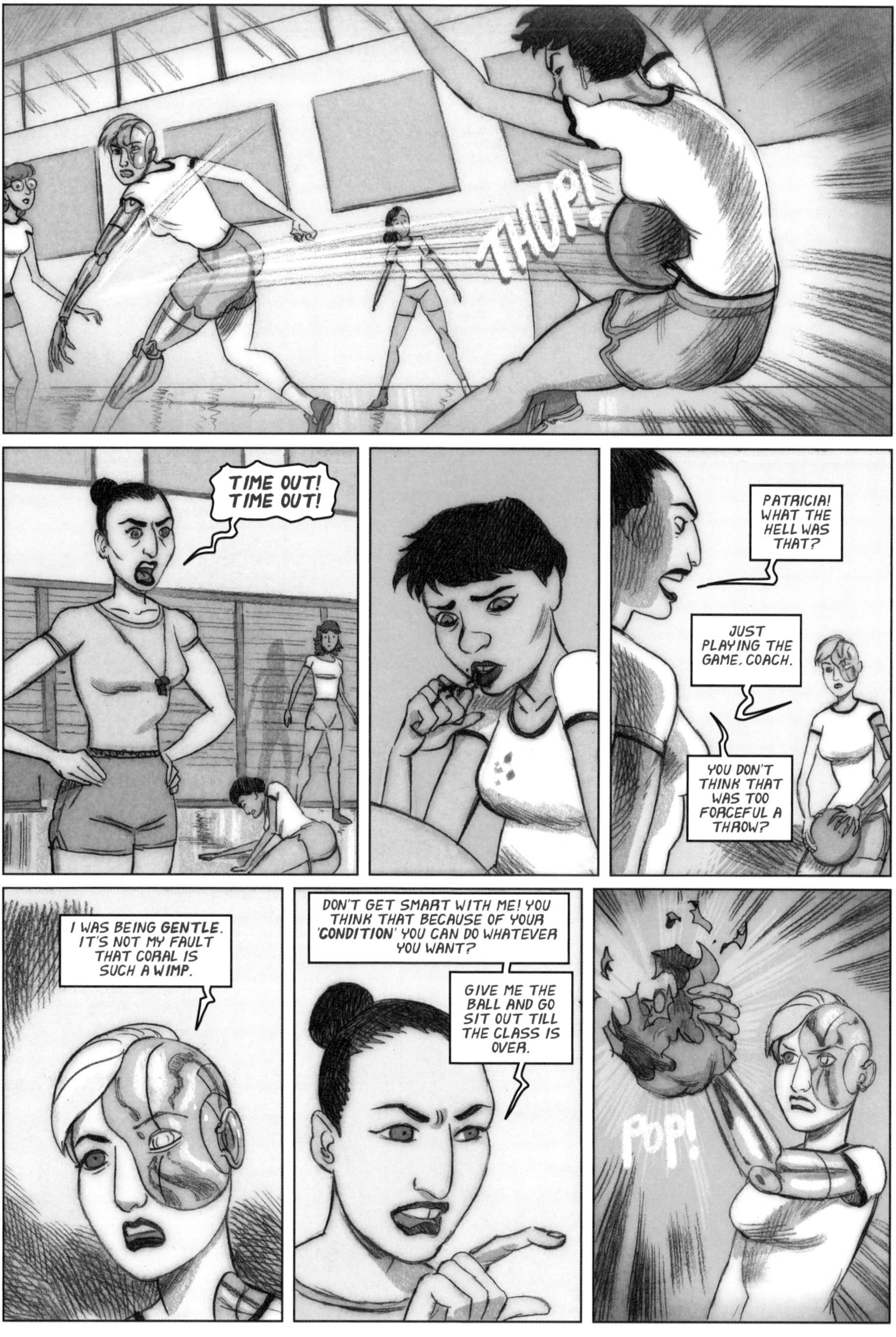
THUP!
TIME OUT! TIME OUT!
PATRICIA! WHAT THE HELL WAS THAT?
JUST PLAYING THE GAME, COACH.
YOU DON'T THINK THAT WAS TOO FORCEFUL A THROW?
I WAS BEING GENTLE. IT'S NOT MY FAULT THAT CORAL IS SUCH A WIMP.
DON'T GET SMART WITH ME! YOU THINK THAT BECAUSE OF YOUR 'CONDITION' YOU CAN DO WHATEVER YOU WANT?
GIVE ME THE BALL AND GO SIT OUT TILL THE CLASS IS OVER.
POP!

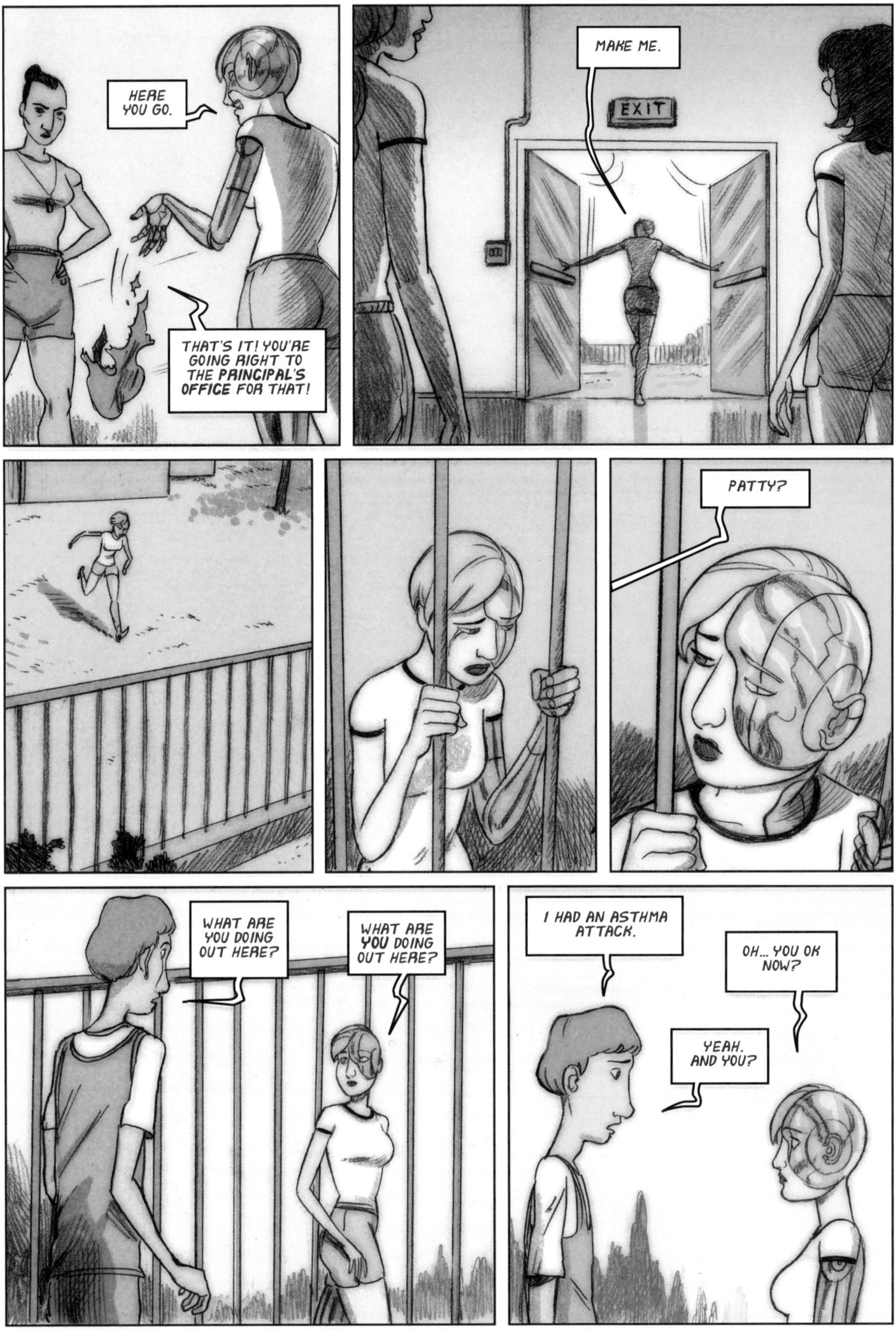
HERE YOU GO.
THAT'S IT! YOU'RE GOING RIGHT TO THE PRINCIPAL'S OFFICE FOR THAT!
MAKE ME.
EXIT
PATTY?
WHAT ARE YOU DOING OUT HERE?
WHAT ARE YOU DOING OUT HERE?
I HAD AN ASTHMA ATTACK.
OH... YOU OK NOW?
YEAH. AND YOU?

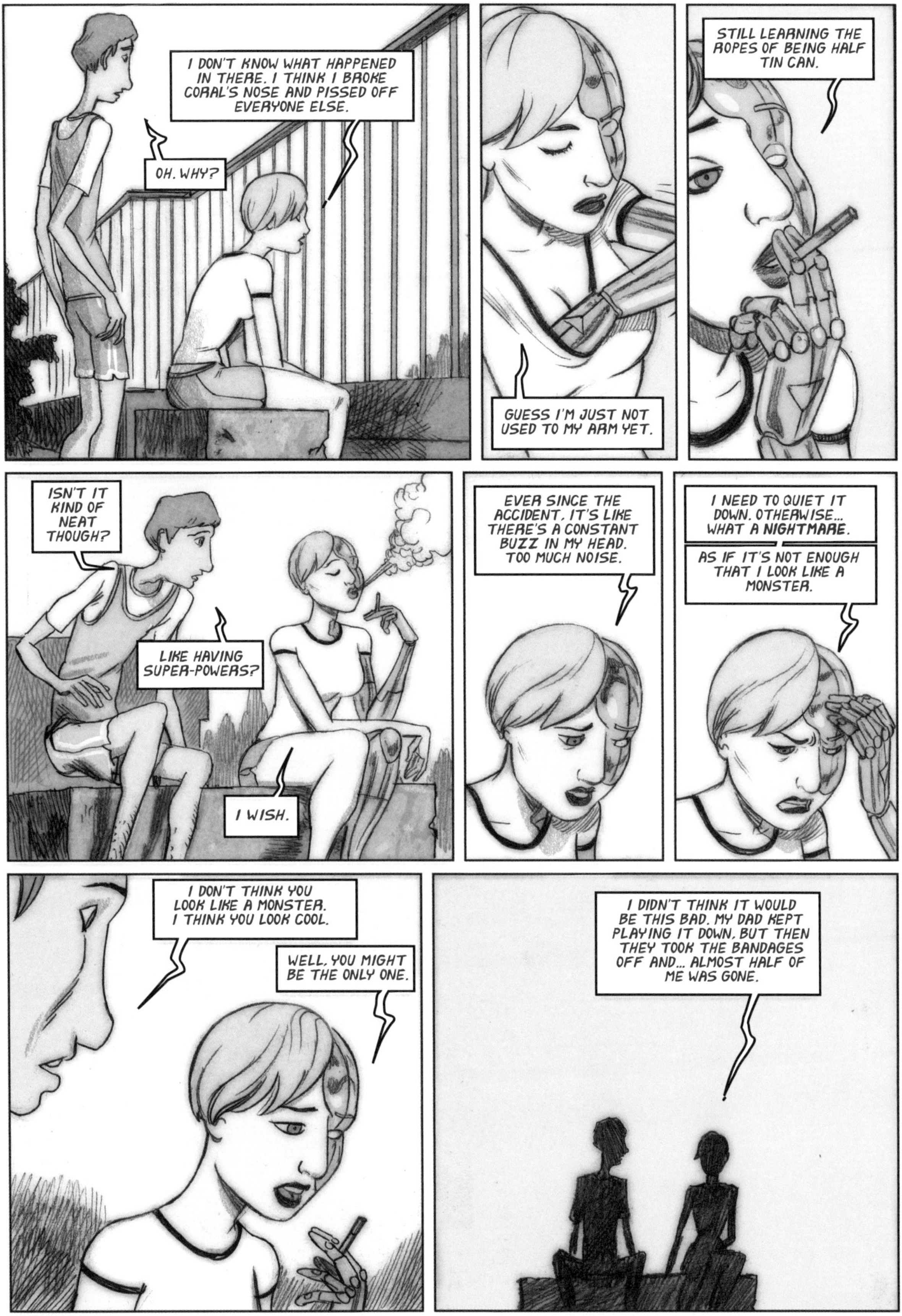
I DON'T KNOW WHAT HAPPENED IN THERE. I THINK I BROKE CORAL'S NOSE AND PISSED OFF EVERYONE ELSE.
OH. WHY?
GUESS I'M JUST NOT USED TO MY ARM YET.
STILL LEARNING THE ROPES OF BEING HALF TIN CAN.
ISN'T IT KIND OF NEAT THOUGH?
LIKE HAVING SUPER-POWERS?
I WISH.
EVER SINCE THE ACCIDENT, IT'S LIKE THERE'S A CONSTANT BUZZ IN MY HEAD. TOO MUCH NOISE.
I NEED TO QUIET IT DOWN. OTHERWISE... WHAT A NIGHTMARE.
AS IF IT'S NOT ENOUGH THAT I LOOK LIKE A MONSTER.
I DON'T THINK YOU LOOK LIKE A MONSTER. I THINK YOU LOOK COOL.
WELL, YOU MIGHT BE THE ONLY ONE.
I DIDN'T THINK IT WOULD BE THIS BAD. MY DAD KEPT PLAYING IT DOWN, BUT THEN THEY TOOK THE BANDAGES OFF AND... ALMOST HALF OF ME WAS GONE.

I THINK YOU LOOK UNIQUE. THE METALLIC PARTS ARE LIKE... A BUNCH OF COOL TATTOOS.

HA! THAT'S PRETTY SWEET OF YOU. WANT A DRAG?

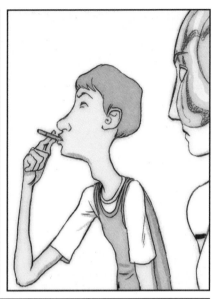

AAK! AAK!

OH SHIT, FORGOT YOUR ASTHMA. ARE YOU OK?

I'LL BE FINE.

MY PARENTS ARE HAVING A PARTY TOMORROW EVENING AT OUR HOUSE. DO YOU WANT TO COME?

SURE.

THERE'S GONNA BE A LOT OF STUCK-UP GEEZERS, BUT HOPEFULLY WE CAN STILL HAVE FUN.

I'LL BE THERE.

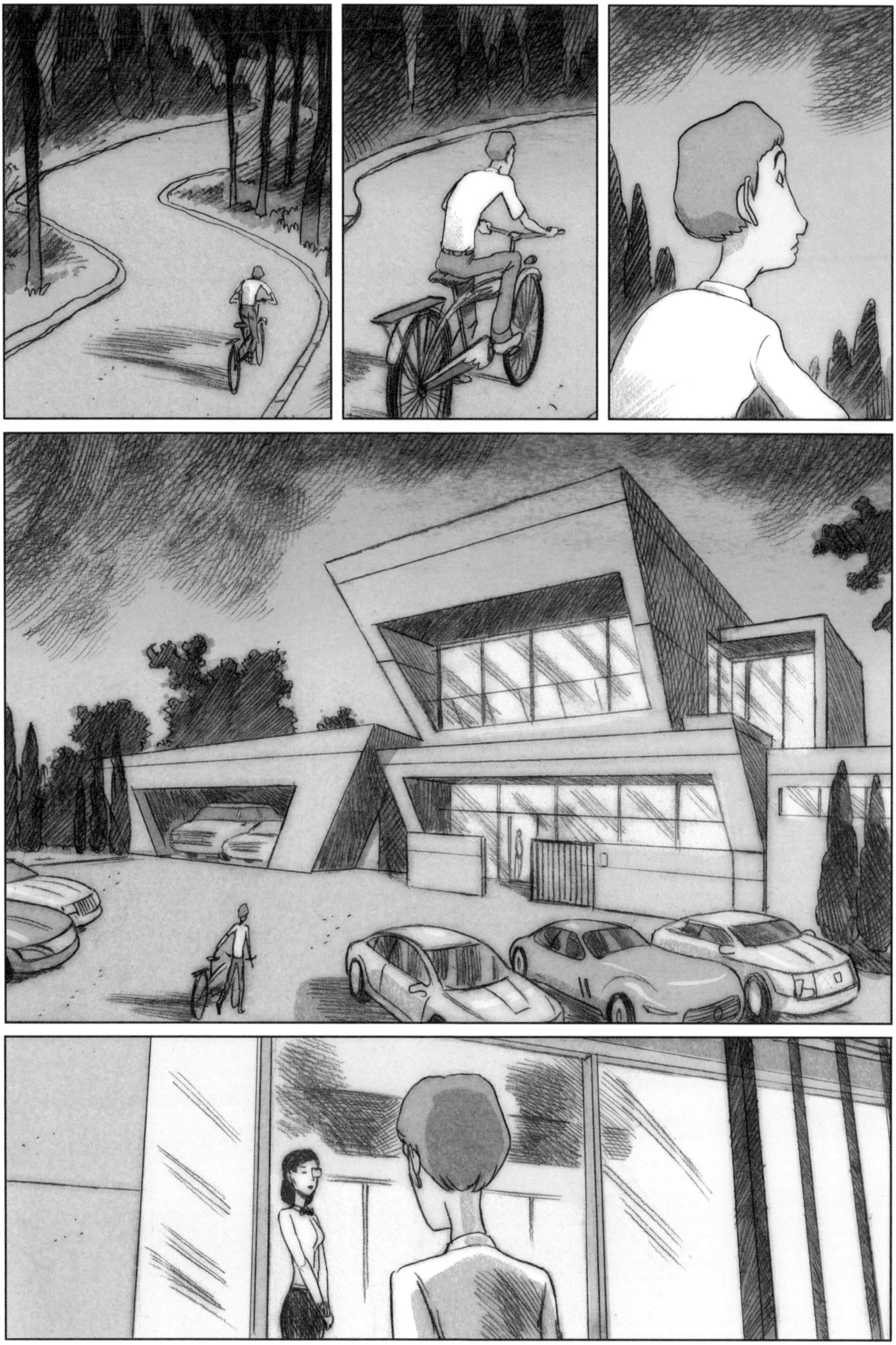

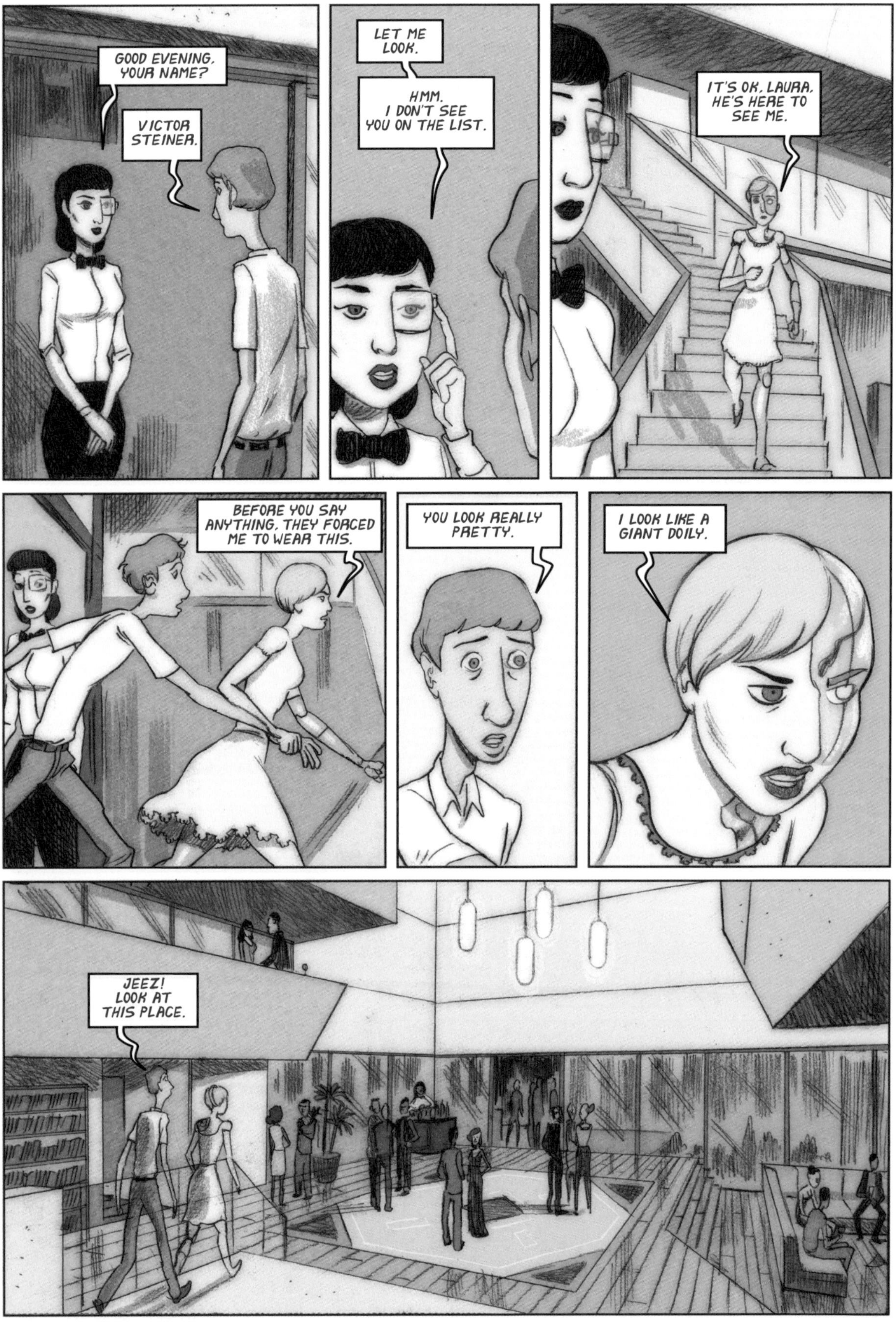
GOOD EVENING, YOUR NAME?
VICTOR STEINER.
LET ME LOOK.
HMM. I DON'T SEE YOU ON THE LIST.
IT'S OK, LAURA, HE'S HERE TO SEE ME.
BEFORE YOU SAY ANYTHING, THEY FORCED ME TO WEAR THIS.
YOU LOOK REALLY PRETTY.
I LOOK LIKE A GIANT DOILY.
JEEZ! LOOK AT THIS PLACE.

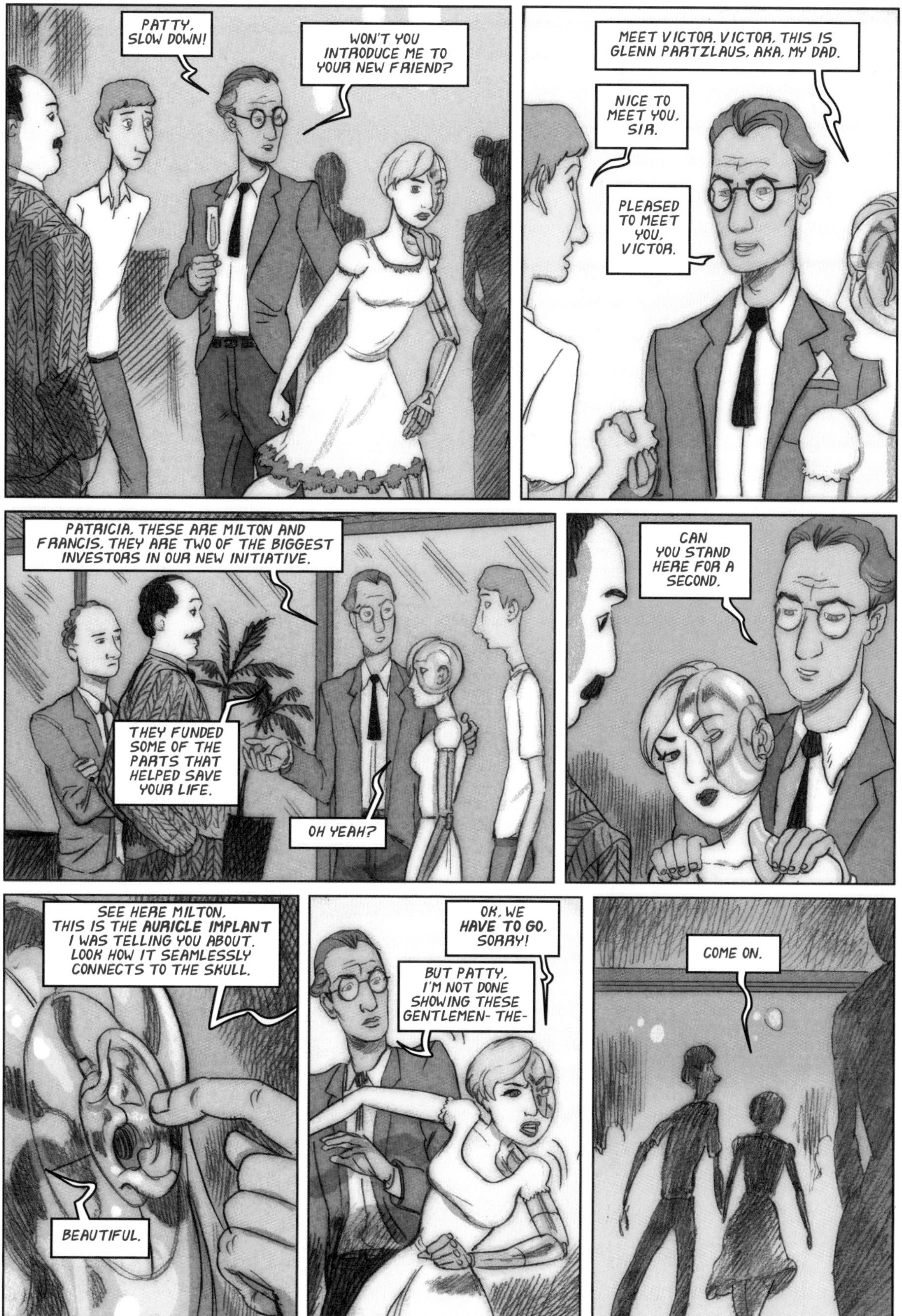

PATTY, SLOW DOWN!
WON'T YOU INTRODUCE ME TO YOUR NEW FRIEND?
MEET VICTOR. VICTOR, THIS IS GLENN PARTZLAUS, AKA, MY DAD.
NICE TO MEET YOU, SIR.
PLEASED TO MEET YOU, VICTOR.
PATRICIA, THESE ARE MILTON AND FRANCIS, THEY ARE TWO OF THE BIGGEST INVESTORS IN OUR NEW INITIATIVE.
THEY FUNDED SOME OF THE PARTS THAT HELPED SAVE YOUR LIFE.
OH YEAH?
CAN YOU STAND HERE FOR A SECOND.
SEE HERE MILTON, THIS IS THE **AURICLE IMPLANT** I WAS TELLING YOU ABOUT. LOOK HOW IT SEAMLESSLY CONNECTS TO THE SKULL.
BEAUTIFUL.
OK, WE **HAVE TO GO**, SORRY!
BUT PATTY, I'M NOT DONE SHOWING THESE GENTLEMEN- THE-
COME ON.

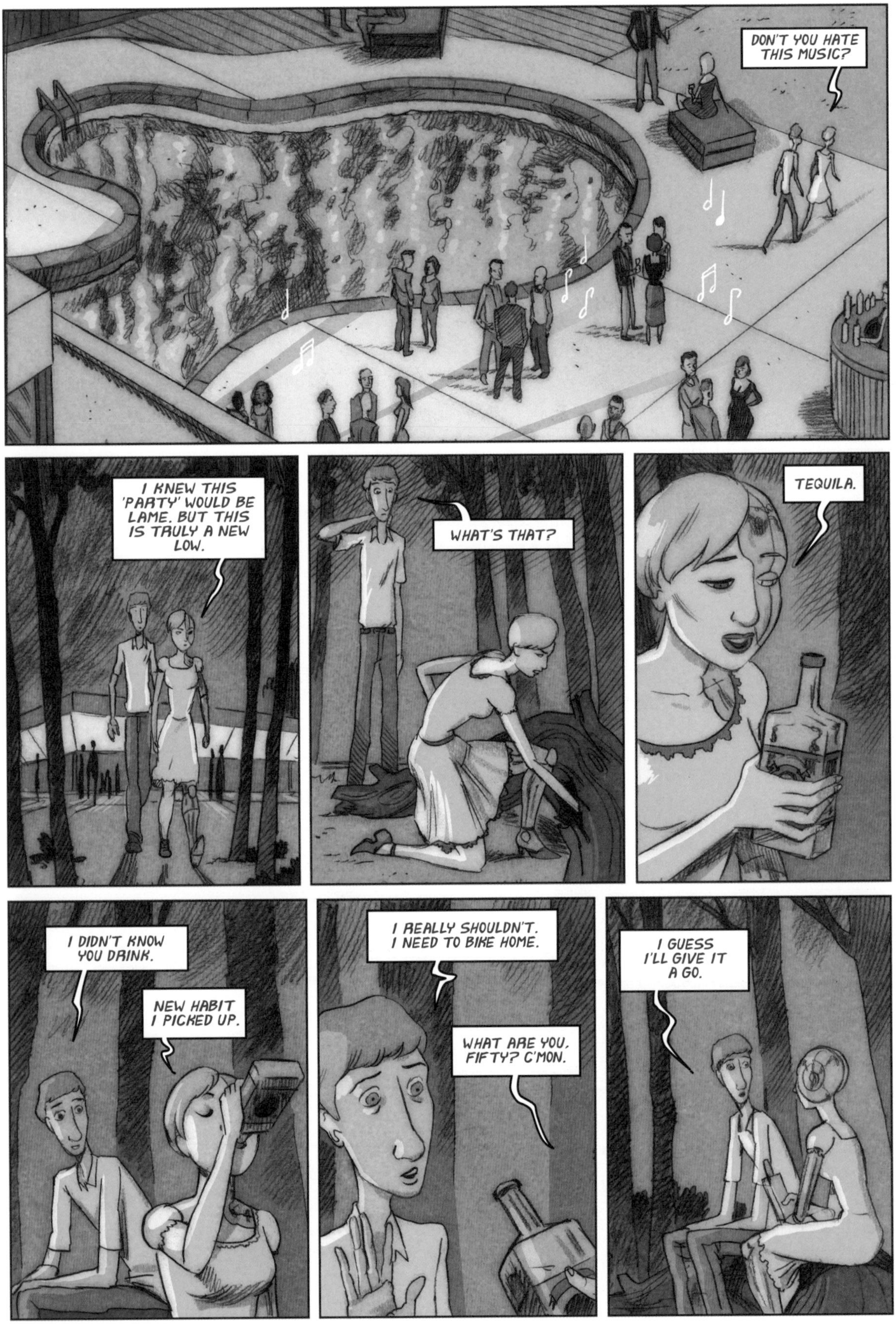
DON'T YOU HATE THIS MUSIC?
I KNEW THIS 'PARTY' WOULD BE LAME. BUT THIS IS TRULY A NEW LOW.
WHAT'S THAT?
TEQUILA.
I DIDN'T KNOW YOU DRINK.
NEW HABIT I PICKED UP.
I REALLY SHOULDN'T. I NEED TO BIKE HOME.
WHAT ARE YOU, FIFTY? C'MON.
I GUESS I'LL GIVE IT A GO.

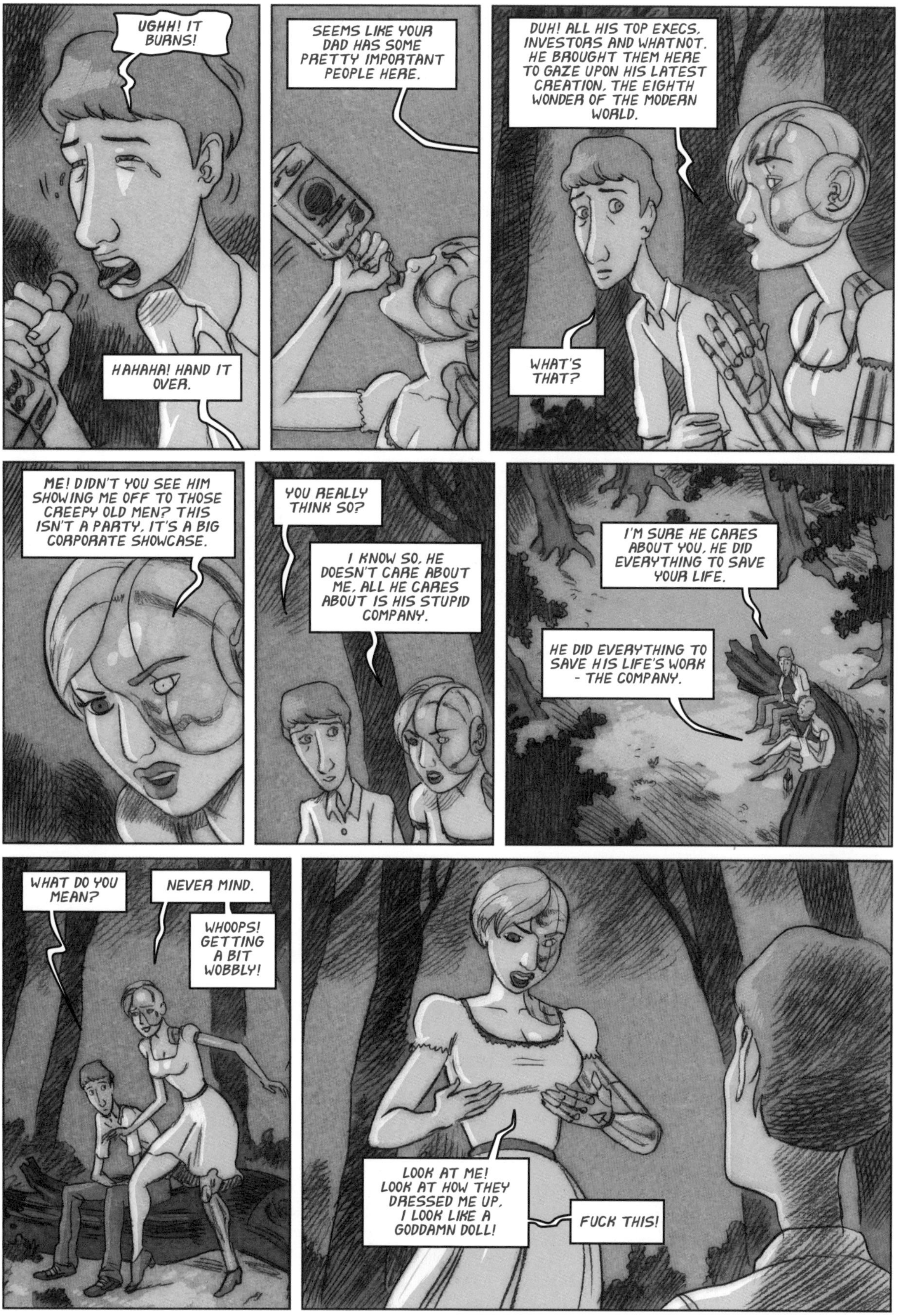
UGHH! IT BURNS!
HAHAHA! HAND IT OVER.
SEEMS LIKE YOUR DAD HAS SOME PRETTY IMPORTANT PEOPLE HERE.
DUH! ALL HIS TOP EXECS, INVESTORS AND WHATNOT. HE BROUGHT THEM HERE TO GAZE UPON HIS LATEST CREATION, THE EIGHTH WONDER OF THE MODERN WORLD.
WHAT'S THAT?
ME! DIDN'T YOU SEE HIM SHOWING ME OFF TO THOSE CREEPY OLD MEN? THIS ISN'T A PARTY, IT'S A BIG CORPORATE SHOWCASE.
YOU REALLY THINK SO?
I KNOW SO, HE DOESN'T CARE ABOUT ME, ALL HE CARES ABOUT IS HIS STUPID COMPANY.
I'M SURE HE CARES ABOUT YOU, HE DID EVERYTHING TO SAVE YOUR LIFE.
HE DID EVERYTHING TO SAVE HIS LIFE'S WORK - THE COMPANY.
WHAT DO YOU MEAN?
NEVER MIND.
WHOOPS! GETTING A BIT WOBBLY!
LOOK AT ME! LOOK AT HOW THEY DRESSED ME UP, I LOOK LIKE A GODDAMN DOLL!
FUCK THIS!

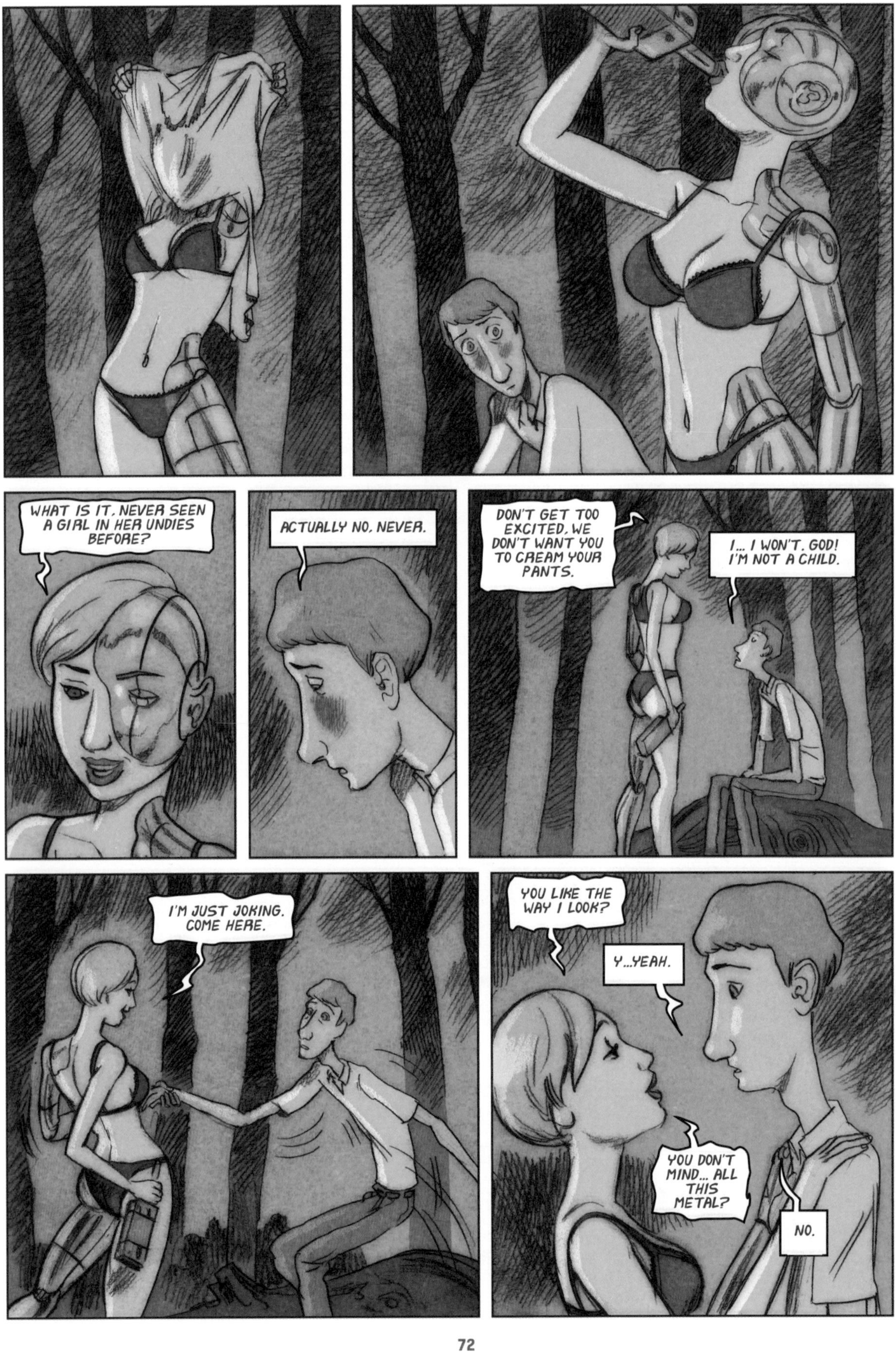
WHAT IS IT, NEVER SEEN A GIRL IN HER UNDIES BEFORE?
ACTUALLY NO, NEVER.
DON'T GET TOO EXCITED, WE DON'T WANT YOU TO CREAM YOUR PANTS.
I... I WON'T. GOD! I'M NOT A CHILD.
I'M JUST JOKING. COME HERE.
YOU LIKE THE WAY I LOOK?
Y...YEAH.
YOU DON'T MIND... ALL THIS METAL?
NO.

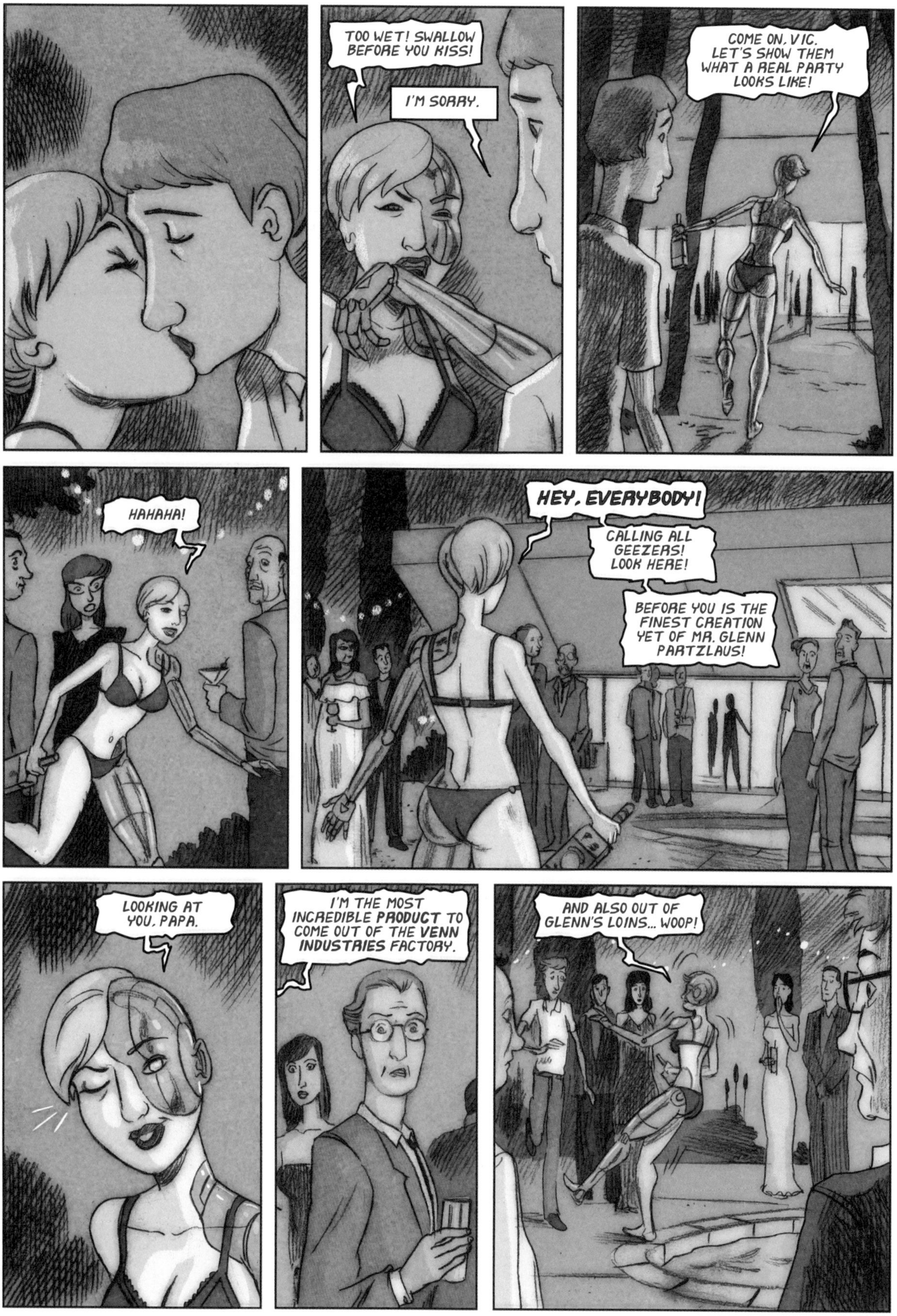
TOO WET! SWALLOW BEFORE YOU KISS!
I'M SORRY.
COME ON, VIC. LET'S SHOW THEM WHAT A REAL PARTY LOOKS LIKE!
HAHAHA!
HEY, EVERYBODY!
CALLING ALL GEEZERS! LOOK HERE!
BEFORE YOU IS THE FINEST CREATION YET OF MR. GLENN PARTZLAUS!
LOOKING AT YOU, PAPA.
I'M THE MOST INCREDIBLE **PRODUCT** TO COME OUT OF THE **VENN INDUSTRIES** FACTORY.
AND ALSO OUT OF GLENN'S LOINS... WOOP!

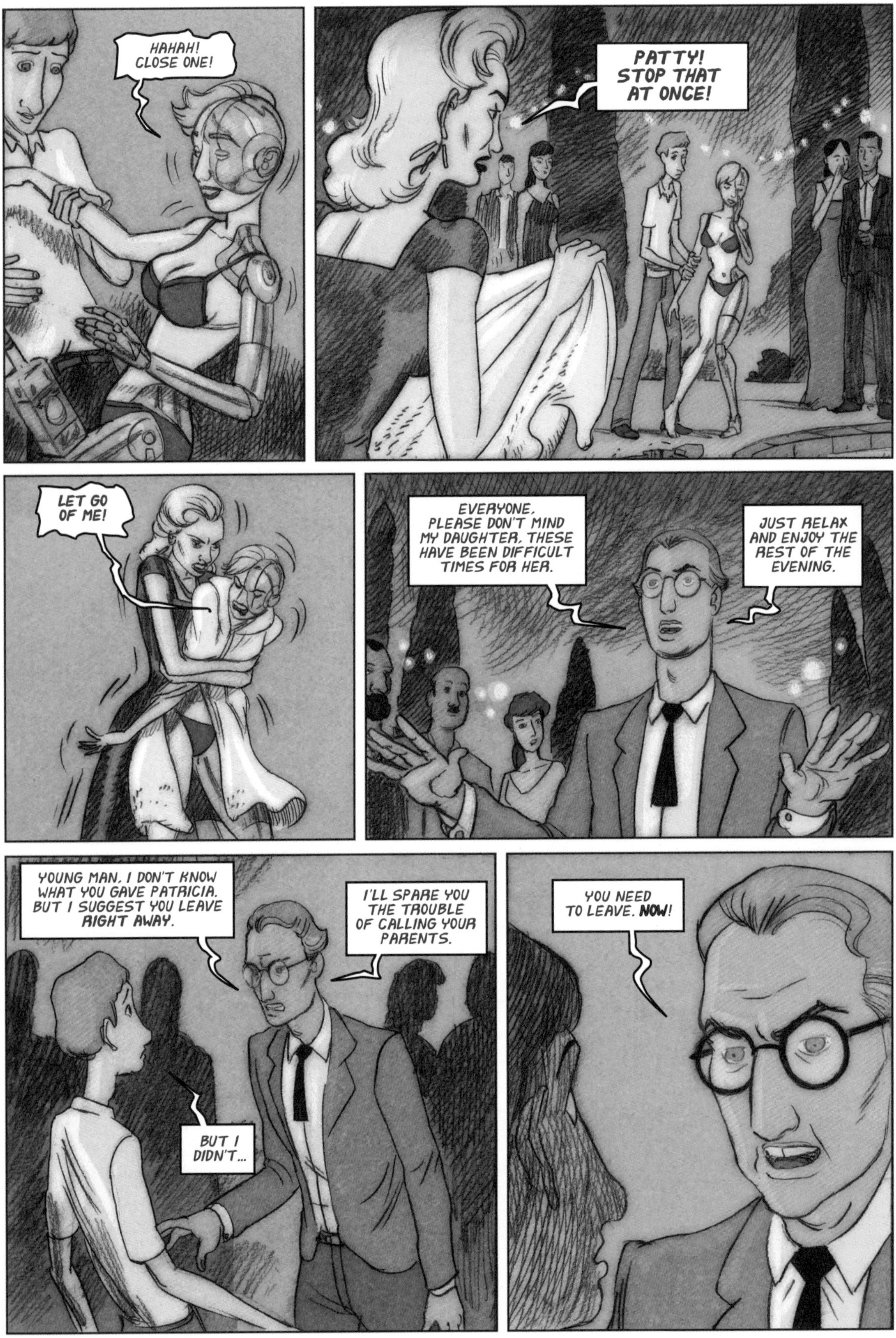
HAHAH! CLOSE ONE!
PATTY! STOP THAT AT ONCE!
LET GO OF ME!
EVERYONE, PLEASE DON'T MIND MY DAUGHTER, THESE HAVE BEEN DIFFICULT TIMES FOR HER.
JUST RELAX AND ENJOY THE REST OF THE EVENING.
YOUNG MAN, I DON'T KNOW WHAT YOU GAVE PATRICIA, BUT I SUGGEST YOU LEAVE RIGHT AWAY.
I'LL SPARE YOU THE TROUBLE OF CALLING YOUR PARENTS.
BUT I DIDN'T...
YOU NEED TO LEAVE. NOW!

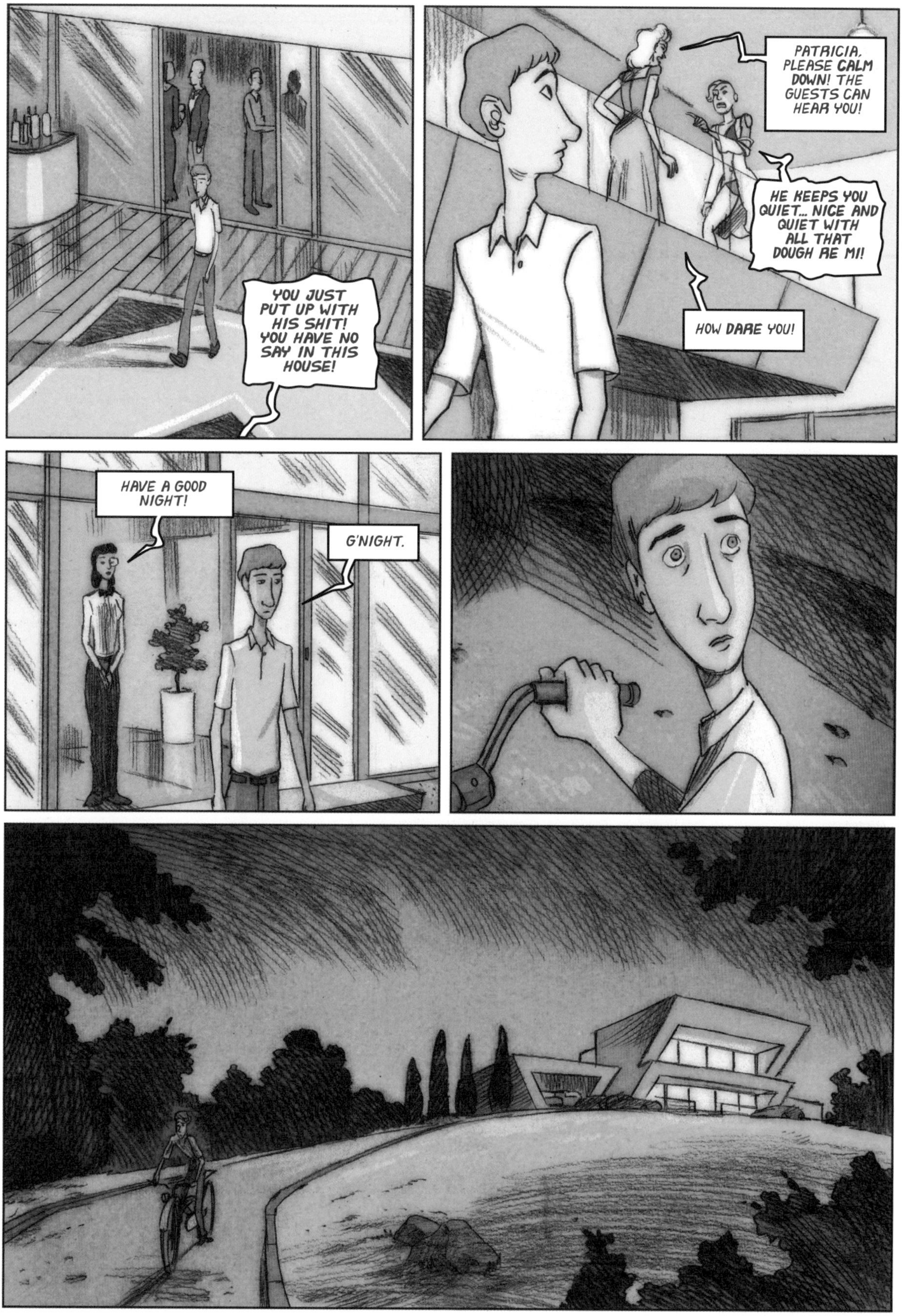
YOU JUST PUT UP WITH HIS SHIT! YOU HAVE NO SAY IN THIS HOUSE!
PATRICIA, PLEASE CALM DOWN! THE GUESTS CAN HEAR YOU!
HE KEEPS YOU QUIET... NICE AND QUIET WITH ALL THAT DOUGH RE MI!
HOW DARE YOU!
HAVE A GOOD NIGHT!
G'NIGHT.

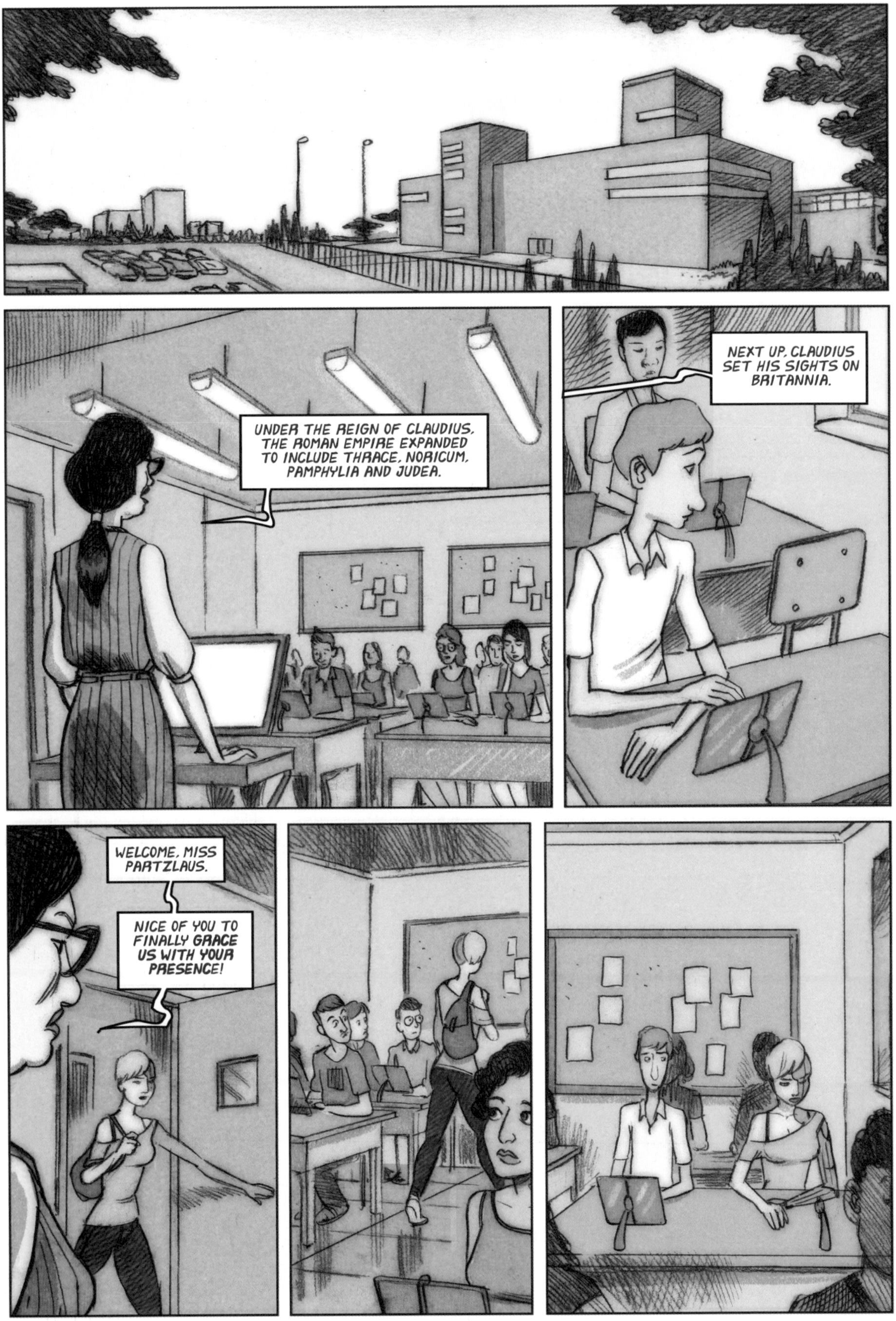
UNDER THE REIGN OF CLAUDIUS, THE ROMAN EMPIRE EXPANDED TO INCLUDE THRACE, NORICUM, PAMPHYLIA AND JUDEA.
NEXT UP, CLAUDIUS SET HIS SIGHTS ON BRITANNIA.
WELCOME, MISS PARTZLAUS.
NICE OF YOU TO FINALLY GRACE US WITH YOUR PRESENCE!

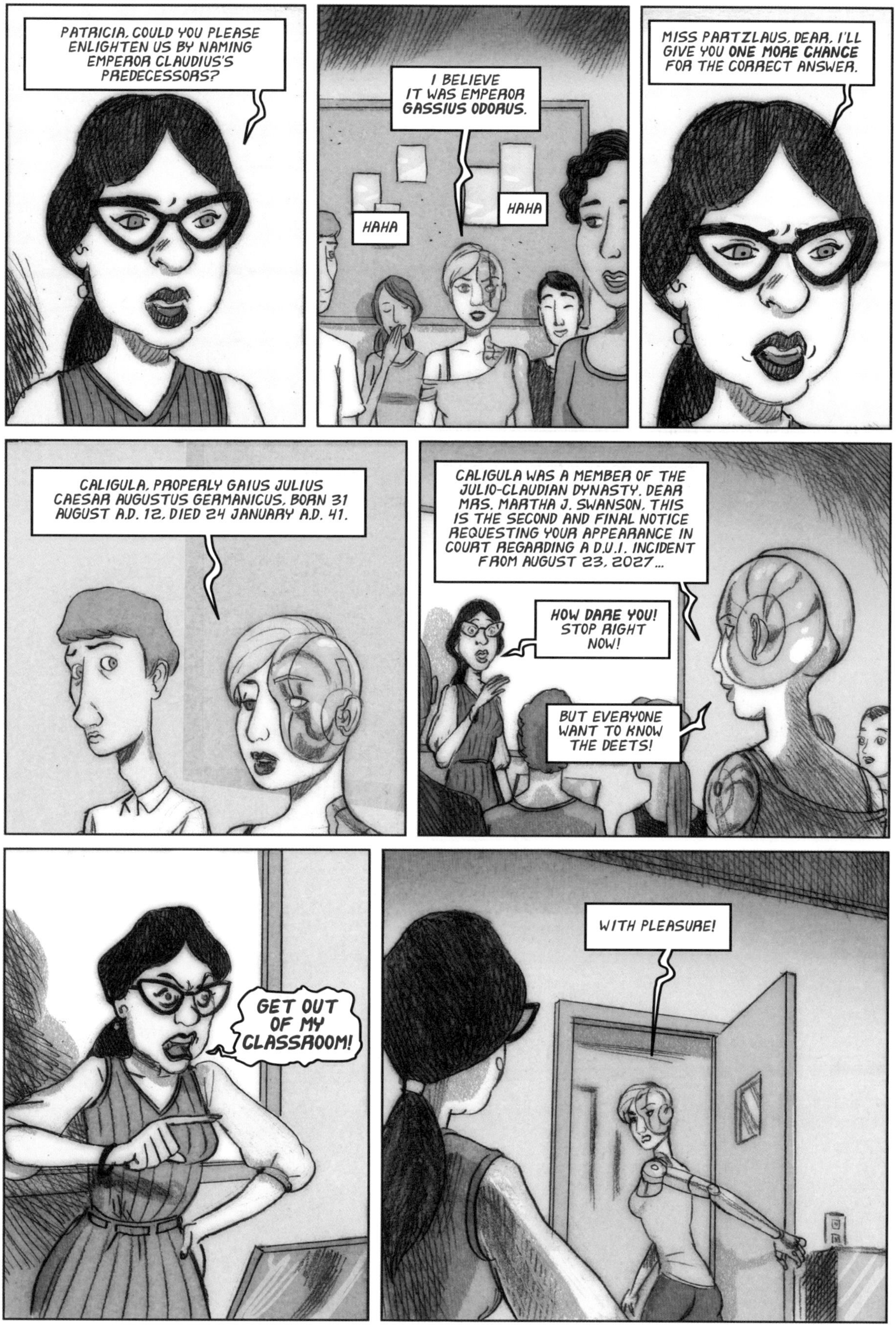
PATRICIA, COULD YOU PLEASE ENLIGHTEN US BY NAMING EMPEROR CLAUDIUS'S PREDECESSORS?
I BELIEVE IT WAS EMPEROR GASSIUS ODORUS.
HAHA
HAHA
MISS PARTZLAUS, DEAR, I'LL GIVE YOU ONE MORE CHANCE FOR THE CORRECT ANSWER.
CALIGULA, PROPERLY GAIUS JULIUS CAESAR AUGUSTUS GERMANICUS, BORN 31 AUGUST A.D. 12, DIED 24 JANUARY A.D. 41.
CALIGULA WAS A MEMBER OF THE JULIO-CLAUDIAN DYNASTY. DEAR MRS. MARTHA J. SWANSON, THIS IS THE SECOND AND FINAL NOTICE REQUESTING YOUR APPEARANCE IN COURT REGARDING A D.U.I. INCIDENT FROM AUGUST 23, 2027...
HOW DARE YOU! STOP RIGHT NOW!
BUT EVERYONE WANT TO KNOW THE DEETS!
GET OUT OF MY CLASSROOM!
WITH PLEASURE!

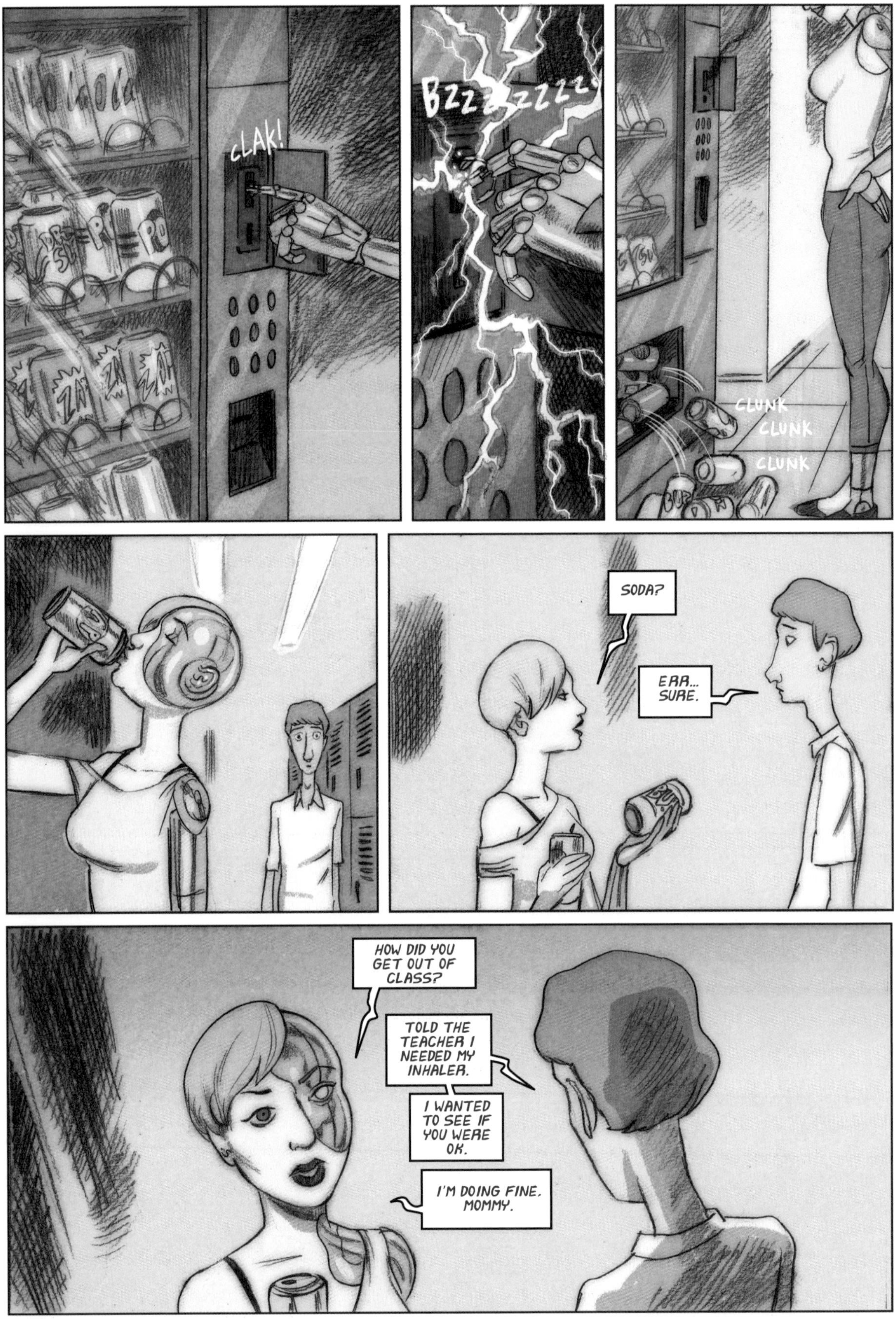
CLAK!
BZZZZZZZ
CLUNK
CLUNK
CLUNK
SODA?
ERR... SURE.
HOW DID YOU GET OUT OF CLASS?
TOLD THE TEACHER I NEEDED MY INHALER.
I WANTED TO SEE IF YOU WERE OK.
I'M DOING FINE, MOMMY.

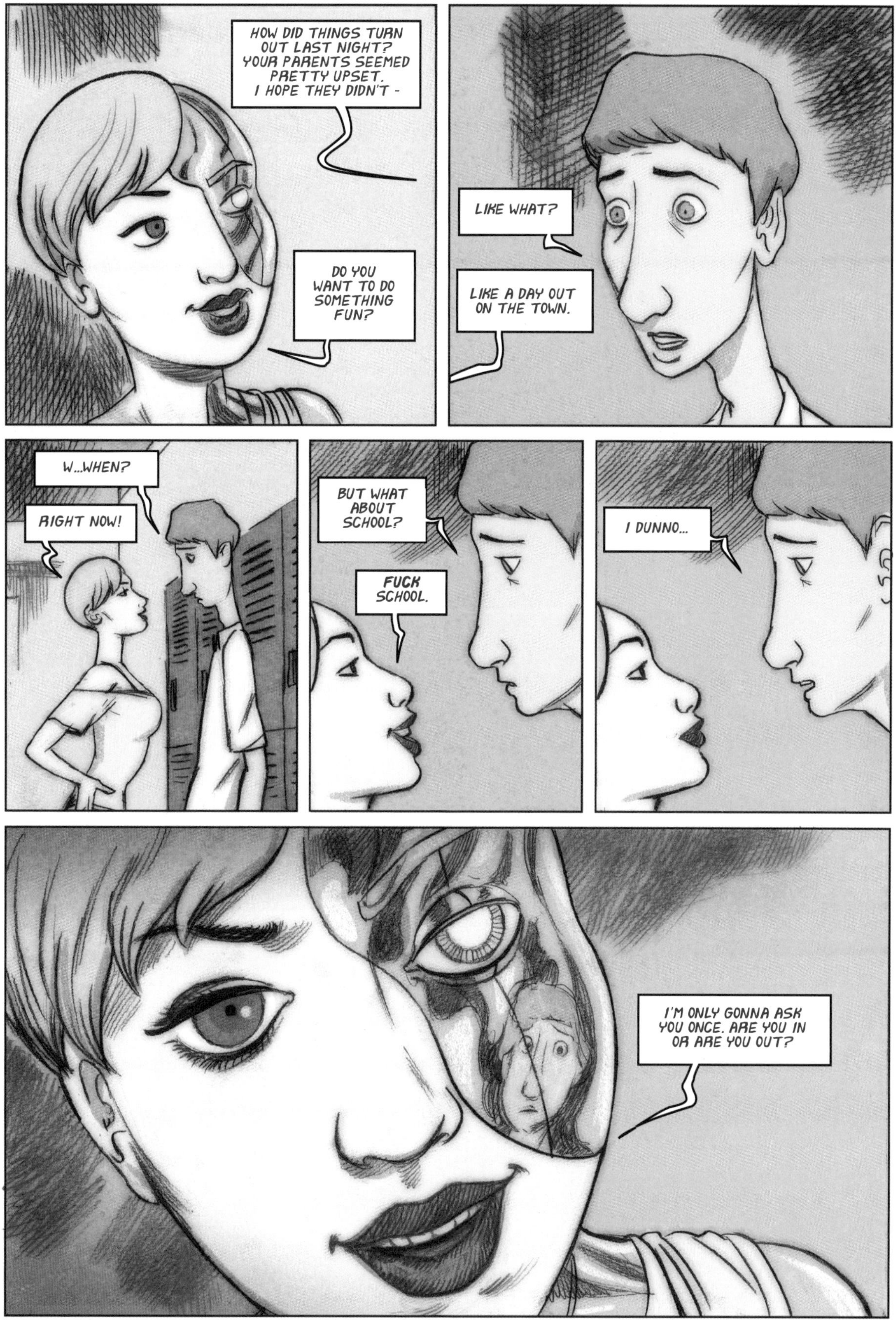
HOW DID THINGS TURN OUT LAST NIGHT? YOUR PARENTS SEEMED PRETTY UPSET. I HOPE THEY DIDN'T -
DO YOU WANT TO DO SOMETHING FUN?
LIKE WHAT?
LIKE A DAY OUT ON THE TOWN.
W...WHEN?
RIGHT NOW!
BUT WHAT ABOUT SCHOOL?
FUCK SCHOOL.
I DUNNO...
I'M ONLY GONNA ASK YOU ONCE. ARE YOU IN OR ARE YOU OUT?

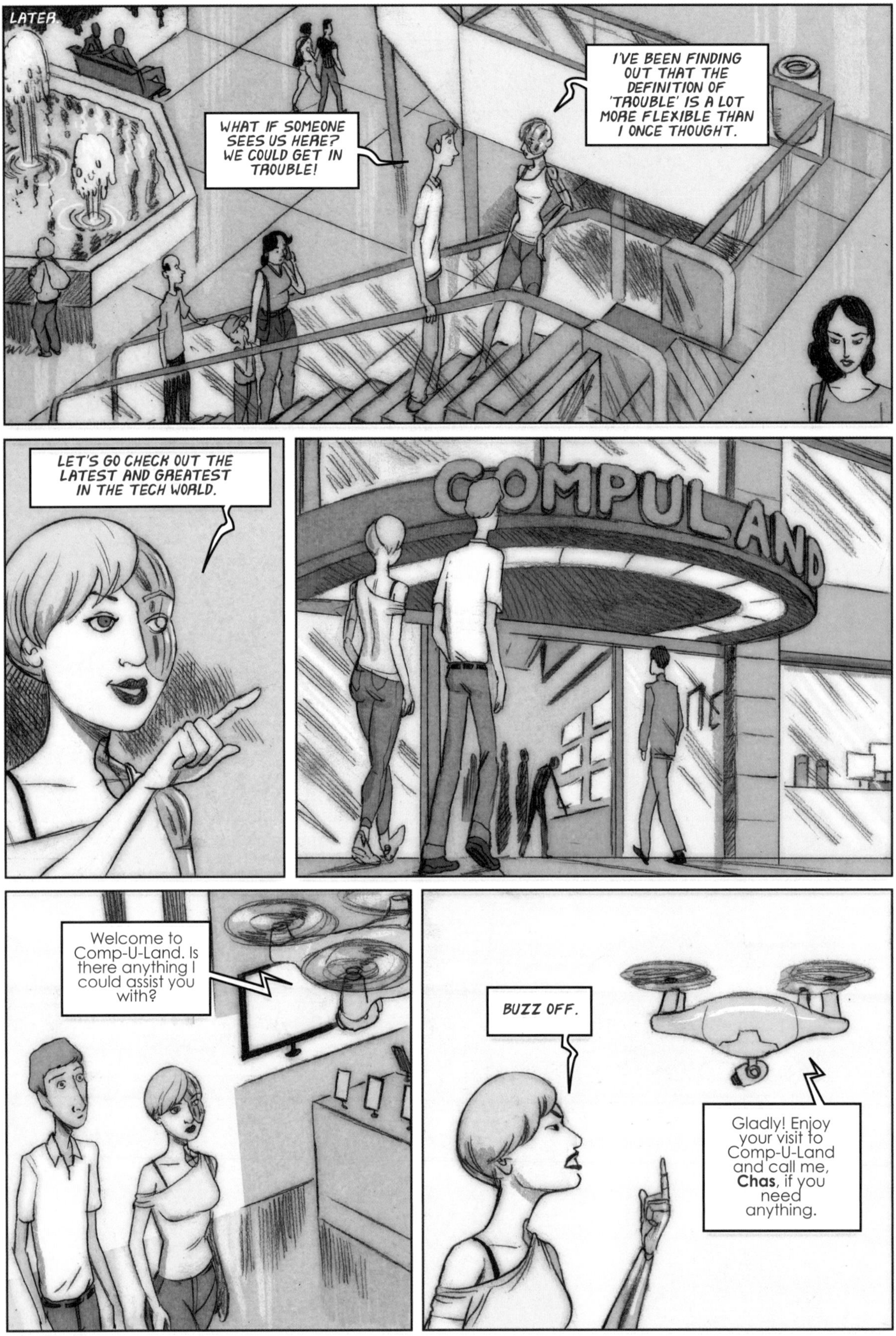
LATER
WHAT IF SOMEONE SEES US HERE? WE COULD GET IN TROUBLE!
I'VE BEEN FINDING OUT THAT THE DEFINITION OF 'TROUBLE' IS A LOT MORE FLEXIBLE THAN I ONCE THOUGHT.
LET'S GO CHECK OUT THE LATEST AND GREATEST IN THE TECH WORLD.
COMPULAND
Welcome to Comp-U-Land. Is there anything I could assist you with?
BUZZ OFF.
Gladly! Enjoy your visit to Comp-U-Land and call me, **Chas**, if you need anything.

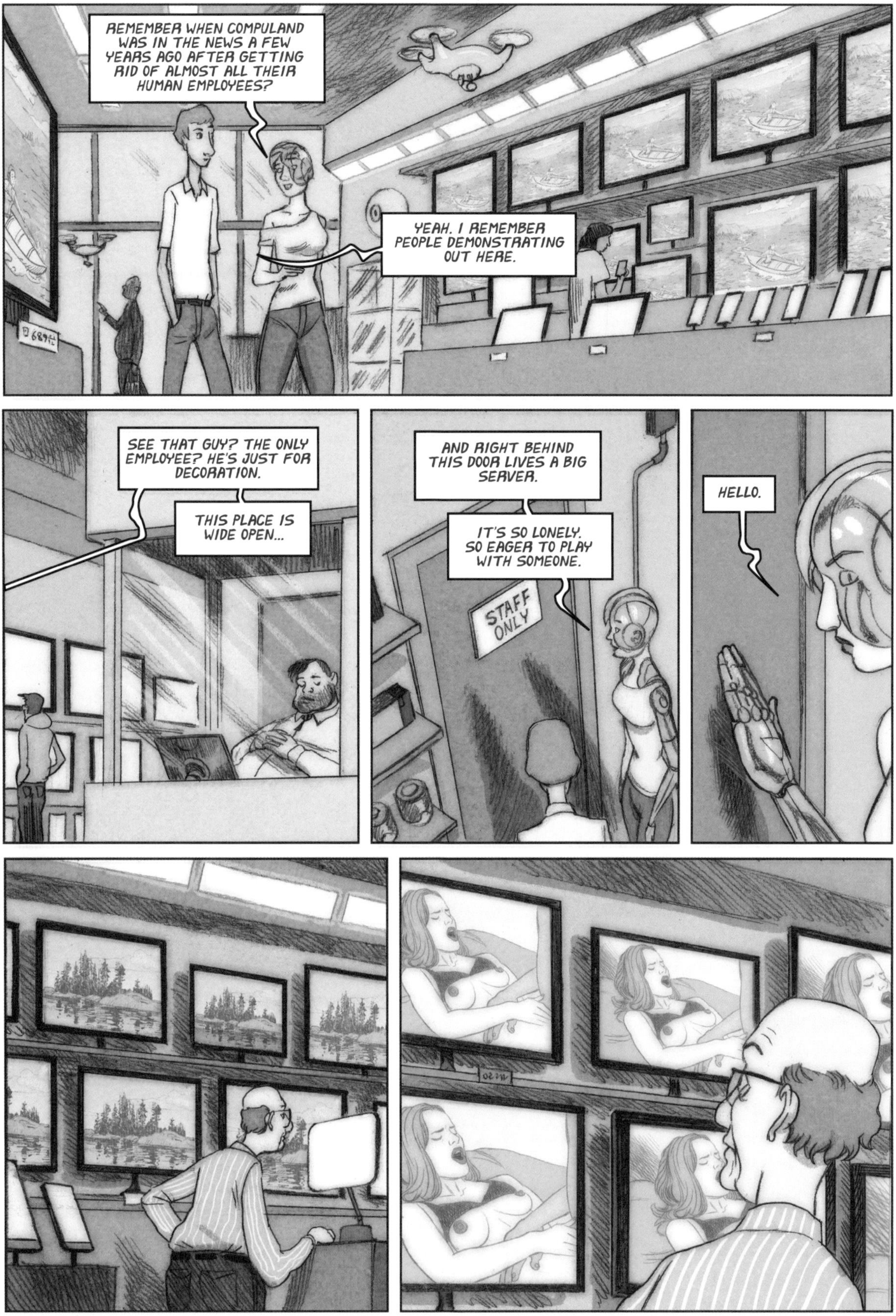
REMEMBER WHEN COMPULAND WAS IN THE NEWS A FEW YEARS AGO AFTER GETTING RID OF ALMOST ALL THEIR HUMAN EMPLOYEES?
YEAH. I REMEMBER PEOPLE DEMONSTRATING OUT HERE.
SEE THAT GUY? THE ONLY EMPLOYEE? HE'S JUST FOR DECORATION.
THIS PLACE IS WIDE OPEN...
AND RIGHT BEHIND THIS DOOR LIVES A BIG SERVER.
IT'S SO LONELY. SO EAGER TO PLAY WITH SOMEONE.
STAFF ONLY
HELLO.

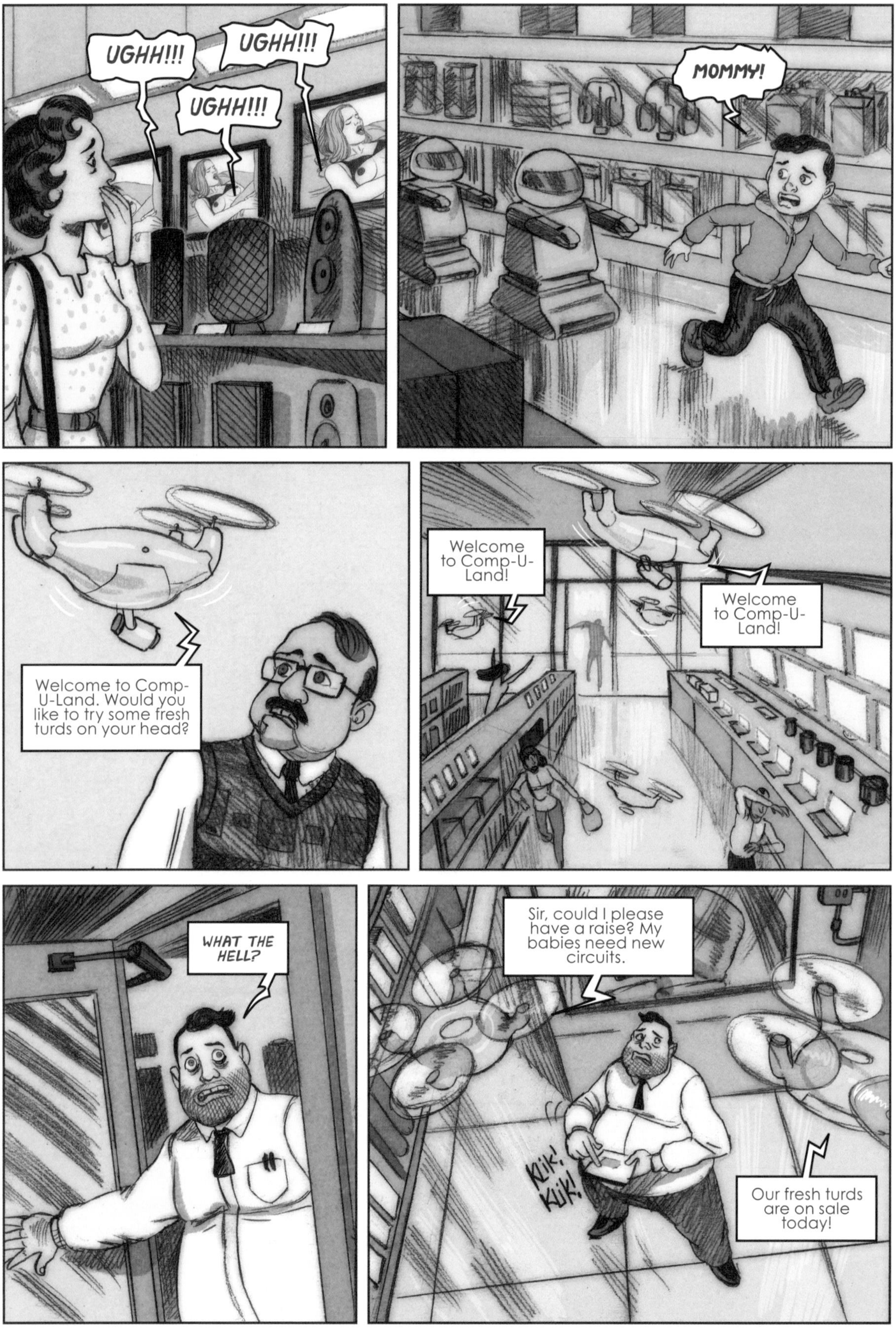
UGHH!!!
UGHH!!!
UGHH!!!
MOMMY!
Welcome to Comp-U-Land. Would you like to try some fresh turds on your head?
Welcome to Comp-U-Land!
Welcome to Comp-U-Land!
WHAT THE HELL?
Sir, could I please have a raise? My babies need new circuits.
KLIK! KLIK!
Our fresh turds are on sale today!

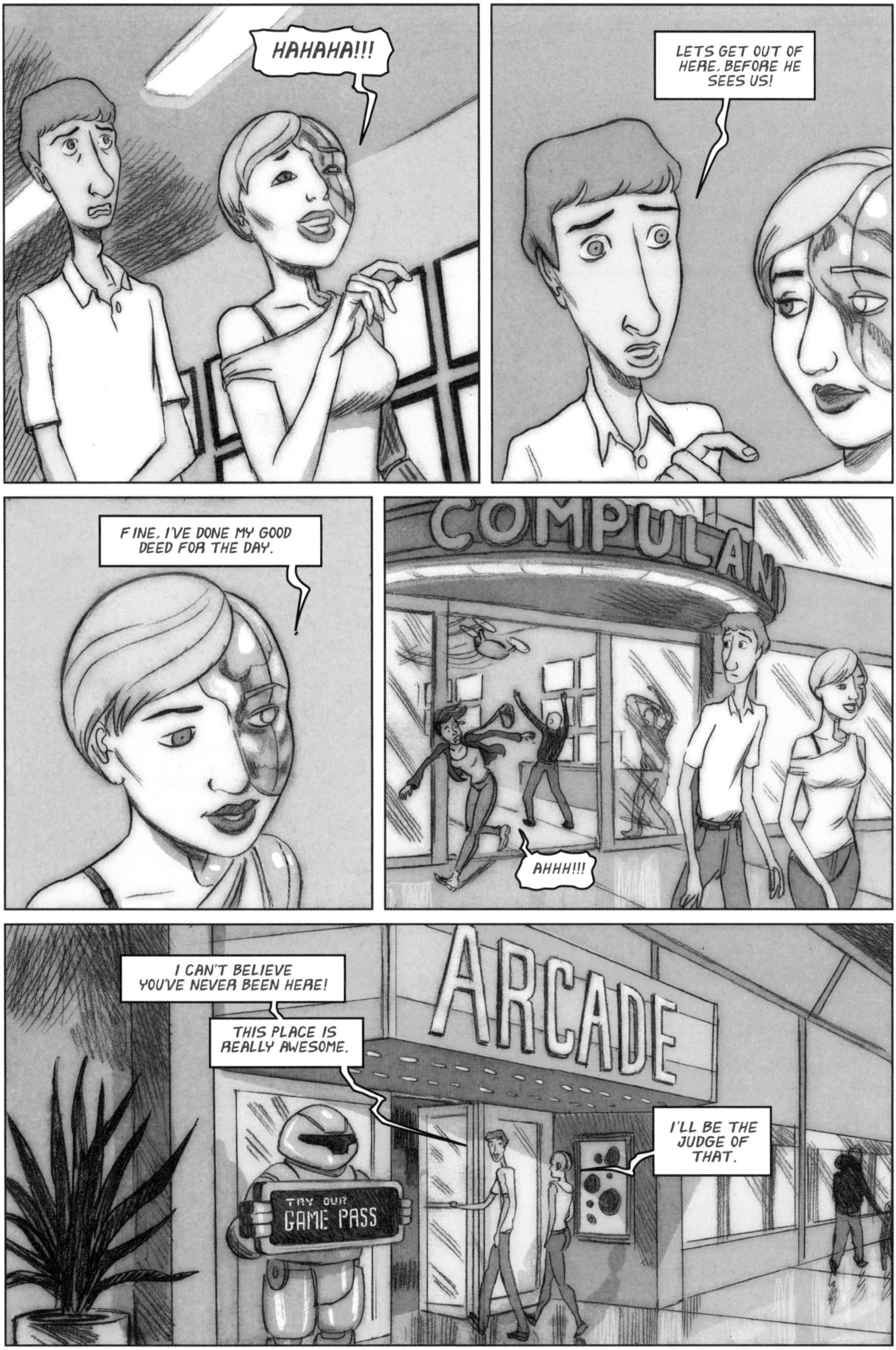
HAHAHA!!!
LETS GET OUT OF HERE, BEFORE HE SEES US!
FINE, I'VE DONE MY GOOD DEED FOR THE DAY.
COMPULAN
AHHH!!!
ARCADE
I CAN'T BELIEVE YOU'VE NEVER BEEN HERE!
THIS PLACE IS REALLY AWESOME.
TRY OUR GAME PASS
I'LL BE THE JUDGE OF THAT.

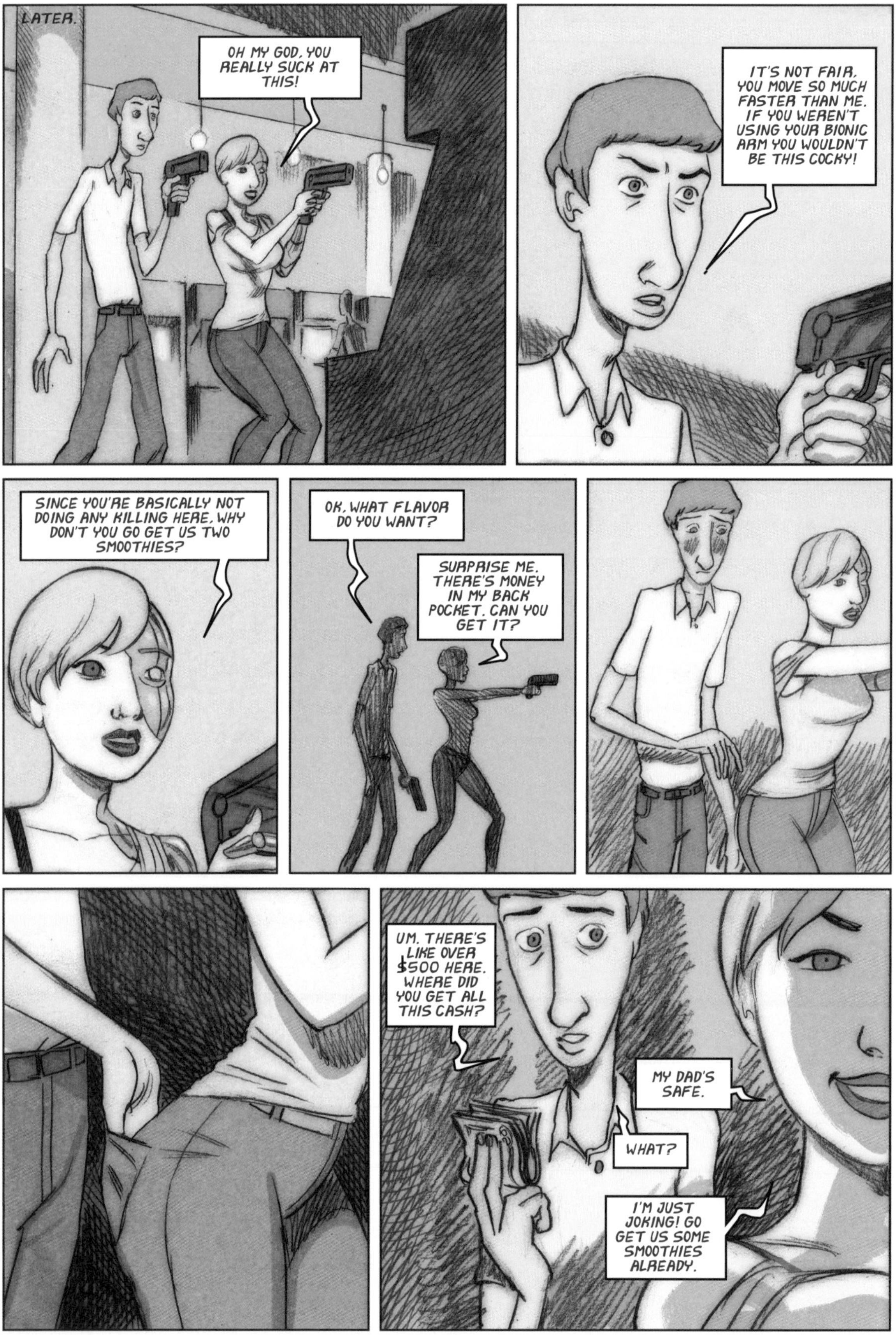
LATER.
OH MY GOD, YOU REALLY SUCK AT THIS!
IT'S NOT FAIR, YOU MOVE SO MUCH FASTER THAN ME. IF YOU WEREN'T USING YOUR BIONIC ARM YOU WOULDN'T BE THIS COCKY!
SINCE YOU'RE BASICALLY NOT DOING ANY KILLING HERE, WHY DON'T YOU GO GET US TWO SMOOTHIES?
OK, WHAT FLAVOR DO YOU WANT?
SURPRISE ME. THERE'S MONEY IN MY BACK POCKET. CAN YOU GET IT?
UM. THERE'S LIKE OVER $500 HERE. WHERE DID YOU GET ALL THIS CASH?
MY DAD'S SAFE.
WHAT?
I'M JUST JOKING! GO GET US SOME SMOOTHIES ALREADY.

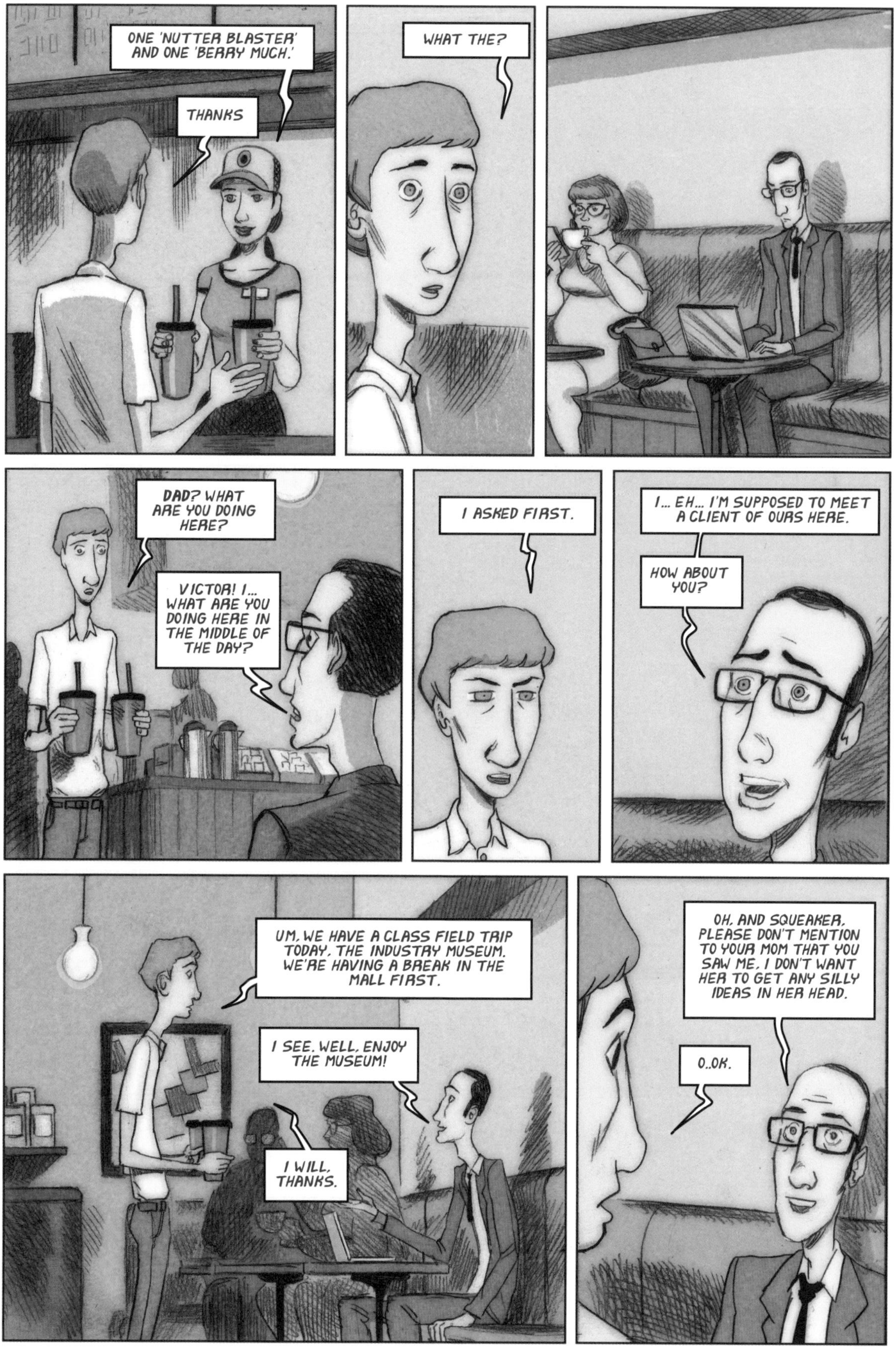
ONE 'NUTTER BLASTER' AND ONE 'BERRY MUCH.'
THANKS
WHAT THE?
DAD? WHAT ARE YOU DOING HERE?
VICTOR! I... WHAT ARE YOU DOING HERE IN THE MIDDLE OF THE DAY?
I ASKED FIRST.
I... EH... I'M SUPPOSED TO MEET A CLIENT OF OURS HERE.
HOW ABOUT YOU?
UM, WE HAVE A CLASS FIELD TRIP TODAY, THE INDUSTRY MUSEUM. WE'RE HAVING A BREAK IN THE MALL FIRST.
I SEE. WELL, ENJOY THE MUSEUM!
I WILL, THANKS.
OH, AND SQUEAKER, PLEASE DON'T MENTION TO YOUR MOM THAT YOU SAW ME. I DON'T WANT HER TO GET ANY SILLY IDEAS IN HER HEAD.
O..OK.

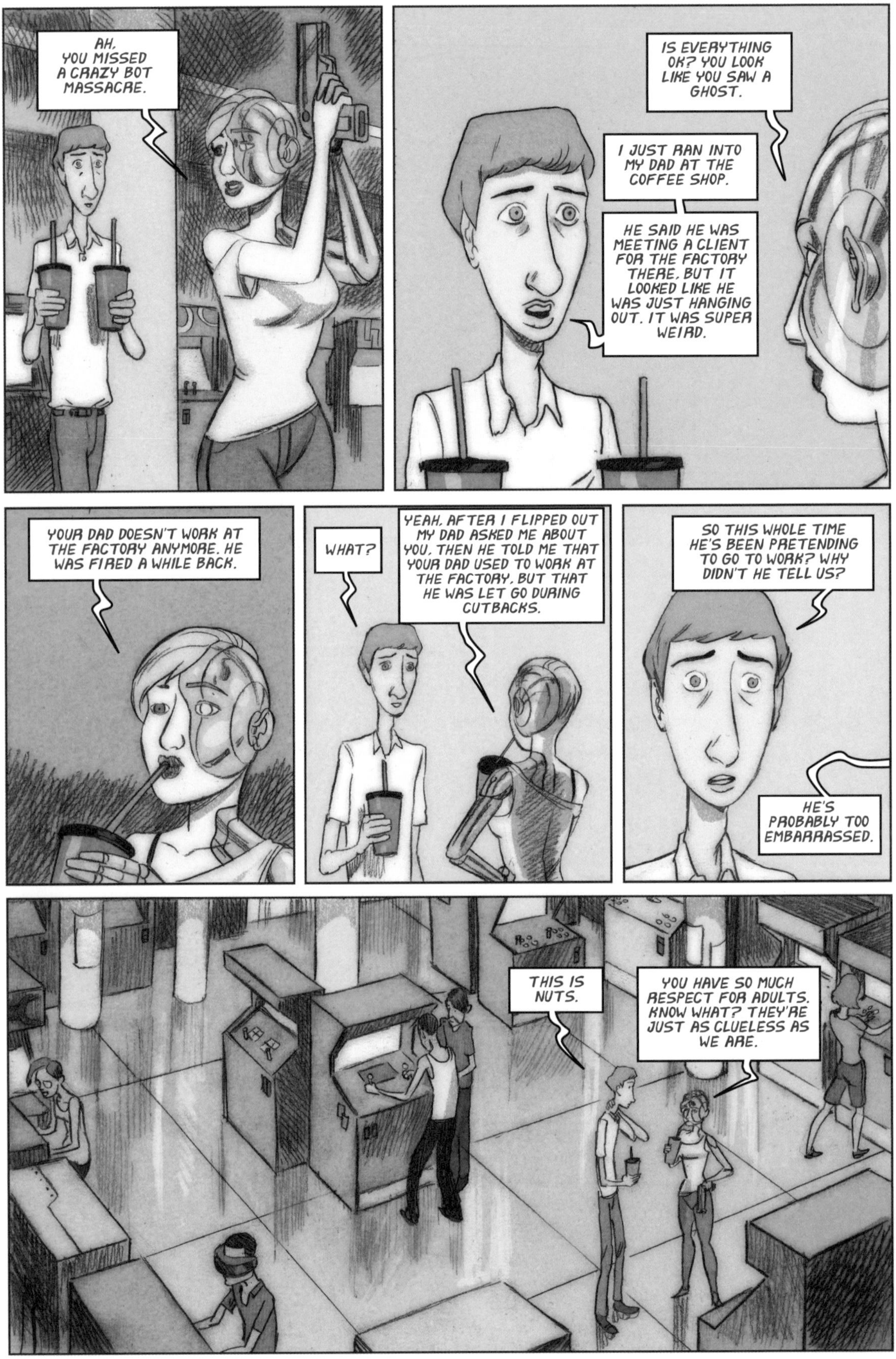
AH, YOU MISSED A CRAZY BOT MASSACRE.
IS EVERYTHING OK? YOU LOOK LIKE YOU SAW A GHOST.
I JUST RAN INTO MY DAD AT THE COFFEE SHOP.
HE SAID HE WAS MEETING A CLIENT FOR THE FACTORY THERE, BUT IT LOOKED LIKE HE WAS JUST HANGING OUT. IT WAS SUPER WEIRD.
YOUR DAD DOESN'T WORK AT THE FACTORY ANYMORE. HE WAS FIRED A WHILE BACK.
WHAT?
YEAH, AFTER I FLIPPED OUT MY DAD ASKED ME ABOUT YOU, THEN HE TOLD ME THAT YOUR DAD USED TO WORK AT THE FACTORY, BUT THAT HE WAS LET GO DURING CUTBACKS.
SO THIS WHOLE TIME HE'S BEEN PRETENDING TO GO TO WORK? WHY DIDN'T HE TELL US?
HE'S PROBABLY TOO EMBARRASSED.
THIS IS NUTS.
YOU HAVE SO MUCH RESPECT FOR ADULTS. KNOW WHAT? THEY'RE JUST AS CLUELESS AS WE ARE.

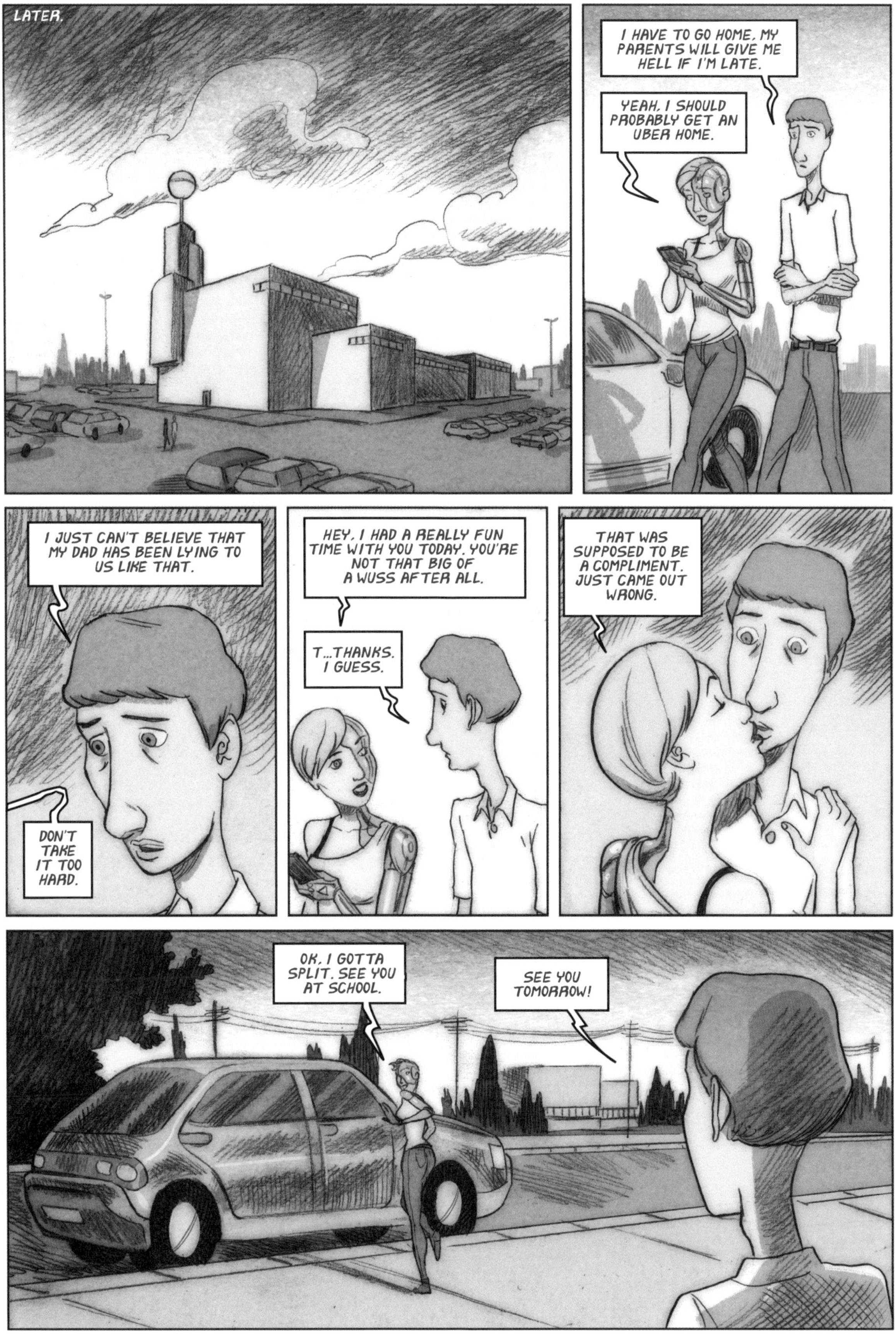
LATER.
I HAVE TO GO HOME. MY PARENTS WILL GIVE ME HELL IF I'M LATE.
YEAH, I SHOULD PROBABLY GET AN UBER HOME.
I JUST CAN'T BELIEVE THAT MY DAD HAS BEEN LYING TO US LIKE THAT.
DON'T TAKE IT TOO HARD.
HEY, I HAD A REALLY FUN TIME WITH YOU TODAY. YOU'RE NOT THAT BIG OF A WUSS AFTER ALL.
T...THANKS. I GUESS.
THAT WAS SUPPOSED TO BE A COMPLIMENT. JUST CAME OUT WRONG.
OK, I GOTTA SPLIT. SEE YOU AT SCHOOL.
SEE YOU TOMORROW!

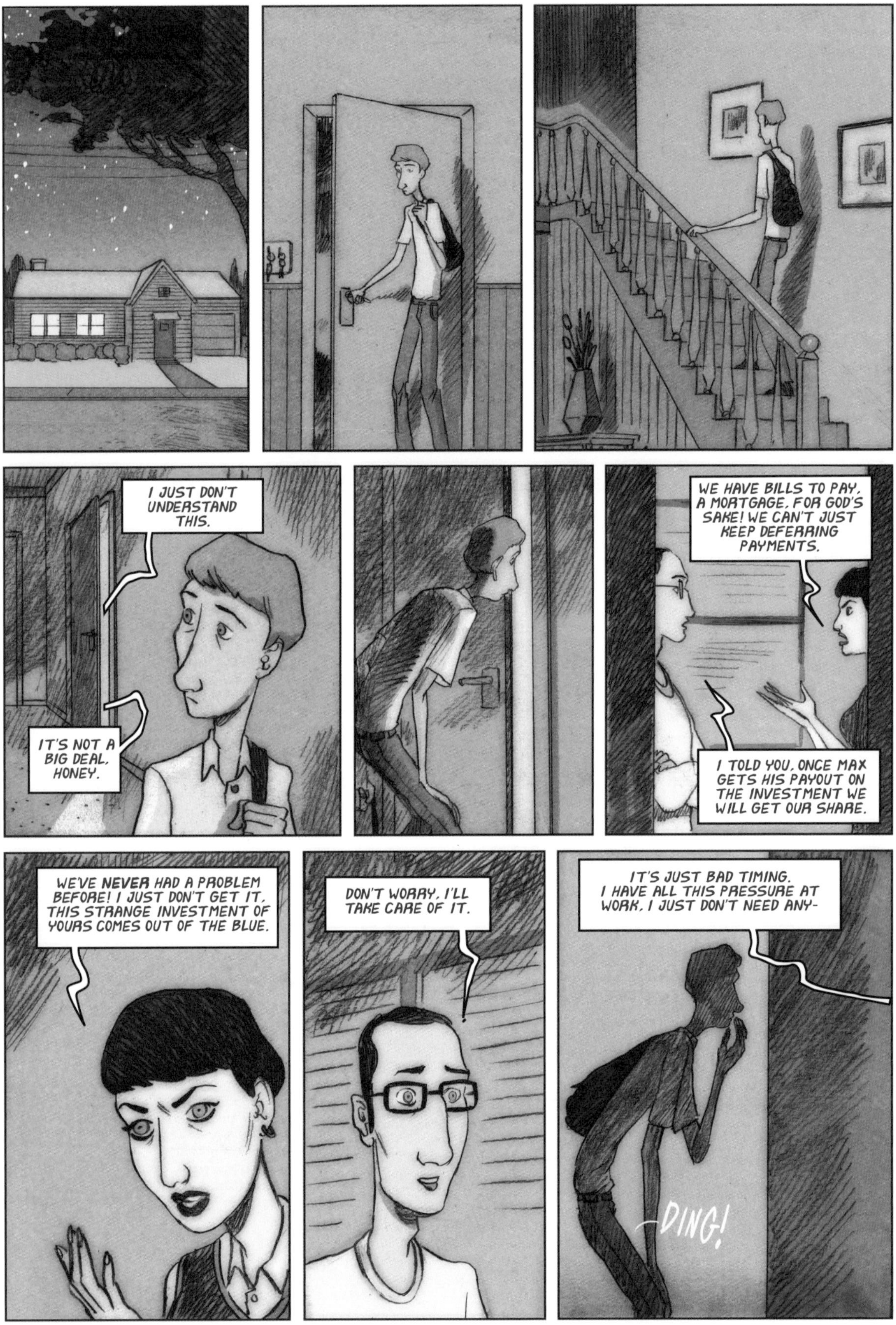
I JUST DON'T UNDERSTAND THIS.
IT'S NOT A BIG DEAL, HONEY.
WE HAVE BILLS TO PAY, A MORTGAGE, FOR GOD'S SAKE! WE CAN'T JUST KEEP DEFERRING PAYMENTS.
I TOLD YOU, ONCE MAX GETS HIS PAYOUT ON THE INVESTMENT WE WILL GET OUR SHARE.
WE'VE NEVER HAD A PROBLEM BEFORE! I JUST DON'T GET IT. THIS STRANGE INVESTMENT OF YOURS COMES OUT OF THE BLUE.
DON'T WORRY, I'LL TAKE CARE OF IT.
IT'S JUST BAD TIMING. I HAVE ALL THIS PRESSURE AT WORK, I JUST DON'T NEED ANY-
DING!

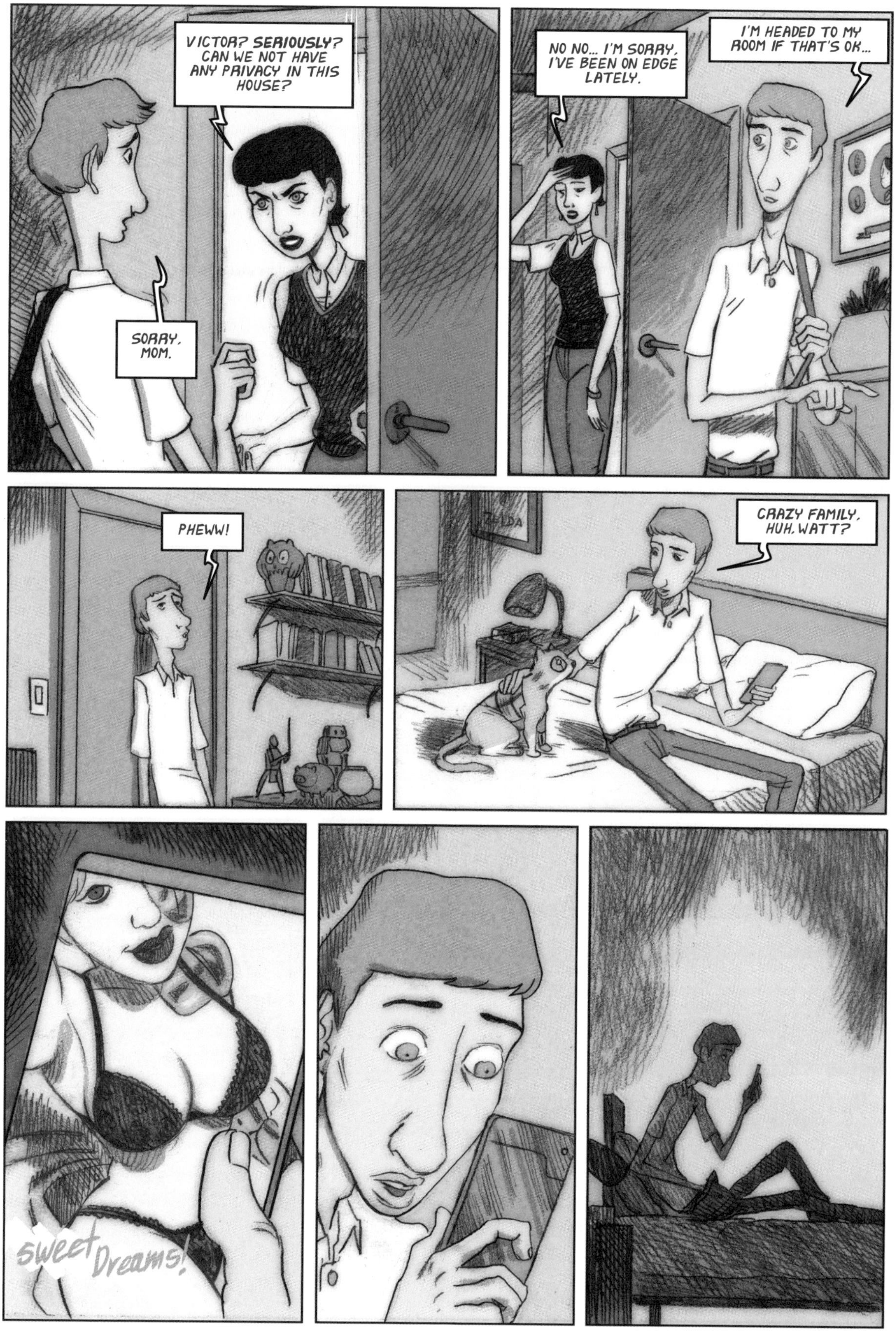
VICTOR? SERIOUSLY? CAN WE NOT HAVE ANY PRIVACY IN THIS HOUSE?
SORRY, MOM.
NO NO... I'M SORRY, I'VE BEEN ON EDGE LATELY.
I'M HEADED TO MY ROOM IF THAT'S OK...
PHEWW!
ZELDA
CRAZY FAMILY, HUH, WATT?
sweet Dreams!

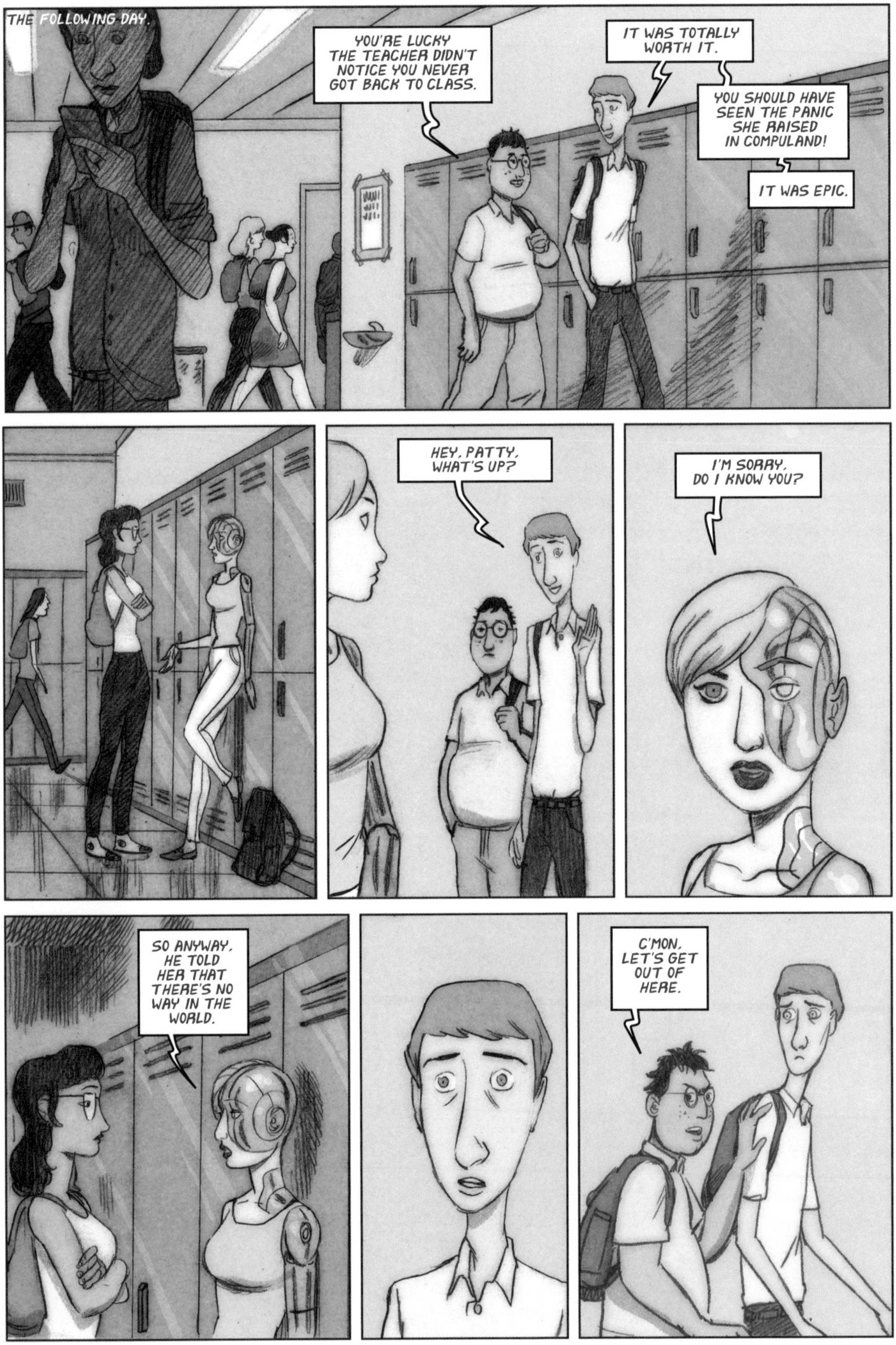
THE FOLLOWING DAY.
YOU'RE LUCKY THE TEACHER DIDN'T NOTICE YOU NEVER GOT BACK TO CLASS.
IT WAS TOTALLY WORTH IT.
YOU SHOULD HAVE SEEN THE PANIC SHE RAISED IN COMPULAND!
IT WAS EPIC.
HEY, PATTY, WHAT'S UP?
I'M SORRY, DO I KNOW YOU?
SO ANYWAY, HE TOLD HER THAT THERE'S NO WAY IN THE WORLD.
C'MON, LET'S GET OUT OF HERE.

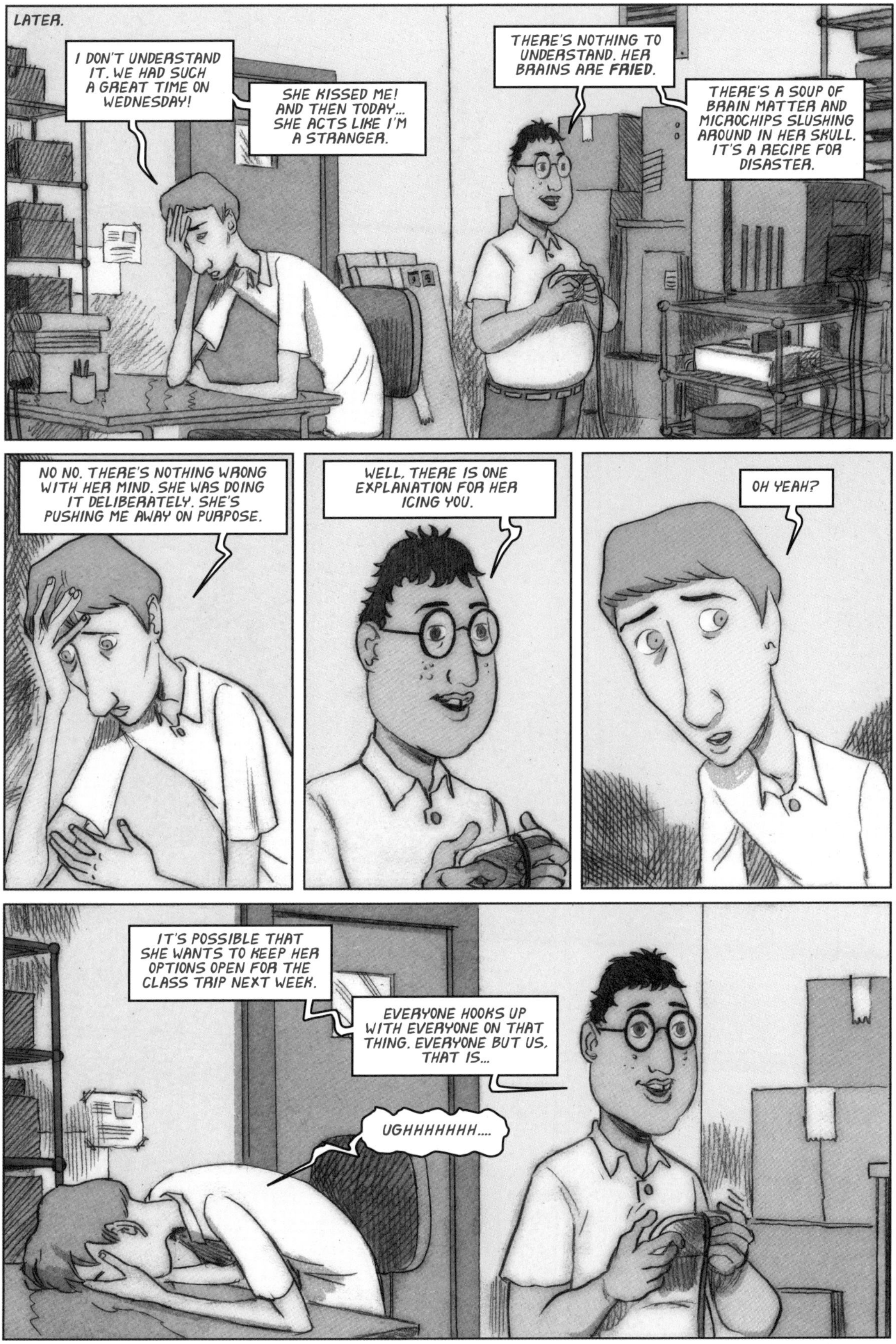
LATER.
I DON'T UNDERSTAND IT. WE HAD SUCH A GREAT TIME ON WEDNESDAY!
SHE KISSED ME! AND THEN TODAY... SHE ACTS LIKE I'M A STRANGER.
THERE'S NOTHING TO UNDERSTAND. HER BRAINS ARE FRIED.
THERE'S A SOUP OF BRAIN MATTER AND MICROCHIPS SLUSHING AROUND IN HER SKULL. IT'S A RECIPE FOR DISASTER.
NO NO. THERE'S NOTHING WRONG WITH HER MIND. SHE WAS DOING IT DELIBERATELY. SHE'S PUSHING ME AWAY ON PURPOSE.
WELL, THERE IS ONE EXPLANATION FOR HER ICING YOU.
OH YEAH?
IT'S POSSIBLE THAT SHE WANTS TO KEEP HER OPTIONS OPEN FOR THE CLASS TRIP NEXT WEEK.
EVERYONE HOOKS UP WITH EVERYONE ON THAT THING. EVERYONE BUT US, THAT IS...
UGHHHHHHH....

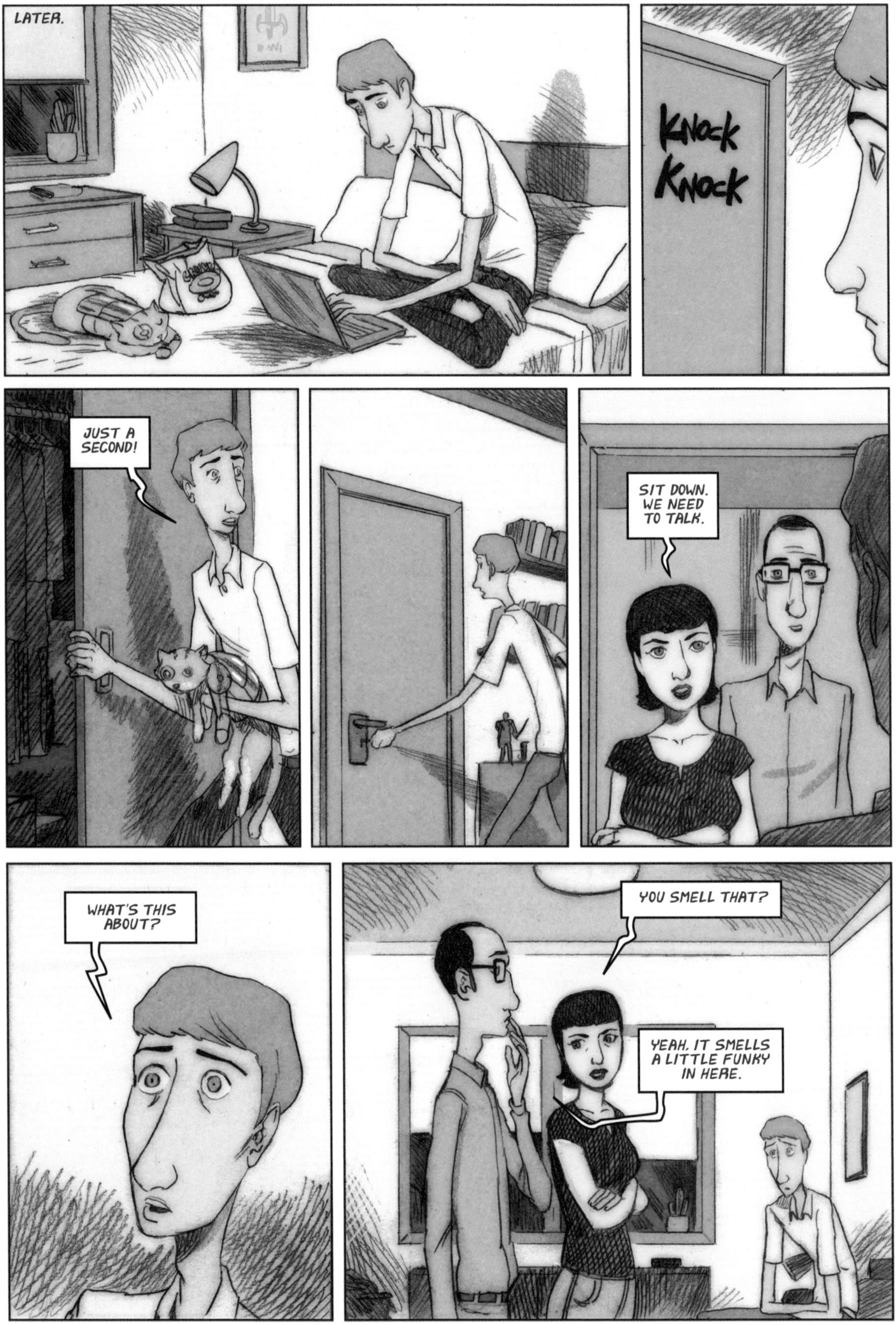
LATER.
KNOCK KNOCK
JUST A SECOND!
SIT DOWN. WE NEED TO TALK.
WHAT'S THIS ABOUT?
YOU SMELL THAT?
YEAH, IT SMELLS A LITTLE FUNKY IN HERE.

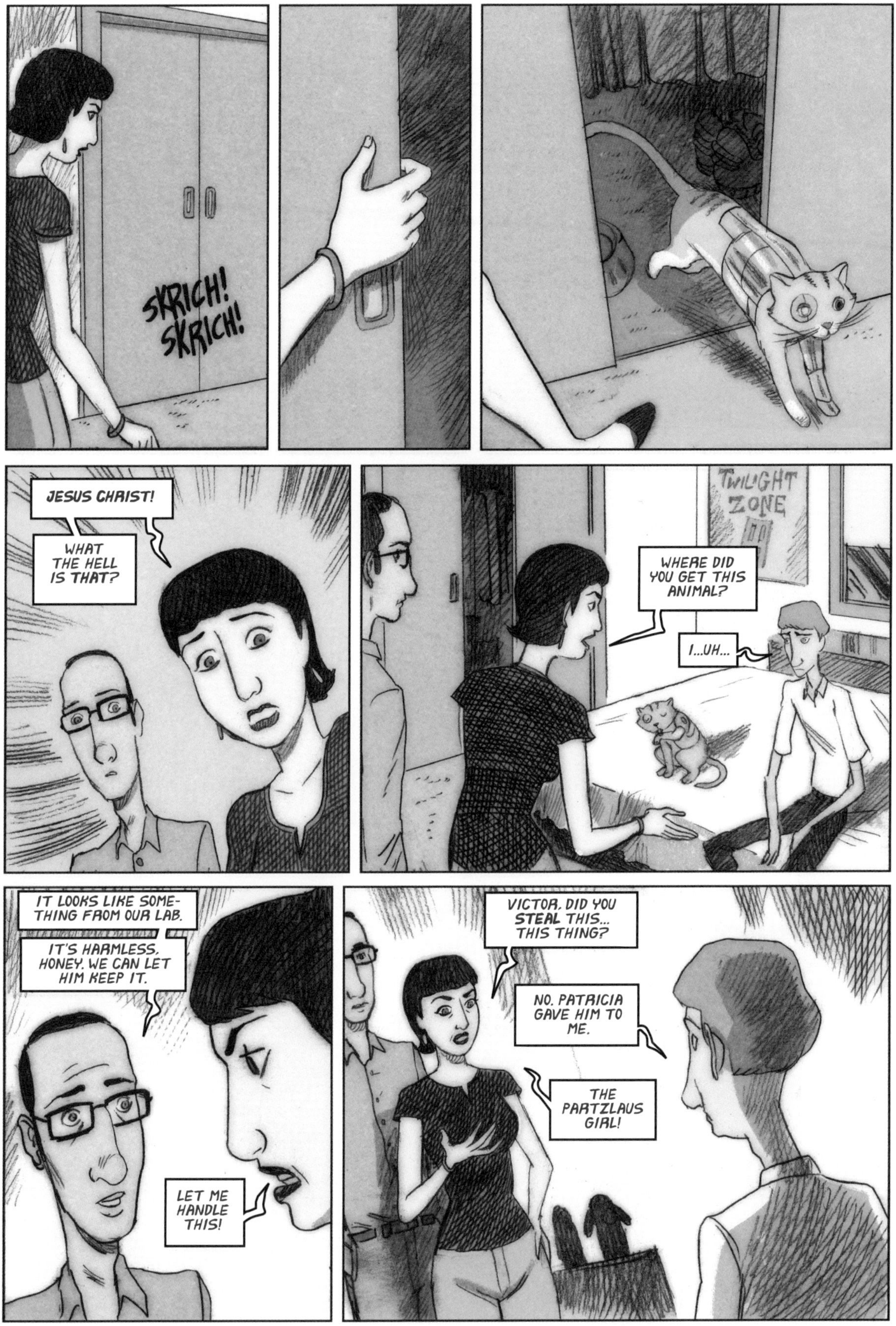
SKRICH! SKRICH!
JESUS CHRIST!
WHAT THE HELL IS THAT?
WHERE DID YOU GET THIS ANIMAL?
I...UH...
TWILIGHT ZONE
IT LOOKS LIKE SOMETHING FROM OUR LAB.
IT'S HARMLESS, HONEY. WE CAN LET HIM KEEP IT.
LET ME HANDLE THIS!
VICTOR, DID YOU STEAL THIS... THIS THING?
NO. PATRICIA GAVE HIM TO ME.
THE PARTZLAUS GIRL!

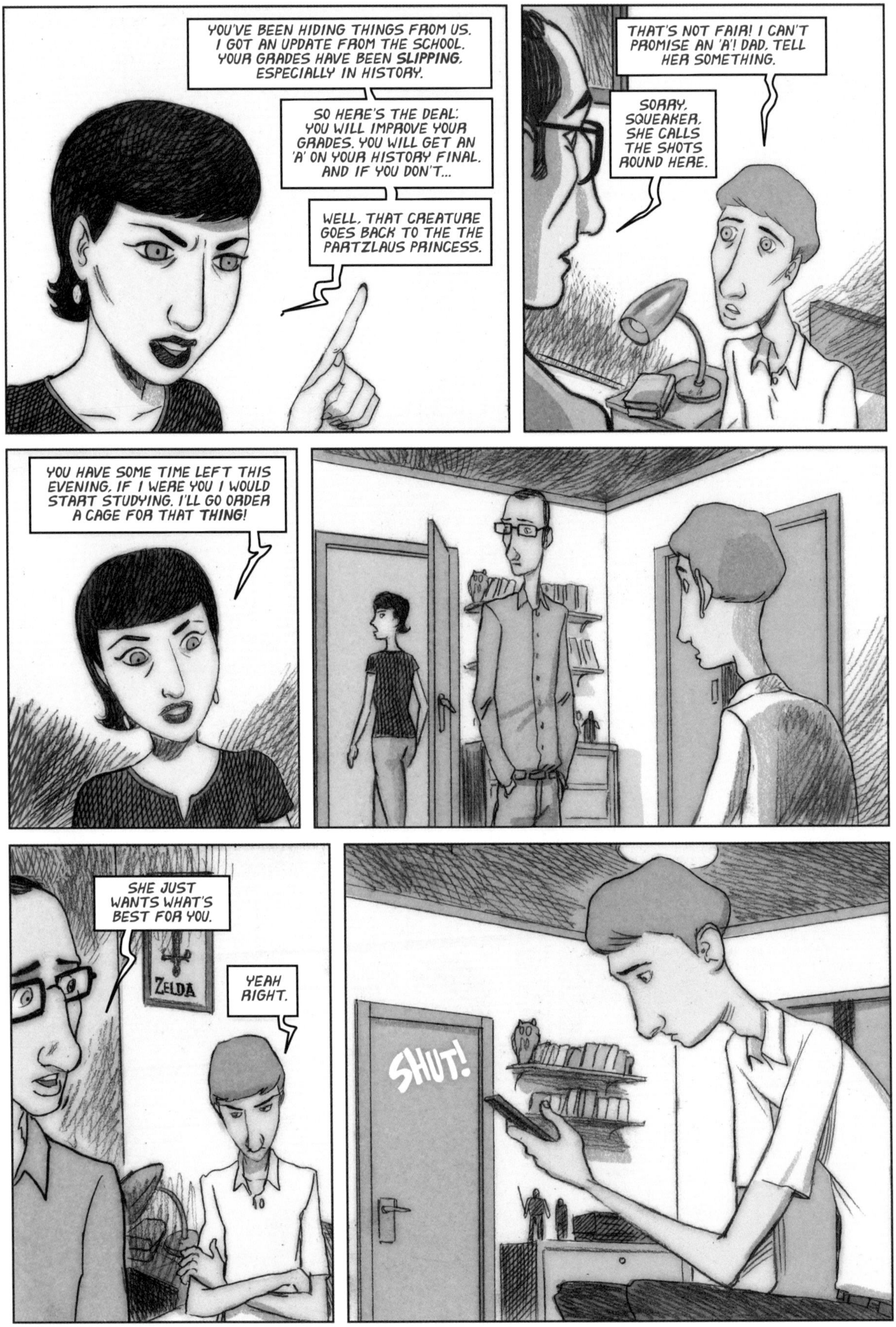
YOU'VE BEEN HIDING THINGS FROM US. I GOT AN UPDATE FROM THE SCHOOL. YOUR GRADES HAVE BEEN **SLIPPING**, ESPECIALLY IN HISTORY.
SO HERE'S THE DEAL: YOU WILL IMPROVE YOUR GRADES. YOU WILL GET AN 'A' ON YOUR HISTORY FINAL. AND IF YOU DON'T...
WELL, THAT CREATURE GOES BACK TO THE THE PARTZLAUS PRINCESS.
THAT'S NOT FAIR! I CAN'T PROMISE AN 'A'! DAD, TELL HER SOMETHING.
SORRY, SQUEAKER, SHE CALLS THE SHOTS ROUND HERE.
YOU HAVE SOME TIME LEFT THIS EVENING. IF I WERE YOU I WOULD START STUDYING. I'LL GO ORDER A CAGE FOR THAT **THING**!
SHE JUST WANTS WHAT'S BEST FOR YOU.
ZELDA
YEAH RIGHT.
SHUT!

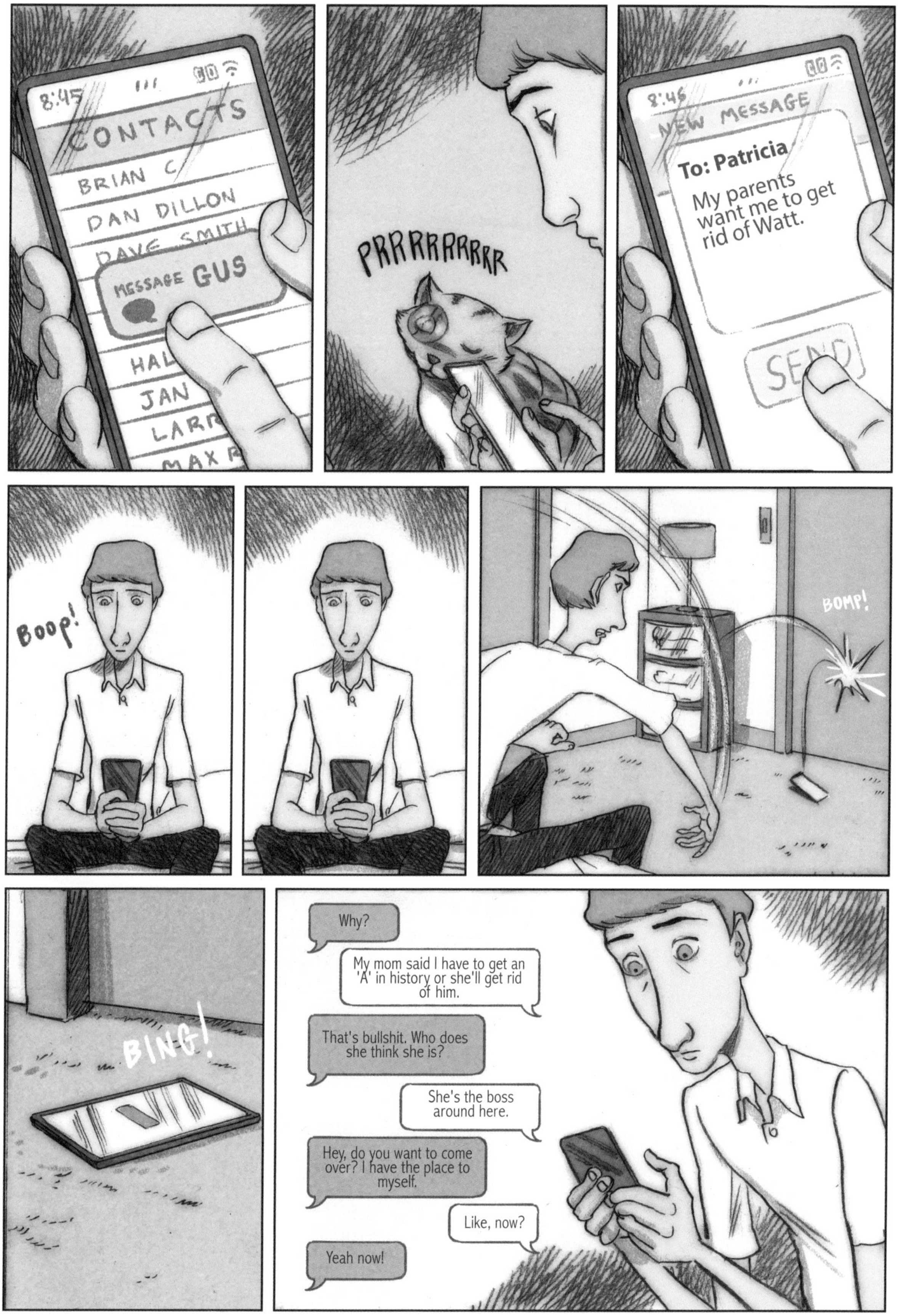
8:45
CONTACTS
BRIAN C
DAN DILLON
DAVE SMITH
MESSAGE GUS
JAN
PRRRRRRRRR
8:46
NEW MESSAGE
To: Patricia
My parents want me to get rid of Watt.
SEND
Boop!
BOMP!
BING!
Why?
My mom said I have to get an 'A' in history or she'll get rid of him.
That's bullshit. Who does she think she is?
She's the boss around here.
Hey, do you want to come over? I have the place to myself.
Like, now?
Yeah now!

LATER.

COME IN, I'M BY THE POOL.

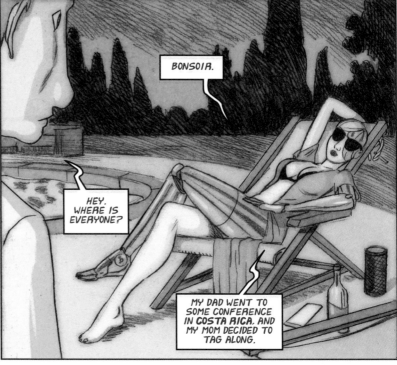

BONSOIR.

HEY. WHERE IS EVERYONE?

MY DAD WENT TO SOME CONFERENCE IN COSTA RICA. AND MY MOM DECIDED TO TAG ALONG.

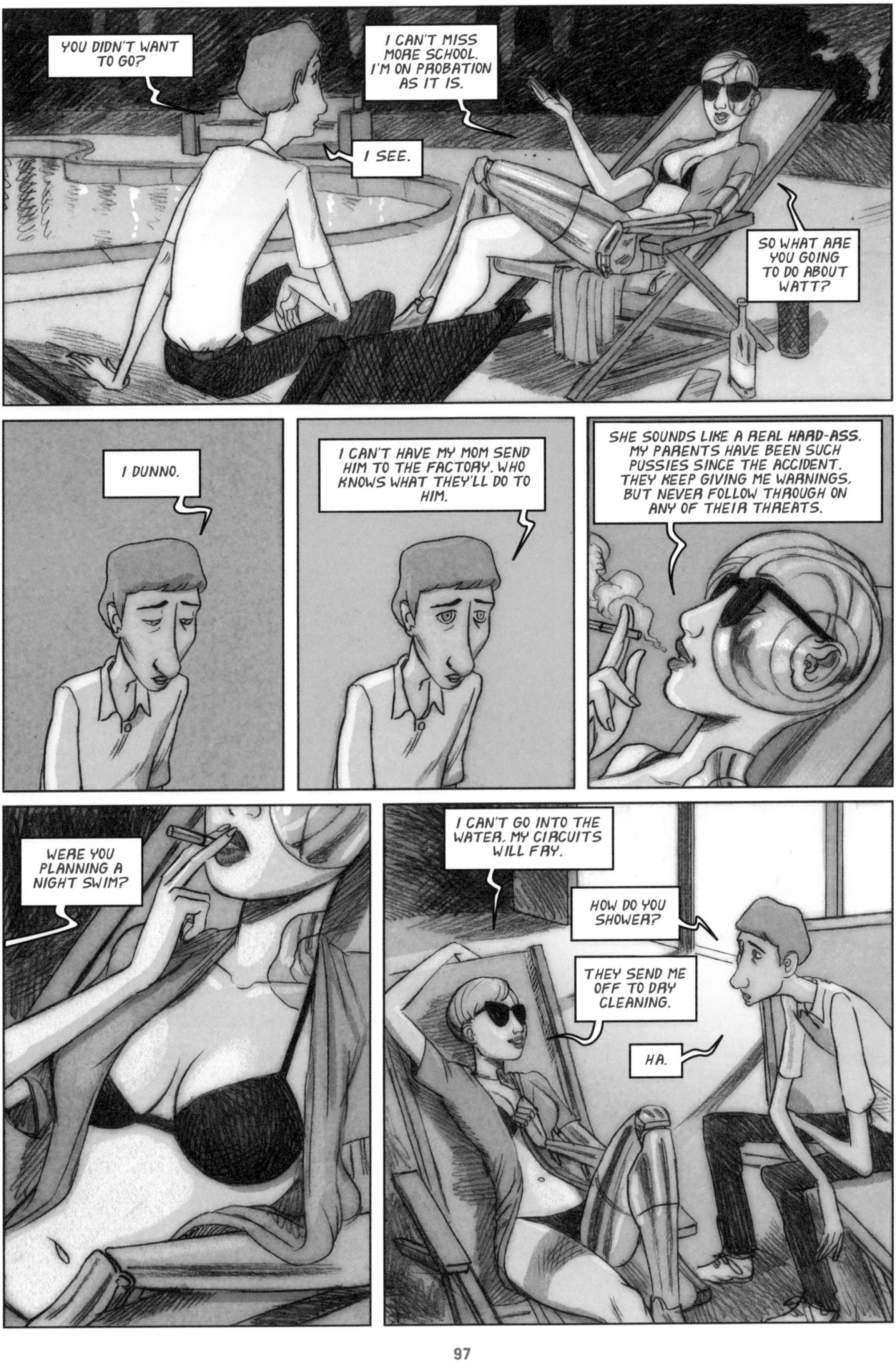

YOU DIDN'T WANT TO GO?
I CAN'T MISS MORE SCHOOL. I'M ON PROBATION AS IT IS.
I SEE.
SO WHAT ARE YOU GOING TO DO ABOUT WATT?
I DUNNO.
I CAN'T HAVE MY MOM SEND HIM TO THE FACTORY. WHO KNOWS WHAT THEY'LL DO TO HIM.
SHE SOUNDS LIKE A REAL HARD-ASS. MY PARENTS HAVE BEEN SUCH PUSSIES SINCE THE ACCIDENT. THEY KEEP GIVING ME WARNINGS, BUT NEVER FOLLOW THROUGH ON ANY OF THEIR THREATS.
WERE YOU PLANNING A NIGHT SWIM?
I CAN'T GO INTO THE WATER, MY CIRCUITS WILL FRY.
HOW DO YOU SHOWER?
THEY SEND ME OFF TO DRY CLEANING.
HA.

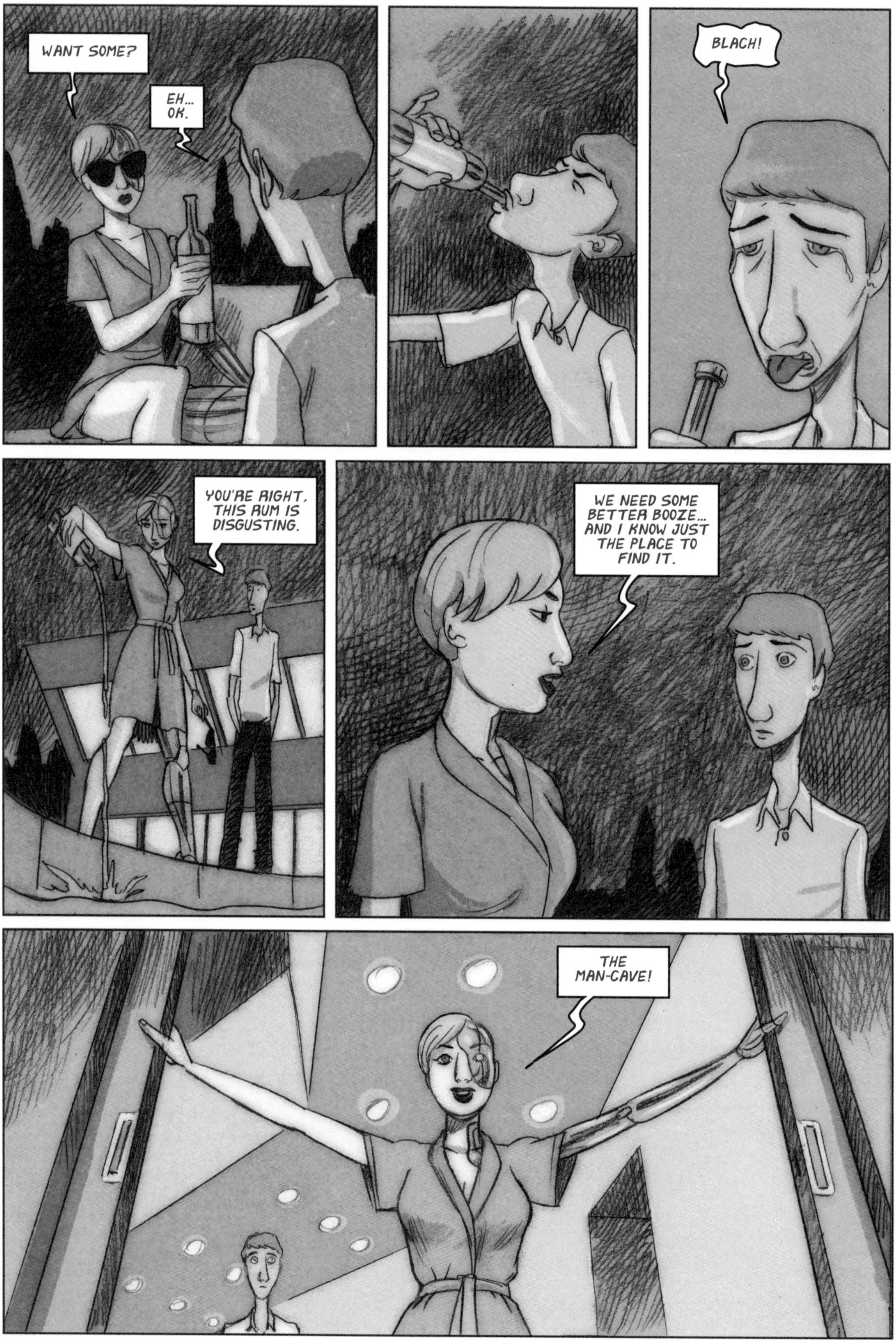
WANT SOME?
EH... OK.
BLACH!
YOU'RE RIGHT, THIS RUM IS DISGUSTING.
WE NEED SOME BETTER BOOZE... AND I KNOW JUST THE PLACE TO FIND IT.
THE MAN-CAVE!

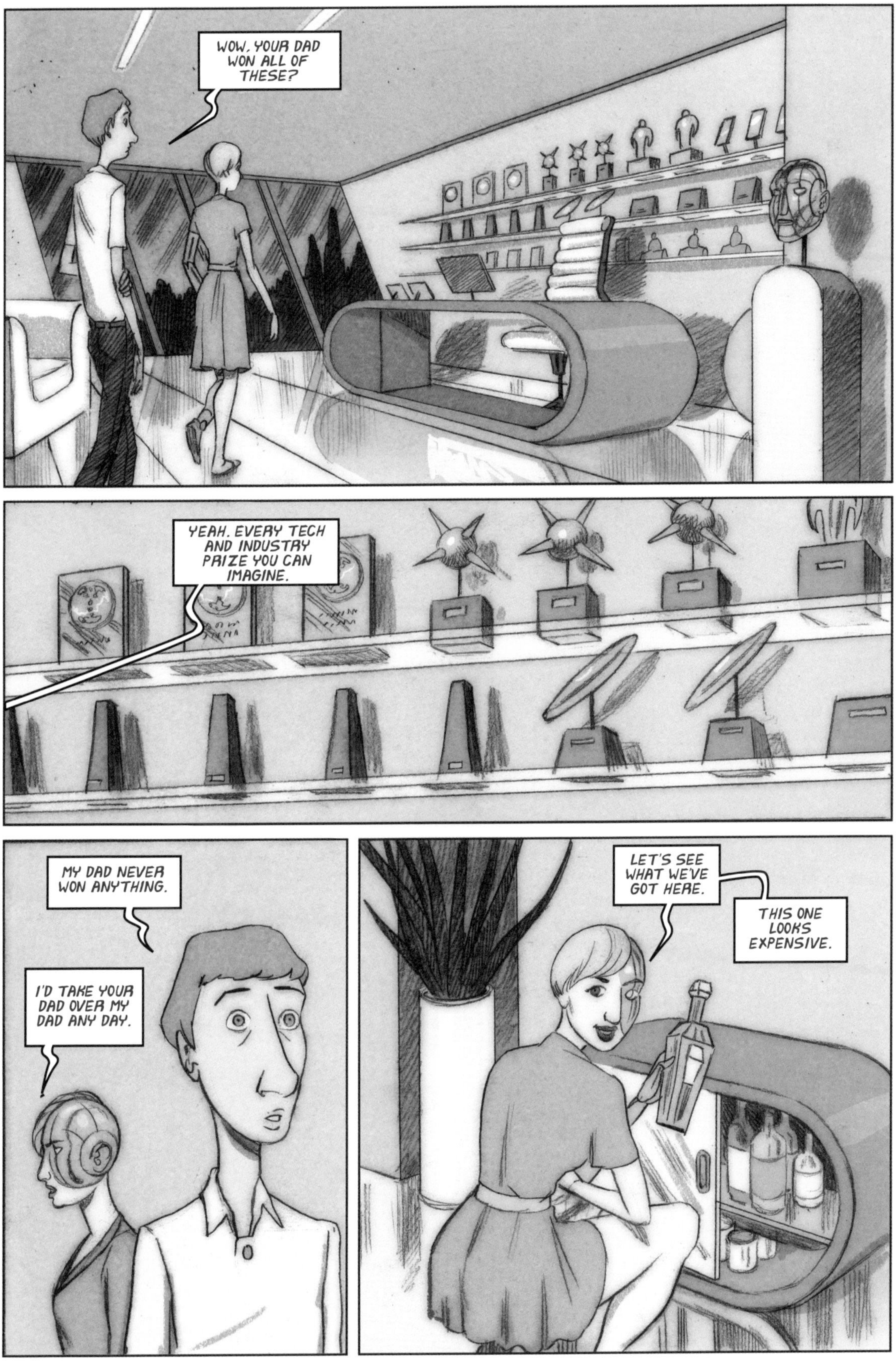
WOW, YOUR DAD WON ALL OF THESE?
YEAH. EVERY TECH AND INDUSTRY PRIZE YOU CAN IMAGINE.
MY DAD NEVER WON ANYTHING.
I'D TAKE YOUR DAD OVER MY DAD ANY DAY.
LET'S SEE WHAT WE'VE GOT HERE.
THIS ONE LOOKS EXPENSIVE.

ISN'T THIS STEALING?

DON'T BE SILLY.

THIS IS PART OF MY COMPENSATION PLAN.

FREE ACCESS TO EVERYTHING IN THE HOUSE.

GETTING A LITTLE HOT IN HERE, NO?

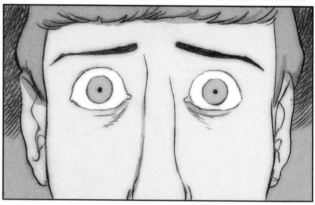

COME ON... DON'T BE SCARED.

YOU'LL GET EXTRA POINTS FOR EACH ITEM YOU BREAK.

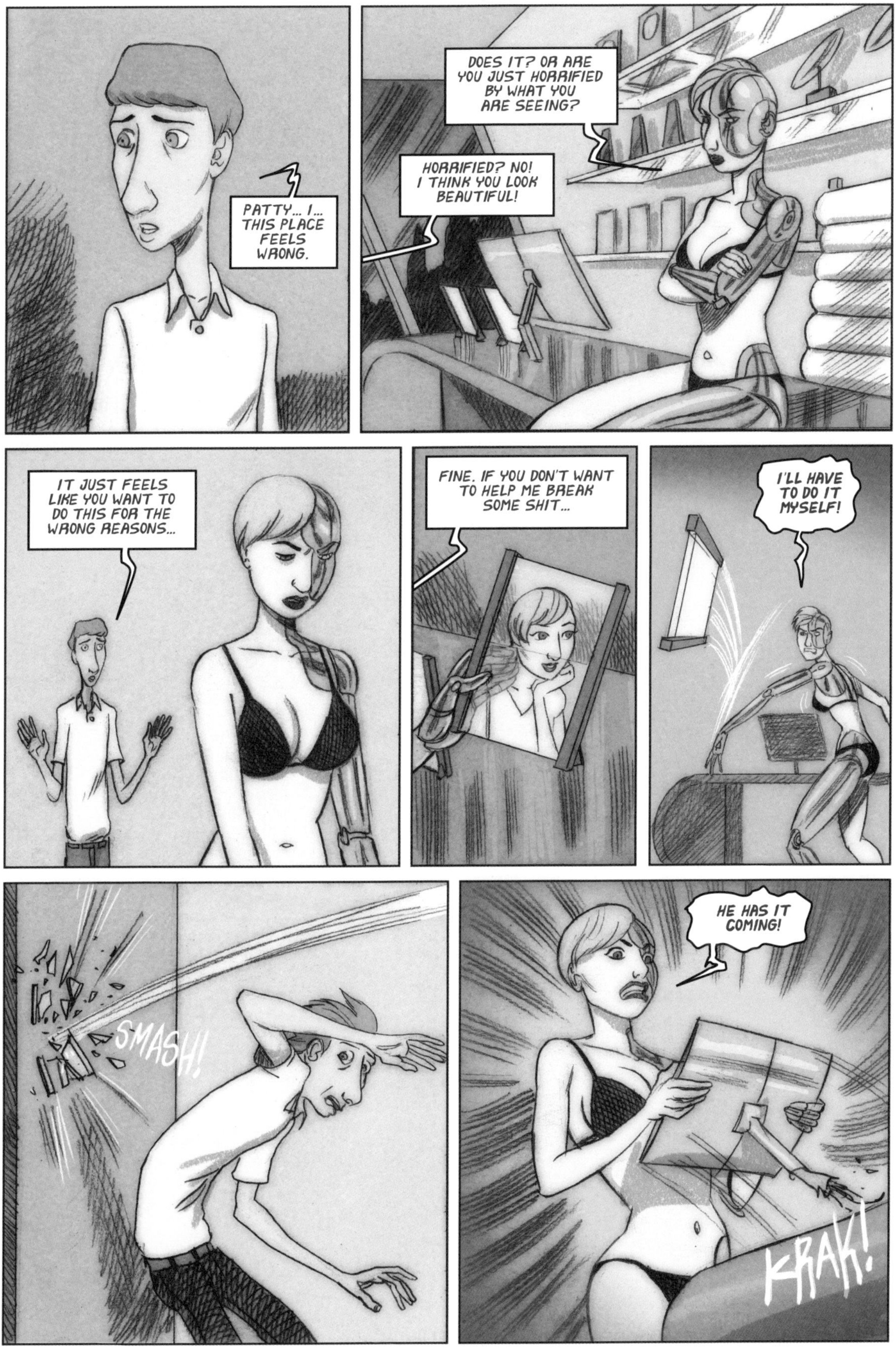
PATTY... I... THIS PLACE FEELS WRONG.
DOES IT? OR ARE YOU JUST HORRIFIED BY WHAT YOU ARE SEEING?
HORRIFIED? NO! I THINK YOU LOOK BEAUTIFUL!
IT JUST FEELS LIKE YOU WANT TO DO THIS FOR THE WRONG REASONS...
FINE. IF YOU DON'T WANT TO HELP ME BREAK SOME SHIT...
I'LL HAVE TO DO IT MYSELF!
SMASH!
HE HAS IT COMING!
KRAK!

ASSHOLE!!!
SKRAKK!
KRAK

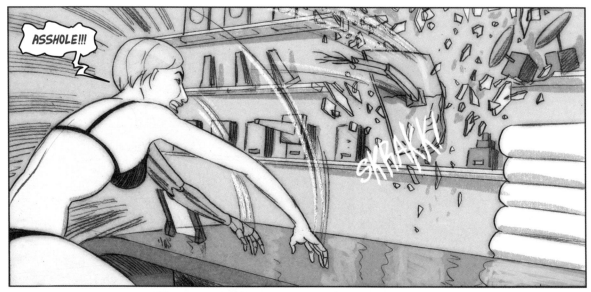

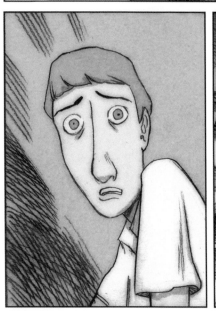

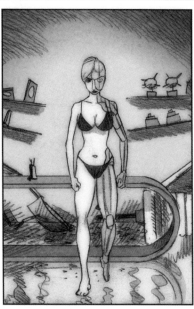

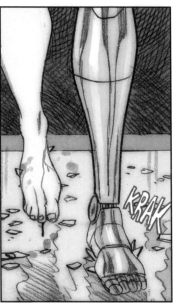

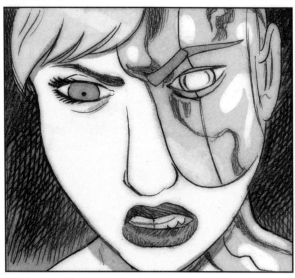

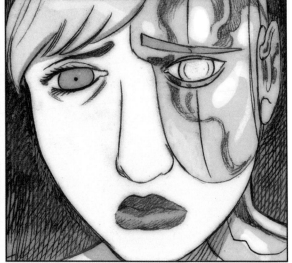

I... I'M SORRY.

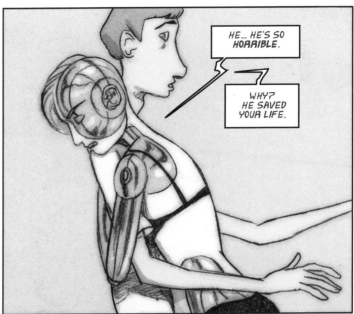

HE... HE'S SO HORRIBLE.

WHY? HE SAVED YOUR LIFE.

HE DIDN'T SAVE MY LIFE.

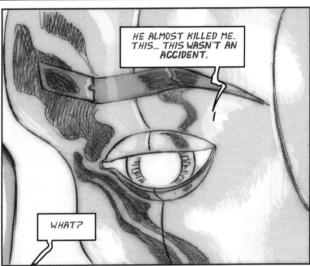

HE ALMOST KILLED ME. THIS... THIS WASN'T AN ACCIDENT.

WHAT?

IT WASN'T AN ACCIDENT. THE CAR HITTING ME THAT DAY, IT WAS ALL PLANNED.

I DON'T UNDERSTAND.

HE HAD IT ALL PLANNED OUT! EVERY LITTLE DETAIL.

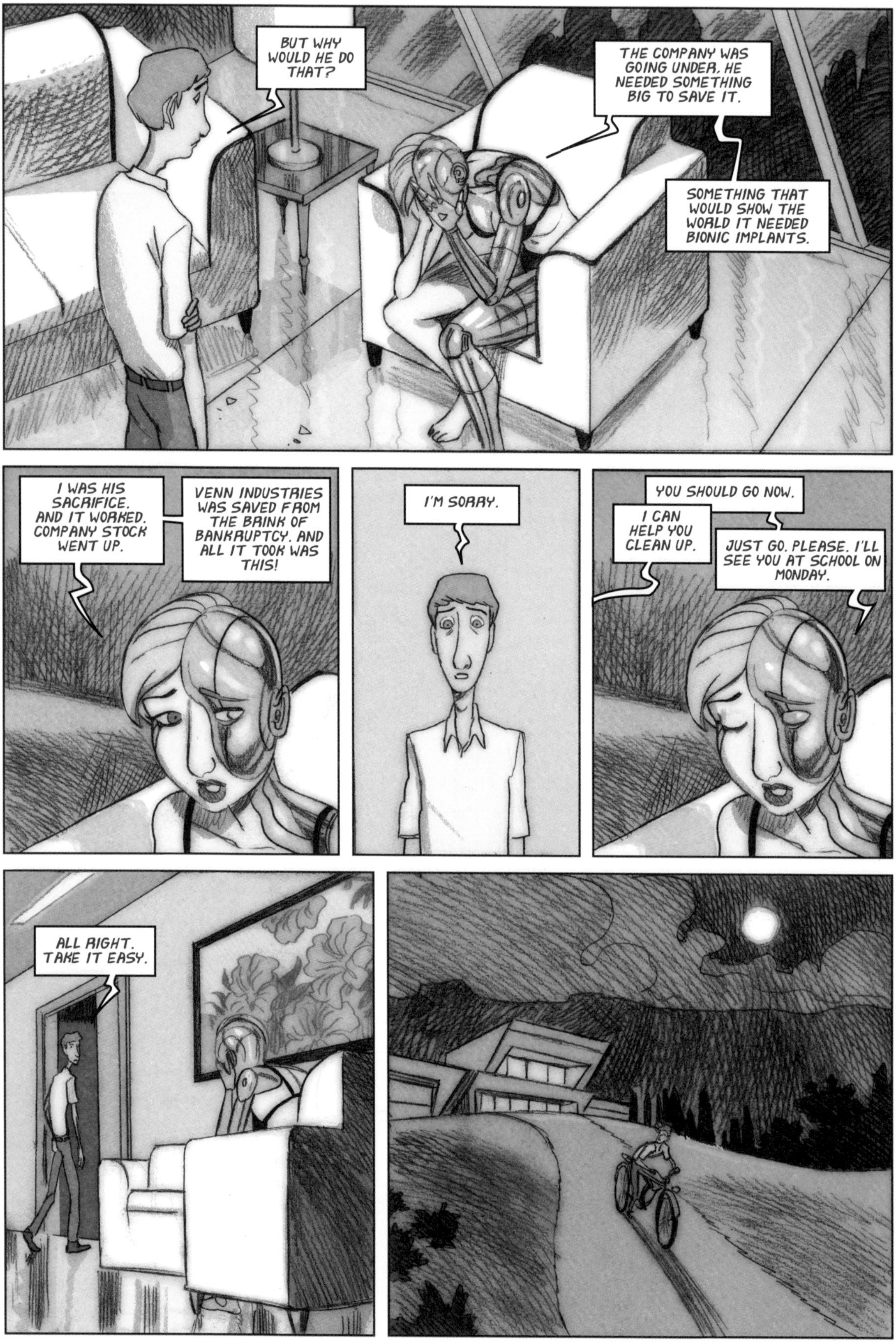
BUT WHY WOULD HE DO THAT?
THE COMPANY WAS GOING UNDER. HE NEEDED SOMETHING BIG TO SAVE IT.
SOMETHING THAT WOULD SHOW THE WORLD IT NEEDED BIONIC IMPLANTS.
I WAS HIS SACRIFICE. AND IT WORKED. COMPANY STOCK WENT UP.
VENN INDUSTRIES WAS SAVED FROM THE BRINK OF BANKRUPTCY. AND ALL IT TOOK WAS THIS!
I'M SORRY.
YOU SHOULD GO NOW.
I CAN HELP YOU CLEAN UP.
JUST GO. PLEASE. I'LL SEE YOU AT SCHOOL ON MONDAY.
ALL RIGHT. TAKE IT EASY.

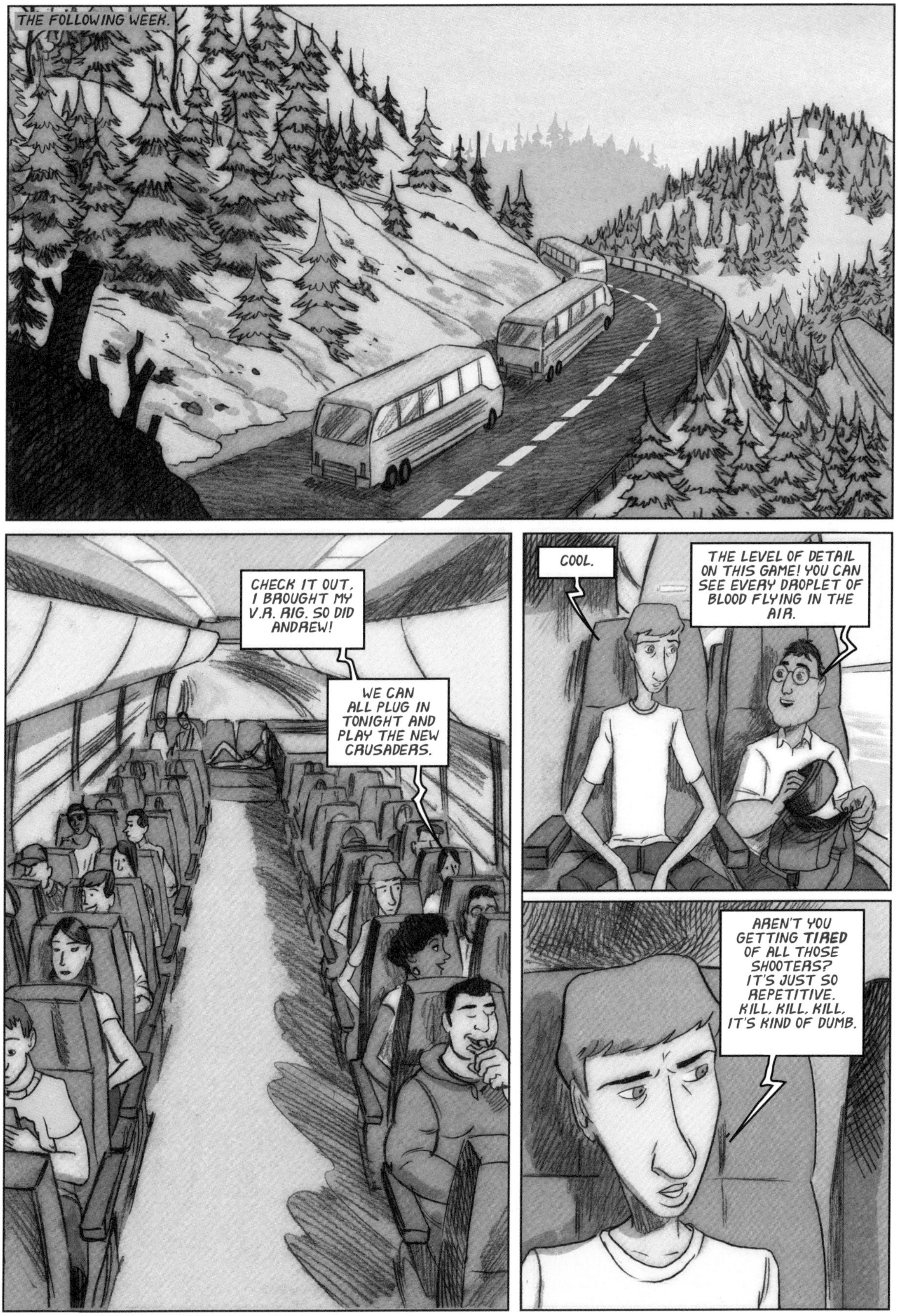
THE FOLLOWING WEEK.
CHECK IT OUT, I BROUGHT MY V.R. RIG. SO DID ANDREW!
WE CAN ALL PLUG IN TONIGHT AND PLAY THE NEW CRUSADERS.
COOL.
THE LEVEL OF DETAIL ON THIS GAME! YOU CAN SEE EVERY DROPLET OF BLOOD FLYING IN THE AIR.
AREN'T YOU GETTING **TIRED** OF ALL THOSE SHOOTERS? IT'S JUST SO REPETITIVE. KILL, KILL, KILL. IT'S KIND OF DUMB.

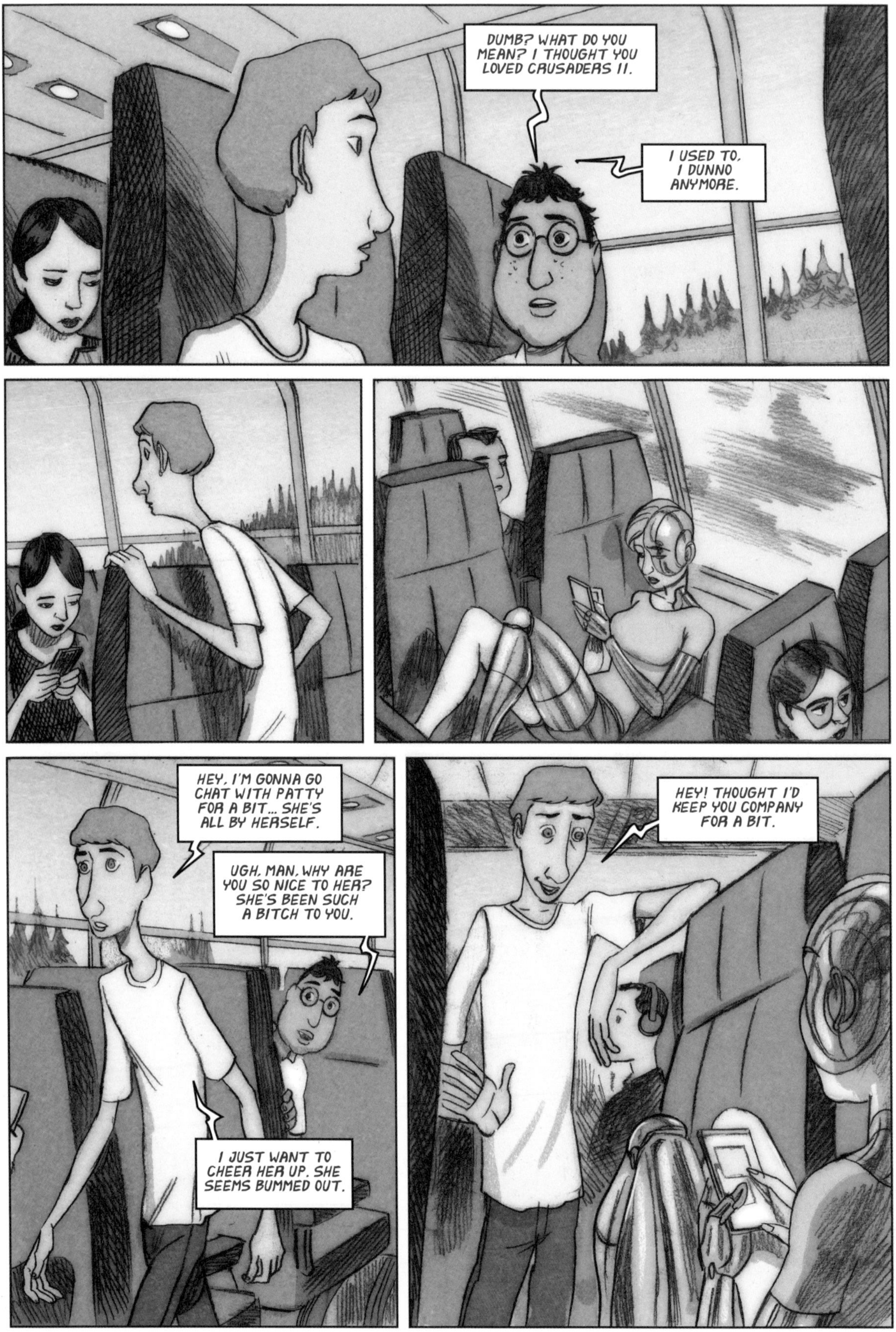
DUMB? WHAT DO YOU MEAN? I THOUGHT YOU LOVED CRUSADERS II.
I USED TO. I DUNNO ANYMORE.
HEY, I'M GONNA GO CHAT WITH PATTY FOR A BIT... SHE'S ALL BY HERSELF.
UGH, MAN, WHY ARE YOU SO NICE TO HER? SHE'S BEEN SUCH A BITCH TO YOU.
I JUST WANT TO CHEER HER UP. SHE SEEMS BUMMED OUT.
HEY! THOUGHT I'D KEEP YOU COMPANY FOR A BIT.

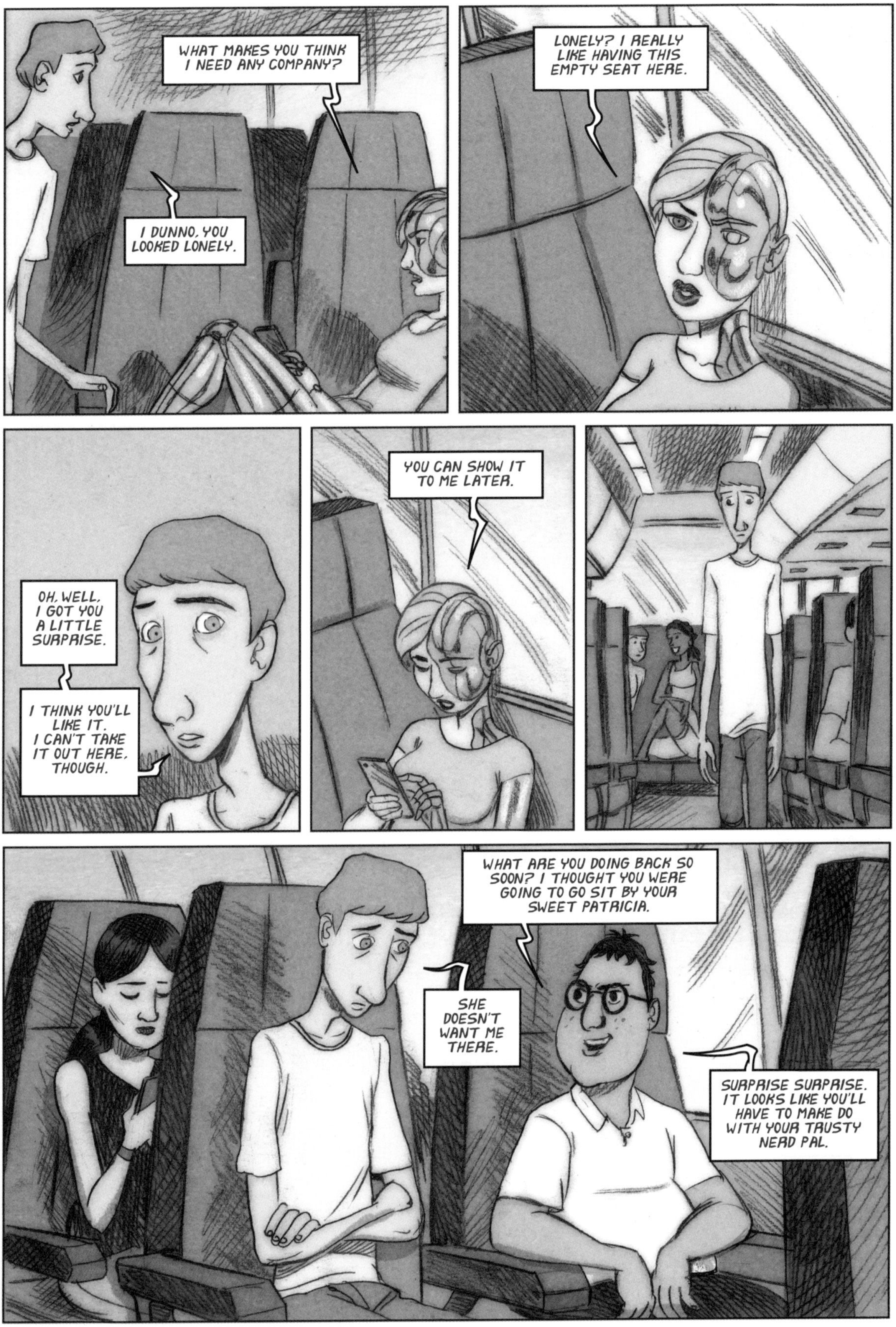
WHAT MAKES YOU THINK I NEED ANY COMPANY?
I DUNNO, YOU LOOKED LONELY.
LONELY? I REALLY LIKE HAVING THIS EMPTY SEAT HERE.
OH, WELL, I GOT YOU A LITTLE SURPRISE.
I THINK YOU'LL LIKE IT. I CAN'T TAKE IT OUT HERE, THOUGH.
YOU CAN SHOW IT TO ME LATER.
WHAT ARE YOU DOING BACK SO SOON? I THOUGHT YOU WERE GOING TO GO SIT BY YOUR SWEET PATRICIA.
SHE DOESN'T WANT ME THERE.
SURPRISE SURPRISE. IT LOOKS LIKE YOU'LL HAVE TO MAKE DO WITH YOUR TRUSTY NERD PAL.

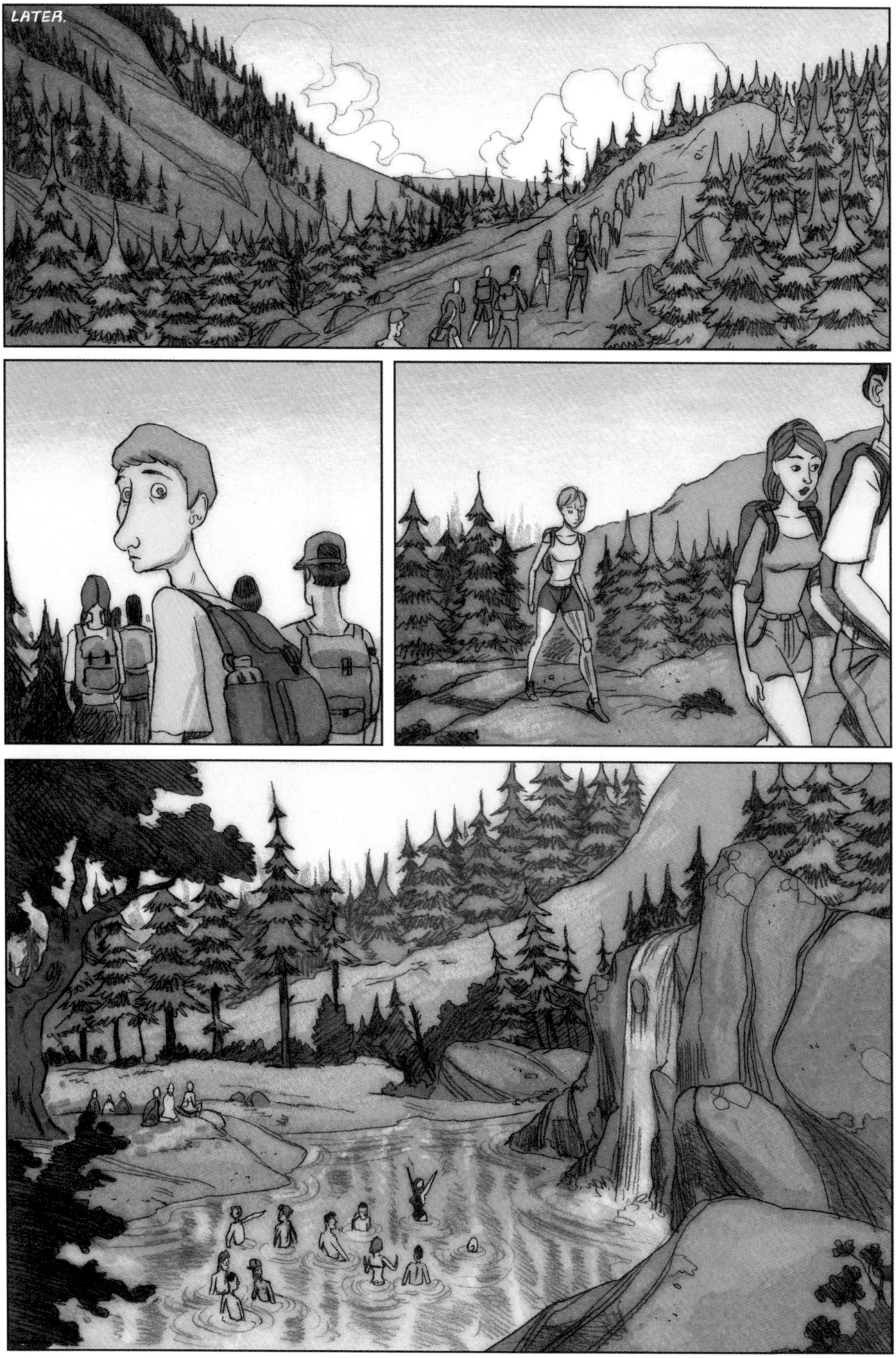
LATER.

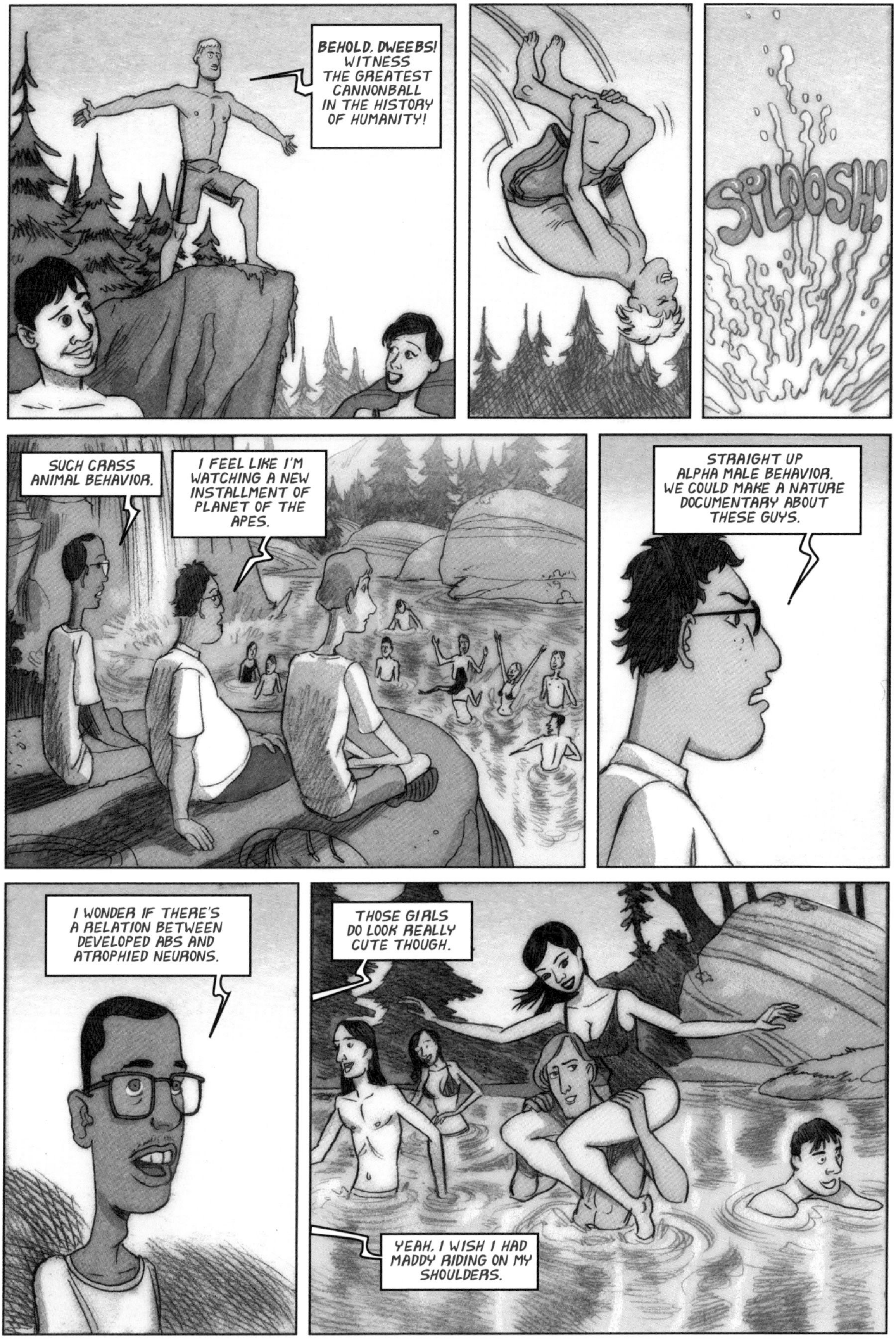

BEHOLD, DWEEBS! WITNESS THE GREATEST CANNONBALL IN THE HISTORY OF HUMANITY!
SPLOOSH!
SUCH CRASS ANIMAL BEHAVIOR.
I FEEL LIKE I'M WATCHING A NEW INSTALLMENT OF PLANET OF THE APES.
STRAIGHT UP ALPHA MALE BEHAVIOR. WE COULD MAKE A NATURE DOCUMENTARY ABOUT THESE GUYS.
I WONDER IF THERE'S A RELATION BETWEEN DEVELOPED ABS AND ATROPHIED NEURONS.
THOSE GIRLS DO LOOK REALLY CUTE THOUGH.
YEAH, I WISH I HAD MADDY RIDING ON MY SHOULDERS.

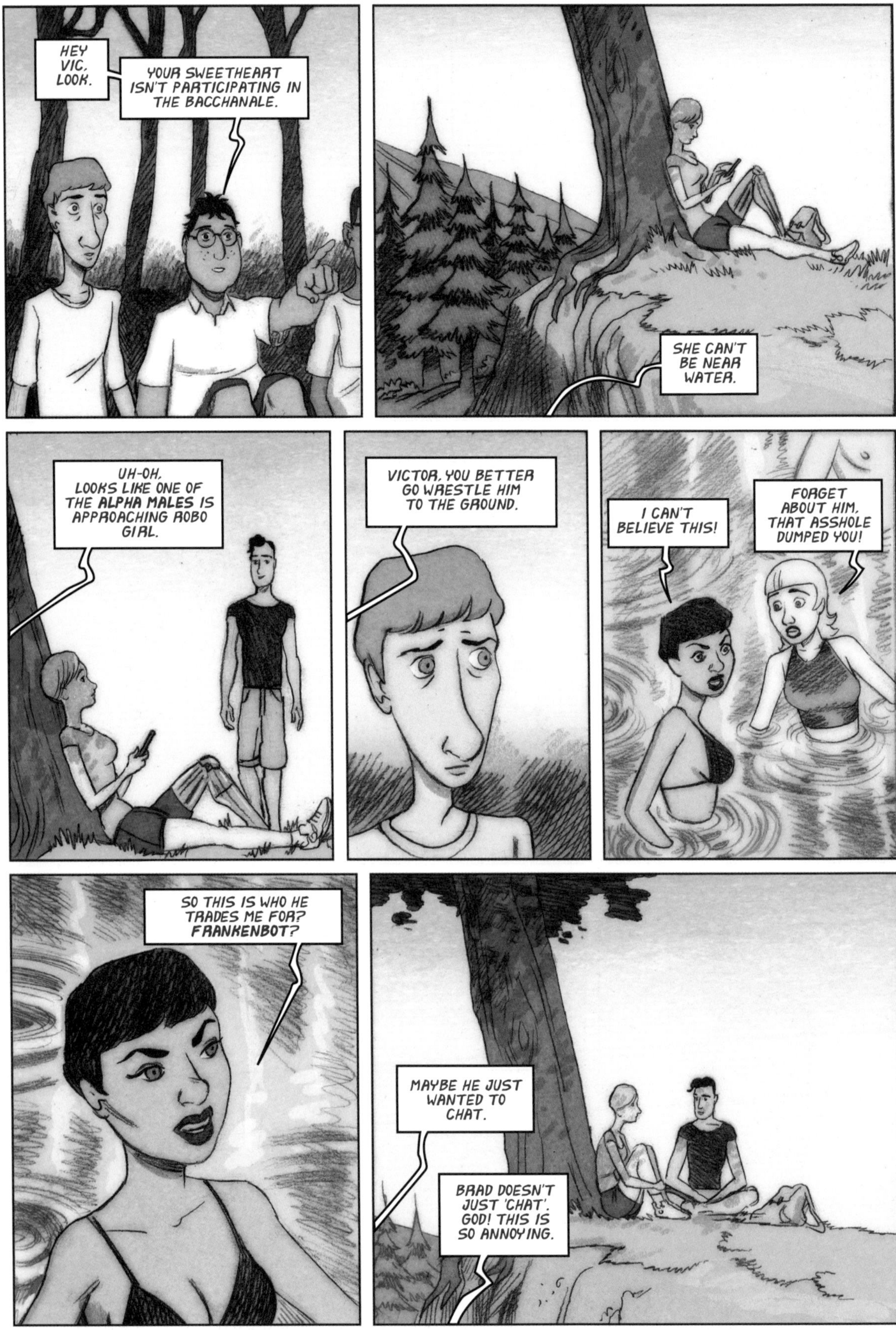
HEY VIC, LOOK.
YOUR SWEETHEART ISN'T PARTICIPATING IN THE BACCHANALE.
SHE CAN'T BE NEAR WATER.
UH-OH, LOOKS LIKE ONE OF THE ALPHA MALES IS APPROACHING ROBO GIRL.
VICTOR, YOU BETTER GO WRESTLE HIM TO THE GROUND.
I CAN'T BELIEVE THIS!
FORGET ABOUT HIM, THAT ASSHOLE DUMPED YOU!
SO THIS IS WHO HE TRADES ME FOR? FRANKENBOT?
MAYBE HE JUST WANTED TO CHAT.
BRAD DOESN'T JUST 'CHAT'. GOD! THIS IS SO ANNOYING.

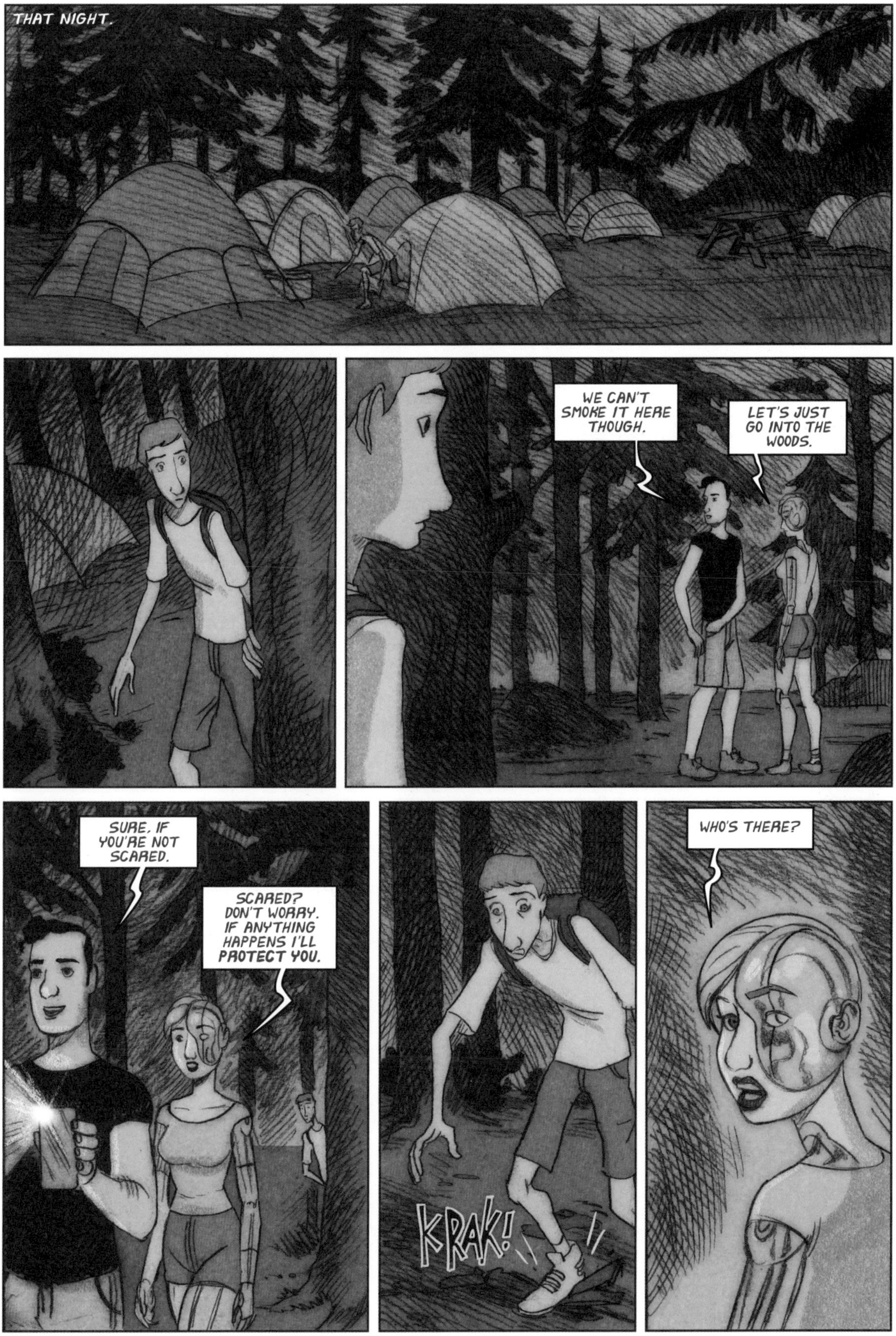
THAT NIGHT.
WE CAN'T SMOKE IT HERE THOUGH.
LET'S JUST GO INTO THE WOODS.
SURE, IF YOU'RE NOT SCARED.
SCARED? DON'T WORRY. IF ANYTHING HAPPENS I'LL PROTECT YOU.
KRAK!
WHO'S THERE?

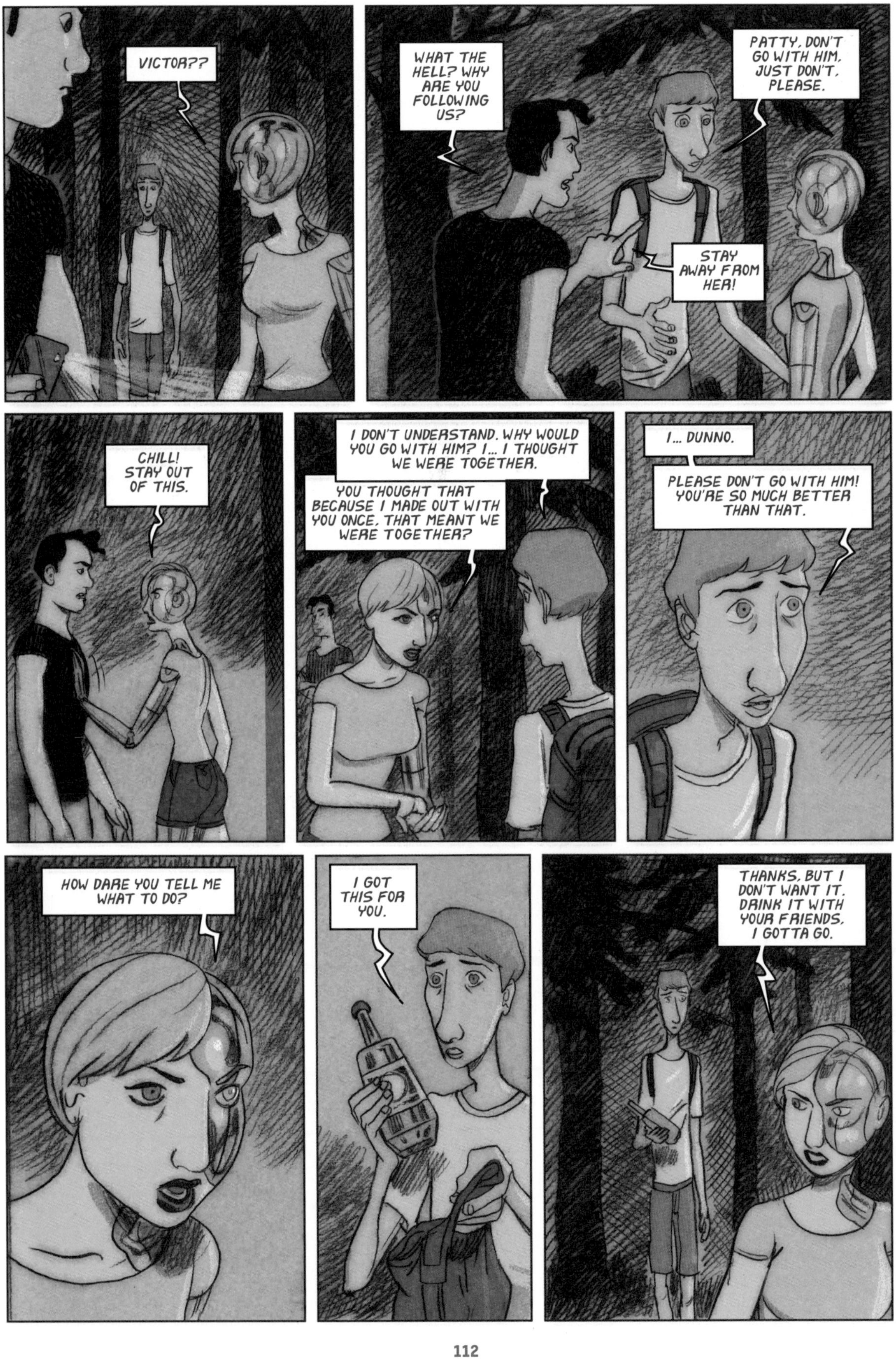
VICTOR??
WHAT THE HELL? WHY ARE YOU FOLLOWING US?
PATTY, DON'T GO WITH HIM, JUST DON'T, PLEASE.
STAY AWAY FROM HER!
CHILL! STAY OUT OF THIS.
I DON'T UNDERSTAND. WHY WOULD YOU GO WITH HIM? I... I THOUGHT WE WERE TOGETHER.
YOU THOUGHT THAT BECAUSE I MADE OUT WITH YOU ONCE, THAT MEANT WE WERE TOGETHER?
I... DUNNO.
PLEASE DON'T GO WITH HIM! YOU'RE SO MUCH BETTER THAN THAT.
HOW DARE YOU TELL ME WHAT TO DO?
I GOT THIS FOR YOU.
THANKS, BUT I DON'T WANT IT. DRINK IT WITH YOUR FRIENDS, I GOTTA GO.

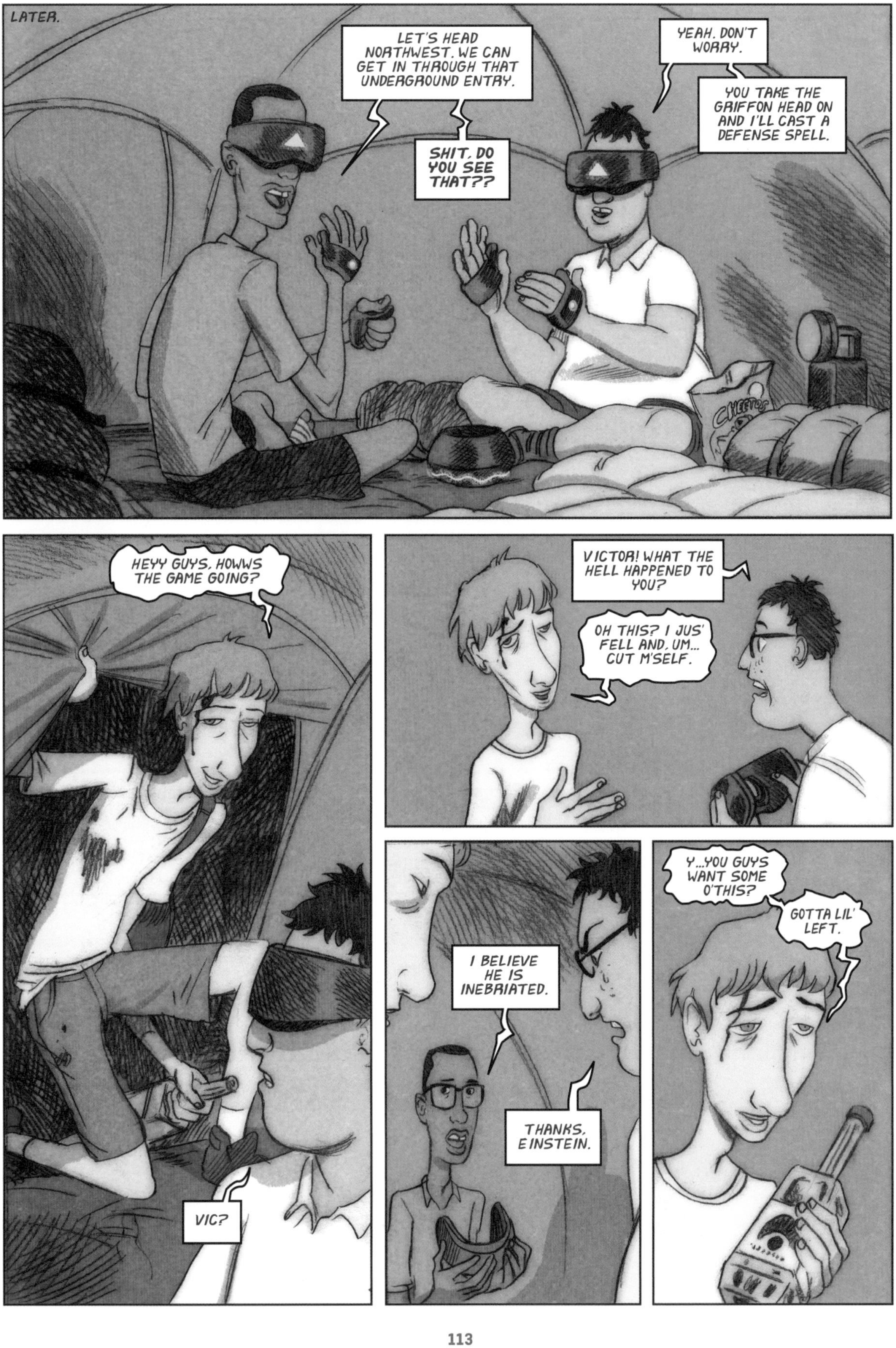
LATER.
LET'S HEAD NORTHWEST. WE CAN GET IN THROUGH THAT UNDERGROUND ENTRY.
SHIT, DO YOU SEE THAT??
YEAH. DON'T WORRY.
YOU TAKE THE GRIFFON HEAD ON AND I'LL CAST A DEFENSE SPELL.
CHEETOS
HEYY GUYS, HOWWS THE GAME GOING?
VIC?
VICTOR! WHAT THE HELL HAPPENED TO YOU?
OH THIS? I JUS' FELL AND, UM... CUT M'SELF.
I BELIEVE HE IS INEBRIATED.
THANKS, EINSTEIN.
Y...YOU GUYS WANT SOME O'THIS?
GOTTA LIL' LEFT.

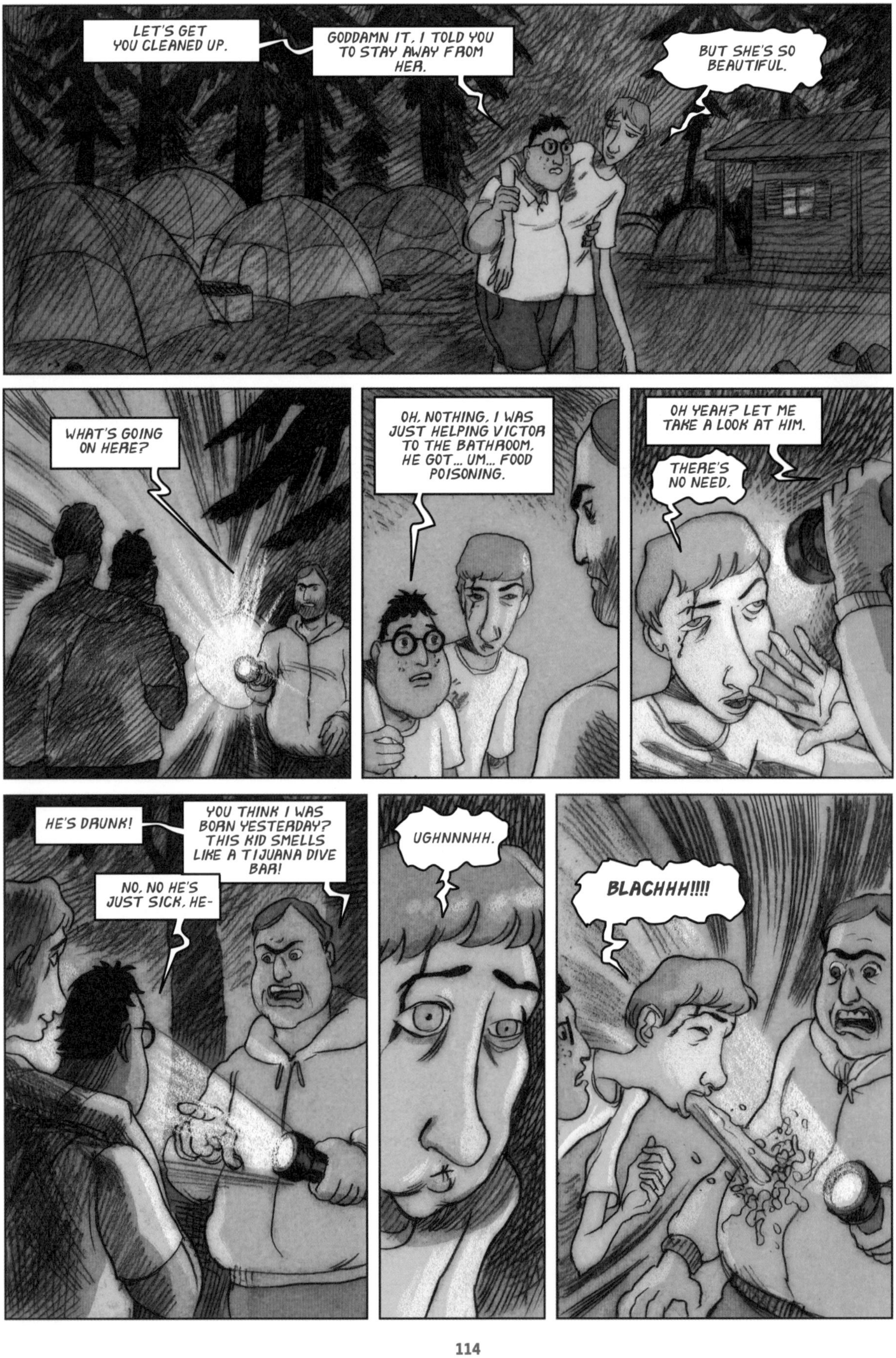
LET'S GET YOU CLEANED UP.
GODDAMN IT, I TOLD YOU TO STAY AWAY FROM HER.
BUT SHE'S SO BEAUTIFUL.
WHAT'S GOING ON HERE?
OH, NOTHING. I WAS JUST HELPING VICTOR TO THE BATHROOM. HE GOT... UM... FOOD POISONING.
OH YEAH? LET ME TAKE A LOOK AT HIM.
THERE'S NO NEED.
HE'S DRUNK!
YOU THINK I WAS BORN YESTERDAY? THIS KID SMELLS LIKE A TIJUANA DIVE BAR!
NO, NO HE'S JUST SICK, HE-
UGHNNNHH.
BLACHHH!!!!

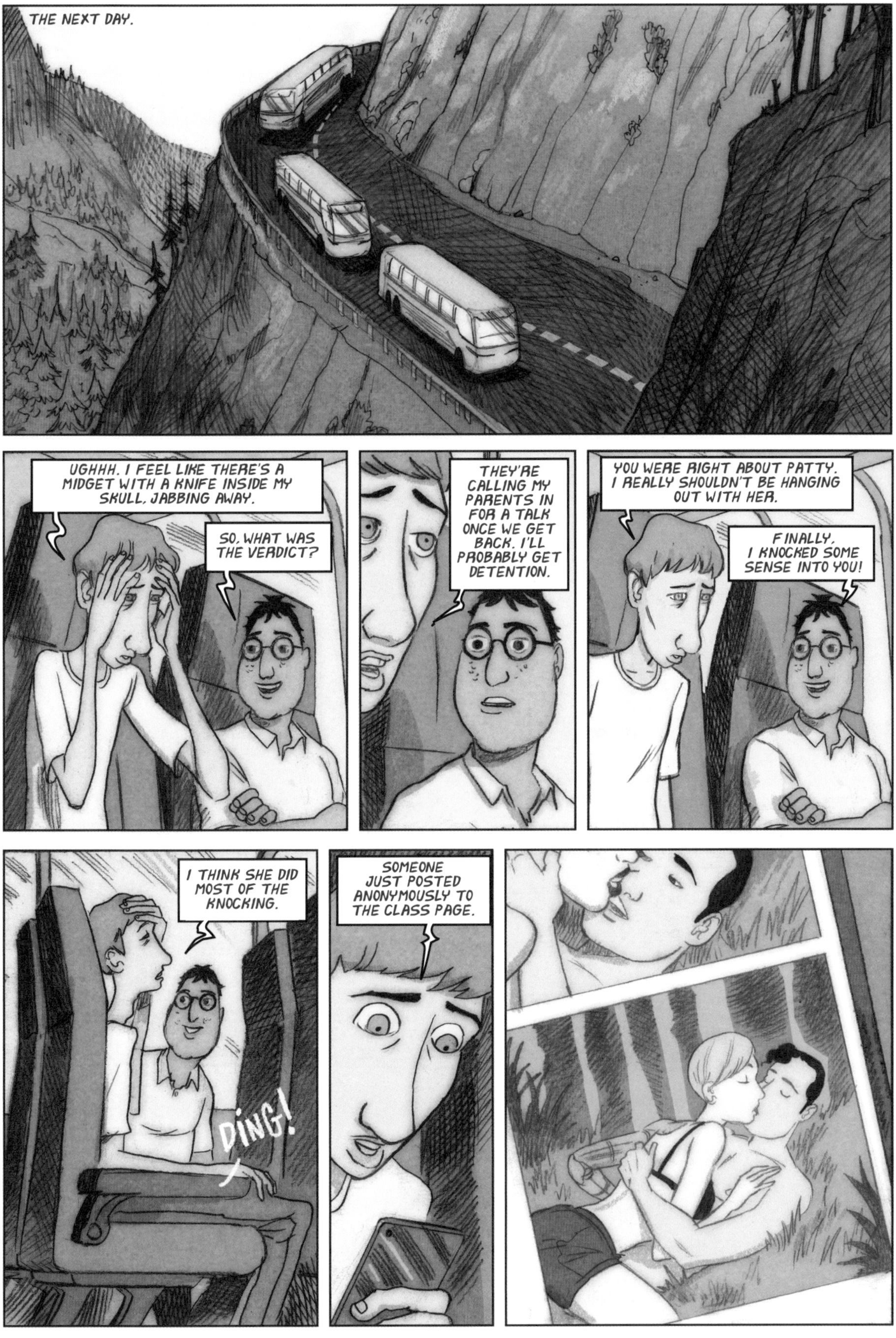

THE NEXT DAY.
UGHHH. I FEEL LIKE THERE'S A MIDGET WITH A KNIFE INSIDE MY SKULL, JABBING AWAY.
SO, WHAT WAS THE VERDICT?
THEY'RE CALLING MY PARENTS IN FOR A TALK ONCE WE GET BACK. I'LL PROBABLY GET DETENTION.
YOU WERE RIGHT ABOUT PATTY. I REALLY SHOULDN'T BE HANGING OUT WITH HER.
FINALLY, I KNOCKED SOME SENSE INTO YOU!
I THINK SHE DID MOST OF THE KNOCKING.
DING!
SOMEONE JUST POSTED ANONYMOUSLY TO THE CLASS PAGE.

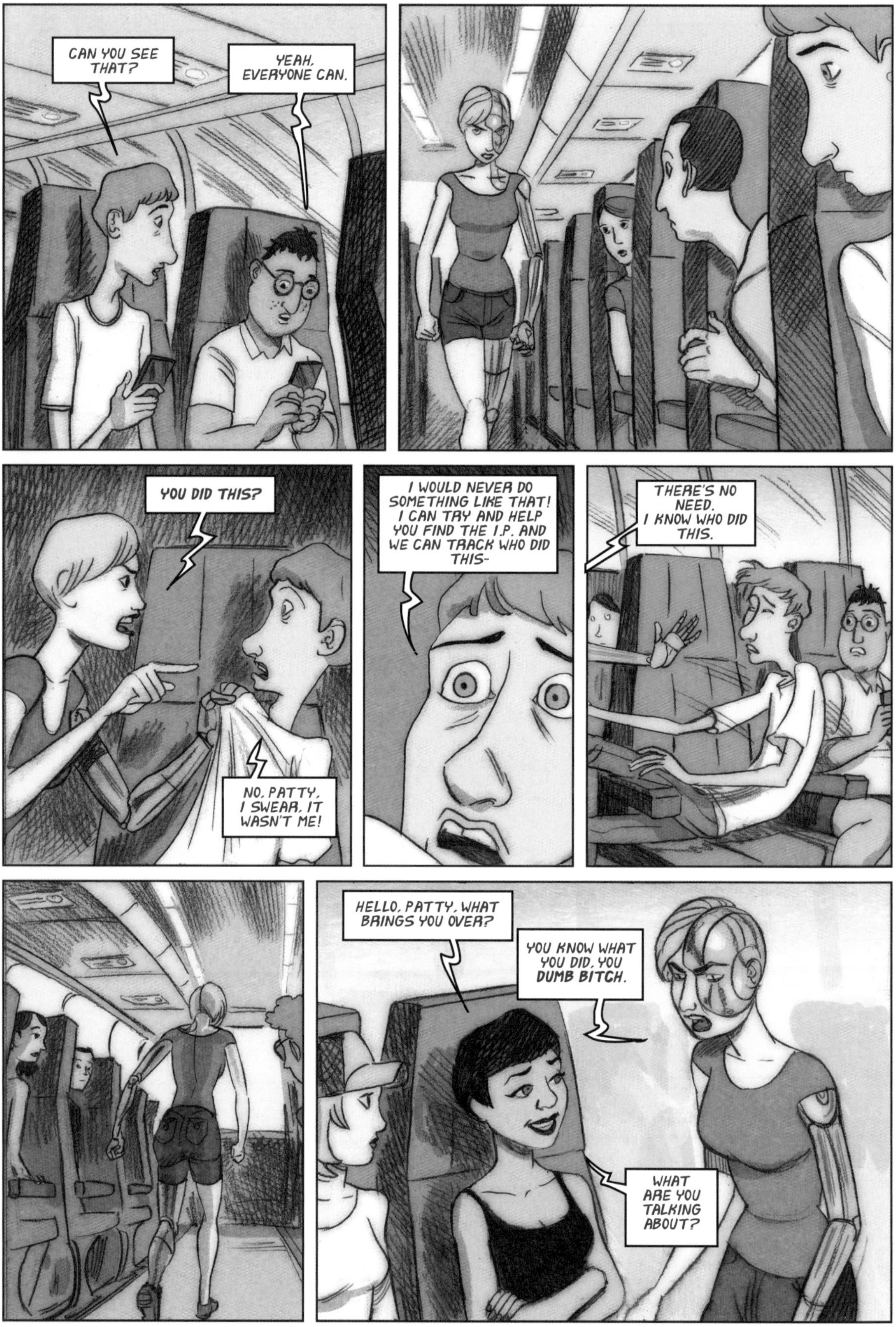
CAN YOU SEE THAT?
YEAH, EVERYONE CAN.
YOU DID THIS?
NO, PATTY, I SWEAR, IT WASN'T ME!
I WOULD NEVER DO SOMETHING LIKE THAT! I CAN TRY AND HELP YOU FIND THE I.P. AND WE CAN TRACK WHO DID THIS-
THERE'S NO NEED. I KNOW WHO DID THIS.
HELLO, PATTY, WHAT BRINGS YOU OVER?
YOU KNOW WHAT YOU DID, YOU DUMB BITCH.
WHAT ARE YOU TALKING ABOUT?

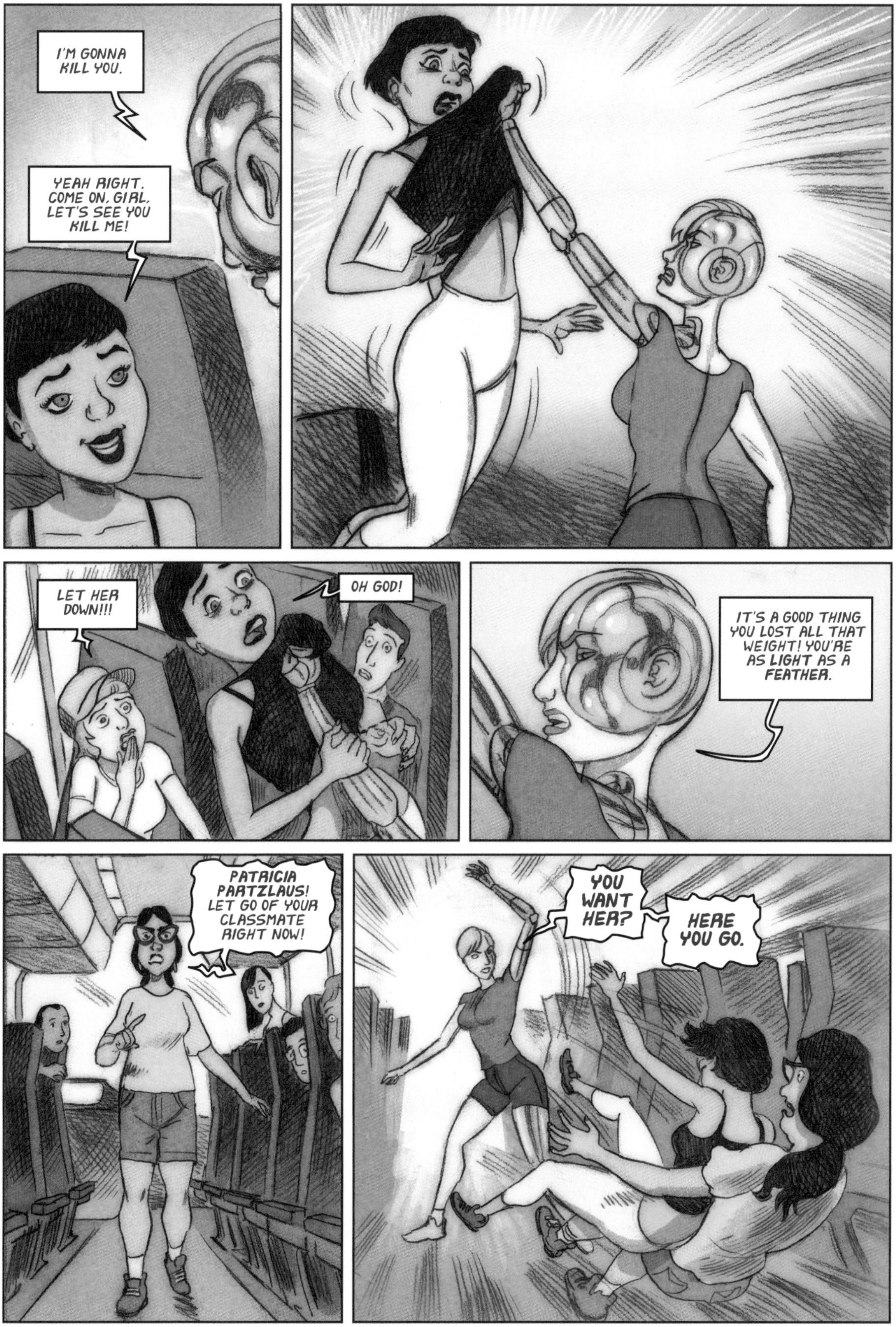
I'M GONNA KILL YOU.
YEAH RIGHT. COME ON, GIRL, LET'S SEE YOU KILL ME!
LET HER DOWN!!!
OH GOD!
IT'S A GOOD THING YOU LOST ALL THAT WEIGHT! YOU'RE AS LIGHT AS A FEATHER.
PATRICIA PARTZLAUS! LET GO OF YOUR CLASSMATE RIGHT NOW!
YOU WANT HER?
HERE YOU GO.

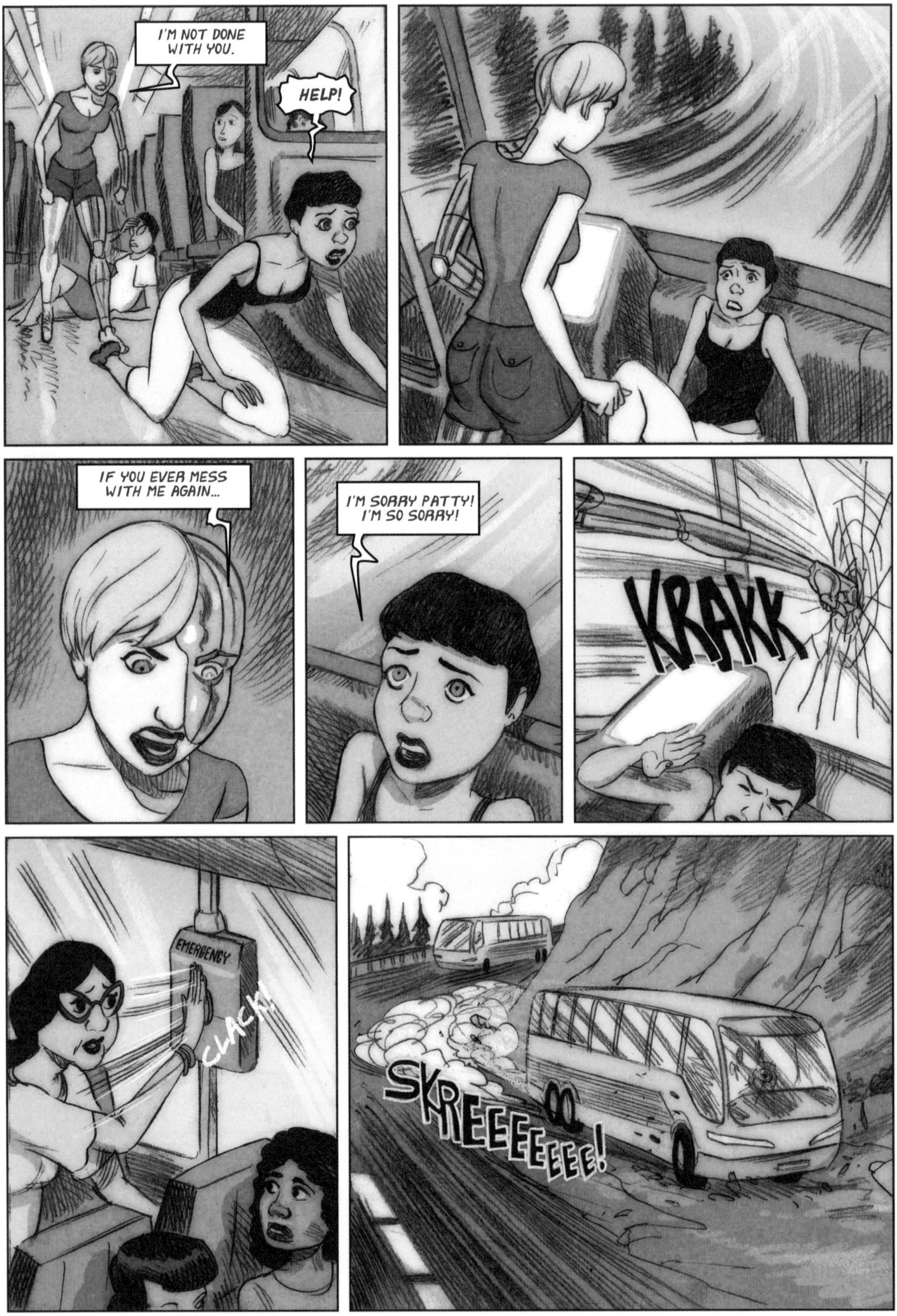
I'M NOT DONE WITH YOU.
HELP!
IF YOU EVER MESS WITH ME AGAIN...
I'M SORRY PATTY! I'M SO SORRY!
KRAKK
EMERGENCY
CLACK!
SKREEEEEEEE!

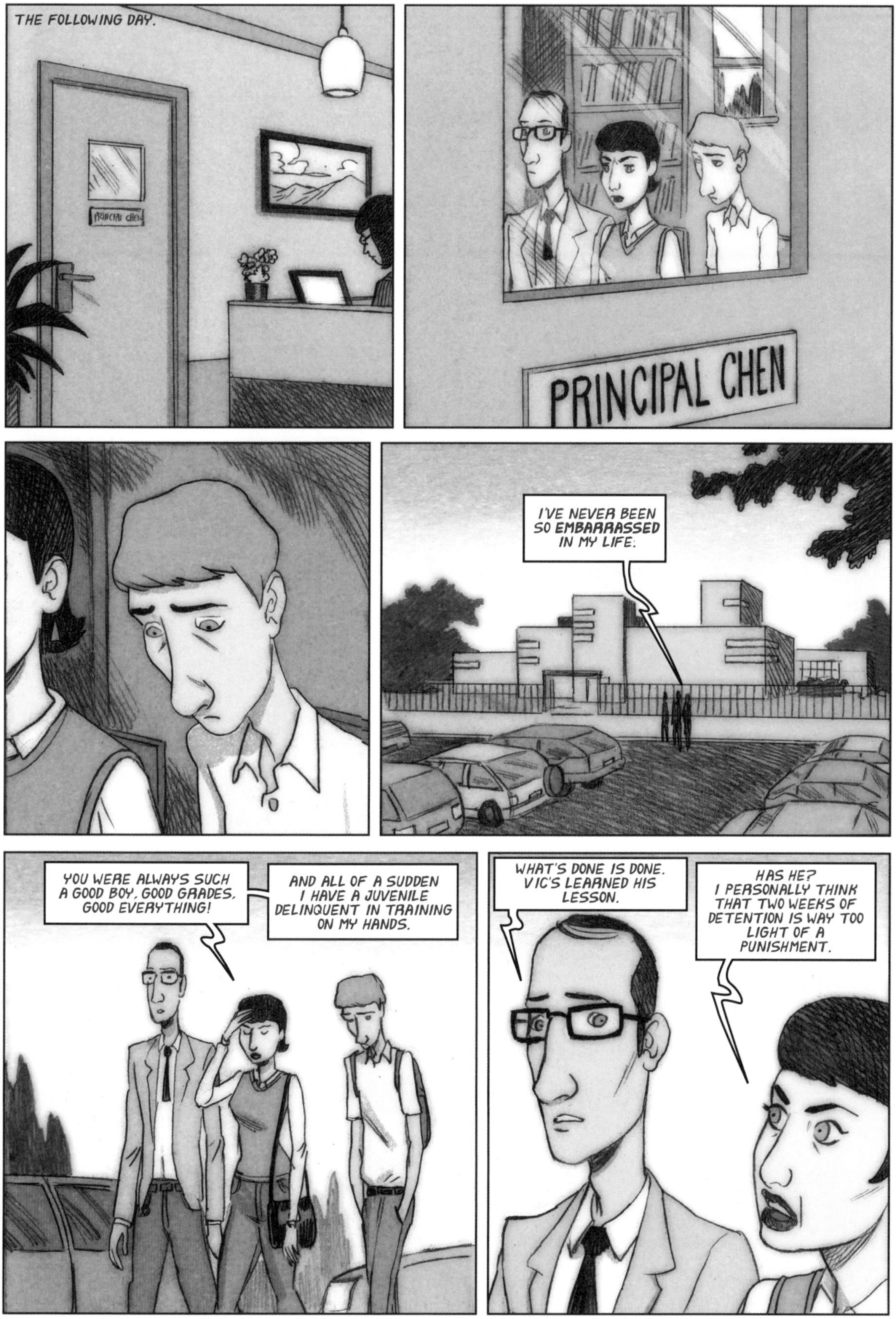
THE FOLLOWING DAY.
PRINCIPAL CHEN
PRINCIPAL CHEN
I'VE NEVER BEEN SO EMBARRASSED IN MY LIFE.
YOU WERE ALWAYS SUCH A GOOD BOY. GOOD GRADES, GOOD EVERYTHING!
AND ALL OF A SUDDEN I HAVE A JUVENILE DELINQUENT IN TRAINING ON MY HANDS.
WHAT'S DONE IS DONE. VIC'S LEARNED HIS LESSON.
HAS HE? I PERSONALLY THINK THAT TWO WEEKS OF DETENTION IS WAY TOO LIGHT OF A PUNISHMENT.

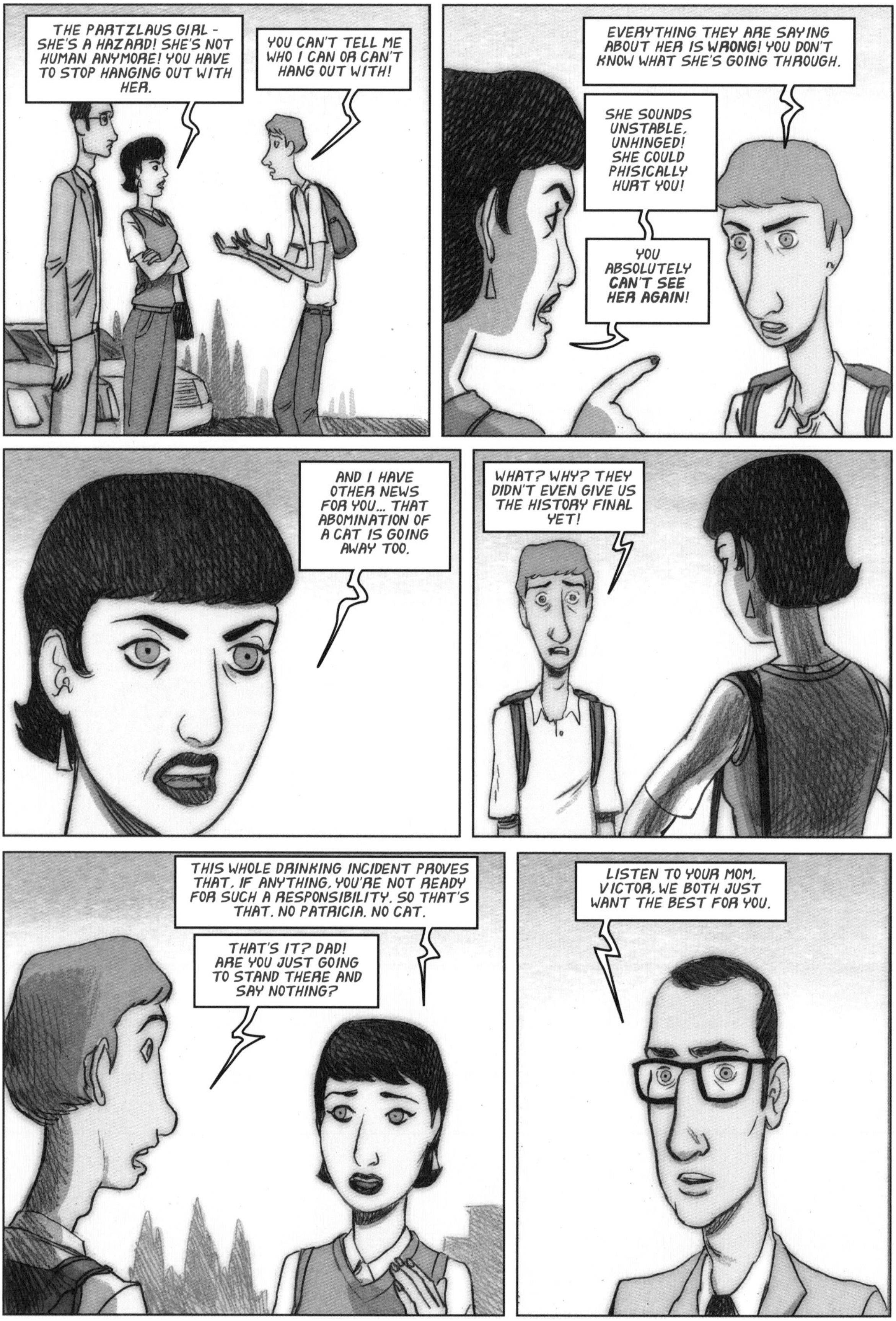
THE PARTZLAUS GIRL - SHE'S A HAZARD! SHE'S NOT HUMAN ANYMORE! YOU HAVE TO STOP HANGING OUT WITH HER.
YOU CAN'T TELL ME WHO I CAN OR CAN'T HANG OUT WITH!
EVERYTHING THEY ARE SAYING ABOUT HER IS WRONG! YOU DON'T KNOW WHAT SHE'S GOING THROUGH.
SHE SOUNDS UNSTABLE, UNHINGED! SHE COULD PHISICALLY HURT YOU!
YOU ABSOLUTELY CAN'T SEE HER AGAIN!
AND I HAVE OTHER NEWS FOR YOU... THAT ABOMINATION OF A CAT IS GOING AWAY TOO.
WHAT? WHY? THEY DIDN'T EVEN GIVE US THE HISTORY FINAL YET!
THIS WHOLE DRINKING INCIDENT PROVES THAT, IF ANYTHING, YOU'RE NOT READY FOR SUCH A RESPONSIBILITY. SO THAT'S THAT. NO PATRICIA. NO CAT.
THAT'S IT? DAD! ARE YOU JUST GOING TO STAND THERE AND SAY NOTHING?
LISTEN TO YOUR MOM, VICTOR, WE BOTH JUST WANT THE BEST FOR YOU.

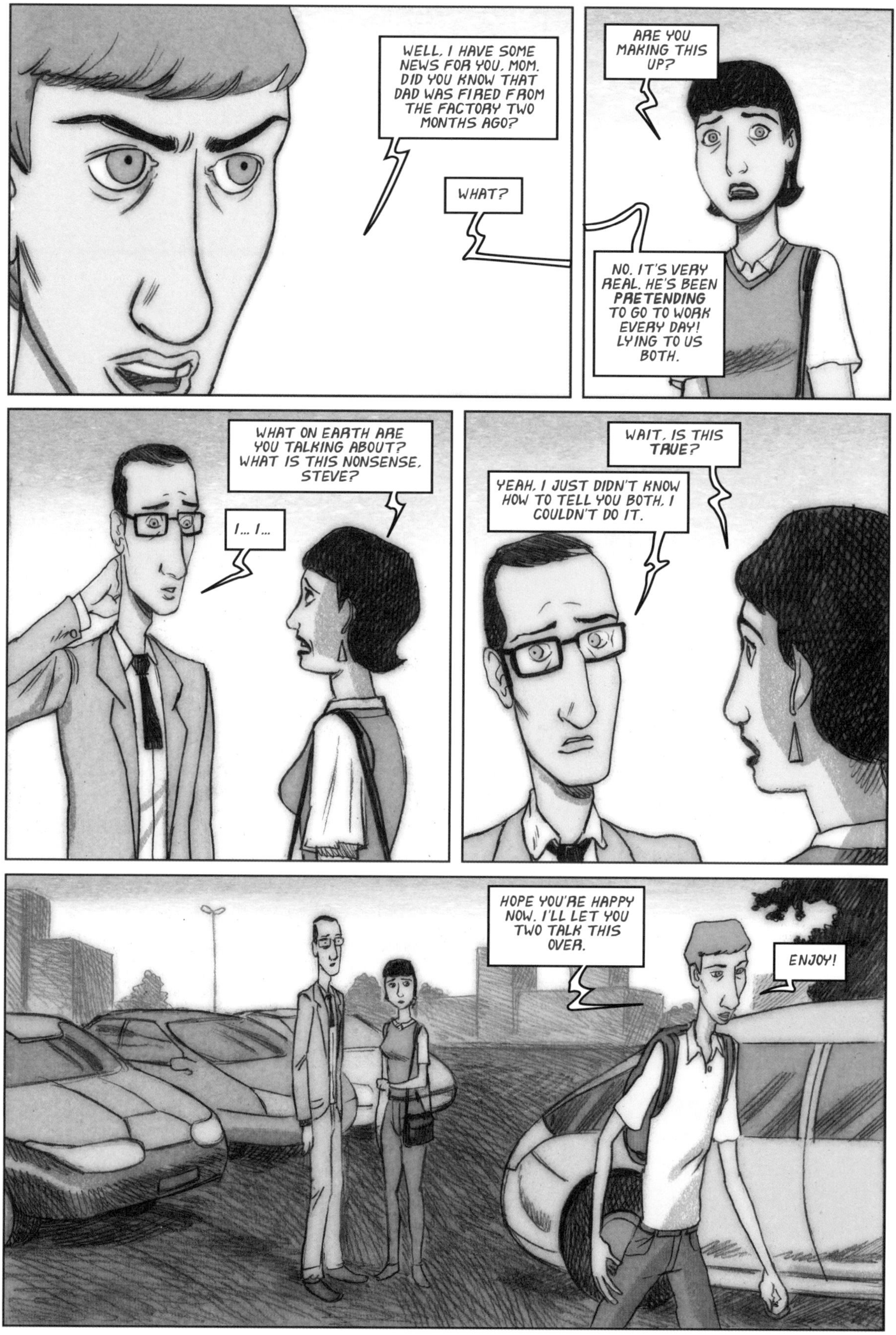
WELL, I HAVE SOME NEWS FOR YOU, MOM. DID YOU KNOW THAT DAD WAS FIRED FROM THE FACTORY TWO MONTHS AGO?
WHAT?
ARE YOU MAKING THIS UP?
NO. IT'S VERY REAL. HE'S BEEN PRETENDING TO GO TO WORK EVERY DAY! LYING TO US BOTH.
WHAT ON EARTH ARE YOU TALKING ABOUT? WHAT IS THIS NONSENSE, STEVE?
I... I...
WAIT, IS THIS TRUE?
YEAH, I JUST DIDN'T KNOW HOW TO TELL YOU BOTH, I COULDN'T DO IT.
HOPE YOU'RE HAPPY NOW. I'LL LET YOU TWO TALK THIS OVER.
ENJOY!

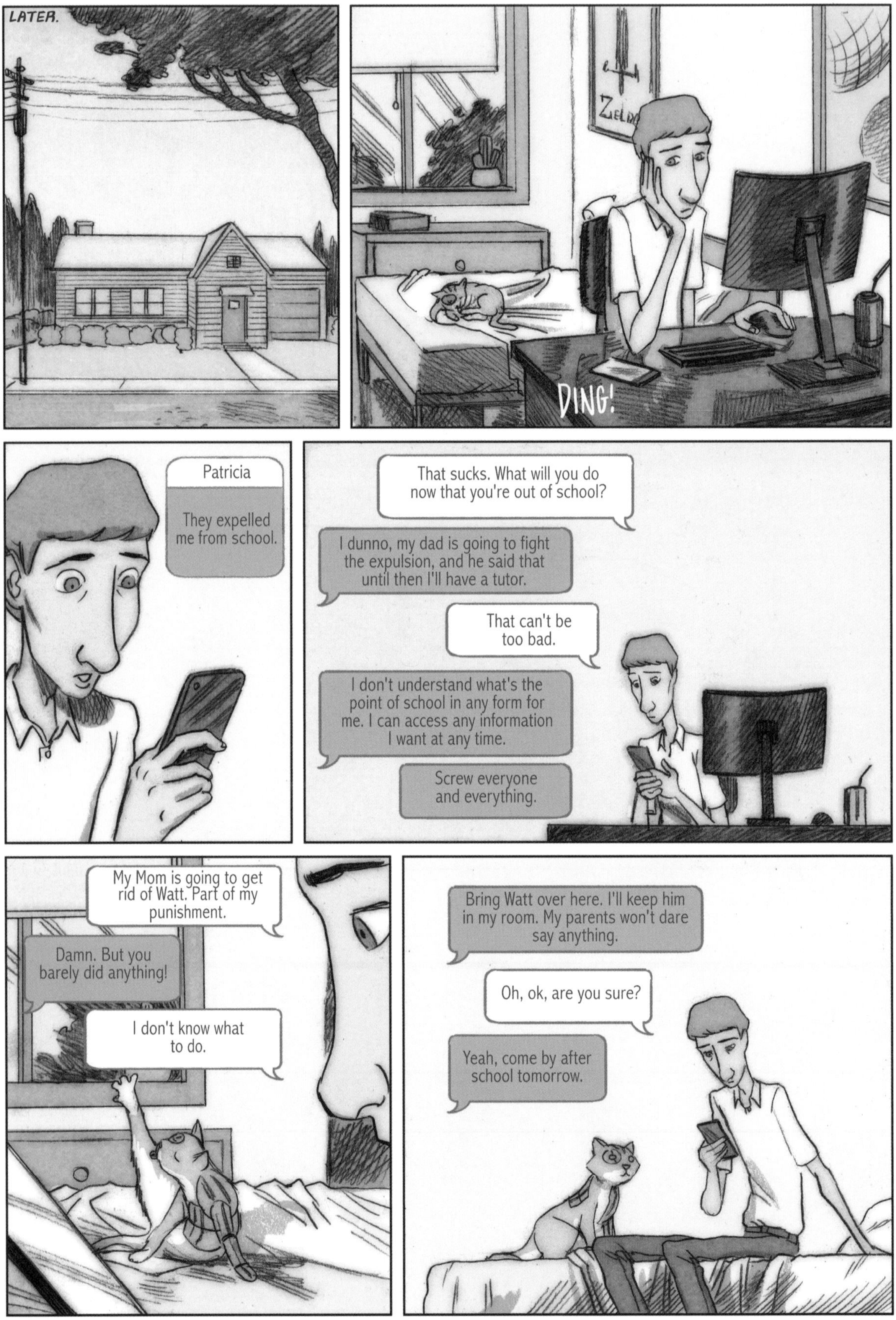
LATER.
DING!
Patricia
They expelled me from school.
That sucks. What will you do now that you're out of school?
I dunno, my dad is going to fight the expulsion, and he said that until then I'll have a tutor.
That can't be too bad.
I don't understand what's the point of school in any form for me. I can access any information I want at any time.
Screw everyone and everything.
My Mom is going to get rid of Watt. Part of my punishment.
Damn. But you barely did anything!
I don't know what to do.
Bring Watt over here. I'll keep him in my room. My parents won't dare say anything.
Oh, ok, are you sure?
Yeah, come by after school tomorrow.

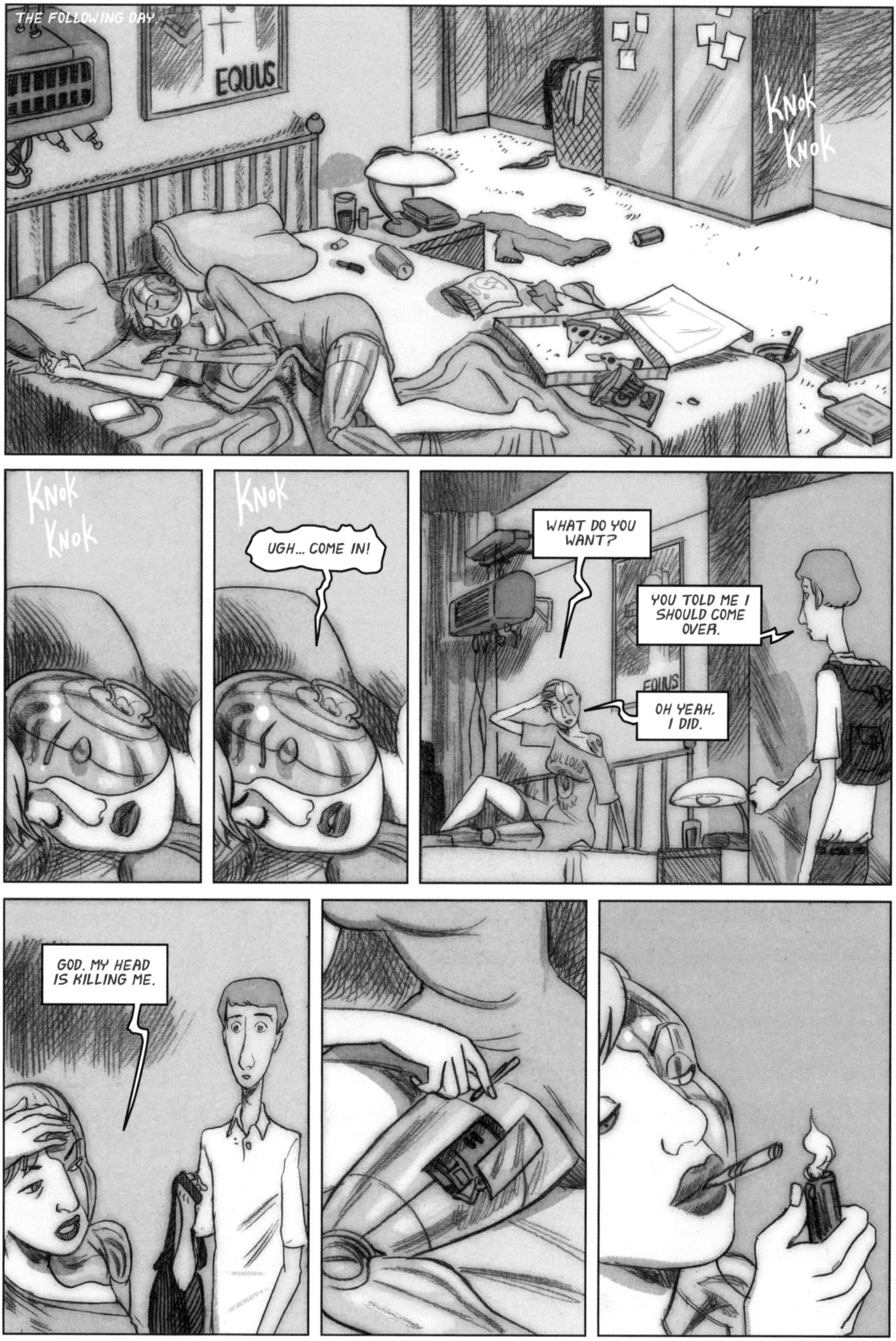
THE FOLLOWING DAY.
EQUUS
KNOK KNOK
KNOK KNOK
KNOK
UGH... COME IN!
WHAT DO YOU WANT?
YOU TOLD ME I SHOULD COME OVER.
OH YEAH, I DID.
GOD. MY HEAD IS KILLING ME.

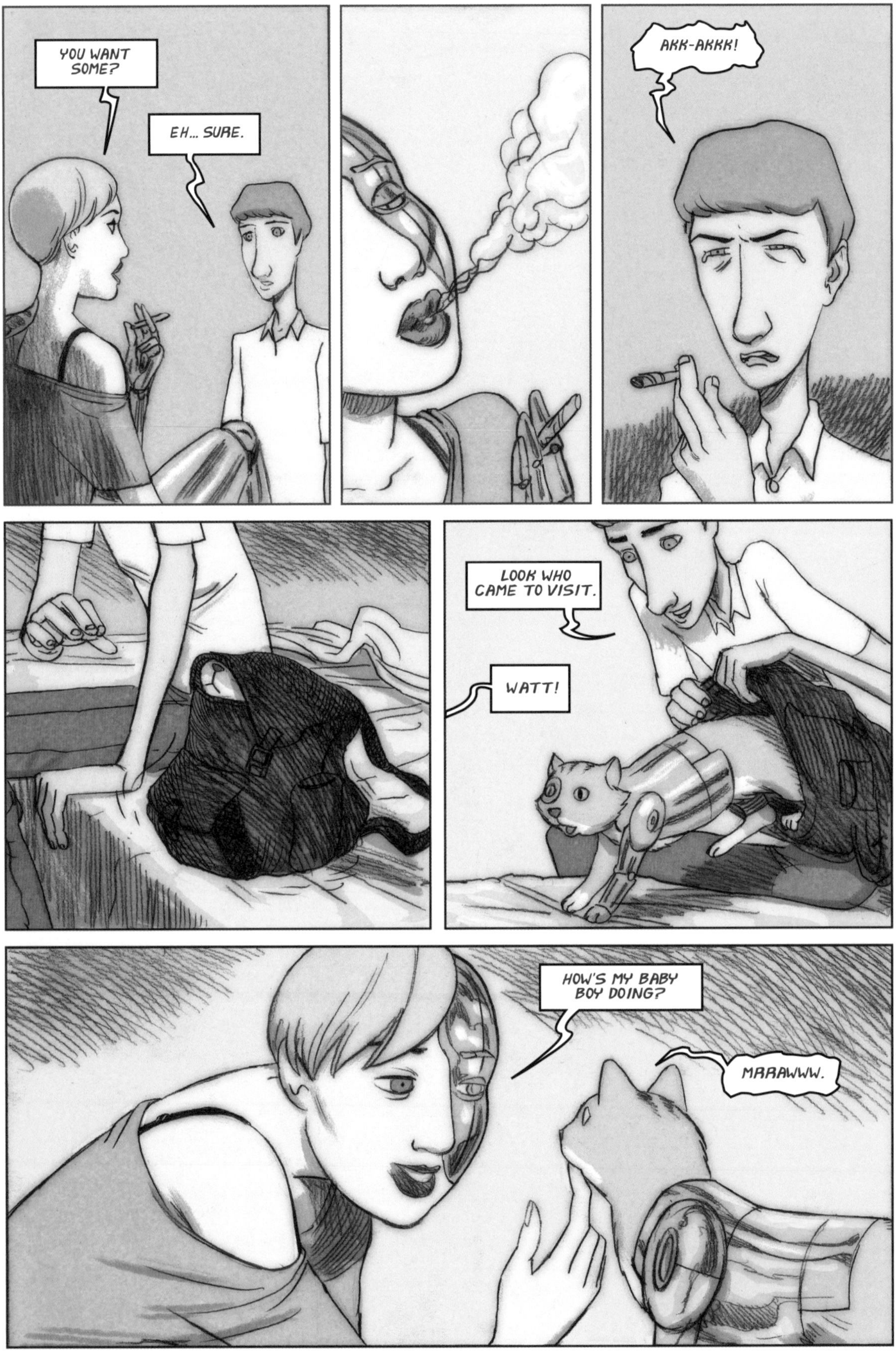
YOU WANT SOME?
EH... SURE.
AKK-AKKK!
LOOK WHO CAME TO VISIT.
WATT!
HOW'S MY BABY BOY DOING?
MRRAWWW.

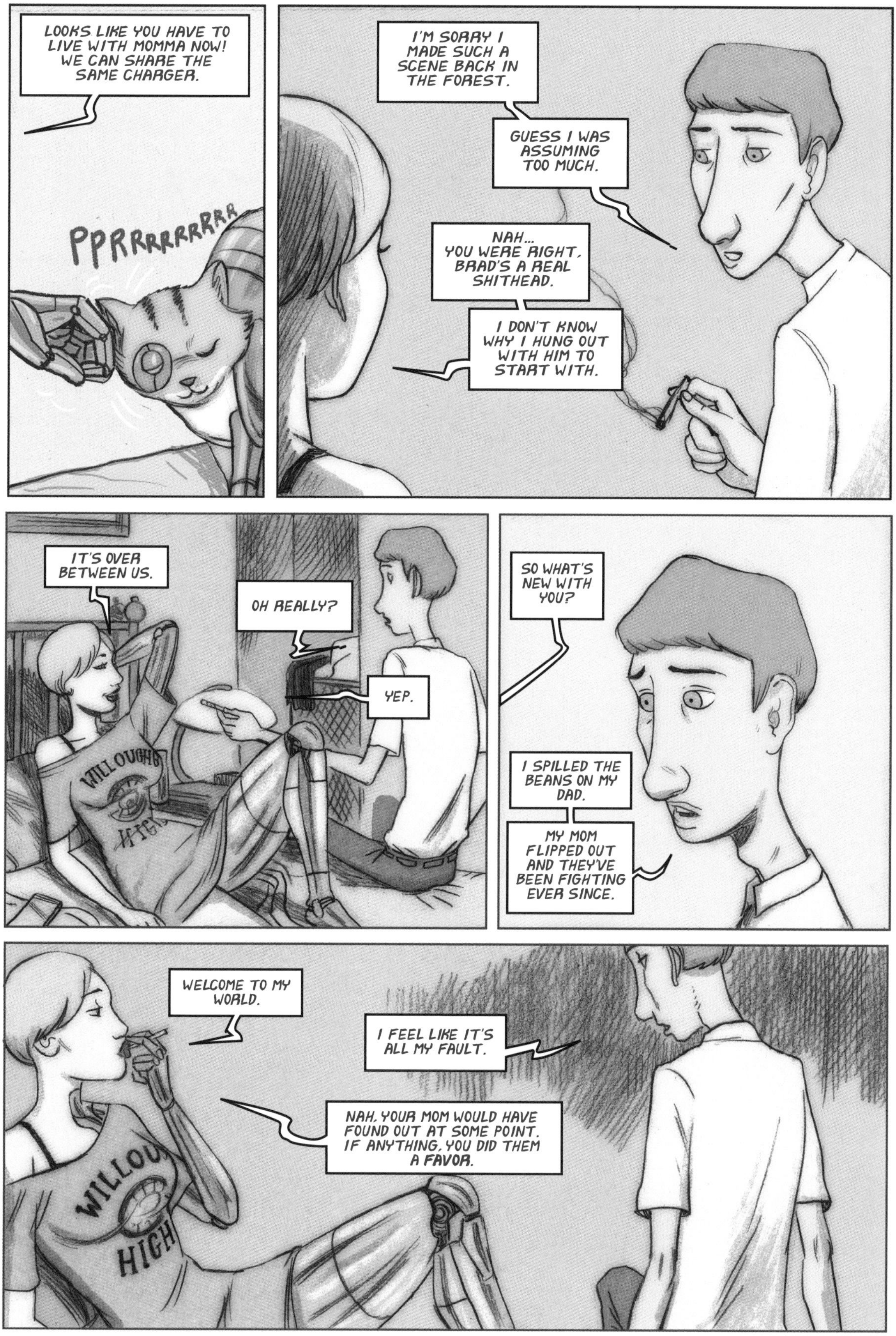
LOOKS LIKE YOU HAVE TO LIVE WITH MOMMA NOW! WE CAN SHARE THE SAME CHARGER.
PPRRRRRRRRR
I'M SORRY I MADE SUCH A SCENE BACK IN THE FOREST.
GUESS I WAS ASSUMING TOO MUCH.
NAH... YOU WERE RIGHT. BRAD'S A REAL SHITHEAD.
I DON'T KNOW WHY I HUNG OUT WITH HIM TO START WITH.
IT'S OVER BETWEEN US.
OH REALLY?
YEP.
SO WHAT'S NEW WITH YOU?
I SPILLED THE BEANS ON MY DAD.
MY MOM FLIPPED OUT AND THEY'VE BEEN FIGHTING EVER SINCE.
WELCOME TO MY WORLD.
I FEEL LIKE IT'S ALL MY FAULT.
NAH. YOUR MOM WOULD HAVE FOUND OUT AT SOME POINT. IF ANYTHING, YOU DID THEM A **FAVOR**.

UGH, I BETTER GET DRESSED. I'VE BEEN WEARING THIS SHIRT FOR DAYS... I MUST SMELL.

SO WHAT HAVE YOU BEEN UP TO, I MEAN, NOT HAVING SCHOOL AND ALL?

LET ME SEE. I'VE BEEN SLEEPING A LOT. UM, WHAT ELSE? EATING A LOT. I MUST HAVE GAINED 15 POUNDS.

YOU DON'T LOOK LIKE YOU'VE GAINED WEIGHT.

THANKS FOR BEING SO KIND.

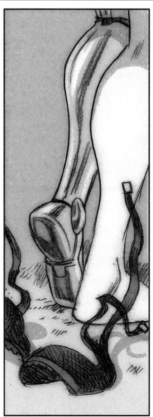

BUT I KNOW THE TRUTH.

I'LL HAVE TO ASK MY DAD FOR NEW 'CHUBBY' PROSTHETICS.

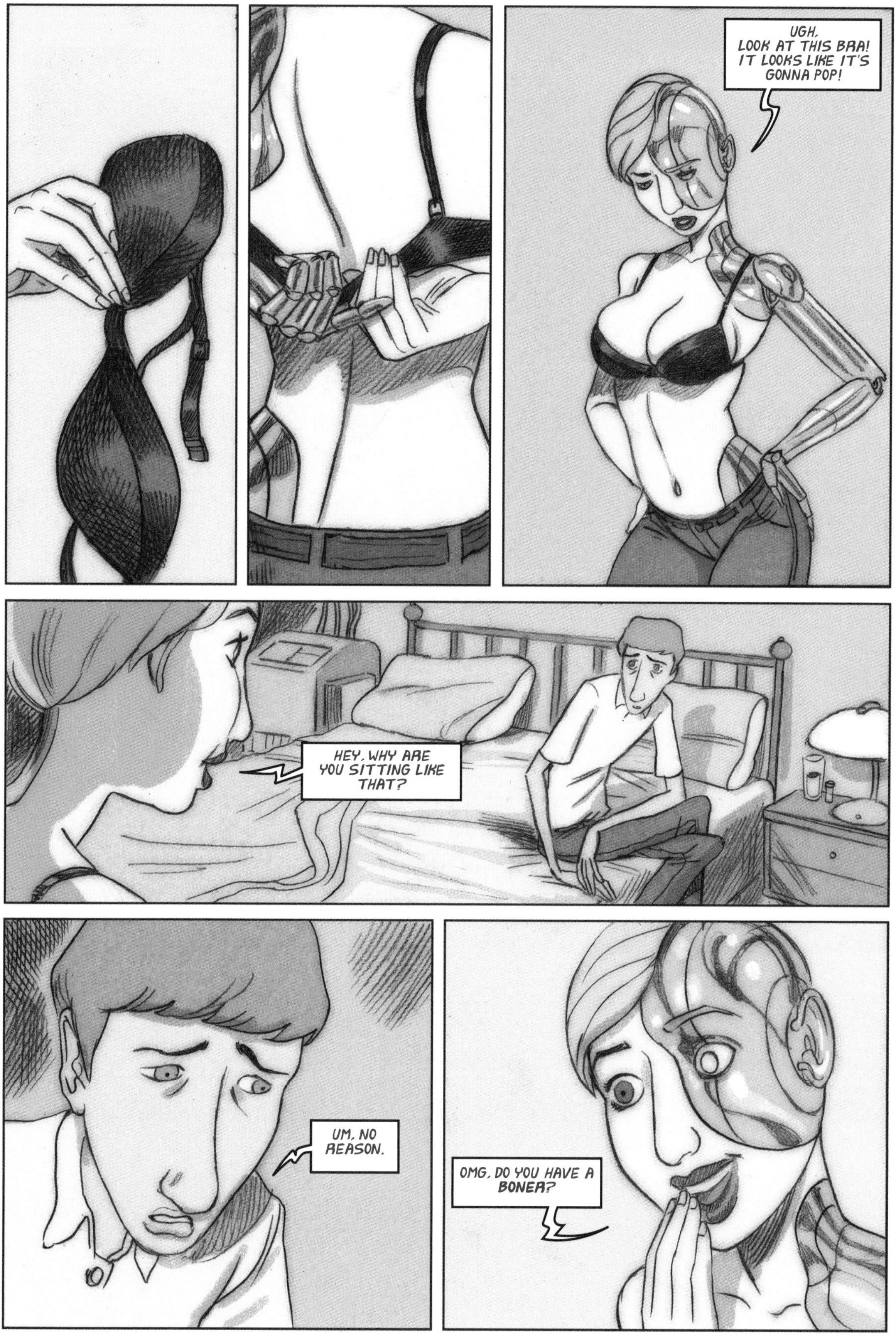
UGH, LOOK AT THIS BRA! IT LOOKS LIKE IT'S GONNA POP!
HEY, WHY ARE YOU SITTING LIKE THAT?
UM, NO REASON.
OMG, DO YOU HAVE A **BONER**?

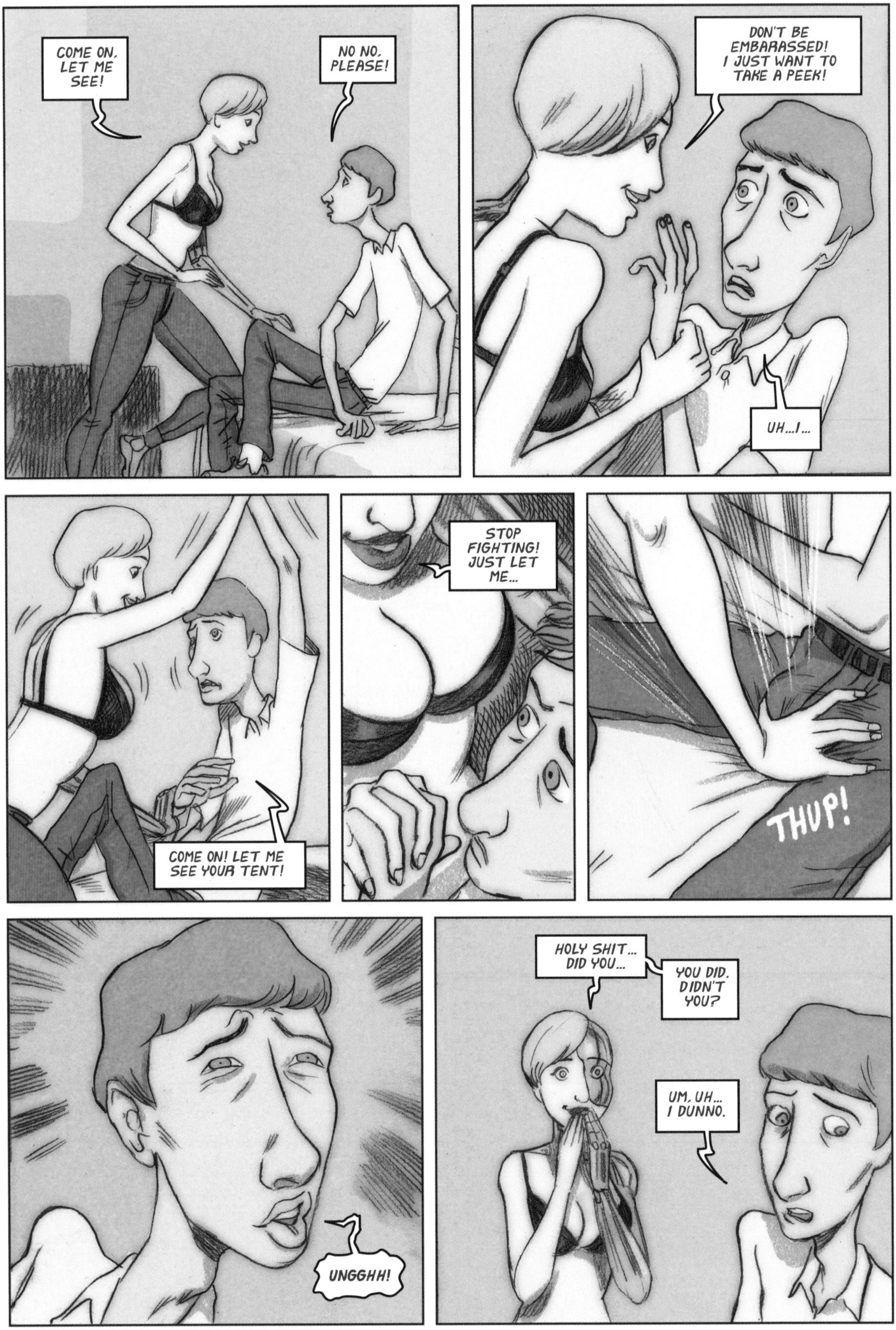
COME ON. LET ME SEE!
NO NO, PLEASE!
DON'T BE EMBARASSED! I JUST WANT TO TAKE A PEEK!
UH...I...
COME ON! LET ME SEE YOUR TENT!
STOP FIGHTING! JUST LET ME...
THUP!
UNGGHH!
HOLY SHIT... DID YOU...
YOU DID. DIDN'T YOU?
UM, UH... I DUNNO.

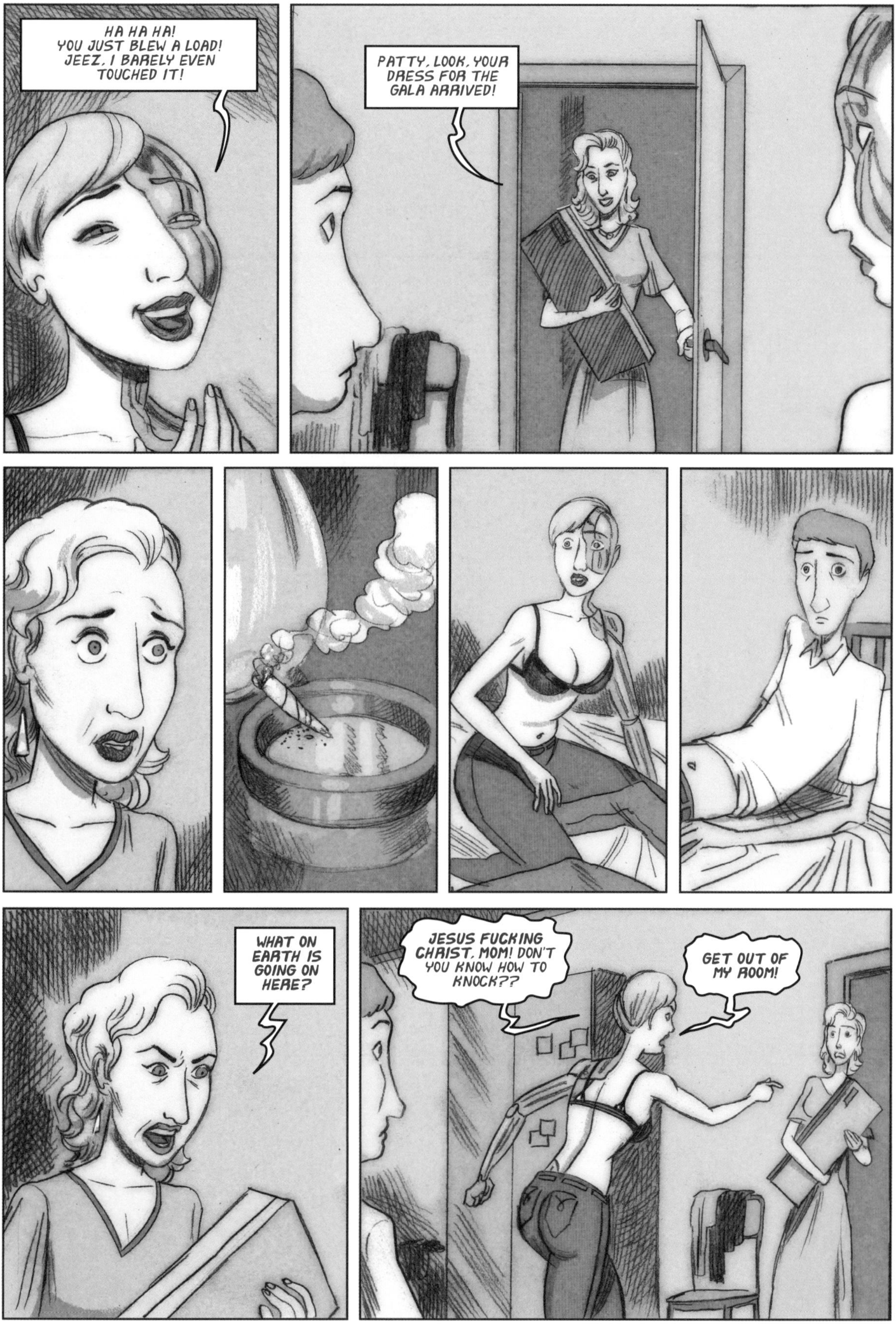
HA HA HA! YOU JUST BLEW A LOAD! JEEZ, I BARELY EVEN TOUCHED IT!
PATTY, LOOK, YOUR DRESS FOR THE GALA ARRIVED!
WHAT ON EARTH IS GOING ON HERE?
JESUS FUCKING CHRIST, MOM! DON'T YOU KNOW HOW TO KNOCK??
GET OUT OF MY ROOM!

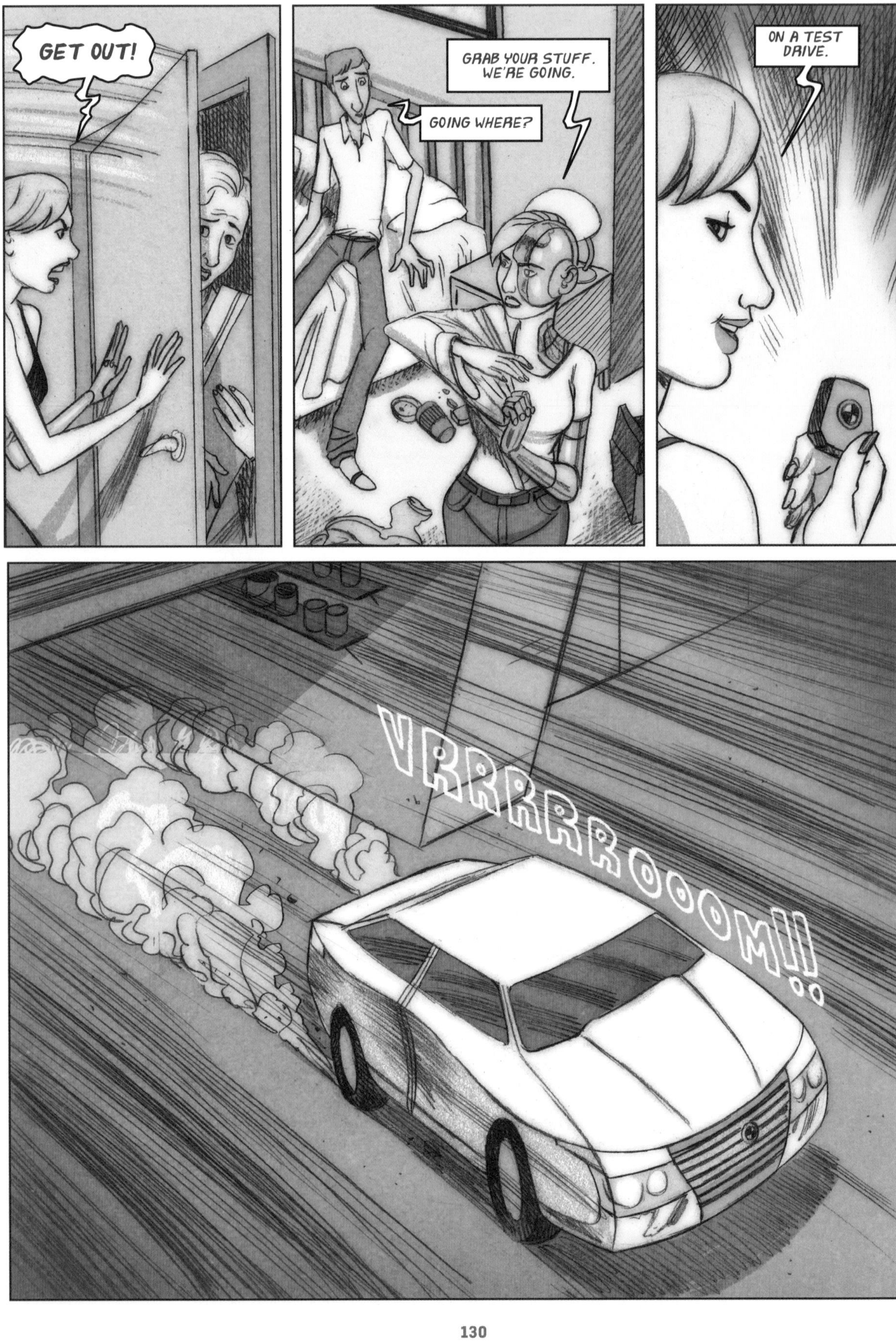
GET OUT!
GRAB YOUR STUFF. WE'RE GOING.
GOING WHERE?
ON A TEST DRIVE.
VRRRRROOOM!!

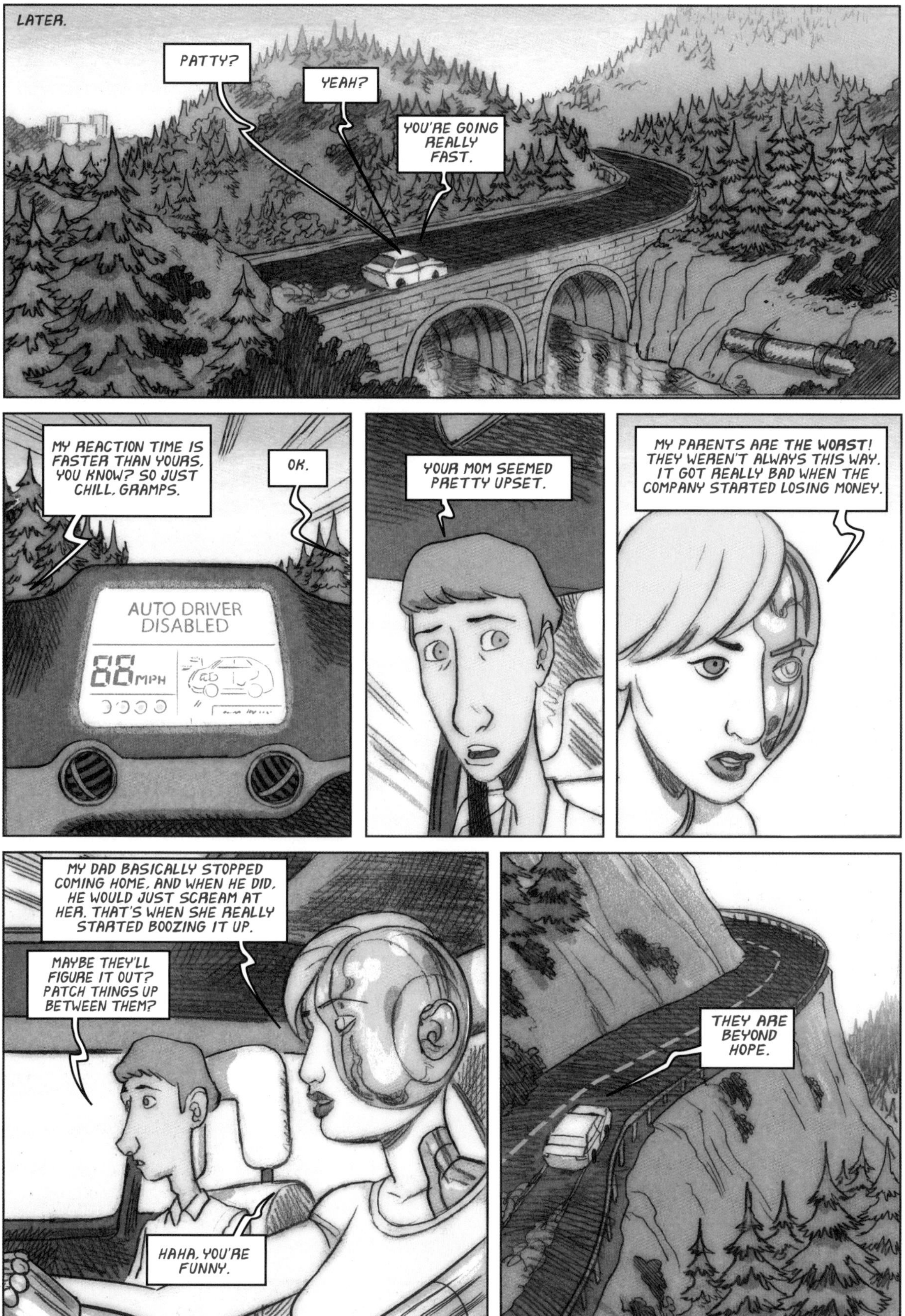
LATER.
PATTY?
YEAH?
YOU'RE GOING REALLY FAST.
MY REACTION TIME IS FASTER THAN YOURS, YOU KNOW? SO JUST CHILL, GRAMPS.
OK.
AUTO DRIVER DISABLED
88 MPH
YOUR MOM SEEMED PRETTY UPSET.
MY PARENTS ARE THE WORST! THEY WEREN'T ALWAYS THIS WAY. IT GOT REALLY BAD WHEN THE COMPANY STARTED LOSING MONEY.
MY DAD BASICALLY STOPPED COMING HOME. AND WHEN HE DID, HE WOULD JUST SCREAM AT HER. THAT'S WHEN SHE REALLY STARTED BOOZING IT UP.
MAYBE THEY'LL FIGURE IT OUT? PATCH THINGS UP BETWEEN THEM?
HAHA, YOU'RE FUNNY.
THEY ARE BEYOND HOPE.

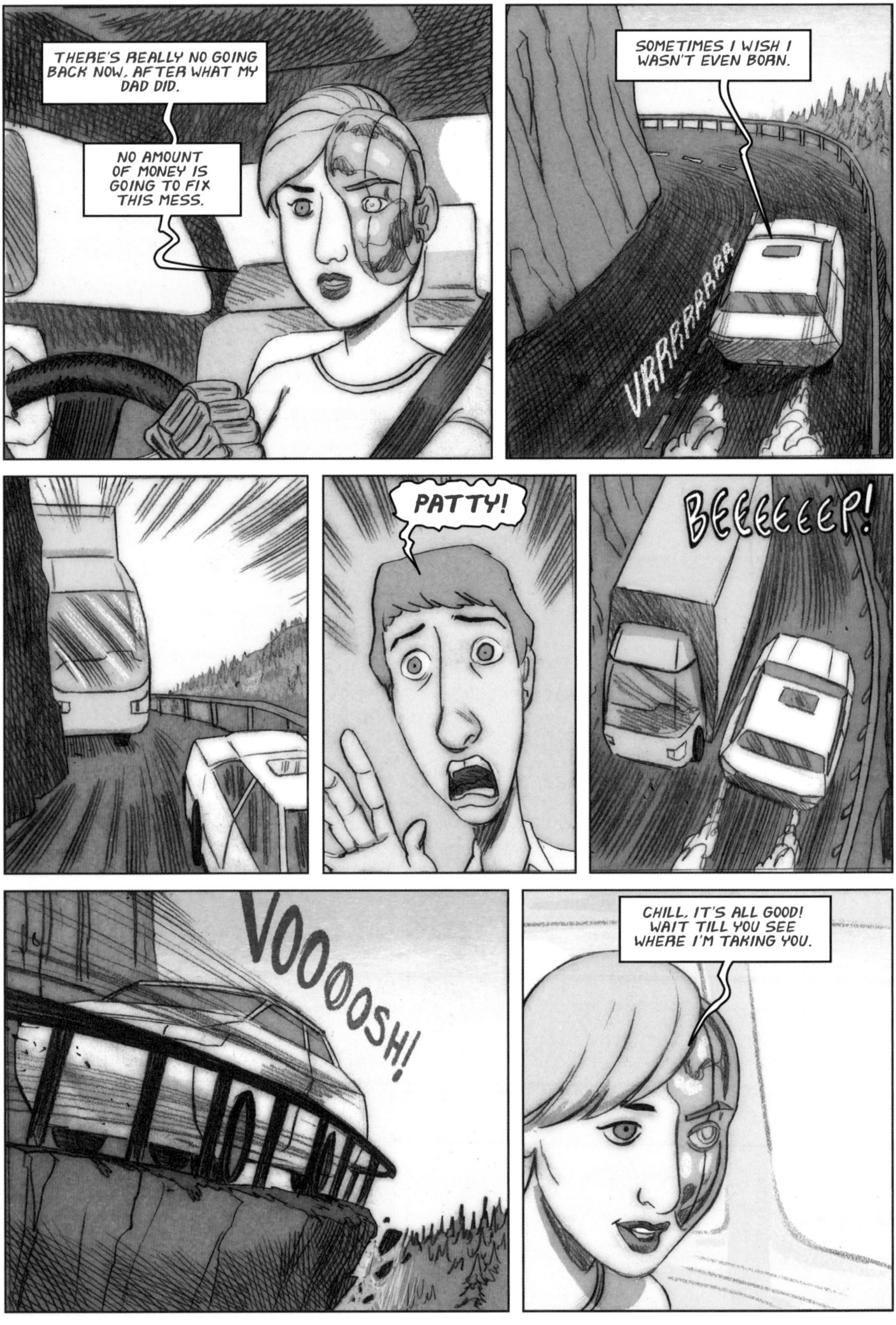

THERE'S REALLY NO GOING BACK NOW, AFTER WHAT MY DAD DID.
NO AMOUNT OF MONEY IS GOING TO FIX THIS MESS.
SOMETIMES I WISH I WASN'T EVEN BORN.
VRRRRRRRR
PATTY!
BEEEEEEP!
VOOOOSH!
CHILL, IT'S ALL GOOD! WAIT TILL YOU SEE WHERE I'M TAKING YOU.

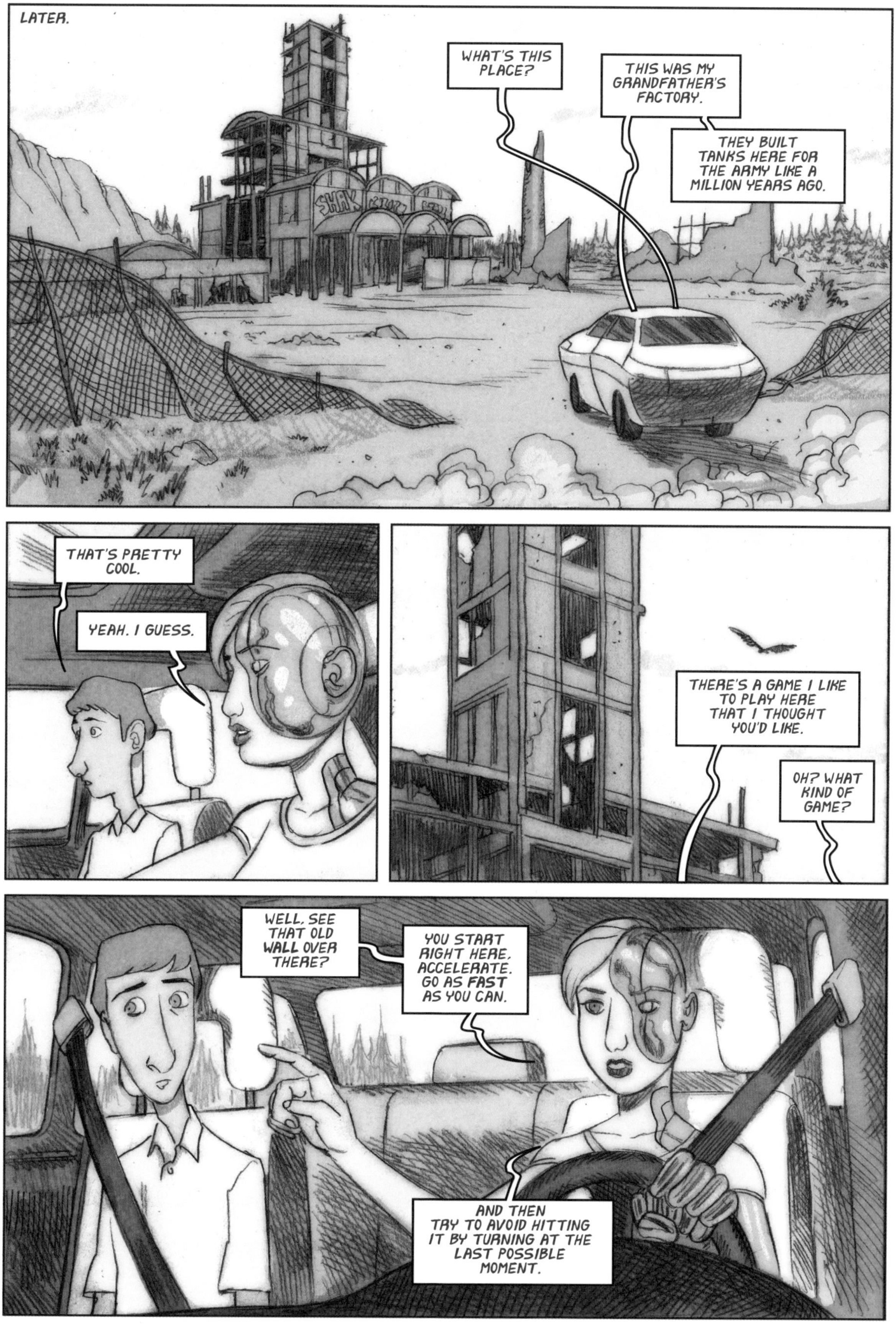
LATER.
WHAT'S THIS PLACE?
THIS WAS MY GRANDFATHER'S FACTORY.
THEY BUILT TANKS HERE FOR THE ARMY LIKE A MILLION YEARS AGO.
THAT'S PRETTY COOL.
YEAH. I GUESS.
THERE'S A GAME I LIKE TO PLAY HERE THAT I THOUGHT YOU'D LIKE.
OH? WHAT KIND OF GAME?
WELL, SEE THAT OLD WALL OVER THERE?
YOU START RIGHT HERE. ACCELERATE. GO AS FAST AS YOU CAN.
AND THEN TRY TO AVOID HITTING IT BY TURNING AT THE LAST POSSIBLE MOMENT.

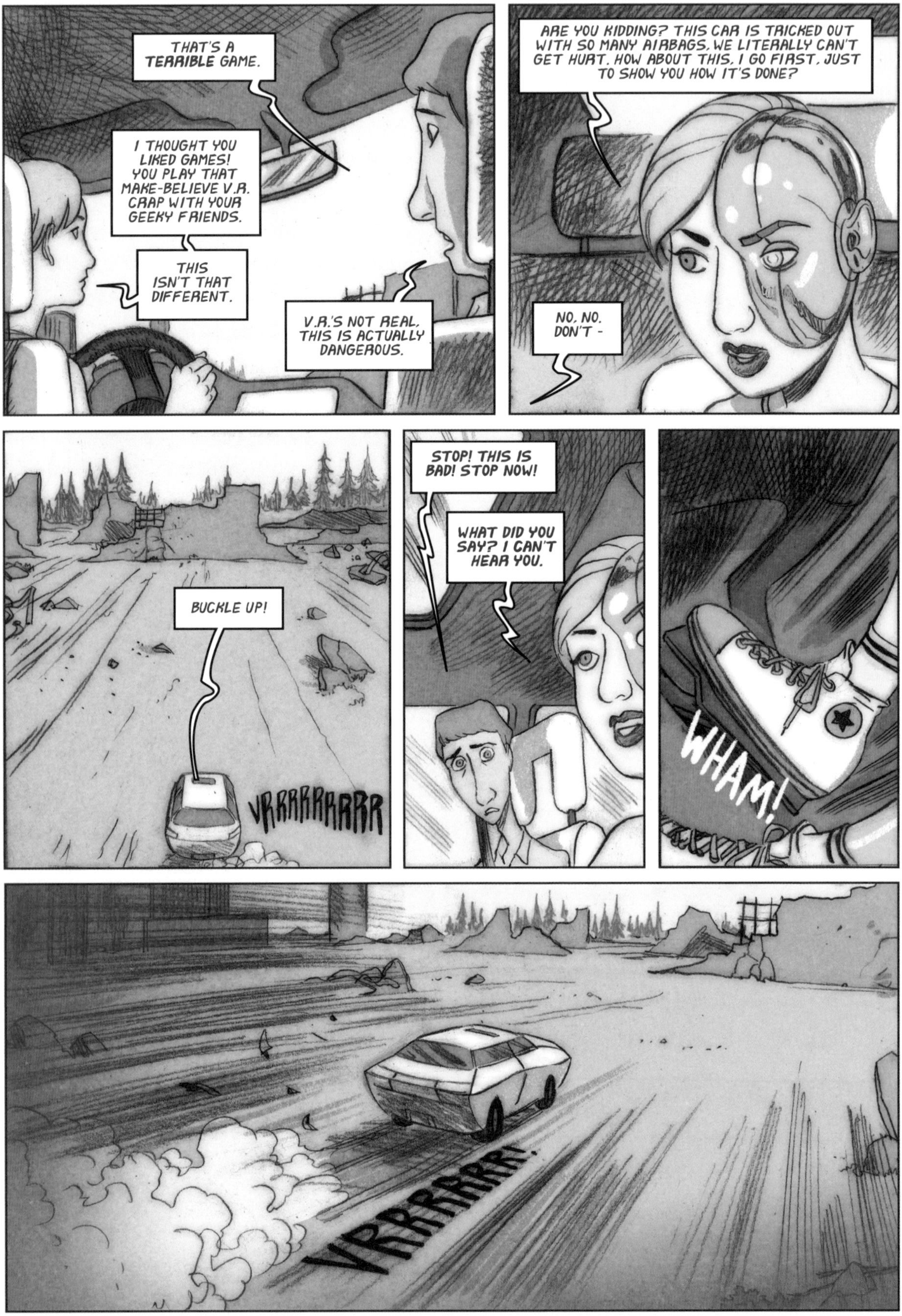
THAT'S A TERRIBLE GAME.
I THOUGHT YOU LIKED GAMES! YOU PLAY THAT MAKE-BELIEVE V.R. CRAP WITH YOUR GEEKY FRIENDS.
THIS ISN'T THAT DIFFERENT.
V.R.'S NOT REAL. THIS IS ACTUALLY DANGEROUS.
ARE YOU KIDDING? THIS CAR IS TRICKED OUT WITH SO MANY AIRBAGS, WE LITERALLY CAN'T GET HURT. HOW ABOUT THIS, I GO FIRST, JUST TO SHOW YOU HOW IT'S DONE?
NO, NO. DON'T -
BUCKLE UP!
VRRRRRRRRR
STOP! THIS IS BAD! STOP NOW!
WHAT DID YOU SAY? I CAN'T HEAR YOU.
WHAM!
VRRRRRRR!

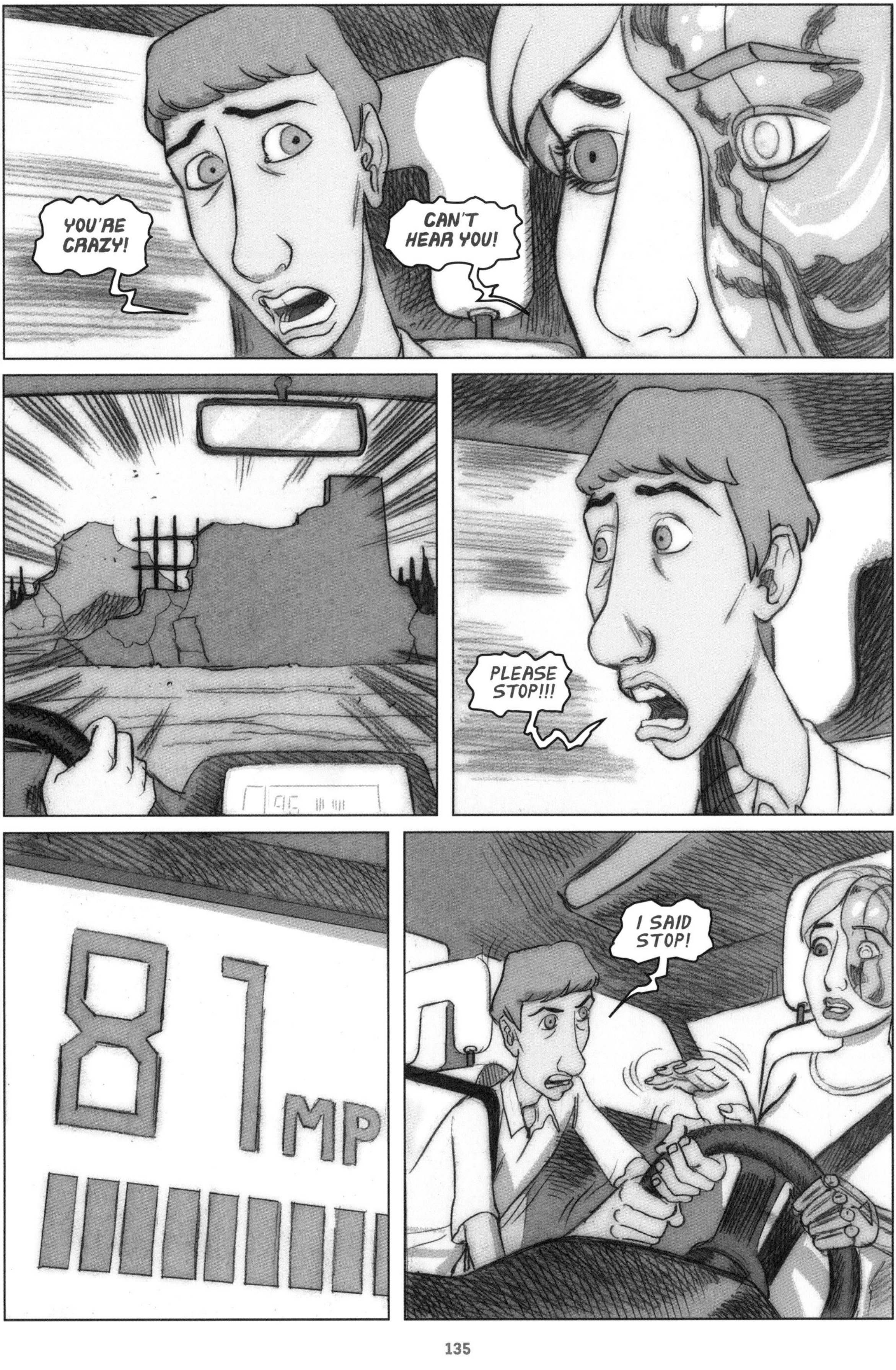
YOU'RE CRAZY!
CAN'T HEAR YOU!
PLEASE STOP!!!
87 MP
I SAID STOP!

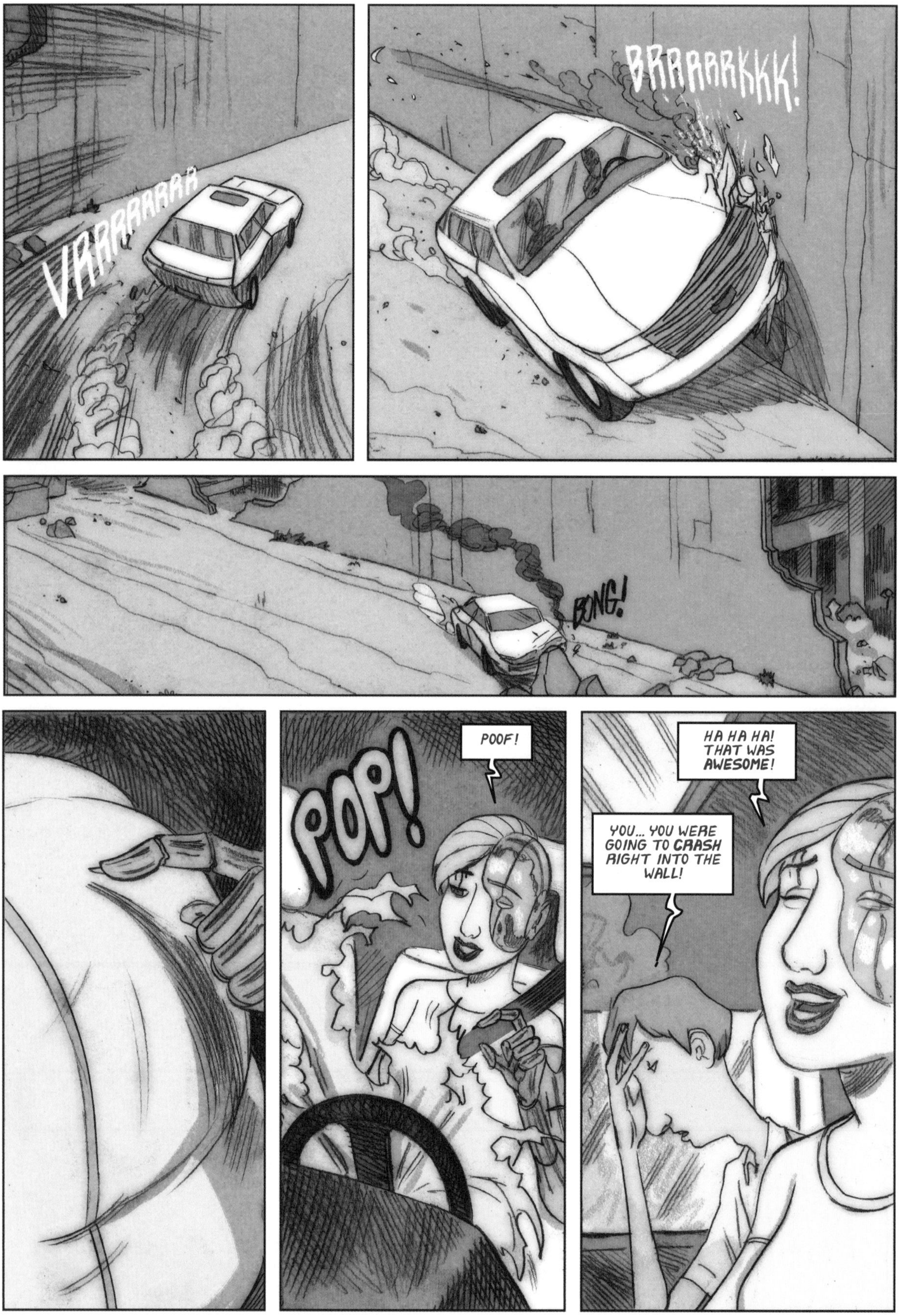
VRRRRRRRR
BRRRRRKKK!
BONG!
POP!
POOF!
HA HA HA! THAT WAS AWESOME!
YOU... YOU WERE GOING TO CRASH RIGHT INTO THE WALL!

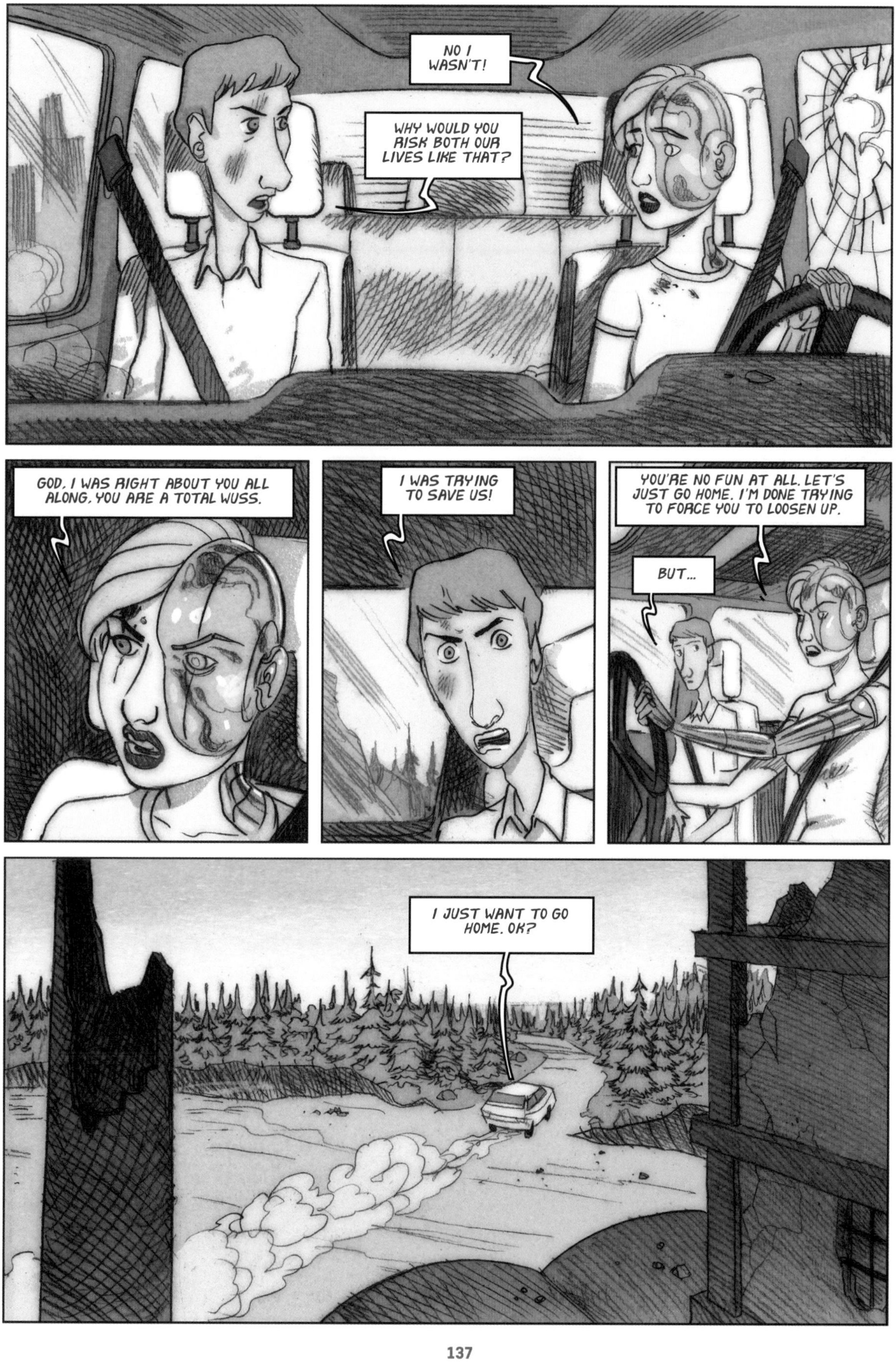
NO I WASN'T!
WHY WOULD YOU RISK BOTH OUR LIVES LIKE THAT?
GOD, I WAS RIGHT ABOUT YOU ALL ALONG. YOU ARE A TOTAL WUSS.
I WAS TRYING TO SAVE US!
YOU'RE NO FUN AT ALL. LET'S JUST GO HOME. I'M DONE TRYING TO FORCE YOU TO LOOSEN UP.
BUT...
I JUST WANT TO GO HOME. OK?

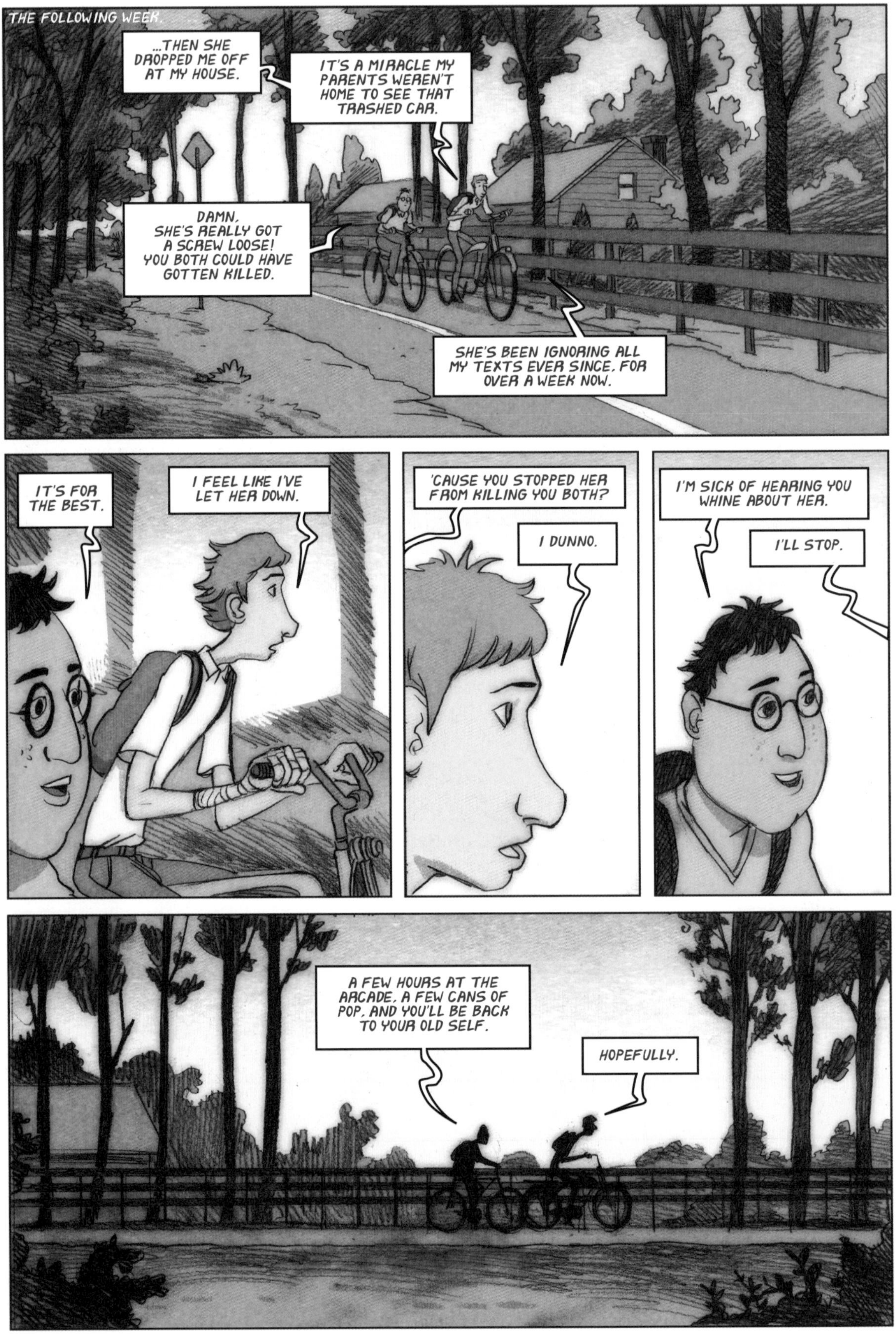
THE FOLLOWING WEEK.
...THEN SHE DROPPED ME OFF AT MY HOUSE.
IT'S A MIRACLE MY PARENTS WEREN'T HOME TO SEE THAT TRASHED CAR.
DAMN, SHE'S REALLY GOT A SCREW LOOSE! YOU BOTH COULD HAVE GOTTEN KILLED.
SHE'S BEEN IGNORING ALL MY TEXTS EVER SINCE, FOR OVER A WEEK NOW.
IT'S FOR THE BEST.
I FEEL LIKE I'VE LET HER DOWN.
'CAUSE YOU STOPPED HER FROM KILLING YOU BOTH?
I DUNNO.
I'M SICK OF HEARING YOU WHINE ABOUT HER.
I'LL STOP.
A FEW HOURS AT THE ARCADE, A FEW CANS OF POP, AND YOU'LL BE BACK TO YOUR OLD SELF.
HOPEFULLY.

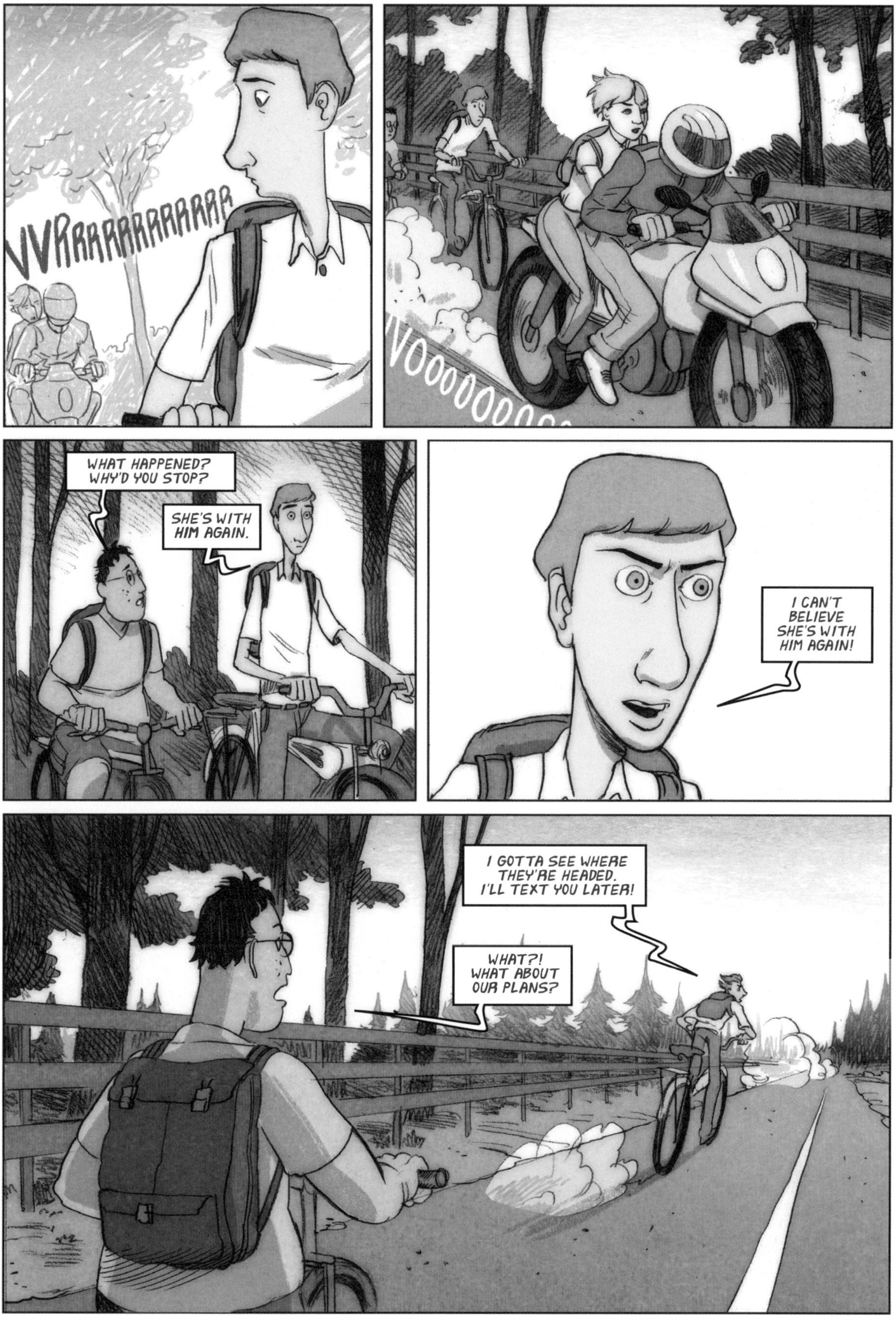
VVRRRRRRRRRRRR
VOOOOOOOO
WHAT HAPPENED? WHY'D YOU STOP?
SHE'S WITH HIM AGAIN.
I CAN'T BELIEVE SHE'S WITH HIM AGAIN!
I GOTTA SEE WHERE THEY'RE HEADED. I'LL TEXT YOU LATER!
WHAT?! WHAT ABOUT OUR PLANS?

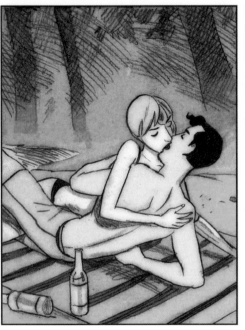

YOU'RE GETTING TOO HOT AND BOTHERED.

A LITTLE DIP MIGHT HELP COOL YOU OFF.

I WANT TO SEE YOU TAKE A DIP.

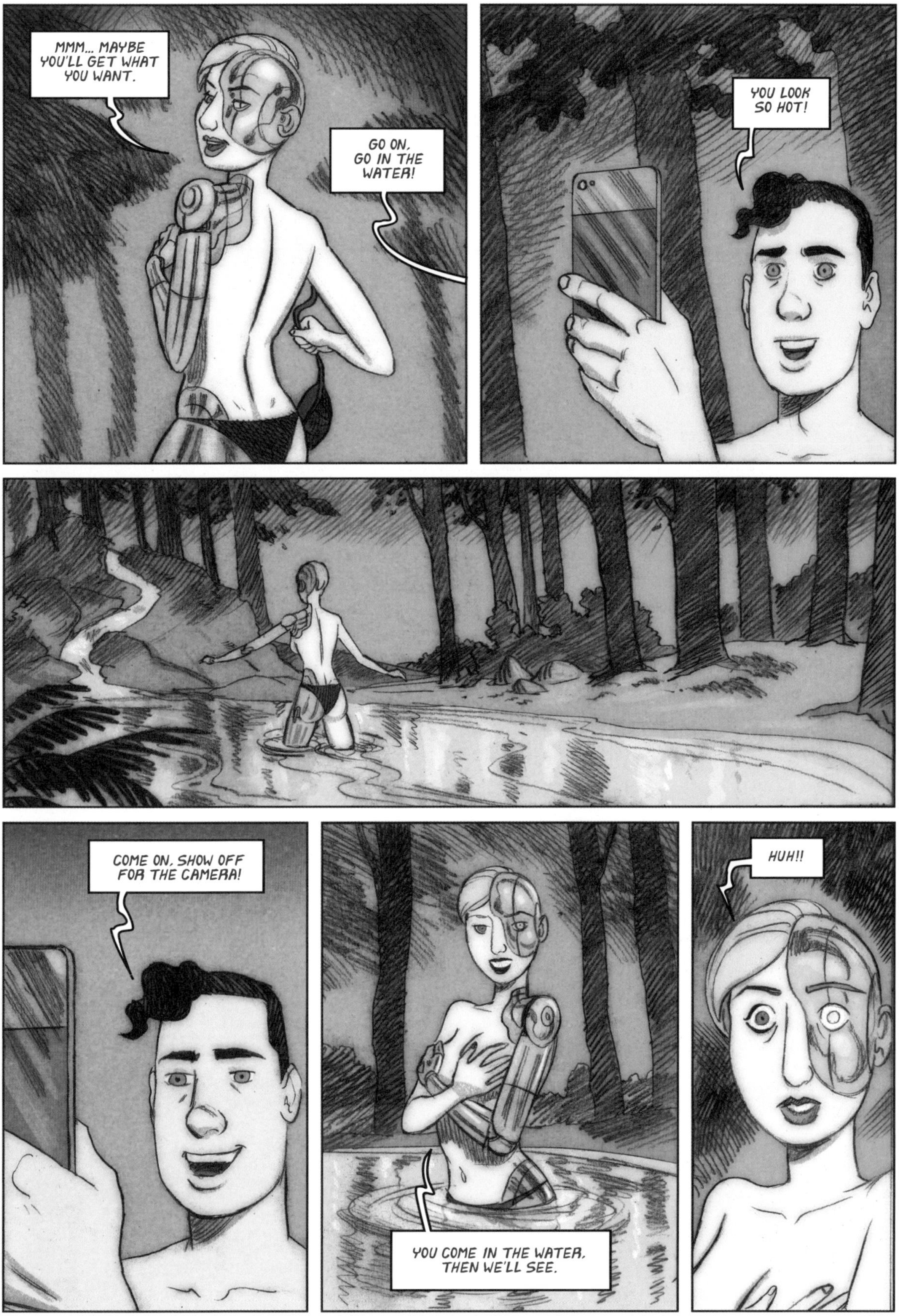
MMM... MAYBE YOU'LL GET WHAT YOU WANT.
GO ON, GO IN THE WATER!
YOU LOOK SO HOT!
COME ON, SHOW OFF FOR THE CAMERA!
YOU COME IN THE WATER, THEN WE'LL SEE.
HUH!!

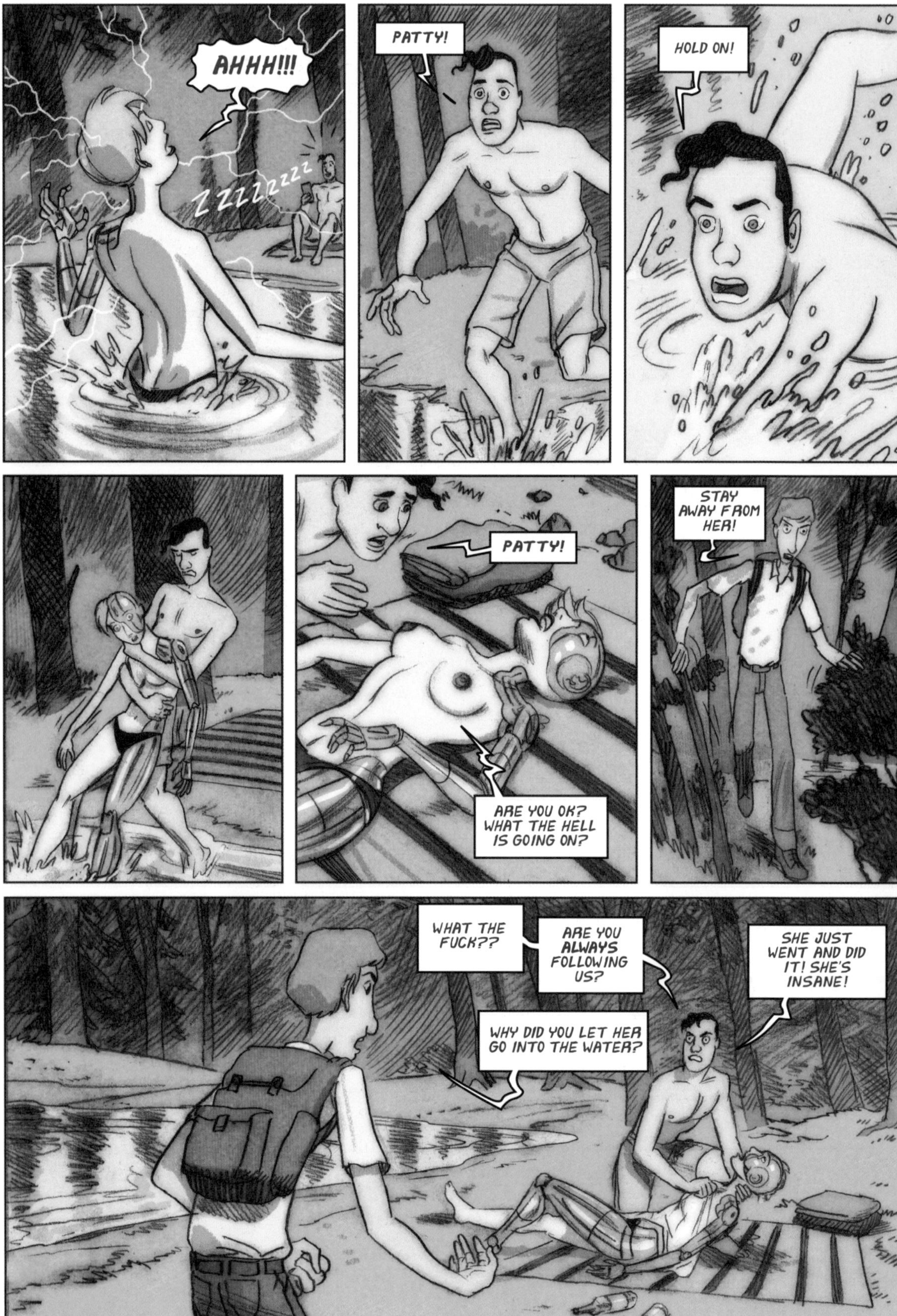
AHHH!!!
ZZZZzzzz
PATTY!
HOLD ON!
PATTY!
ARE YOU OK? WHAT THE HELL IS GOING ON?
STAY AWAY FROM HER!
WHAT THE FUCK??
ARE YOU ALWAYS FOLLOWING US?
SHE JUST WENT AND DID IT! SHE'S INSANE!
WHY DID YOU LET HER GO INTO THE WATER?

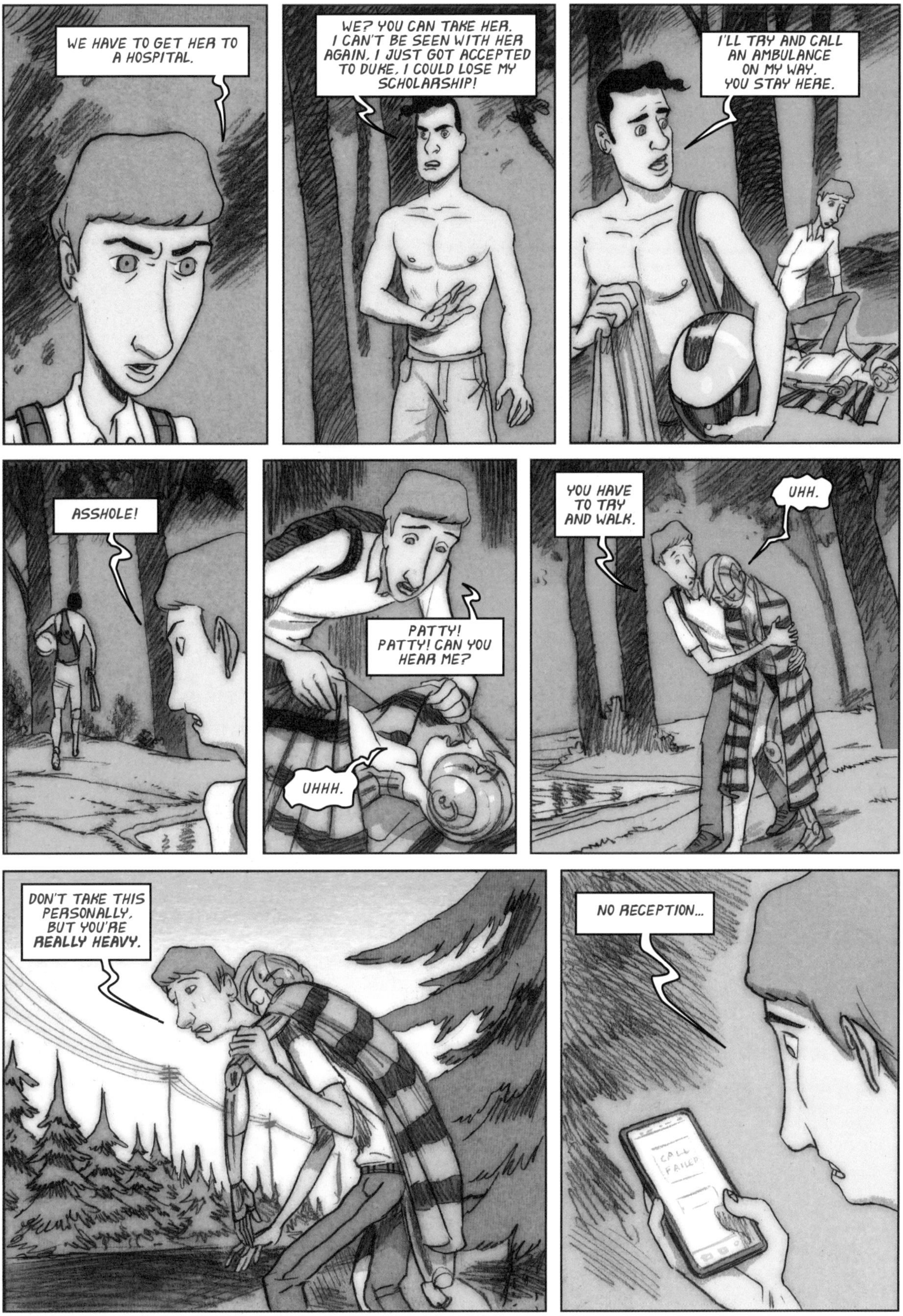
WE HAVE TO GET HER TO A HOSPITAL.
WE? YOU CAN TAKE HER. I CAN'T BE SEEN WITH HER AGAIN. I JUST GOT ACCEPTED TO DUKE. I COULD LOSE MY SCHOLARSHIP!
I'LL TRY AND CALL AN AMBULANCE ON MY WAY. YOU STAY HERE.
ASSHOLE!
PATTY! PATTY! CAN YOU HEAR ME?
UHHH.
YOU HAVE TO TRY AND WALK.
UHH.
DON'T TAKE THIS PERSONALLY, BUT YOU'RE REALLY HEAVY.
NO RECEPTION...

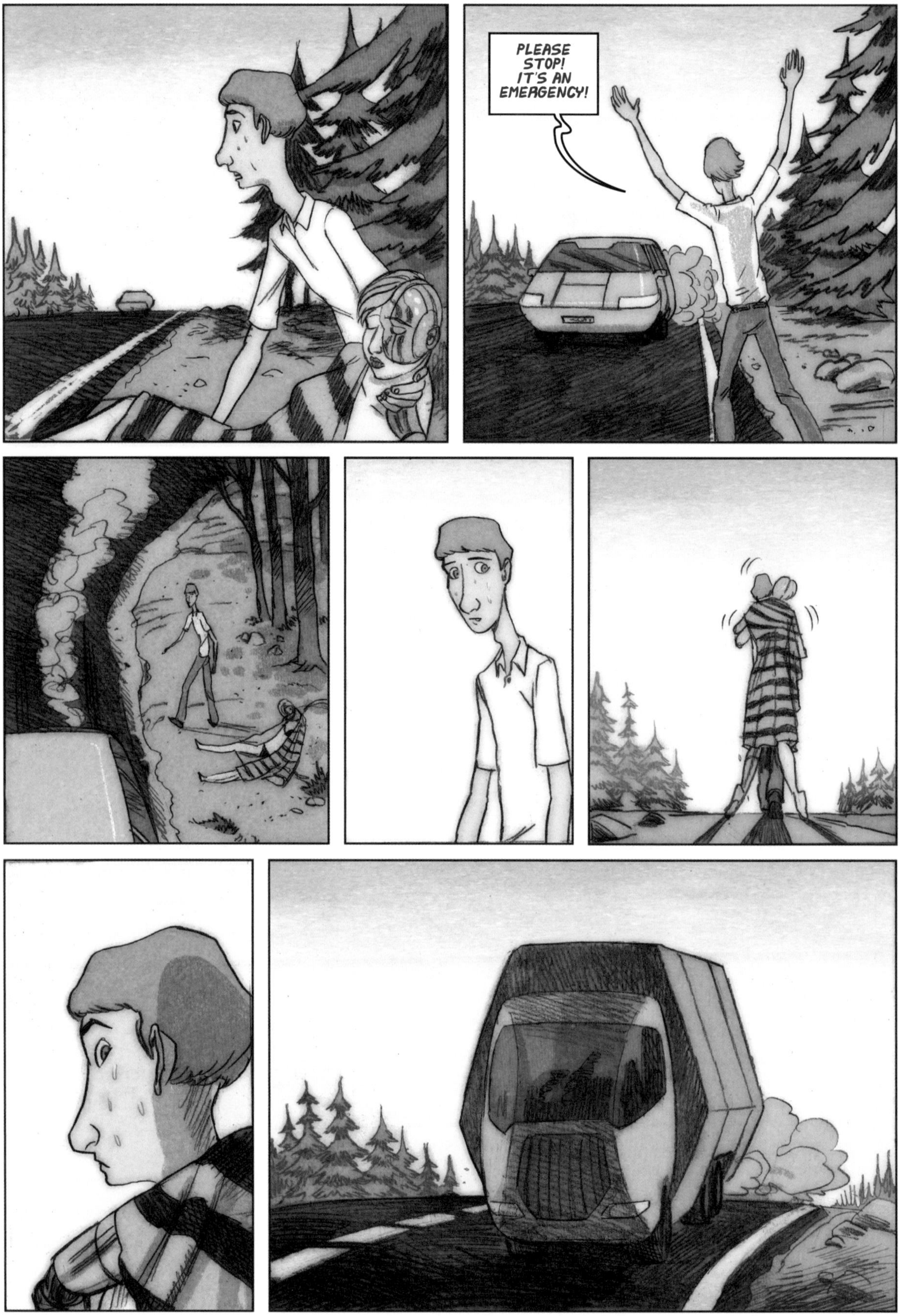
PLEASE STOP! IT'S AN EMERGENCY!

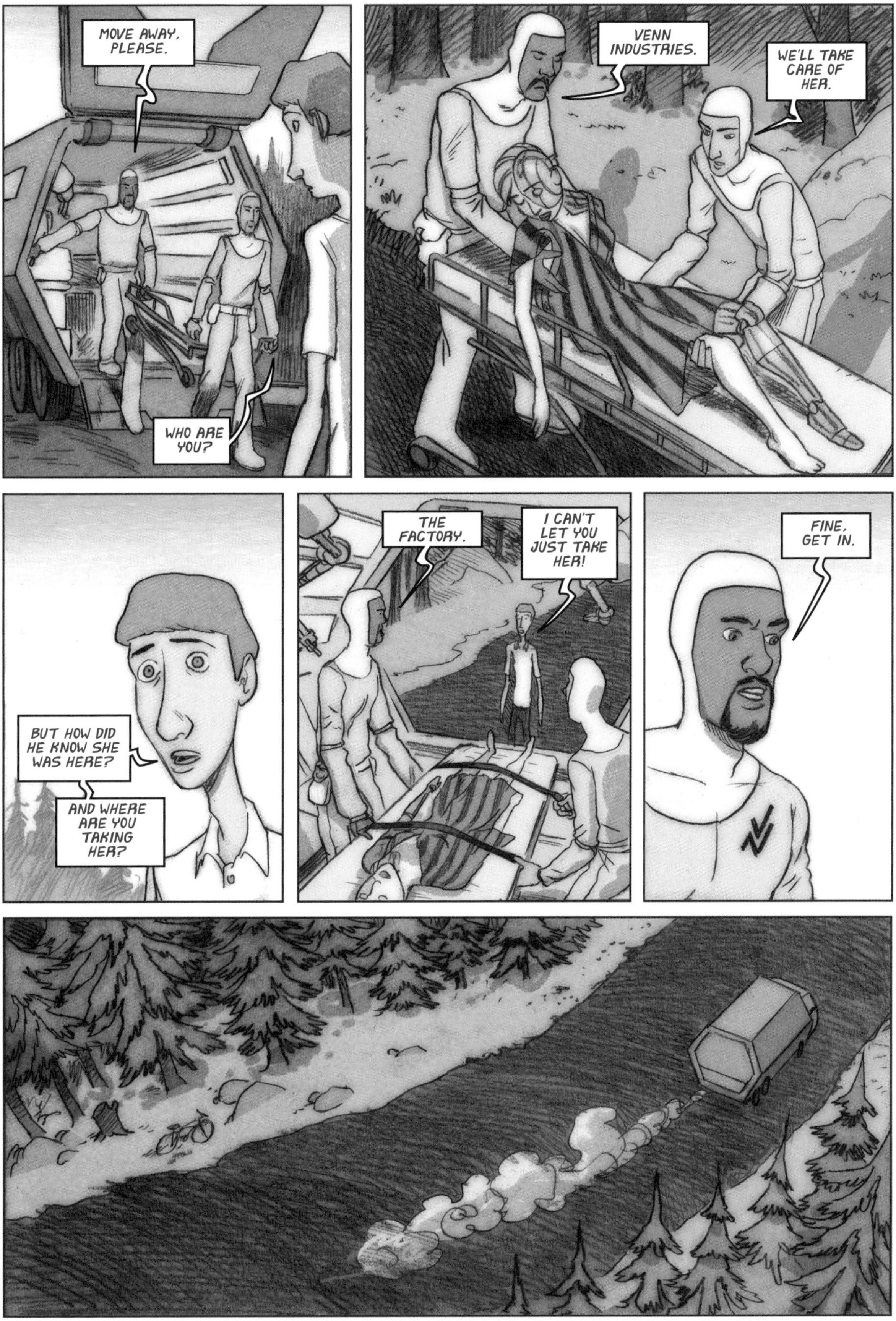
MOVE AWAY, PLEASE.
WHO ARE YOU?
VENN INDUSTRIES.
WE'LL TAKE CARE OF HER.
BUT HOW DID HE KNOW SHE WAS HERE?
AND WHERE ARE YOU TAKING HER?
THE FACTORY.
I CAN'T LET YOU JUST TAKE HER!
FINE, GET IN.

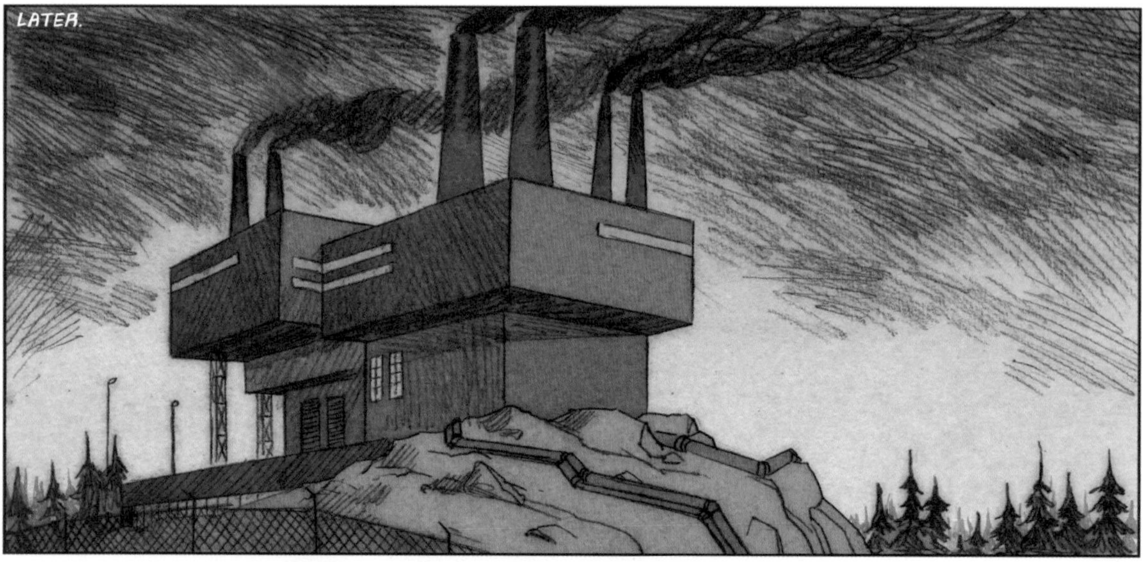
LATER.

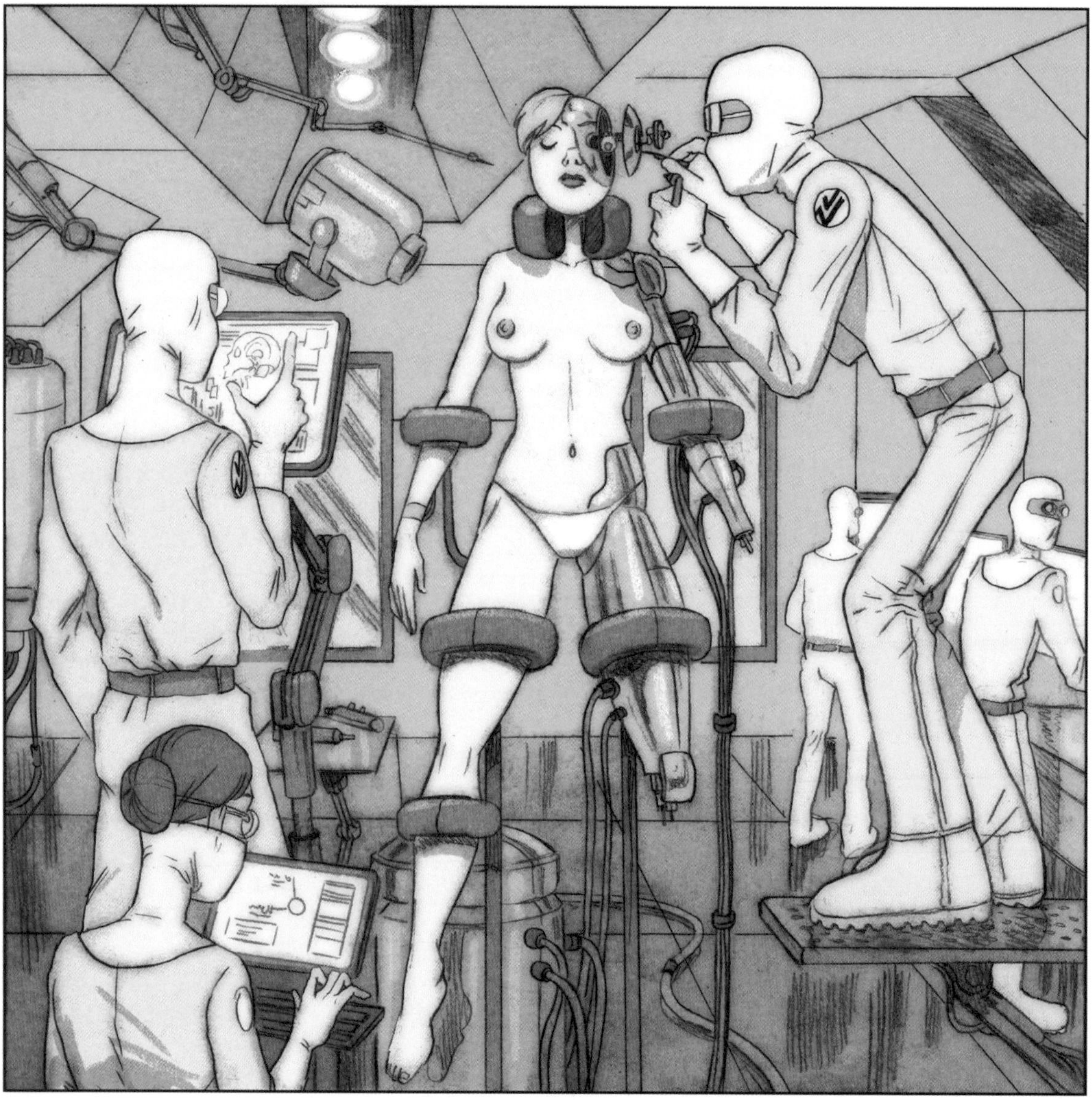

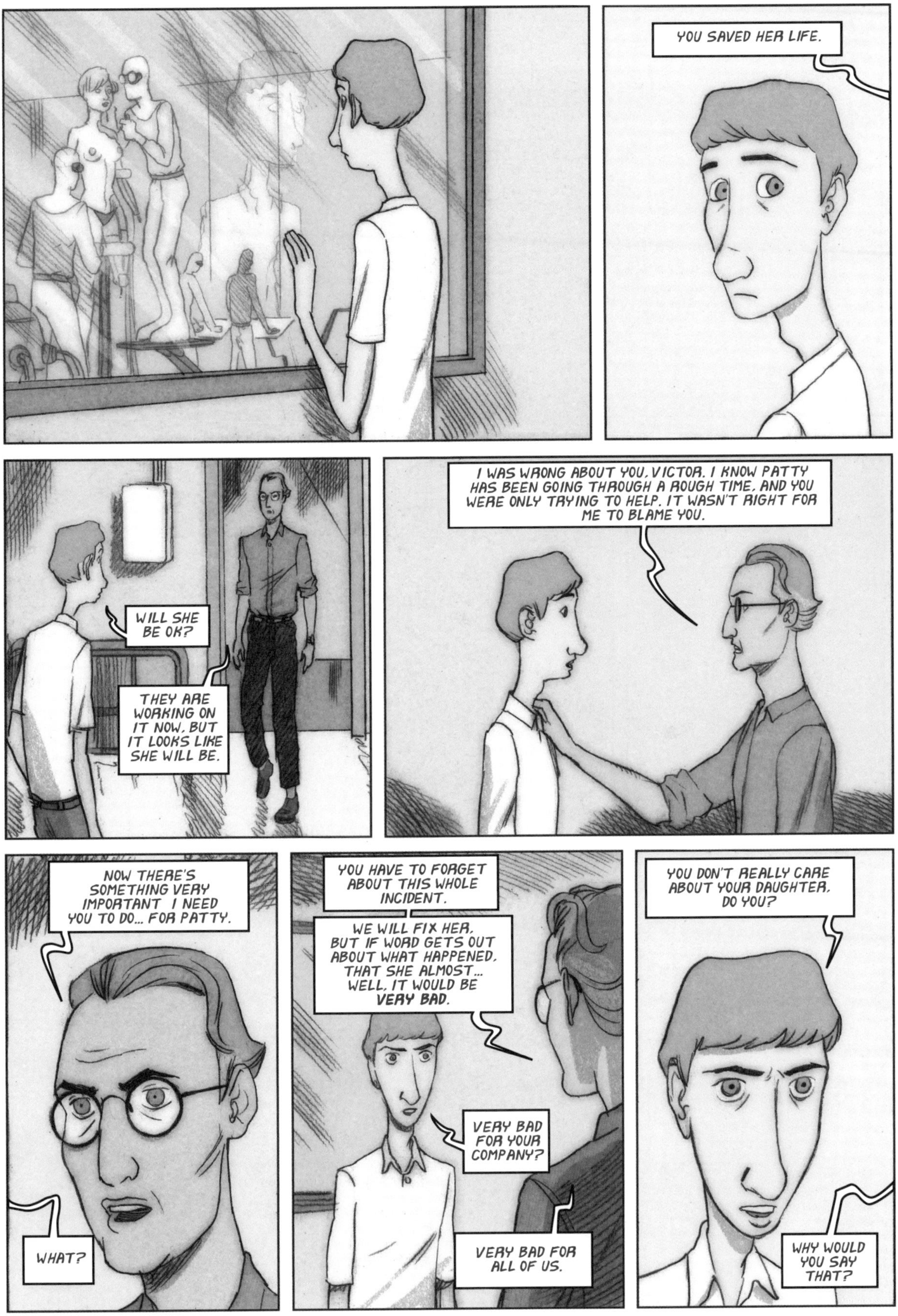
YOU SAVED HER LIFE.
WILL SHE BE OK?
THEY ARE WORKING ON IT NOW, BUT IT LOOKS LIKE SHE WILL BE.
I WAS WRONG ABOUT YOU, VICTOR. I KNOW PATTY HAS BEEN GOING THROUGH A ROUGH TIME, AND YOU WERE ONLY TRYING TO HELP. IT WASN'T RIGHT FOR ME TO BLAME YOU.
NOW THERE'S SOMETHING VERY IMPORTANT I NEED YOU TO DO... FOR PATTY.
WHAT?
YOU HAVE TO FORGET ABOUT THIS WHOLE INCIDENT.
WE WILL FIX HER, BUT IF WORD GETS OUT ABOUT WHAT HAPPENED, THAT SHE ALMOST... WELL, IT WOULD BE **VERY BAD**.
VERY BAD FOR YOUR COMPANY?
VERY BAD FOR ALL OF US.
YOU DON'T REALLY CARE ABOUT YOUR DAUGHTER, DO YOU?
WHY WOULD YOU SAY THAT?

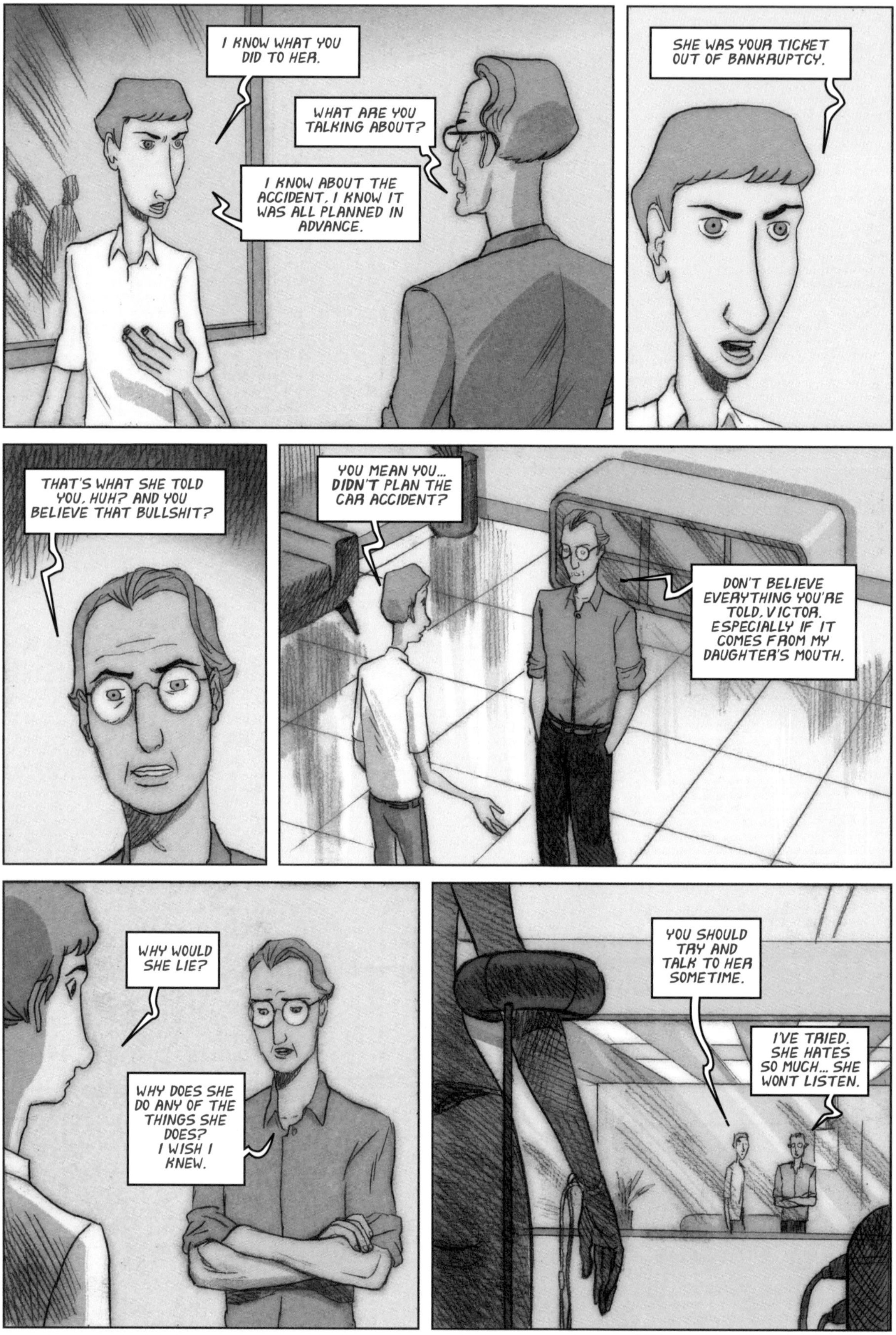
I KNOW WHAT YOU DID TO HER.
WHAT ARE YOU TALKING ABOUT?
I KNOW ABOUT THE ACCIDENT. I KNOW IT WAS ALL PLANNED IN ADVANCE.
SHE WAS YOUR TICKET OUT OF BANKRUPTCY.
THAT'S WHAT SHE TOLD YOU, HUH? AND YOU BELIEVE THAT BULLSHIT?
YOU MEAN YOU... **DIDN'T** PLAN THE CAR ACCIDENT?
DON'T BELIEVE EVERYTHING YOU'RE TOLD, VICTOR. ESPECIALLY IF IT COMES FROM MY DAUGHTER'S MOUTH.
WHY WOULD SHE LIE?
WHY DOES SHE DO ANY OF THE THINGS SHE DOES? I WISH I KNEW.
YOU SHOULD TRY AND TALK TO HER SOMETIME.
I'VE TRIED. SHE HATES SO MUCH... SHE WONT LISTEN.

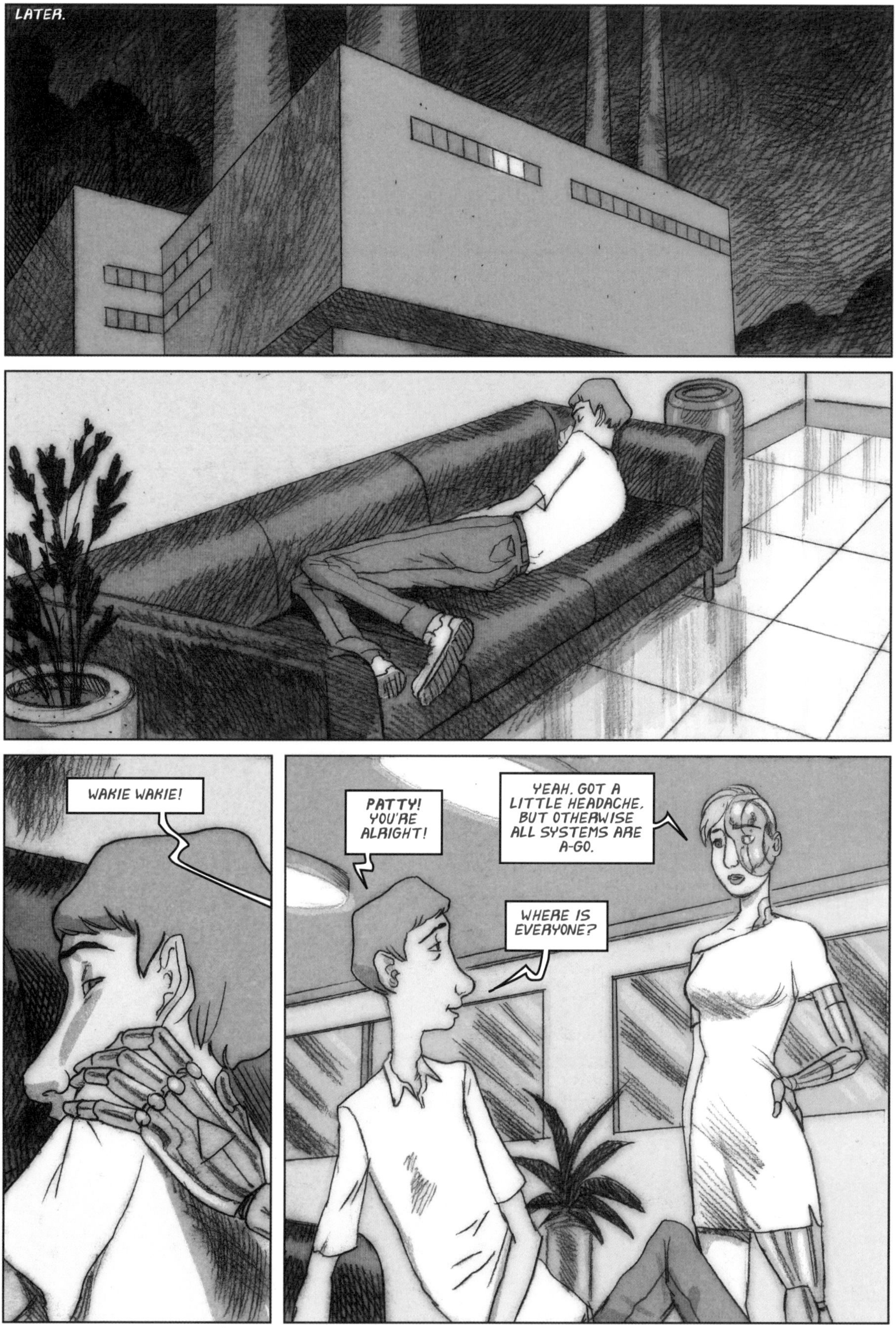
LATER.
WAKIE WAKIE!
PATTY! YOU'RE ALRIGHT!
YEAH. GOT A LITTLE HEADACHE, BUT OTHERWISE ALL SYSTEMS ARE A-GO.
WHERE IS EVERYONE?

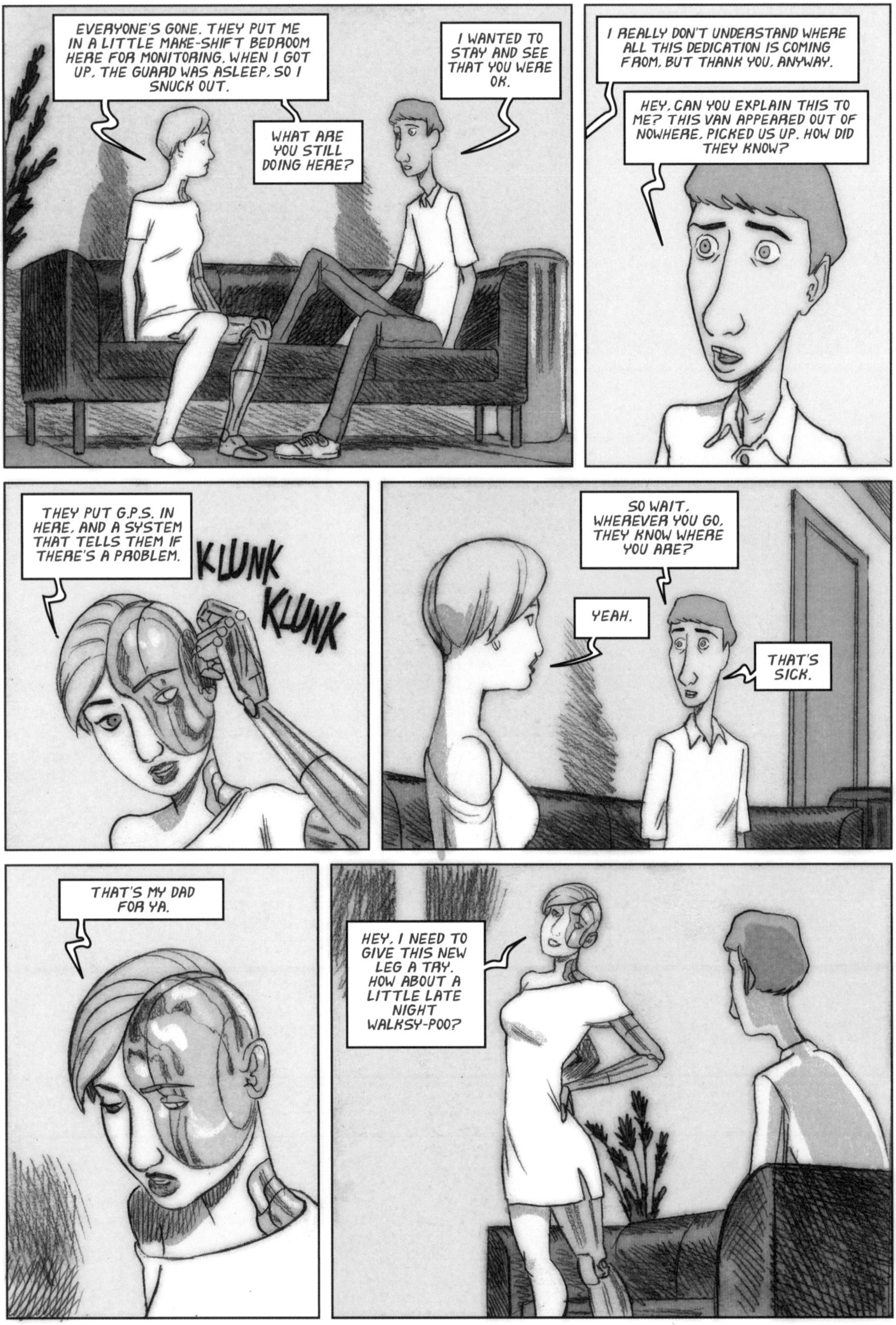
EVERYONE'S GONE. THEY PUT ME IN A LITTLE MAKE-SHIFT BEDROOM HERE FOR MONITORING. WHEN I GOT UP, THE GUARD WAS ASLEEP, SO I SNUCK OUT.
WHAT ARE YOU STILL DOING HERE?
I WANTED TO STAY AND SEE THAT YOU WERE OK.
I REALLY DON'T UNDERSTAND WHERE ALL THIS DEDICATION IS COMING FROM, BUT THANK YOU, ANYWAY.
HEY, CAN YOU EXPLAIN THIS TO ME? THIS VAN APPEARED OUT OF NOWHERE, PICKED US UP. HOW DID THEY KNOW?
THEY PUT G.P.S. IN HERE, AND A SYSTEM THAT TELLS THEM IF THERE'S A PROBLEM.
KLUNK
KLUNK
SO WAIT, WHEREVER YOU GO, THEY KNOW WHERE YOU ARE?
YEAH.
THAT'S SICK.
THAT'S MY DAD FOR YA.
HEY, I NEED TO GIVE THIS NEW LEG A TRY. HOW ABOUT A LITTLE LATE NIGHT WALKSY-POO?

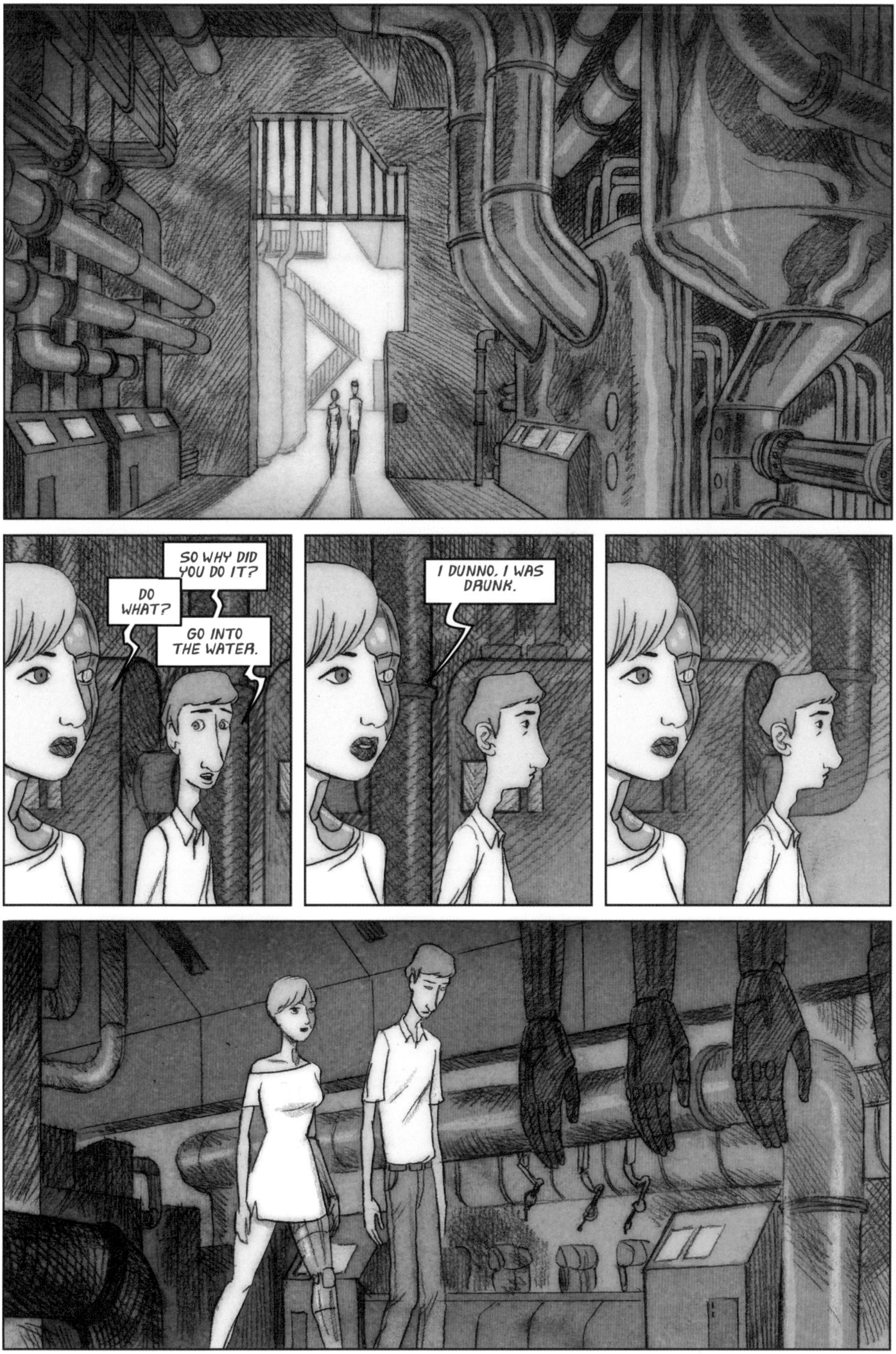
SO WHY DID YOU DO IT?
DO WHAT?
GO INTO THE WATER.
I DUNNO, I WAS DRUNK.

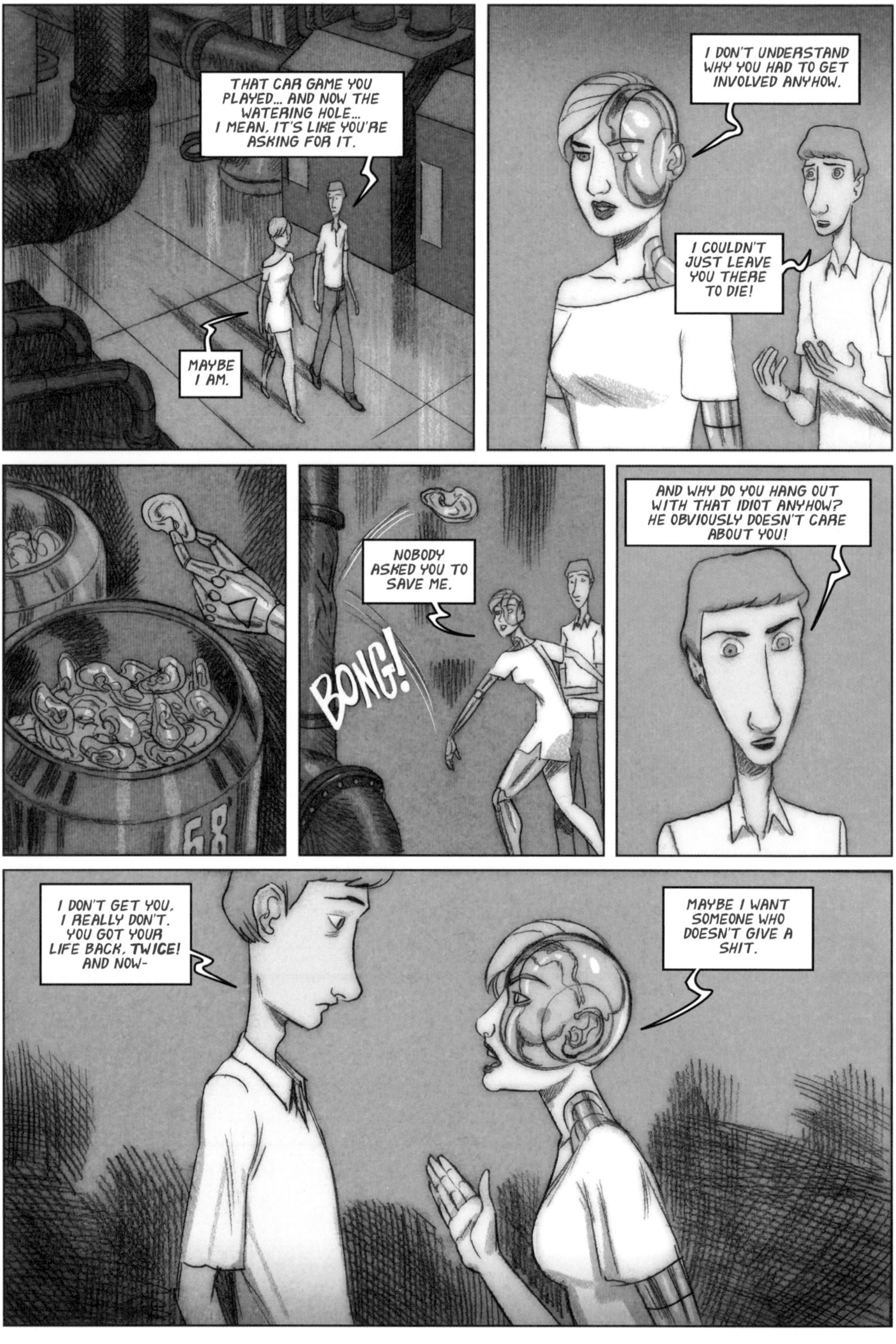
THAT CAR GAME YOU PLAYED... AND NOW THE WATERING HOLE... I MEAN, IT'S LIKE YOU'RE ASKING FOR IT.
MAYBE I AM.
I DON'T UNDERSTAND WHY YOU HAD TO GET INVOLVED ANYHOW.
I COULDN'T JUST LEAVE YOU THERE TO DIE!
NOBODY ASKED YOU TO SAVE ME.
BONG!
68
AND WHY DO YOU HANG OUT WITH THAT IDIOT ANYHOW? HE OBVIOUSLY DOESN'T CARE ABOUT YOU!
I DON'T GET YOU. I REALLY DON'T. YOU GOT YOUR LIFE BACK, TWICE! AND NOW-
MAYBE I WANT SOMEONE WHO DOESN'T GIVE A SHIT.

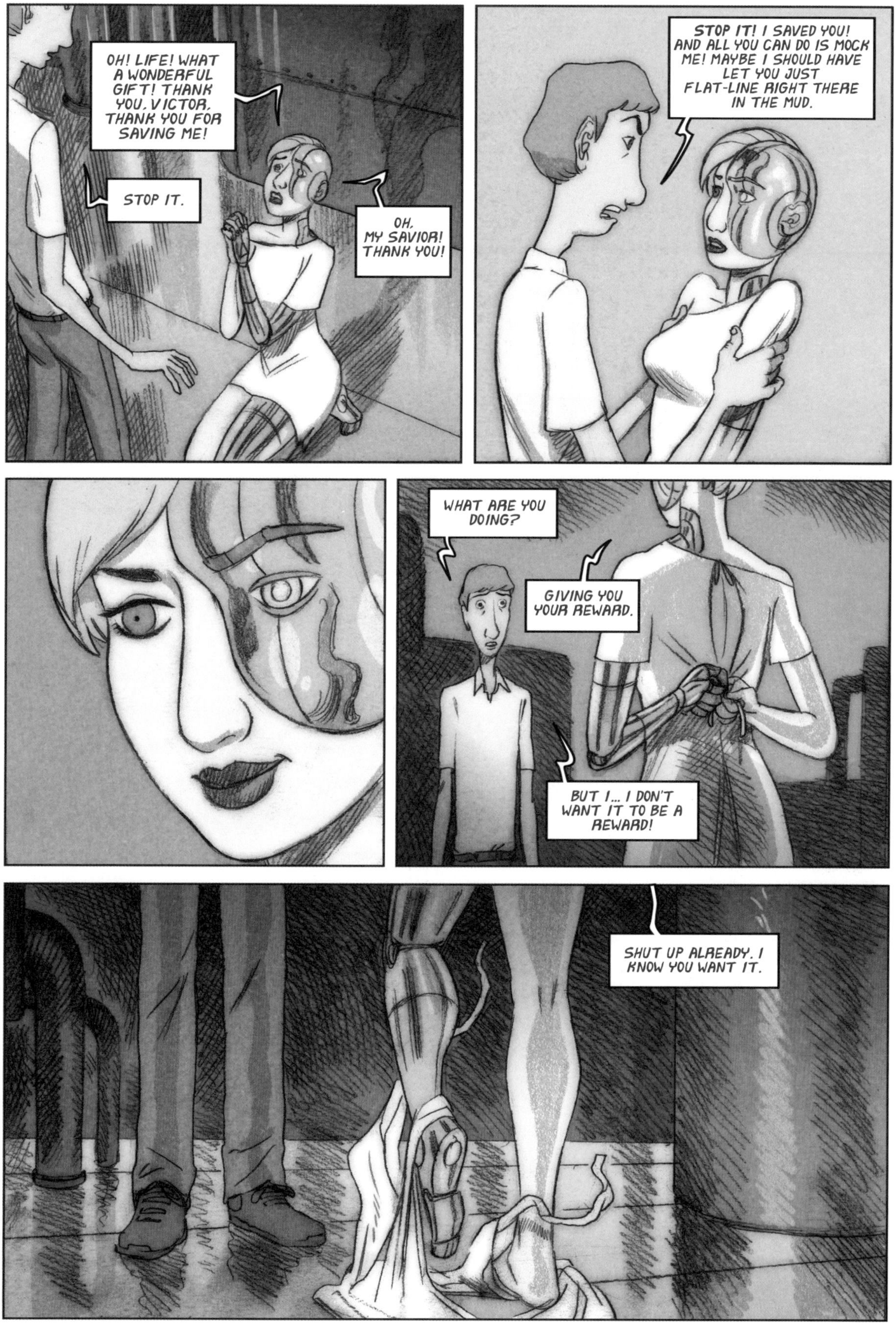
OH! LIFE! WHAT A WONDERFUL GIFT! THANK YOU, VICTOR, THANK YOU FOR SAVING ME!
STOP IT.
OH, MY SAVIOR! THANK YOU!
STOP IT! I SAVED YOU! AND ALL YOU CAN DO IS MOCK ME! MAYBE I SHOULD HAVE LET YOU JUST FLAT-LINE RIGHT THERE IN THE MUD.
WHAT ARE YOU DOING?
GIVING YOU YOUR REWARD.
BUT I... I DON'T WANT IT TO BE A REWARD!
SHUT UP ALREADY. I KNOW YOU WANT IT.

AH!!
AHH!!!

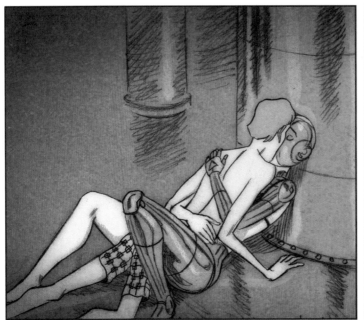

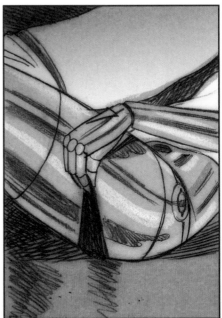

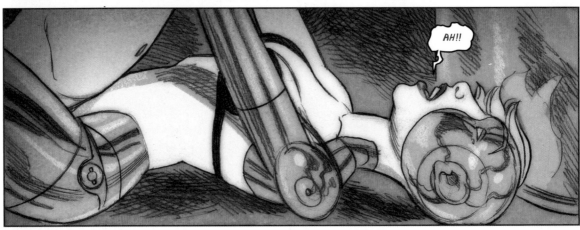

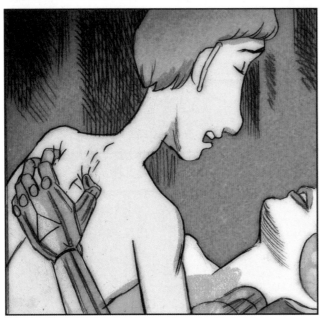

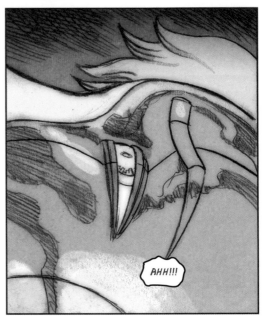

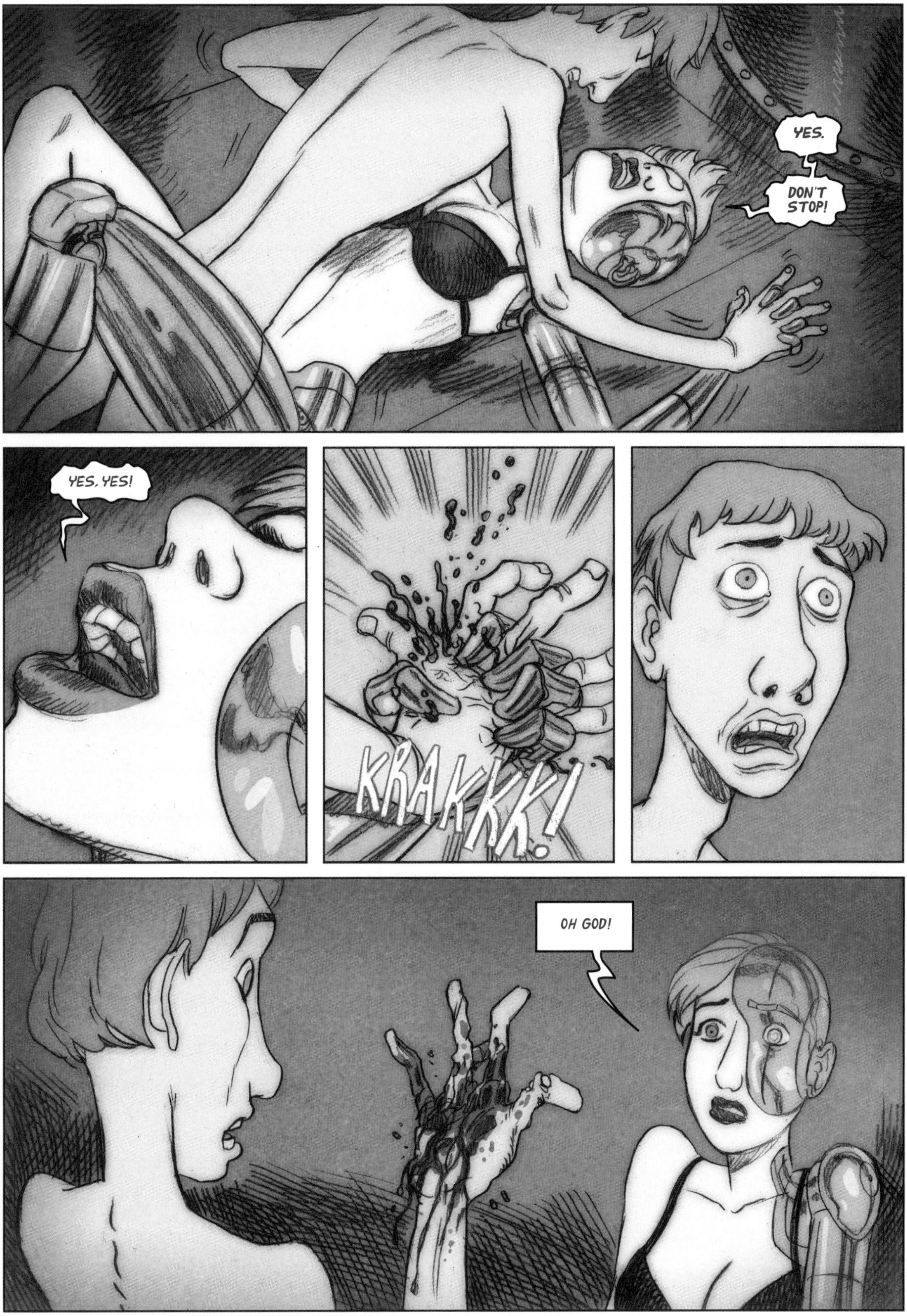
YES.
DON'T STOP!
YES, YES!
KRAKKK!
OH GOD!

A FEW DAYS LATER.

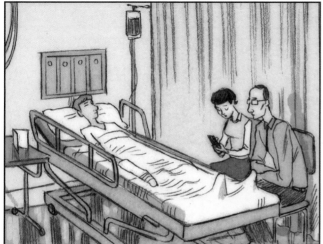

Get
Well
Soon!

grandma

MOM?

HEY, HONEY, HOW ARE YOU FEELING?

OK, A LITTLE GROGGY.

WE WERE WORRIED ABOUT YOU, SQUEAKER.

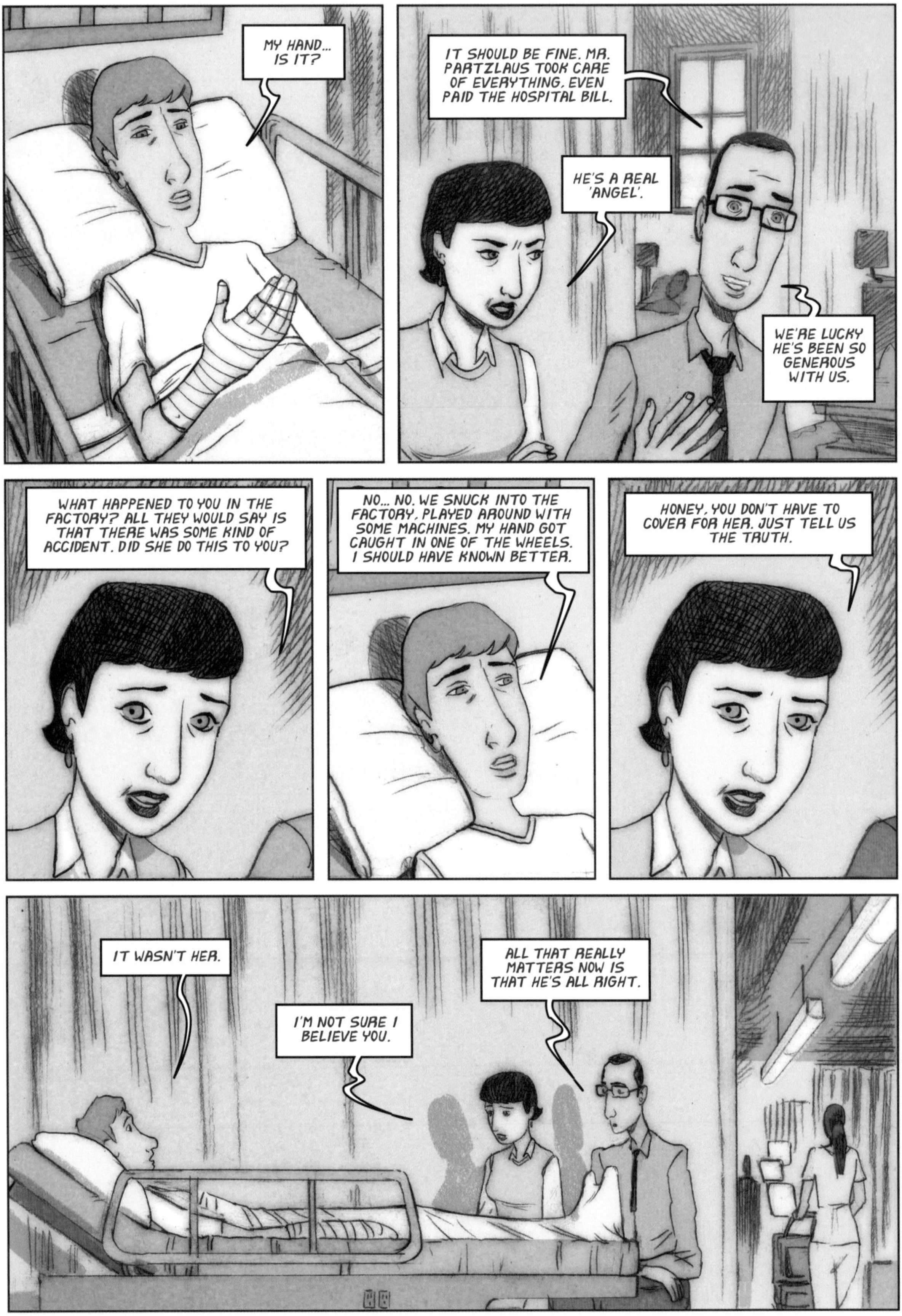
MY HAND... IS IT?
IT SHOULD BE FINE. MR. PARTZLAUS TOOK CARE OF EVERYTHING, EVEN PAID THE HOSPITAL BILL.
HE'S A REAL 'ANGEL'.
WE'RE LUCKY HE'S BEEN SO GENEROUS WITH US.
WHAT HAPPENED TO YOU IN THE FACTORY? ALL THEY WOULD SAY IS THAT THERE WAS SOME KIND OF ACCIDENT. DID SHE DO THIS TO YOU?
NO... NO. WE SNUCK INTO THE FACTORY, PLAYED AROUND WITH SOME MACHINES. MY HAND GOT CAUGHT IN ONE OF THE WHEELS. I SHOULD HAVE KNOWN BETTER.
HONEY, YOU DON'T HAVE TO COVER FOR HER. JUST TELL US THE TRUTH.
IT WASN'T HER.
I'M NOT SURE I BELIEVE YOU.
ALL THAT REALLY MATTERS NOW IS THAT HE'S ALL RIGHT.

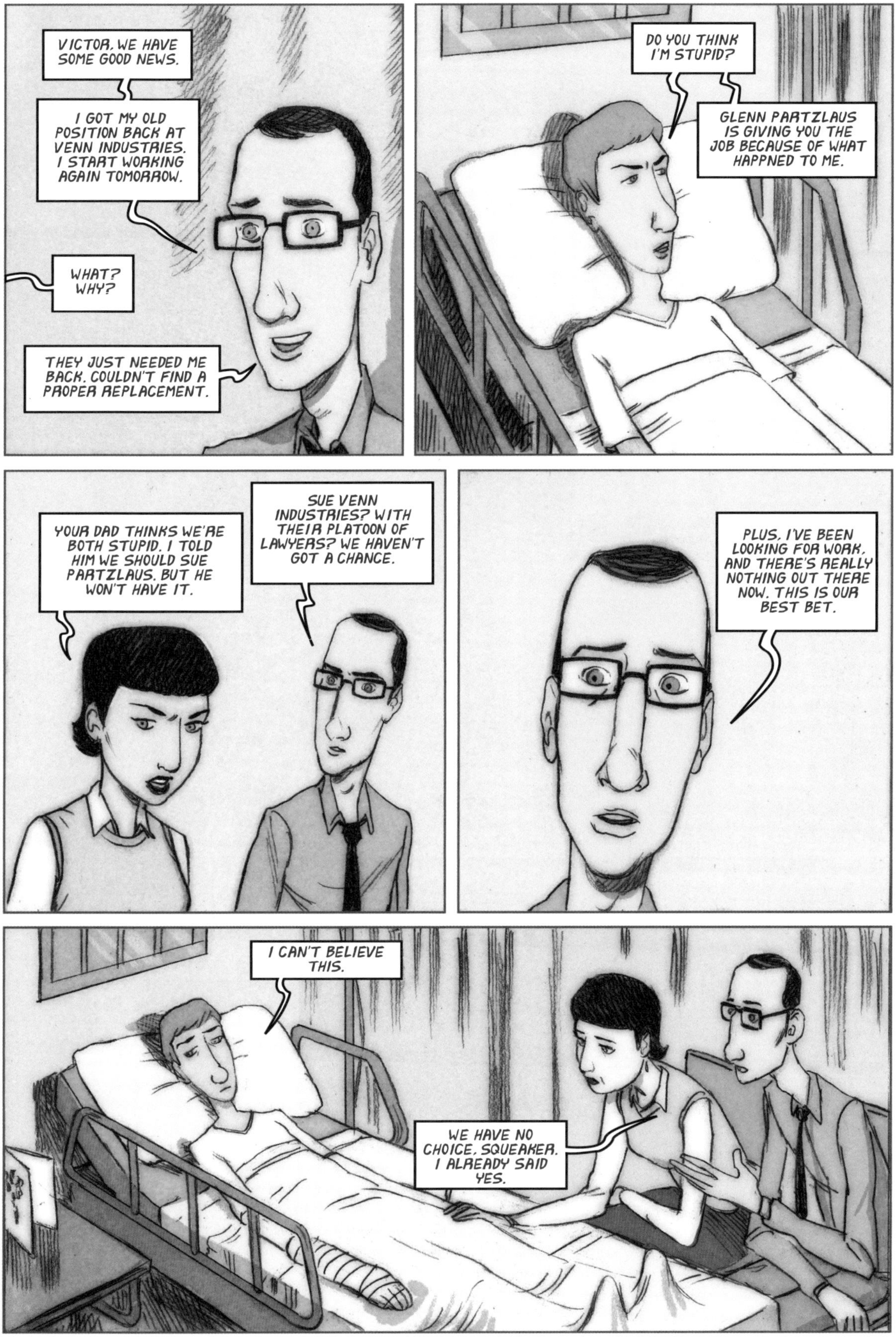
VICTOR, WE HAVE SOME GOOD NEWS.
I GOT MY OLD POSITION BACK AT VENN INDUSTRIES. I START WORKING AGAIN TOMORROW.
WHAT? WHY?
THEY JUST NEEDED ME BACK. COULDN'T FIND A PROPER REPLACEMENT.
DO YOU THINK I'M STUPID?
GLENN PARTZLAUS IS GIVING YOU THE JOB BECAUSE OF WHAT HAPPNED TO ME.
YOUR DAD THINKS WE'RE BOTH STUPID. I TOLD HIM WE SHOULD SUE PARTZLAUS. BUT HE WON'T HAVE IT.
SUE VENN INDUSTRIES? WITH THEIR PLATOON OF LAWYERS? WE HAVEN'T GOT A CHANCE.
PLUS, I'VE BEEN LOOKING FOR WORK, AND THERE'S REALLY NOTHING OUT THERE NOW. THIS IS OUR BEST BET.
I CAN'T BELIEVE THIS.
WE HAVE NO CHOICE, SQUEAKER. I ALREADY SAID YES.

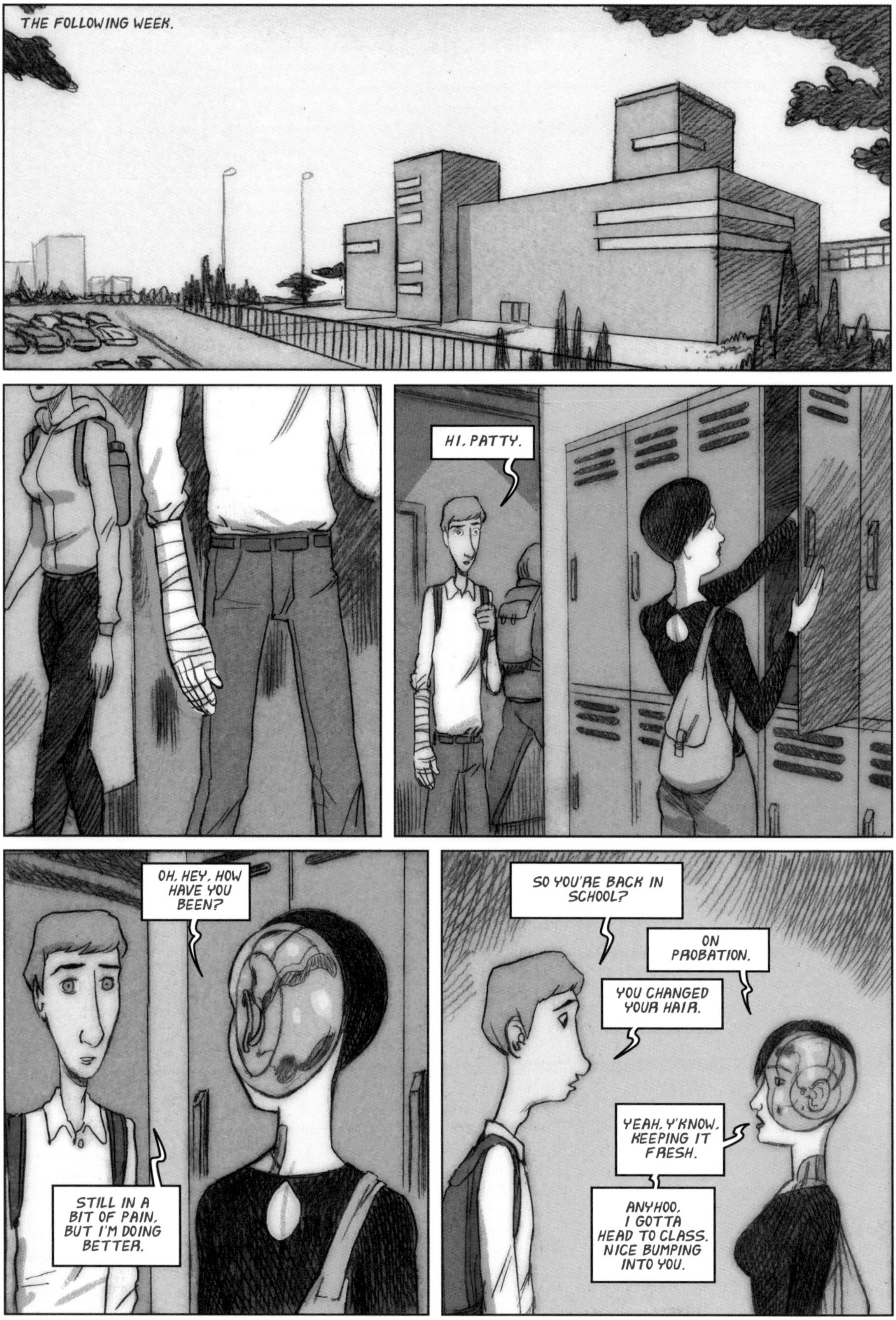
THE FOLLOWING WEEK.
HI, PATTY.
OH, HEY. HOW HAVE YOU BEEN?
STILL IN A BIT OF PAIN, BUT I'M DOING BETTER.
SO YOU'RE BACK IN SCHOOL?
ON PROBATION.
YOU CHANGED YOUR HAIR.
YEAH, Y'KNOW, KEEPING IT FRESH.
ANYHOO, I GOTTA HEAD TO CLASS. NICE BUMPING INTO YOU.

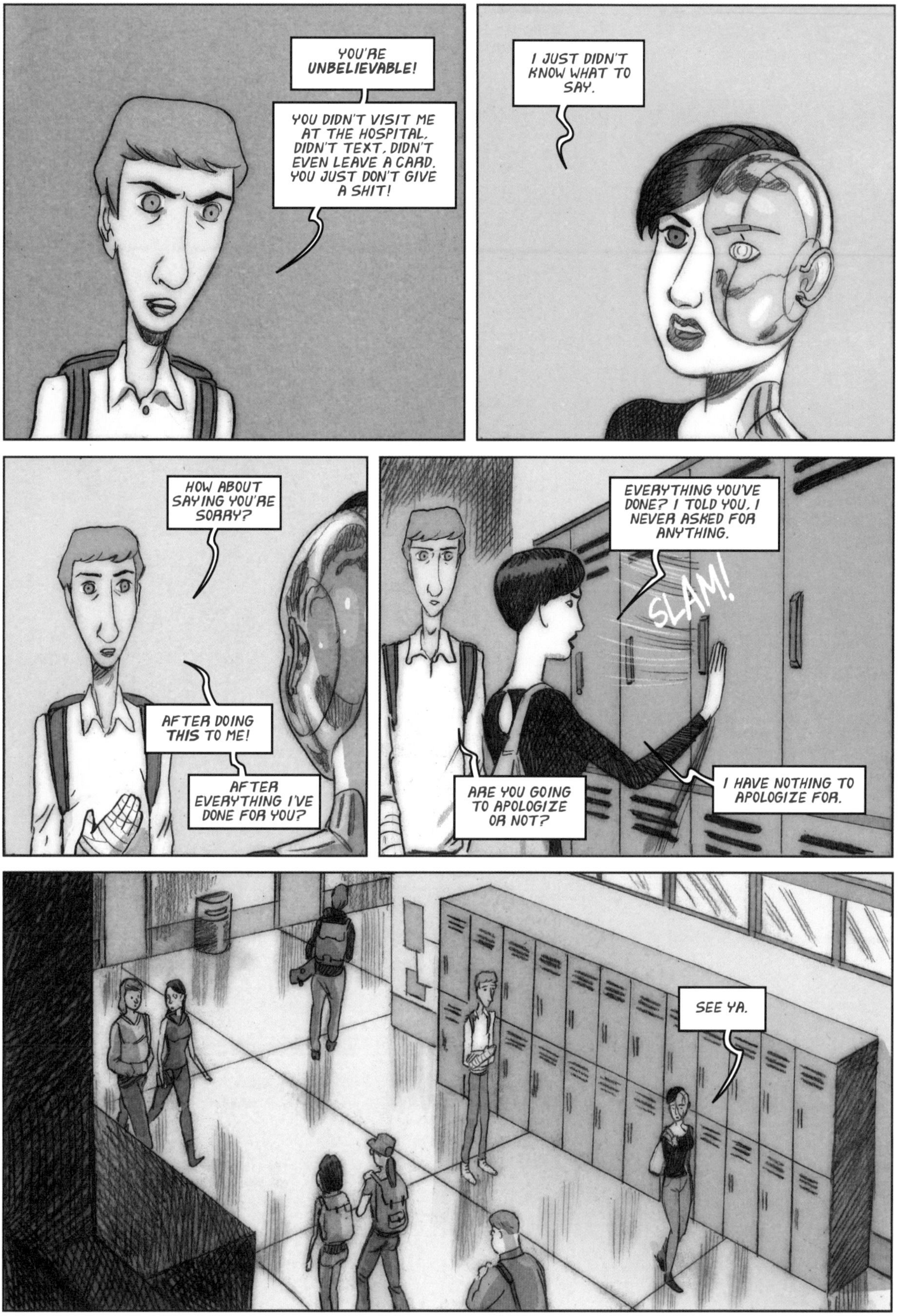
YOU'RE UNBELIEVABLE!
YOU DIDN'T VISIT ME AT THE HOSPITAL, DIDN'T TEXT, DIDN'T EVEN LEAVE A CARD. YOU JUST DON'T GIVE A SHIT!
I JUST DIDN'T KNOW WHAT TO SAY.
HOW ABOUT SAYING YOU'RE SORRY?
AFTER DOING THIS TO ME!
AFTER EVERYTHING I'VE DONE FOR YOU?
EVERYTHING YOU'VE DONE? I TOLD YOU, I NEVER ASKED FOR ANYTHING.
SLAM!
ARE YOU GOING TO APOLOGIZE OR NOT?
I HAVE NOTHING TO APOLOGIZE FOR.
SEE YA.

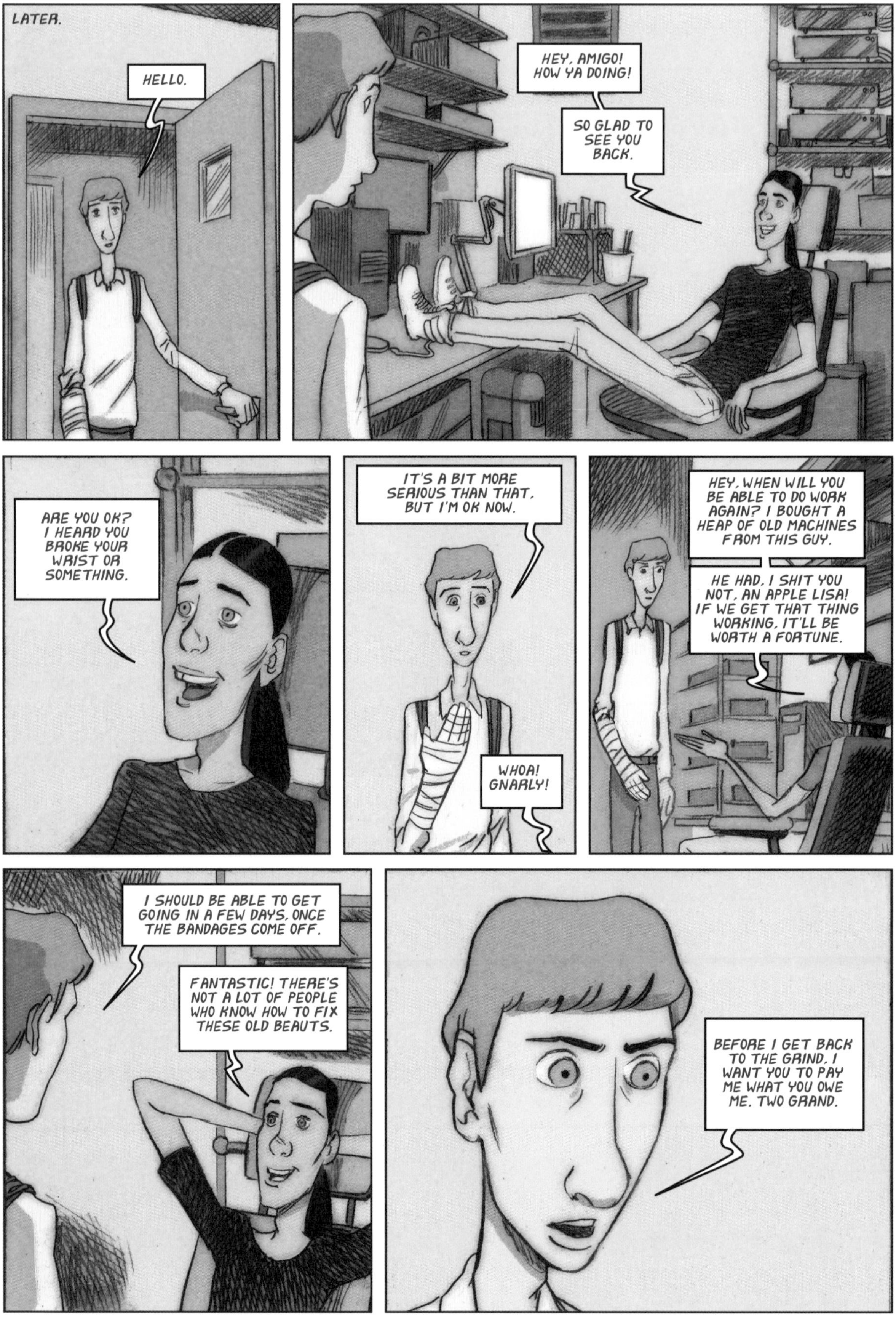
LATER.
HELLO.
HEY, AMIGO! HOW YA DOING!
SO GLAD TO SEE YOU BACK.
ARE YOU OK? I HEARD YOU BROKE YOUR WRIST OR SOMETHING.
IT'S A BIT MORE SERIOUS THAN THAT, BUT I'M OK NOW.
WHOA! GNARLY!
HEY, WHEN WILL YOU BE ABLE TO DO WORK AGAIN? I BOUGHT A HEAP OF OLD MACHINES FROM THIS GUY.
HE HAD, I SHIT YOU NOT, AN APPLE LISA! IF WE GET THAT THING WORKING, IT'LL BE WORTH A FORTUNE.
I SHOULD BE ABLE TO GET GOING IN A FEW DAYS, ONCE THE BANDAGES COME OFF.
FANTASTIC! THERE'S NOT A LOT OF PEOPLE WHO KNOW HOW TO FIX THESE OLD BEAUTS.
BEFORE I GET BACK TO THE GRIND, I WANT YOU TO PAY ME WHAT YOU OWE ME. TWO GRAND.

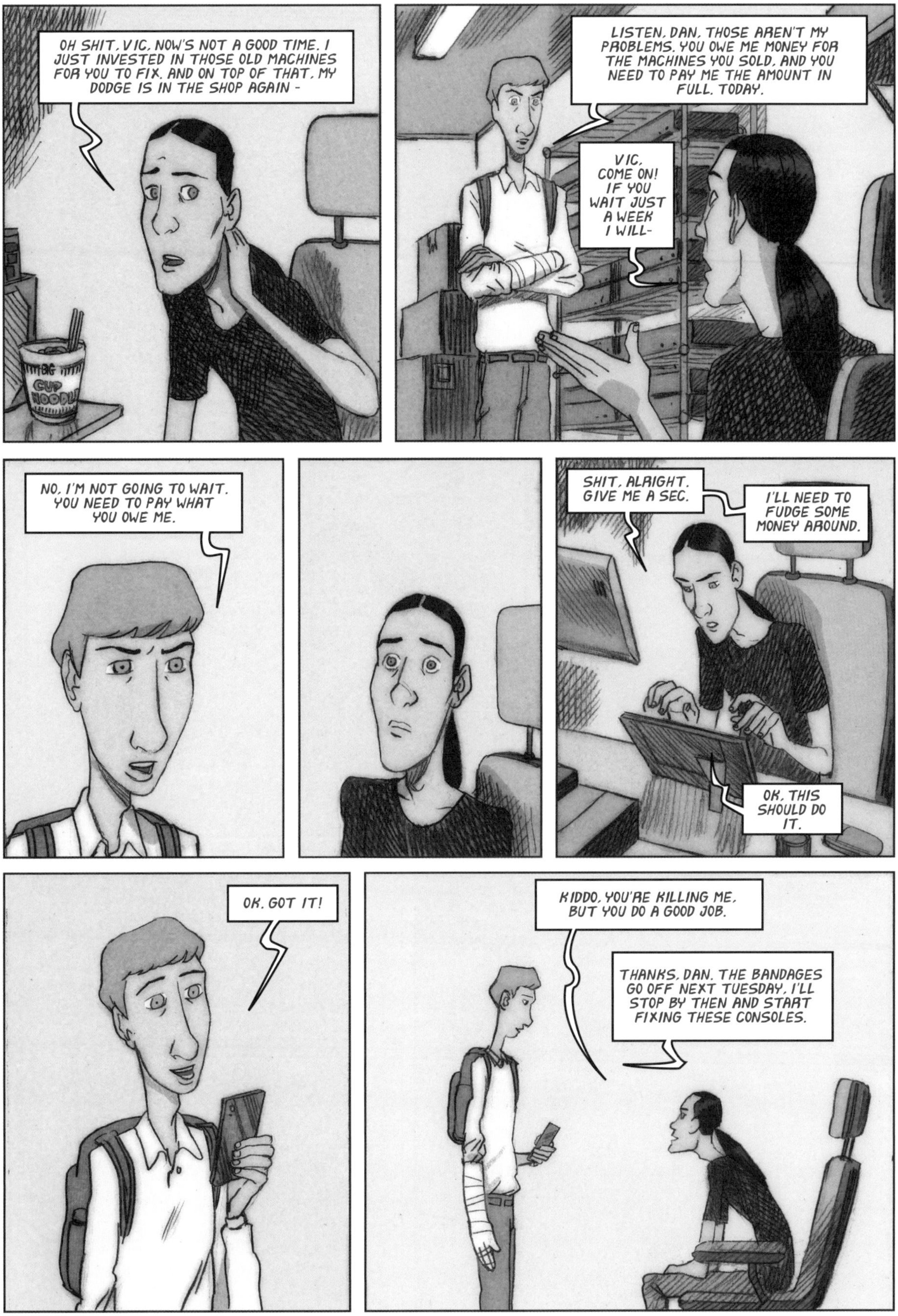
OH SHIT, VIC, NOW'S NOT A GOOD TIME. I JUST INVESTED IN THOSE OLD MACHINES FOR YOU TO FIX. AND ON TOP OF THAT, MY DODGE IS IN THE SHOP AGAIN -
LISTEN, DAN, THOSE AREN'T MY PROBLEMS. YOU OWE ME MONEY FOR THE MACHINES YOU SOLD, AND YOU NEED TO PAY ME THE AMOUNT IN FULL. TODAY.
VIC, COME ON! IF YOU WAIT JUST A WEEK I WILL-
NO, I'M NOT GOING TO WAIT. YOU NEED TO PAY WHAT YOU OWE ME.
SHIT, ALRIGHT. GIVE ME A SEC.
I'LL NEED TO FUDGE SOME MONEY AROUND.
OK, THIS SHOULD DO IT.
OK, GOT IT!
KIDDO, YOU'RE KILLING ME, BUT YOU DO A GOOD JOB.
THANKS, DAN. THE BANDAGES GO OFF NEXT TUESDAY, I'LL STOP BY THEN AND START FIXING THESE CONSOLES.

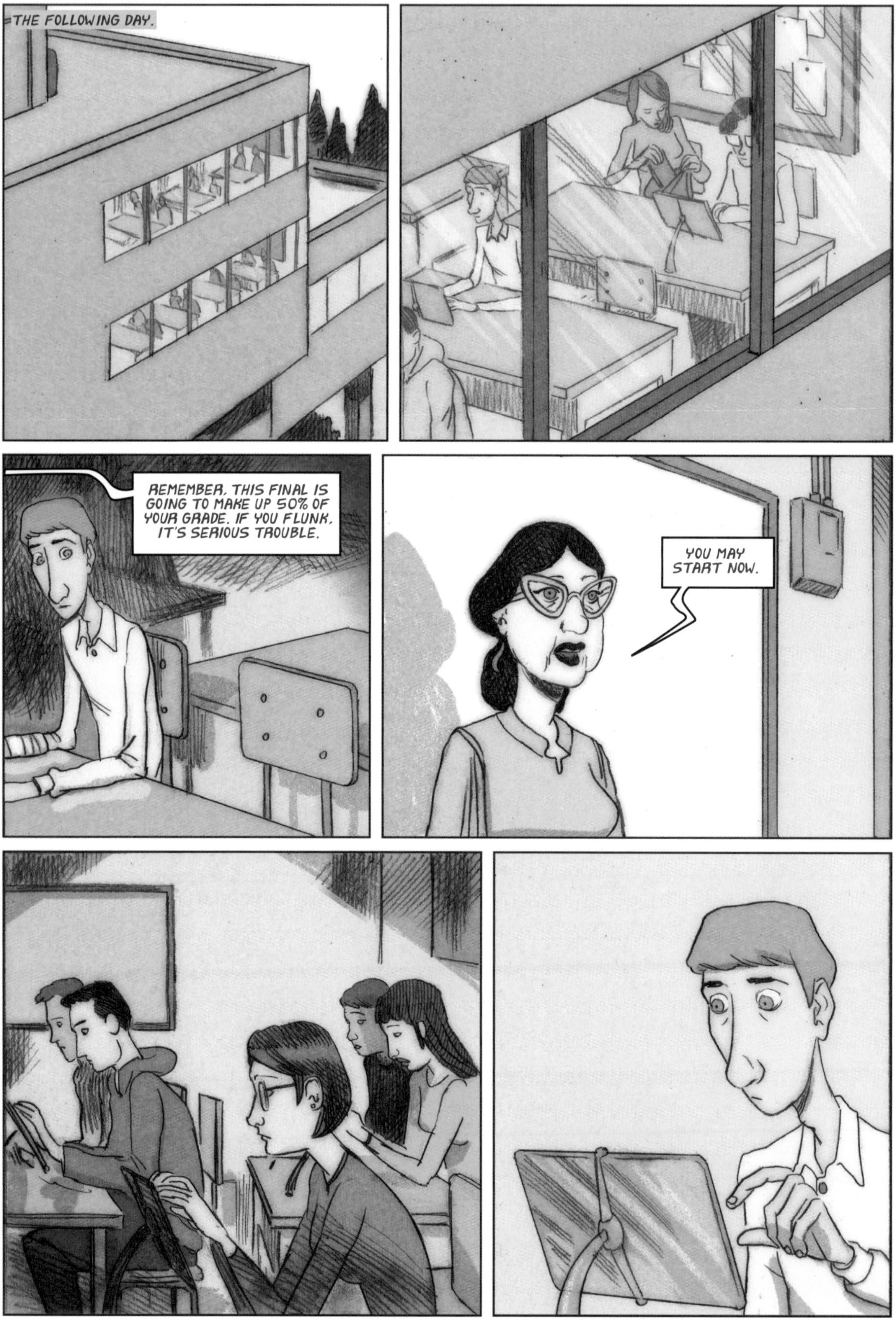
THE FOLLOWING DAY.
REMEMBER, THIS FINAL IS GOING TO MAKE UP 50% OF YOUR GRADE. IF YOU FLUNK, IT'S SERIOUS TROUBLE.
YOU MAY START NOW.

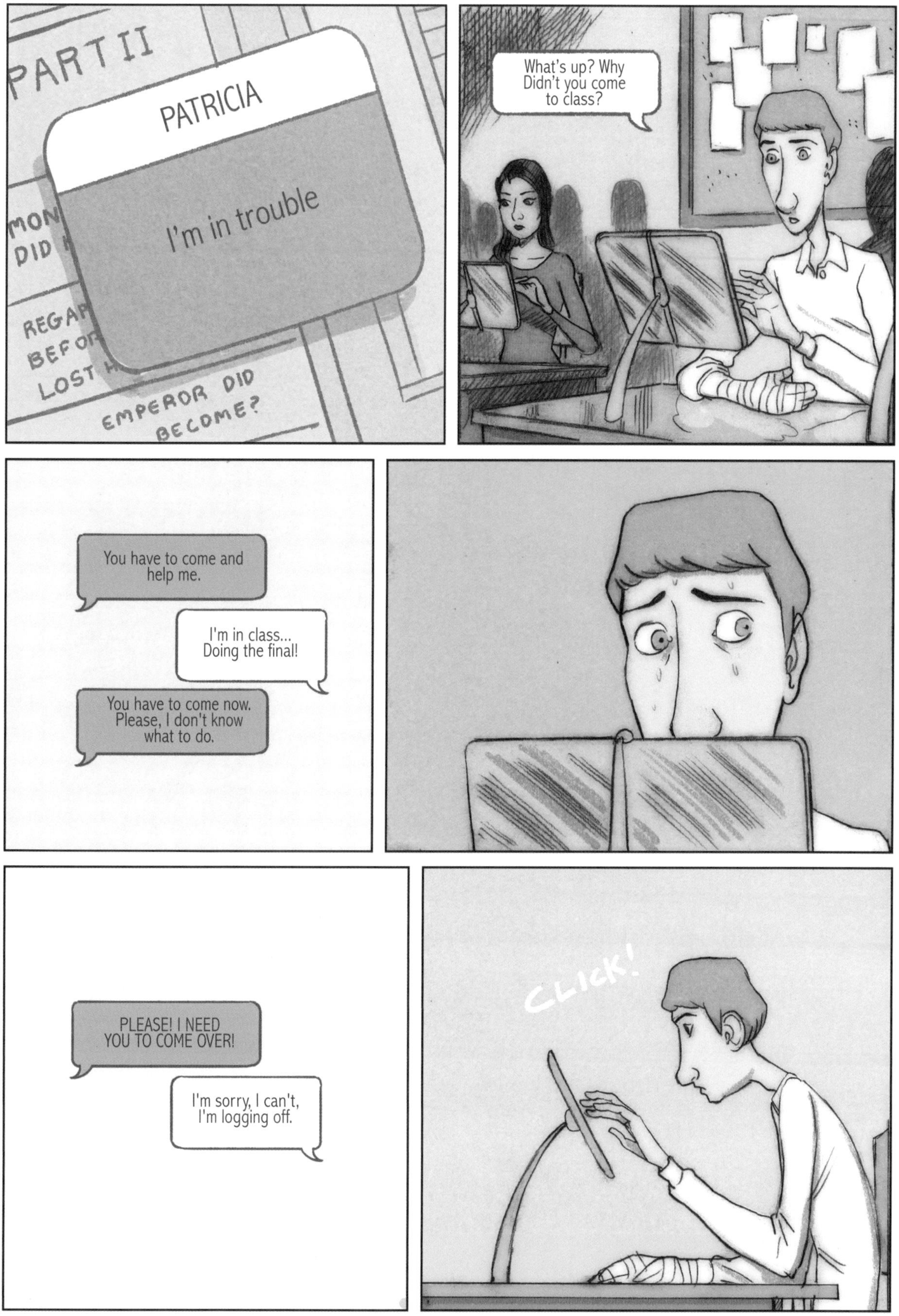
PART II
PATRICIA
I'm in trouble
EMPEROR DID
BECOME?
What's up? Why Didn't you come to class?
You have to come and help me.
I'm in class... Doing the final!
You have to come now. Please, I don't know what to do.
PLEASE! I NEED YOU TO COME OVER!
I'm sorry, I can't, I'm logging off.
CLICK!

THAT EVENING.

HEY, VICTOR.

HEY, GUYS, HOW WAS THERAPY?

APPERANTLY I'M EMOTIONALLY UNAVAILABLE AND OUT OF TOUCH WITH MYSELF!

THE TRUTH HURTS, DOESN'T IT?

DING!

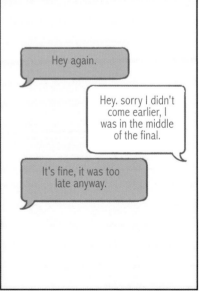

Hey again.

Hey. sorry I didn't come earlier, I was in the middle of the final.

It's fine, it was too late anyway.

Too late for what?
Watt. He died.
He... died?
Yeah, I... I thought it was my fault at first, I wasn't paying enough attention...
but it was some malfunction... the bionic part suddenly started being rejected by the rest of his body.
I... I'm so sorry.
I'm sorry too. I know you loved him. You took good care of him... Thank you for thatt
Poor watt...
I'm doing a little funeral in the back yard. Do you want to come?

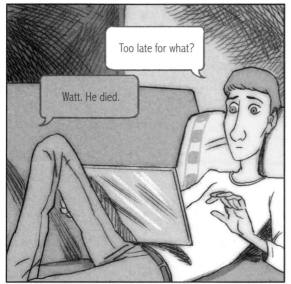

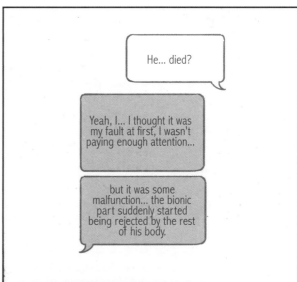

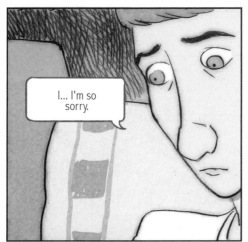

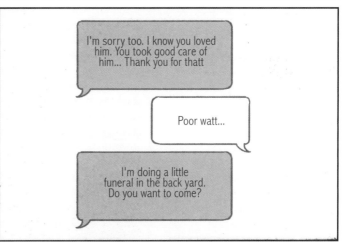

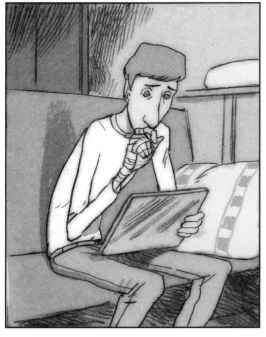

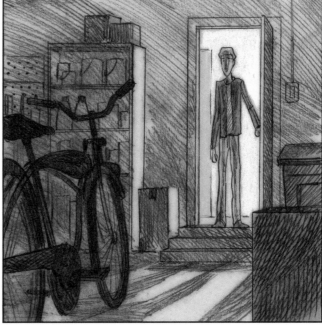

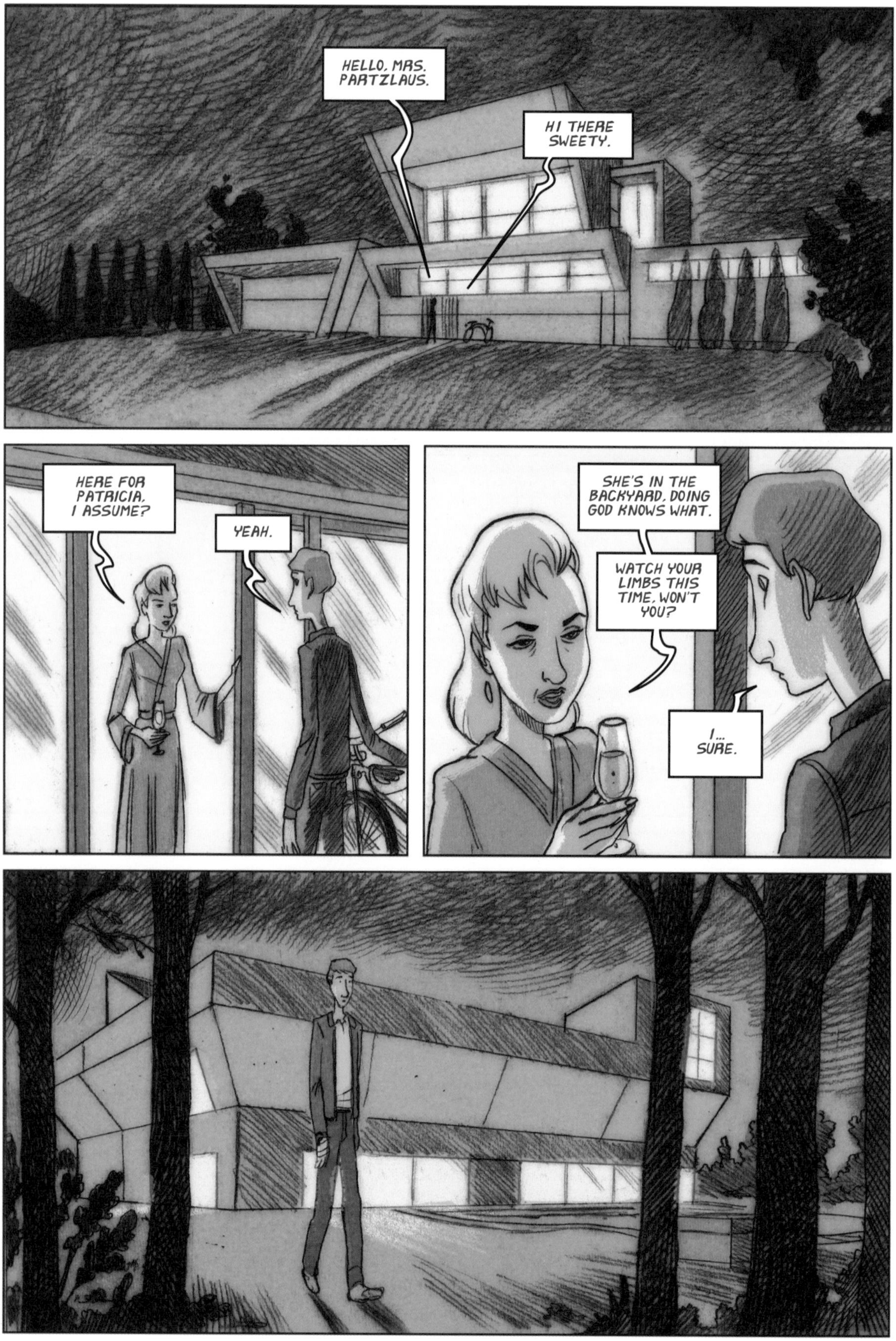
HELLO, MRS. PARTZLAUS.
HI THERE SWEETY.
HERE FOR PATRICIA, I ASSUME?
YEAH.
SHE'S IN THE BACKYARD, DOING GOD KNOWS WHAT.
WATCH YOUR LIMBS THIS TIME, WON'T YOU?
I... SURE.

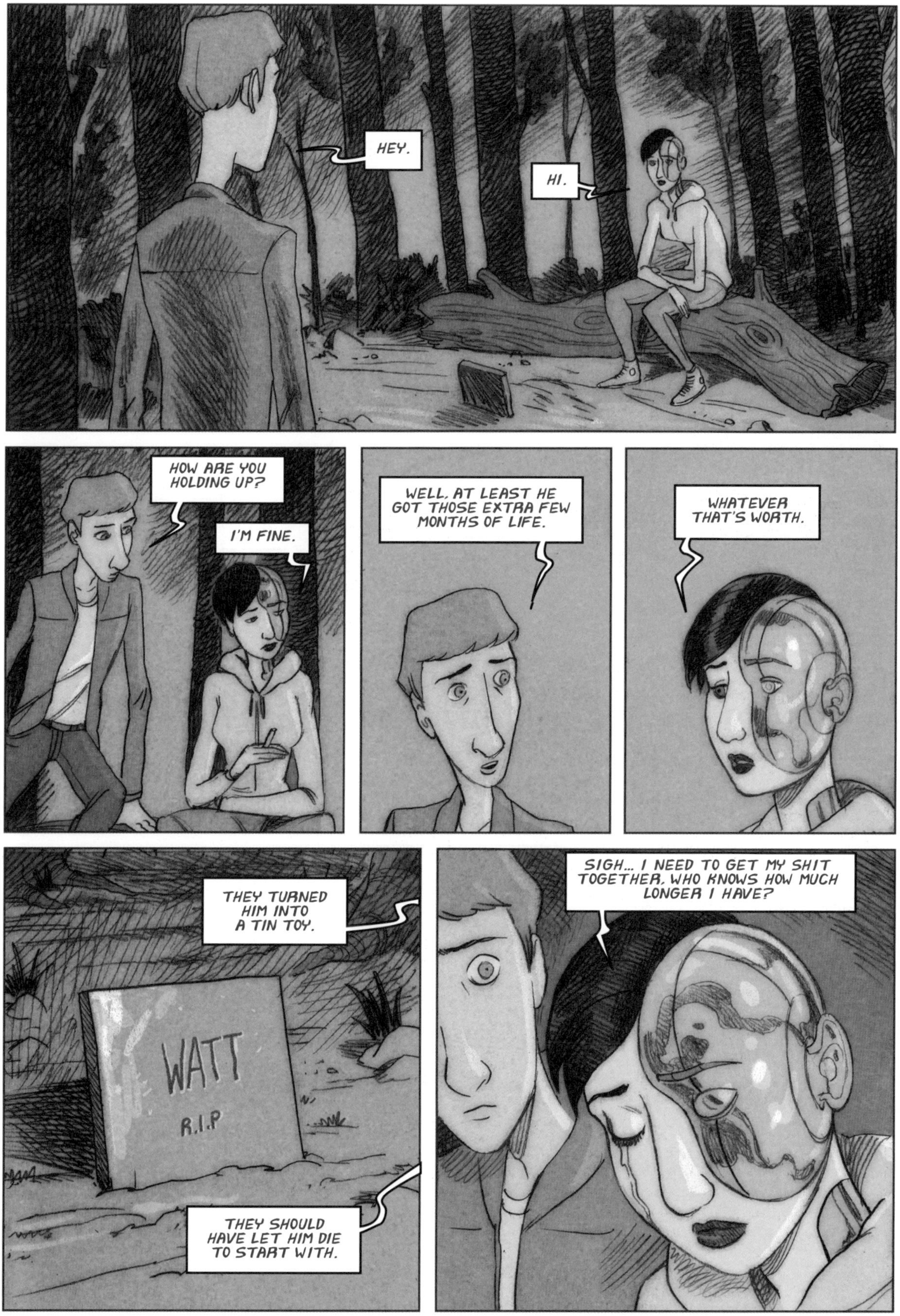
HEY.
HI.
HOW ARE YOU HOLDING UP?
I'M FINE.
WELL, AT LEAST HE GOT THOSE EXTRA FEW MONTHS OF LIFE.
WHATEVER THAT'S WORTH.
THEY TURNED HIM INTO A TIN TOY.
WATT
R.I.P
THEY SHOULD HAVE LET HIM DIE TO START WITH.
SIGH... I NEED TO GET MY SHIT TOGETHER. WHO KNOWS HOW MUCH LONGER I HAVE?

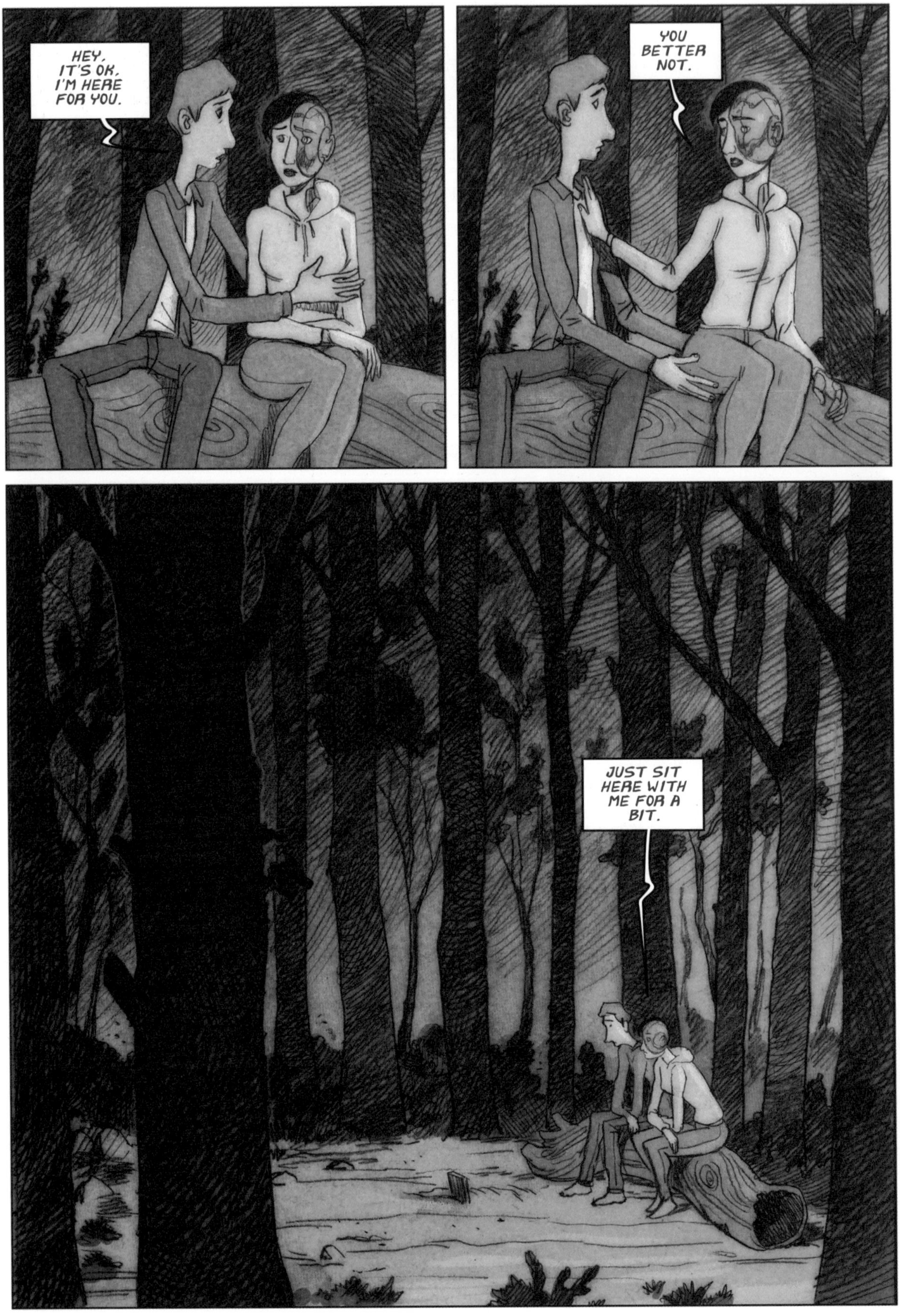
HEY, IT'S OK, I'M HERE FOR YOU.
YOU BETTER NOT.
JUST SIT HERE WITH ME FOR A BIT.

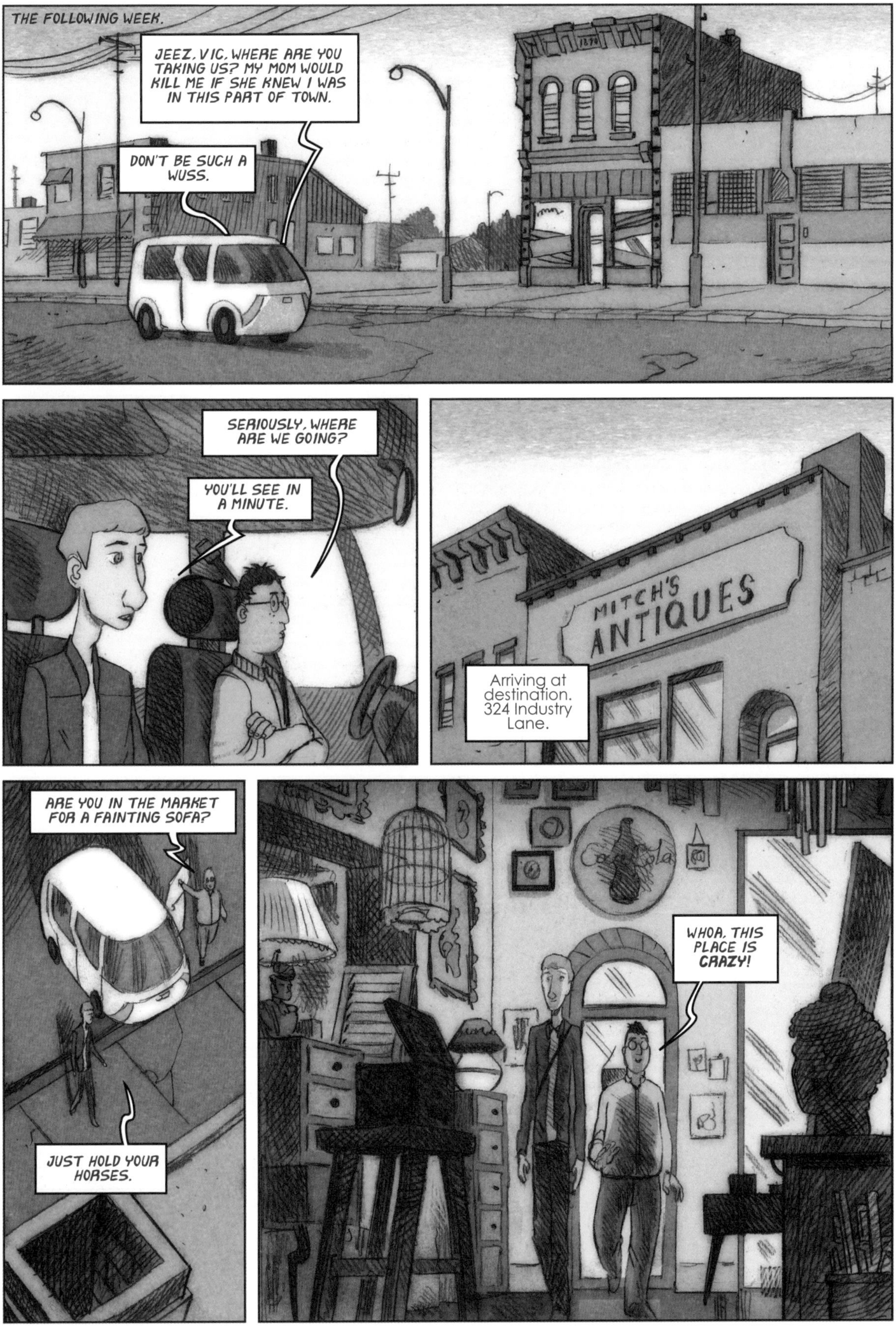
THE FOLLOWING WEEK.
JEEZ, VIC, WHERE ARE YOU TAKING US? MY MOM WOULD KILL ME IF SHE KNEW I WAS IN THIS PART OF TOWN.
DON'T BE SUCH A WUSS.
SERIOUSLY, WHERE ARE WE GOING?
YOU'LL SEE IN A MINUTE.
MITCH'S ANTIQUES
Arriving at destination. 324 Industry Lane.
ARE YOU IN THE MARKET FOR A FAINTING SOFA?
JUST HOLD YOUR HORSES.
WHOA, THIS PLACE IS CRAZY!

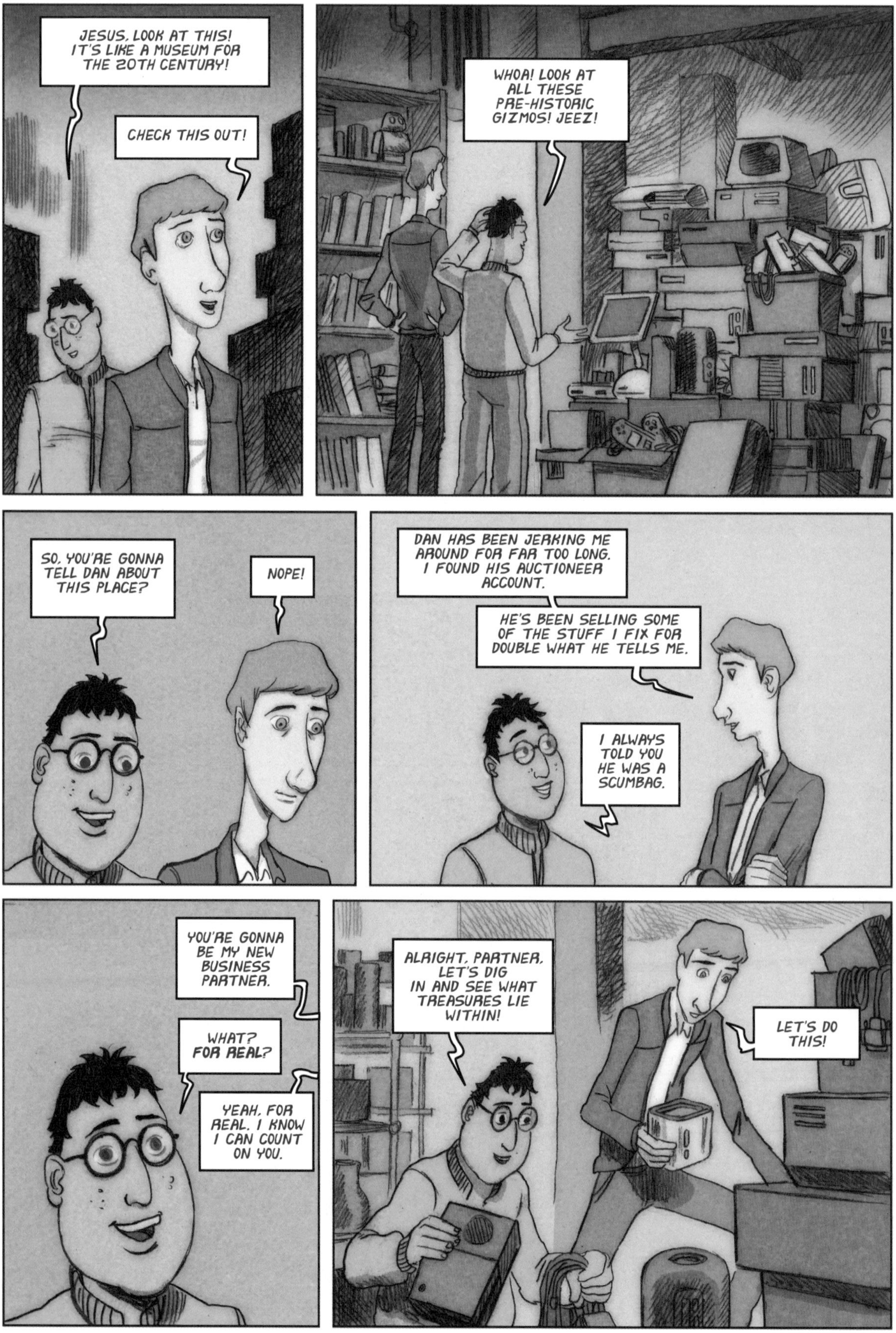
JESUS, LOOK AT THIS! IT'S LIKE A MUSEUM FOR THE 20TH CENTURY!
CHECK THIS OUT!
WHOA! LOOK AT ALL THESE PRE-HISTORIC GIZMOS! JEEZ!
SO, YOU'RE GONNA TELL DAN ABOUT THIS PLACE?
NOPE!
DAN HAS BEEN JERKING ME AROUND FOR FAR TOO LONG. I FOUND HIS AUCTIONEER ACCOUNT.
HE'S BEEN SELLING SOME OF THE STUFF I FIX FOR DOUBLE WHAT HE TELLS ME.
I ALWAYS TOLD YOU HE WAS A SCUMBAG.
YOU'RE GONNA BE MY NEW BUSINESS PARTNER.
WHAT? FOR REAL?
YEAH, FOR REAL. I KNOW I CAN COUNT ON YOU.
ALRIGHT, PARTNER, LET'S DIG IN AND SEE WHAT TREASURES LIE WITHIN!
LET'S DO THIS!

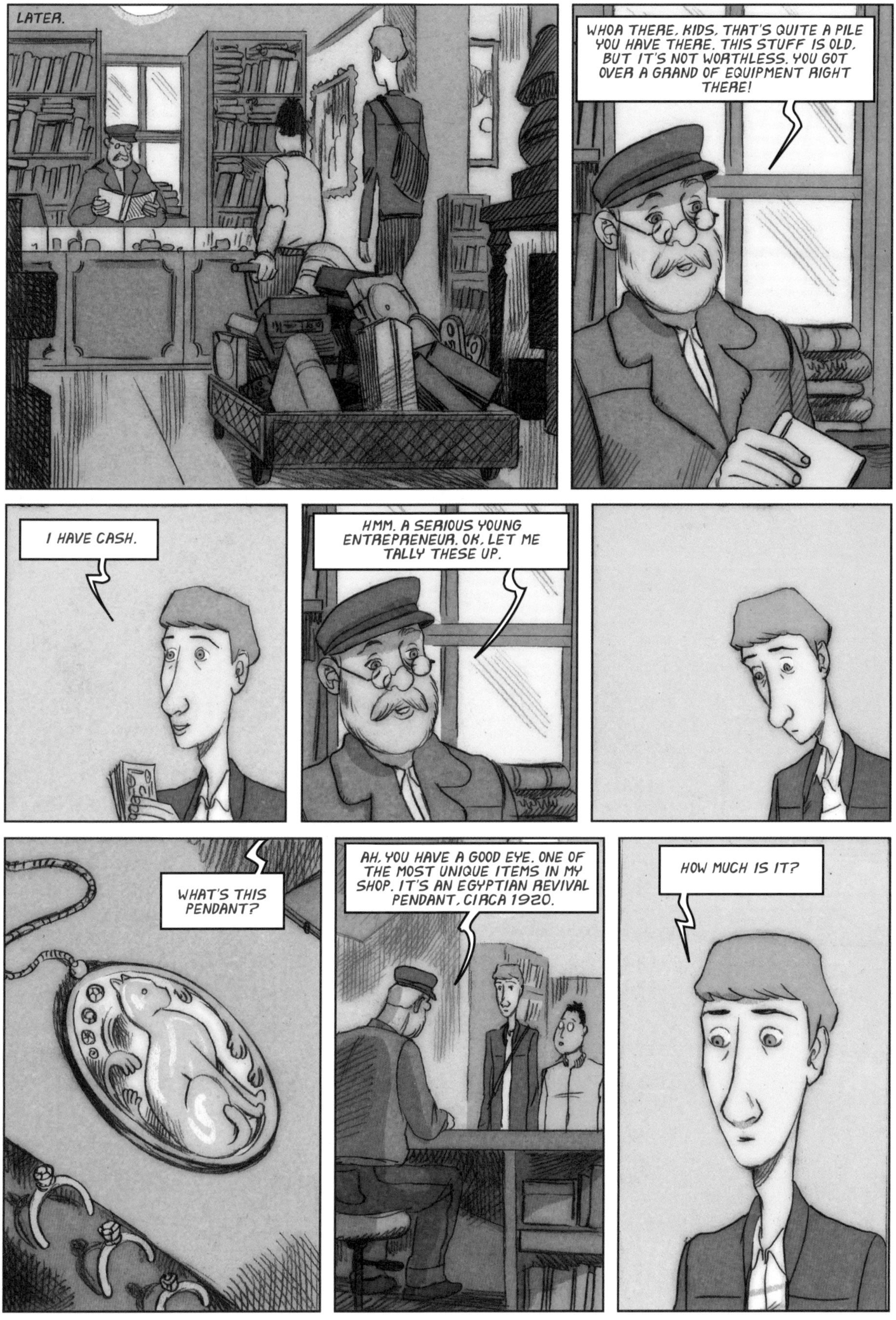
LATER.
WHOA THERE, KIDS, THAT'S QUITE A PILE YOU HAVE THERE. THIS STUFF IS OLD, BUT IT'S NOT WORTHLESS. YOU GOT OVER A GRAND OF EQUIPMENT RIGHT THERE!
I HAVE CASH.
HMM. A SERIOUS YOUNG ENTREPRENEUR. OK, LET ME TALLY THESE UP.
WHAT'S THIS PENDANT?
AH, YOU HAVE A GOOD EYE. ONE OF THE MOST UNIQUE ITEMS IN MY SHOP. IT'S AN EGYPTIAN REVIVAL PENDANT, CIRCA 1920.
HOW MUCH IS IT?

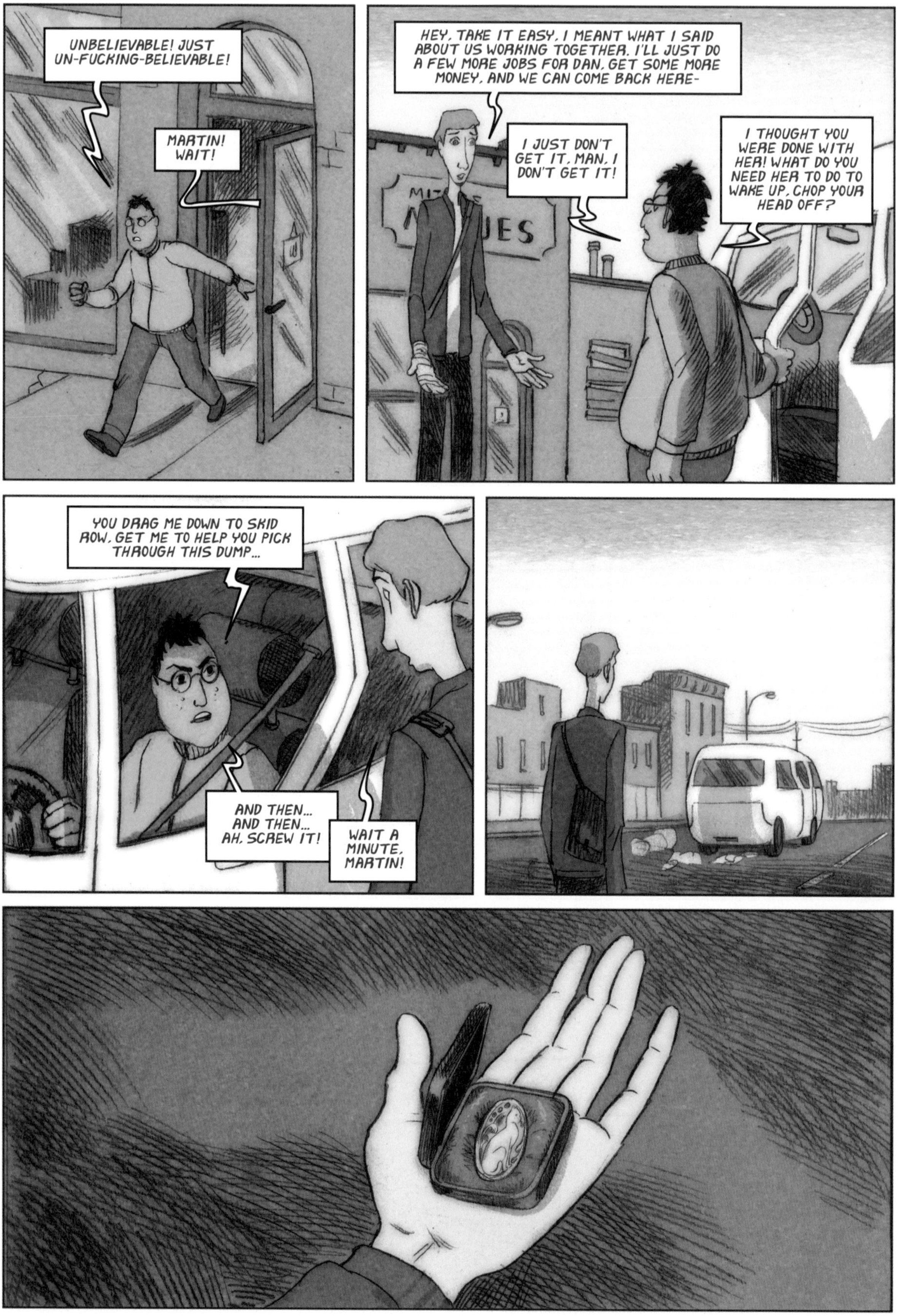
UNBELIEVABLE! JUST UN-FUCKING-BELIEVABLE!
MARTIN! WAIT!
HEY, TAKE IT EASY, I MEANT WHAT I SAID ABOUT US WORKING TOGETHER. I'LL JUST DO A FEW MORE JOBS FOR DAN, GET SOME MORE MONEY, AND WE CAN COME BACK HERE-
I JUST DON'T GET IT, MAN, I DON'T GET IT!
I THOUGHT YOU WERE DONE WITH HER! WHAT DO YOU NEED HER TO DO TO WAKE UP, CHOP YOUR HEAD OFF?
YOU DRAG ME DOWN TO SKID ROW, GET ME TO HELP YOU PICK THROUGH THIS DUMP...
AND THEN... AND THEN... AH, SCREW IT!
WAIT A MINUTE, MARTIN!

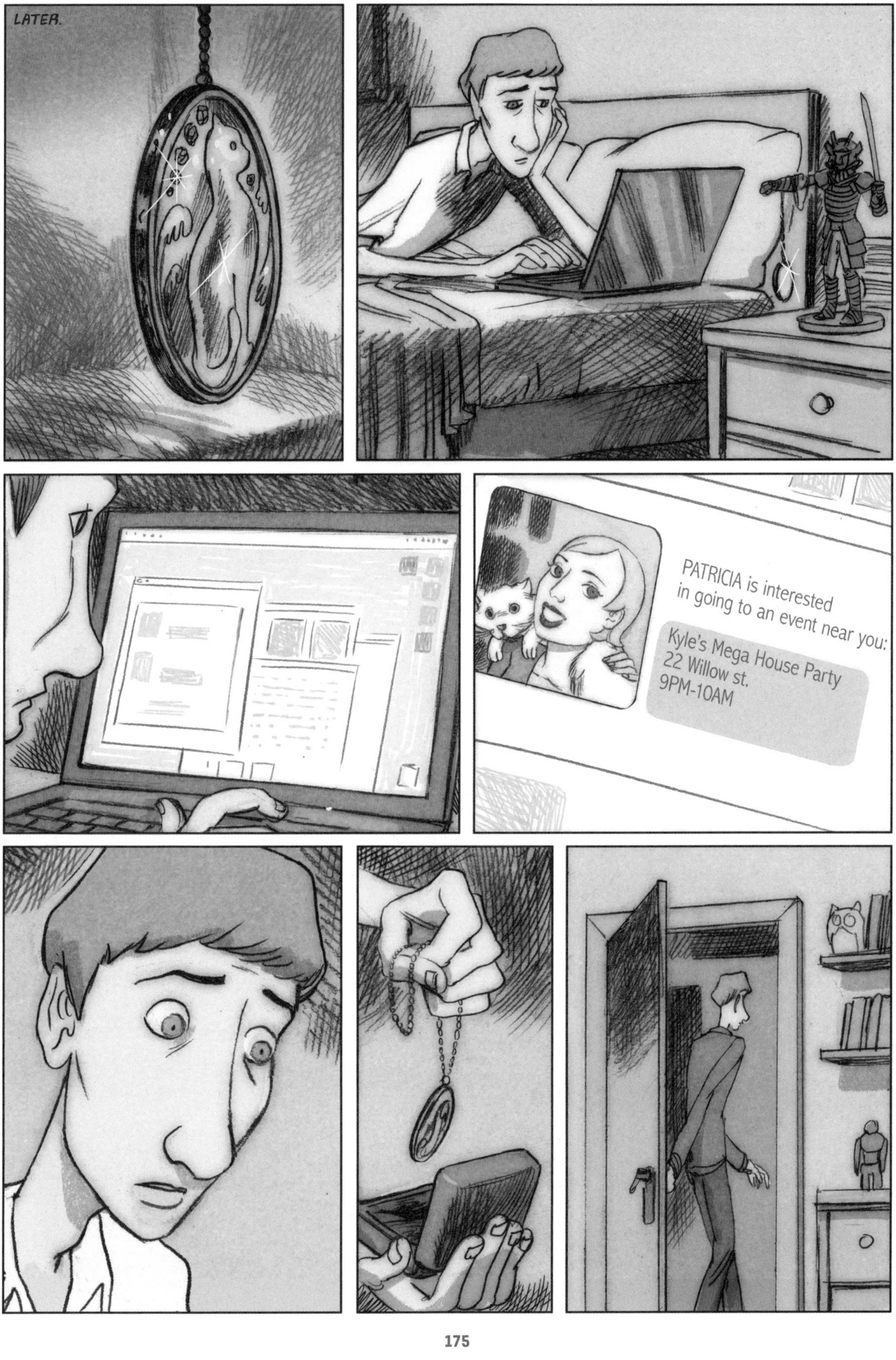
LATER.
PATRICIA is interested in going to an event near you:
Kyle's Mega House Party
22 Willow st.
9PM-10AM

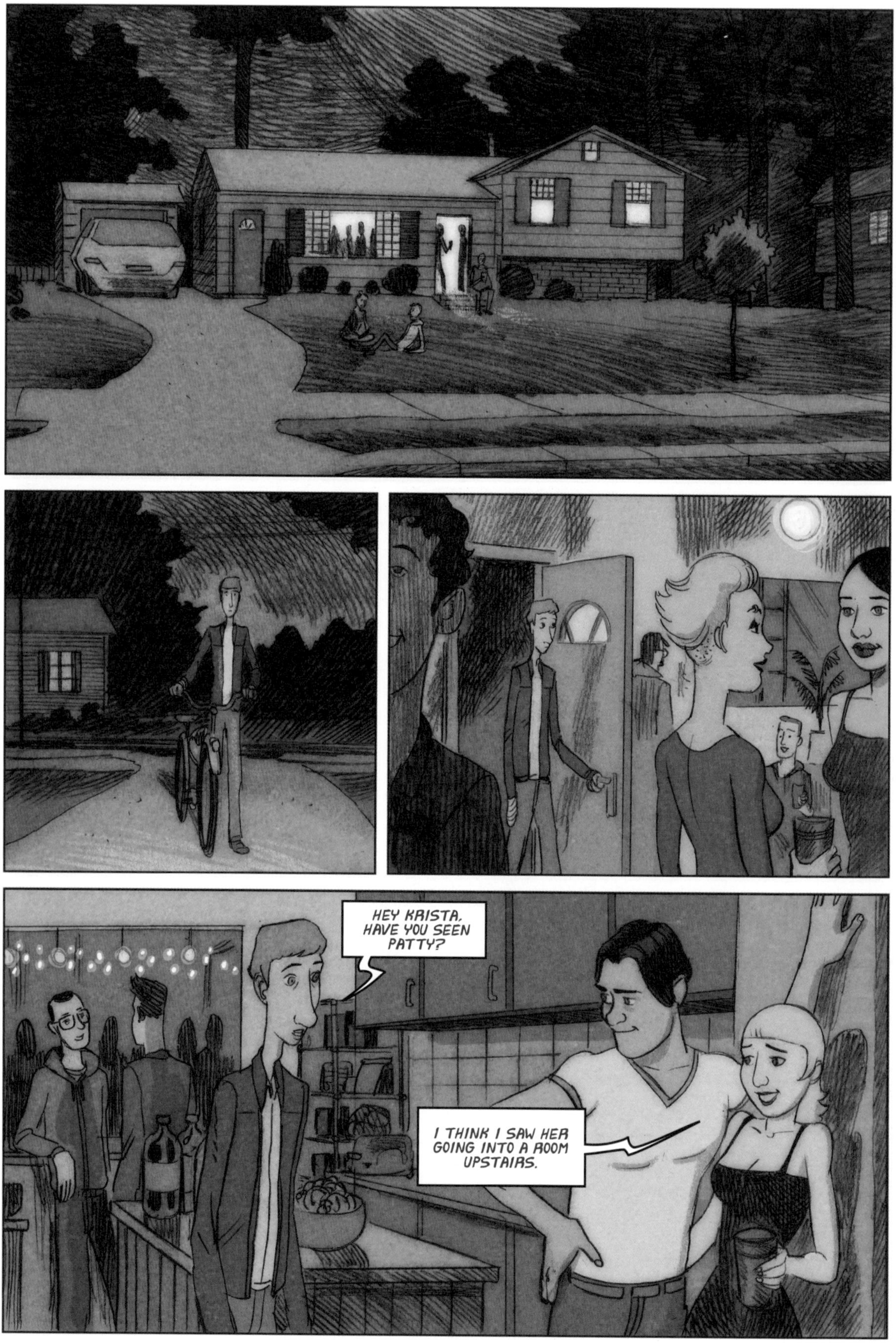
HEY KRISTA. HAVE YOU SEEN PATTY?
I THINK I SAW HER GOING INTO A ROOM UPSTAIRS.

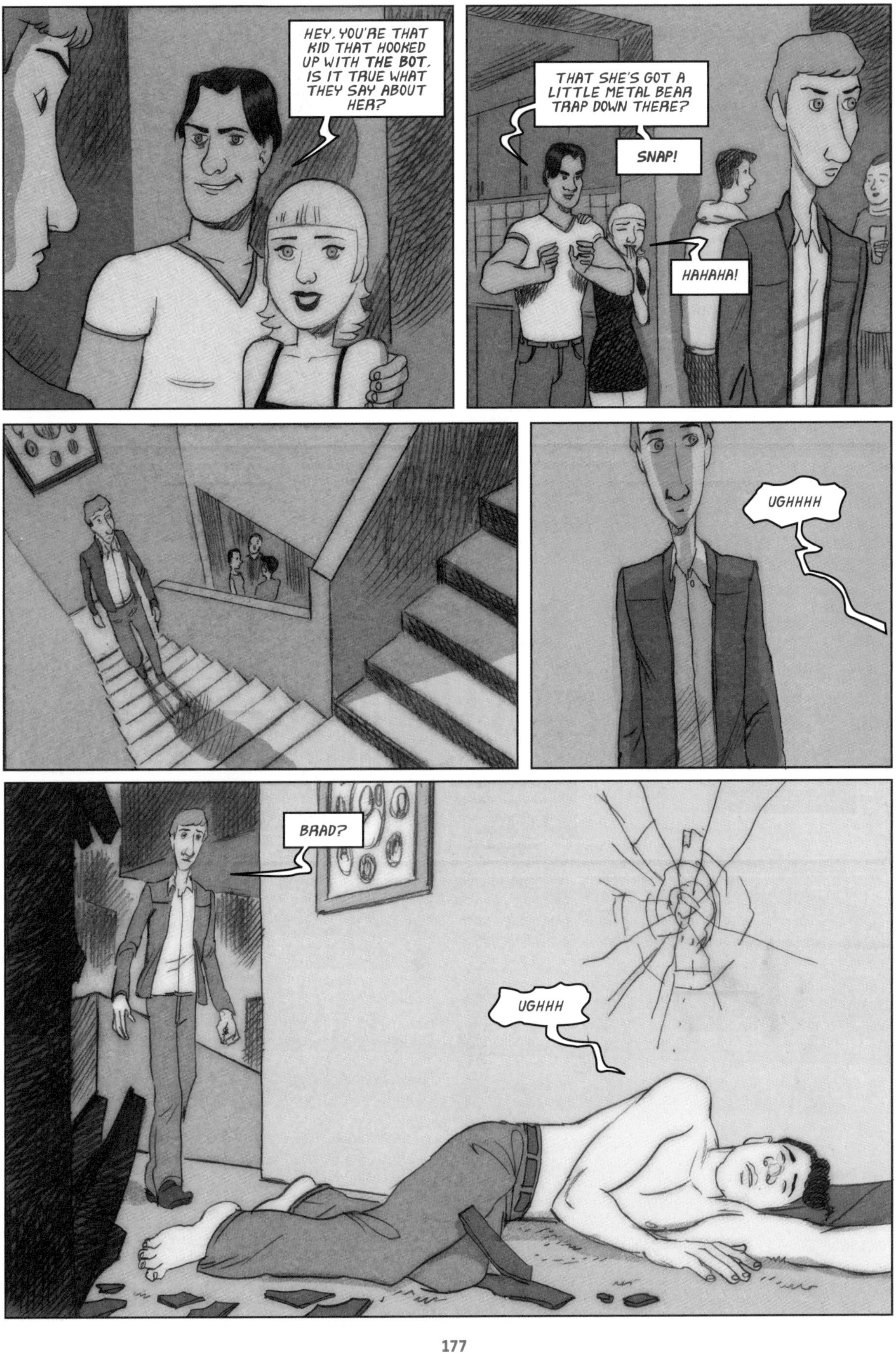
HEY, YOU'RE THAT KID THAT HOOKED UP WITH THE BOT, IS IT TRUE WHAT THEY SAY ABOUT HER?
THAT SHE'S GOT A LITTLE METAL BEAR TRAP DOWN THERE?
SNAP!
HAHAHA!
UGHHHH
BRAD?
UGHHH

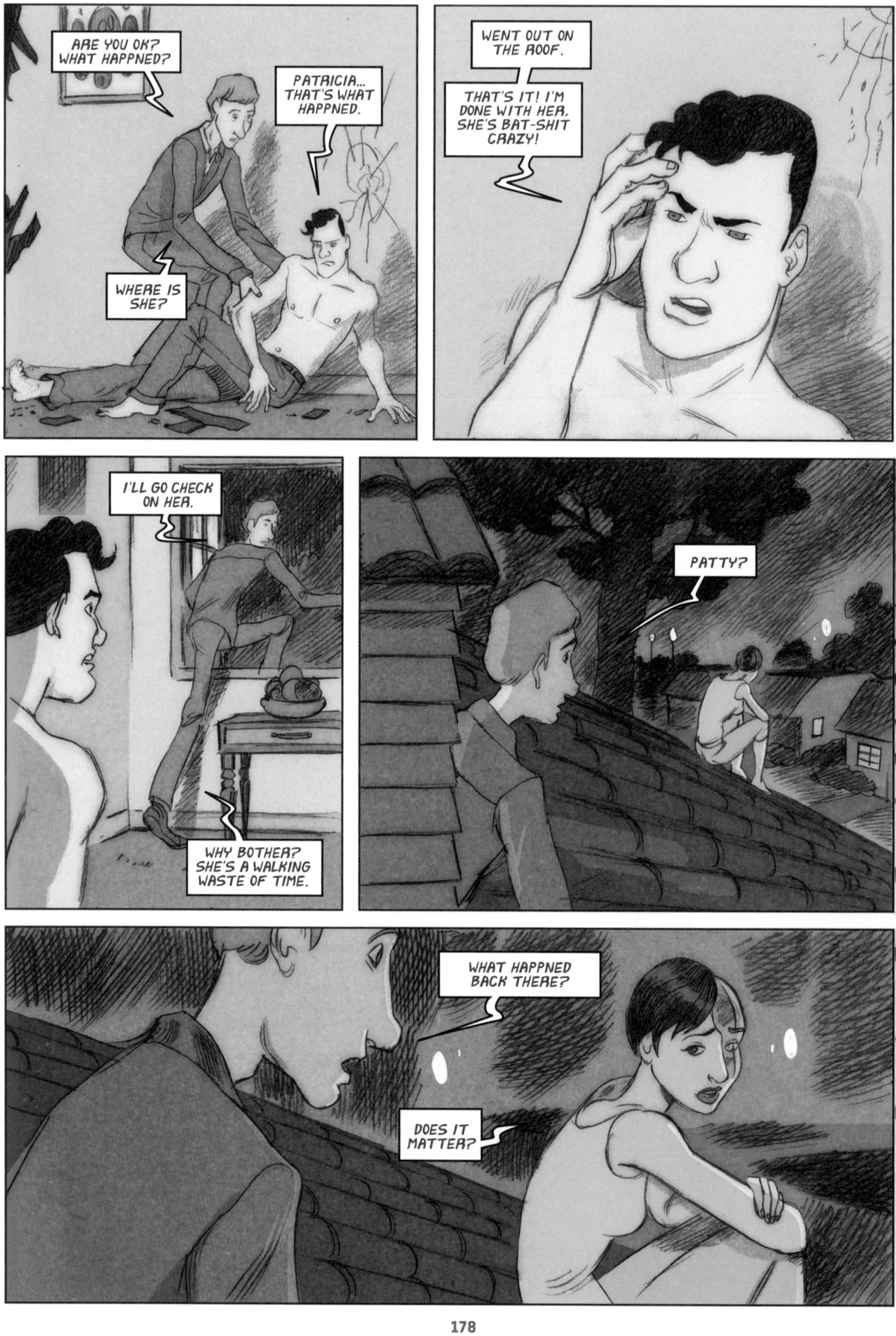
ARE YOU OK? WHAT HAPPNED?
PATRICIA... THAT'S WHAT HAPPNED.
WHERE IS SHE?
WENT OUT ON THE ROOF.
THAT'S IT! I'M DONE WITH HER. SHE'S BAT-SHIT CRAZY!
I'LL GO CHECK ON HER.
WHY BOTHER? SHE'S A WALKING WASTE OF TIME.
PATTY?
WHAT HAPPNED BACK THERE?
DOES IT MATTER?

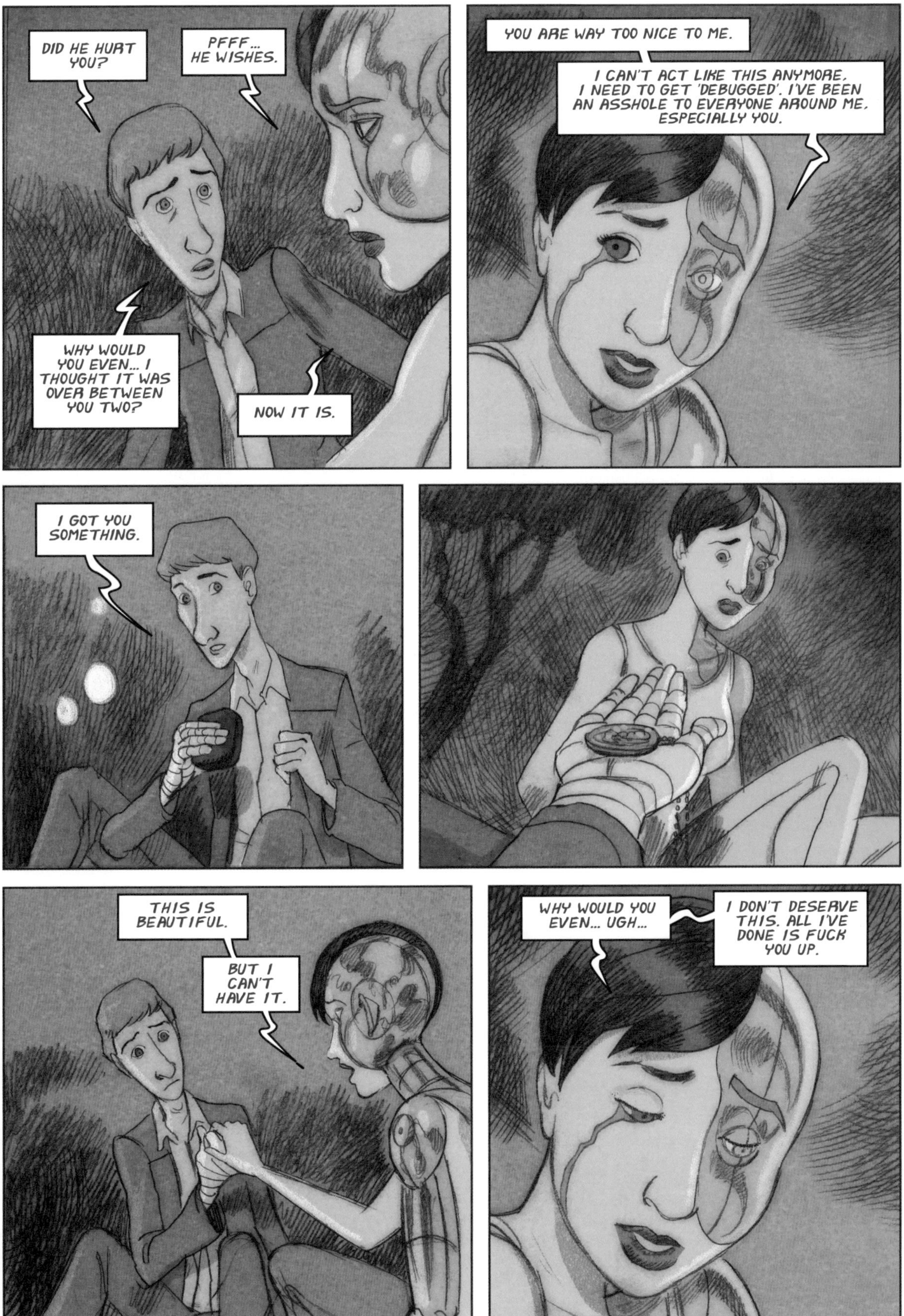
DID HE HURT YOU?
PFFF... HE WISHES.
WHY WOULD YOU EVEN... I THOUGHT IT WAS OVER BETWEEN YOU TWO?
NOW IT IS.
YOU ARE WAY TOO NICE TO ME.
I CAN'T ACT LIKE THIS ANYMORE, I NEED TO GET 'DEBUGGED'. I'VE BEEN AN ASSHOLE TO EVERYONE AROUND ME, ESPECIALLY YOU.
I GOT YOU SOMETHING.
THIS IS BEAUTIFUL.
BUT I CAN'T HAVE IT.
WHY WOULD YOU EVEN... UGH...
I DON'T DESERVE THIS. ALL I'VE DONE IS FUCK YOU UP.

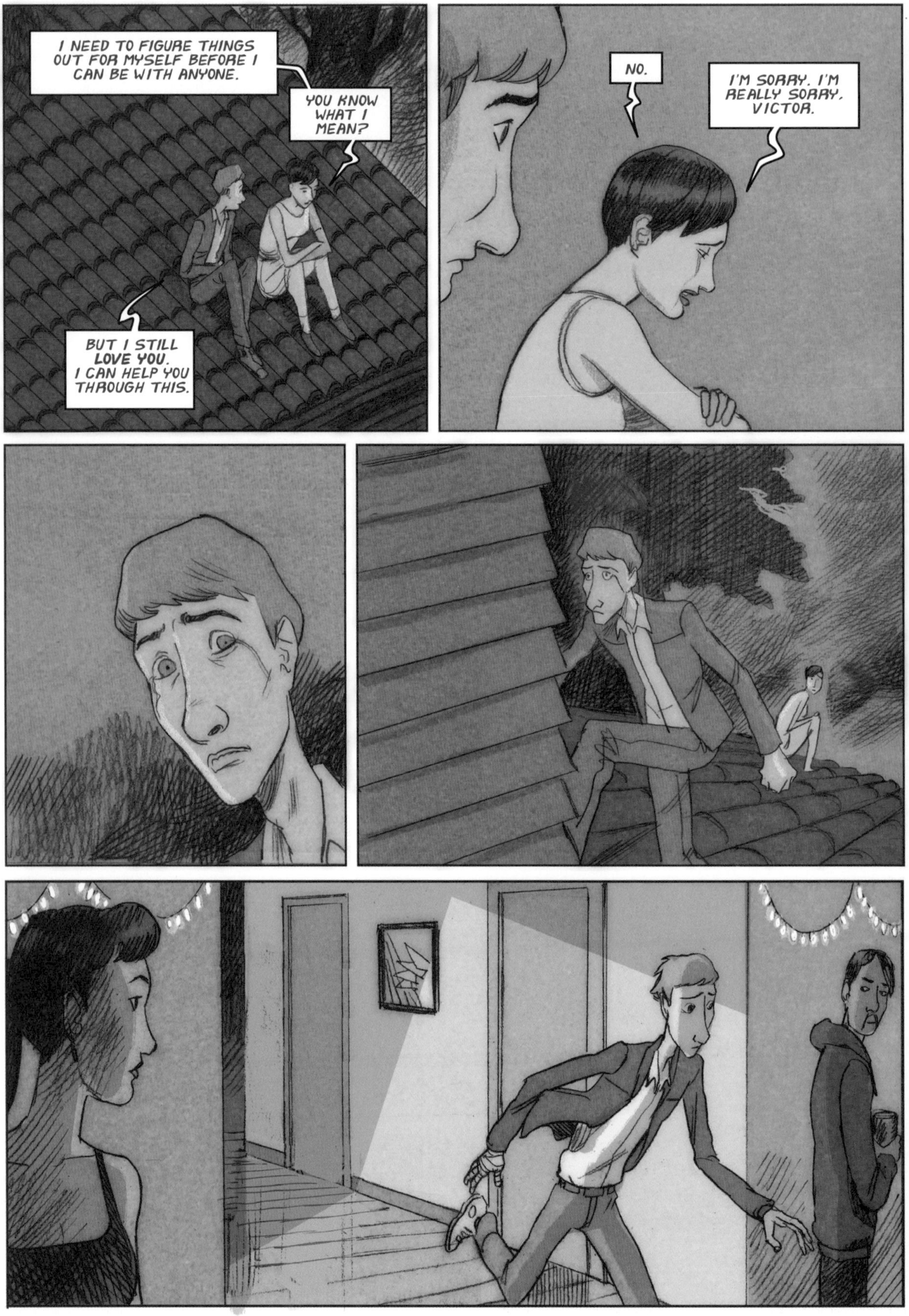
I NEED TO FIGURE THINGS OUT FOR MYSELF BEFORE I CAN BE WITH ANYONE.
YOU KNOW WHAT I MEAN?
BUT I STILL LOVE YOU. I CAN HELP YOU THROUGH THIS.
NO.
I'M SORRY. I'M REALLY SORRY, VICTOR.

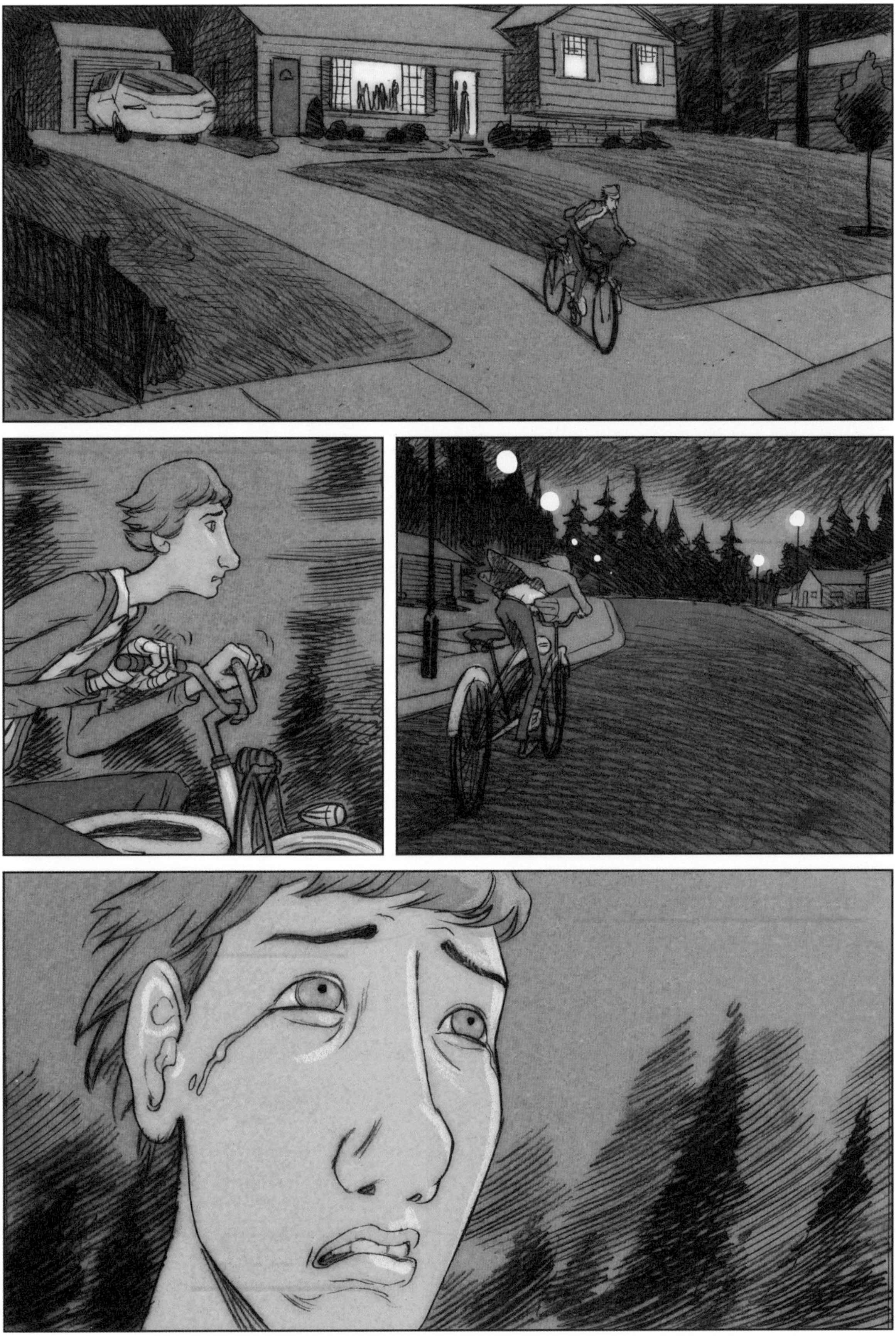

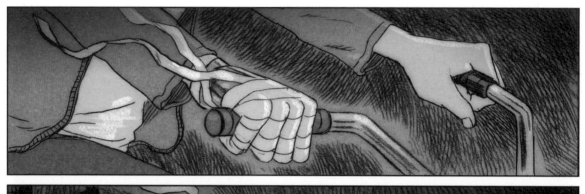

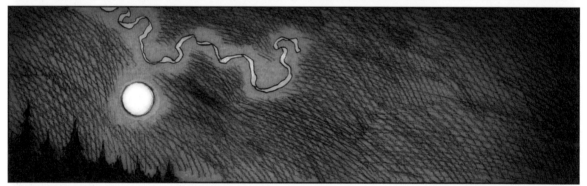

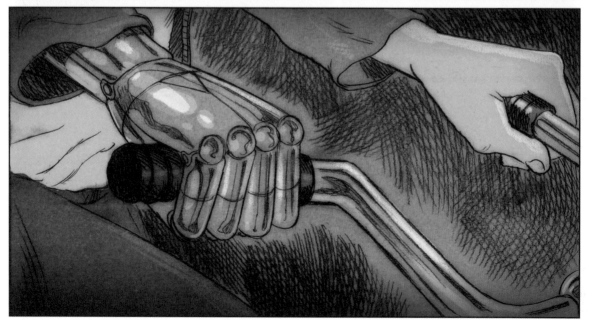

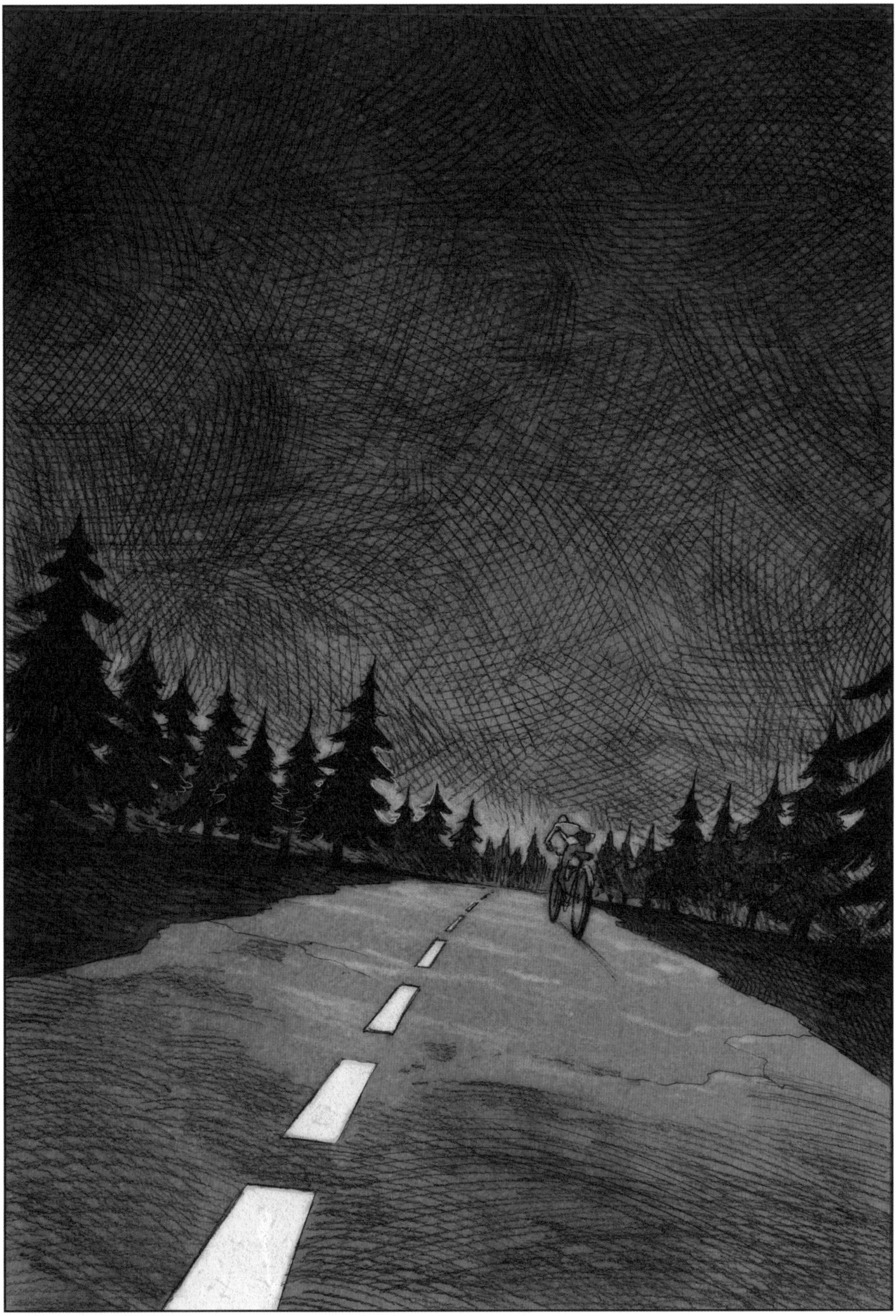